Whulge

Introduction

Millions of years ago, the Cascade Mountains and Puget Sound region were torn from the earth by the thrust of massive glaciers, melting ice sheets, and the upwelling of the sub-crustal mantle from deep within the earth. All of these were brought together by the movement of tectonic plates, some of them were lifted above the surface while others were forced underground where enormous amounts of heat and pressure forced them upward, creating the Cascade Arc and its mighty volcanoes.

After the last ice age, thirteen-thousand years ago, the Puget Lobe of the Cordilleran Ice Sheet began to melt and recede. The ice sheet was an enormously thick single body, ranging from 3,000 to 6,000 feet deep, and covered most of what is now Western Washington. As global temperatures rose, the glacier melted and withdrew. It wore down and blasted apart the earth below it, creating canyons, lakes, and rivers, born to channel the massive quantities of glacial water it released. As the glaciers disappeared, Puget Sound as we know it was created, carved out and filled by this cataclysmic temperature shift. These primordial forces of earth and water were the natural muscle and master architects of the region, the lords of the landscape and progenitors of the territory.

Four deep basins were created, all connected by shallower

submarine sills: long, straight planes of solid rock resting below the surface. Those being at Hood Canal west of the Kitsap Peninsula, Whidbey Basin east of Whidbey Island, the Sound south of Tacoma Narrows, and the Main Basin, which is further subdivided into Admiralty Inlet and the Central Basin. These sills separate the basins from one another, and Puget Sound from the Strait of Juan de Fuca. The sill at Admiralty Inlet checks the flow of saltwater between the Strait of Juan de Fuca and Puget Sound, with another doing the same for the entrance to Hood Canal and at the Tacoma Narrows. Once the ice melted and the water was drained the saltwater of the sea flowed in and our ecosystem developed.

Slowly a mix of microenvironments; tide flats, river deltas and estuaries developed besides vast burgeoning timberlands of cedar, hemlock, fir and maple that grew tall and lush. Varieties of Pacific salmon evolved and flourished along with clams, crab, herring, flounder, rock and bottom fish, sea otter, seals and whales.

On land, animals moved into the area via the Siberia-Alaska land bridge, among them bear, deer, elk, lynx and bobcat. Other smaller inhabitants such as beaver migrated across the Bering Strait. As the natural world and its animals developed, so too did the origins of early man.

First Nation People, who referred to Puget Sound as Whulge, have lived in the area for thousands of years. These Natives, the last known as Puget Salish and Southern Coastal Salish, and distinguished by various spellings of local tribes such as the Snohomish, Snoqualmie, Skykomish, Duwamish, Nisqually, Skagit, Lummi and Stillaguamish are also known as Lushootseed people. Lushootseed comes from two words, one meaning "salt-water," the other meaning "language," and refers to the common language spoken by the people up and down the Northern Pacific

Coast, made up of many local dialects.

Archeologists believe that the Lushootseed people came to the Salish Sea area via Siberia as the glaciers of the ice age melted. These men and women developed a rich culture shaped by the natural wealth and wonder of the northwest — the spirits of the animals and the earth, the ever-shifting seasons, the spectacular, glacier carved mountains and valleys draped in cold fog before being lit ablaze by the piercing rays of the warm sun. The spirits were strong in this land, and the Lushootseed responded to them through legends creating Transformer and Changer Origin Stories.

Dukwibal was a Transformer God in Lushootseed legend who brought balance to the world by using its spiritual powers. *Dukwibal* means "Changer," and it had the ability to take on many different forms to assist or punish individuals or groups of people at times when needed. *Dukwibal* had the power to control the natural world and the elements.

Prior to the white man's arrival in what is known today as Snohomish and Island Counties, there were multiple small summer villages located around Possession Sound, Port Susan, Saratoga Passage and southern Whidbey and Camano Islands. These First Nation People, the *Sdoh-doh-hohbsh*, had a fully formed society with an advanced inter-tribal trading network and traveled with the seasons to hunt, gather and fish.

The largest concentration of Lushootseed people lived during winter months at the north end of the peninsula on the Snohomish River in a winter village of 2,000 people, and now part of Everett. Hibulb was a fortified community with several long houses, a potlatch house, and was an important cultural center with an available bounty of fresh fish and food sources via the cold waters of the Sound and Snohomish River. It was the gathering place for trading, potlatches, diplomacy, weddings, formalities and alliances between different tribes. Because of its estuary location at the mouth of the river on the edge of the saltwater, it was blessed with an abundance of salmon harvests and tall Western Red Cedar trees for canoe construction and other required needs.

Following the British conquest of French Canada in the French and Indian War, more aggressive British business interests began to gradually take ground from and displace the more provincial, less capitalized French fur and Indian traders. After the forced merger of the French Northwest Company with the British Hudson's Bay Company in 1821, the HBC began expanding into what was then the far reaches of the earth.

In November of 1824 an expedition of roughly 40 HBC men from Fort George (Astoria) traveled up the coast to Gray's Harbor, then up the Chehalis and Black Rivers. They eventually reached Puget Sound in mid-December and explored sites for a string of forts along the coastal waters of the Pacific Northwest. In so doing they became the first known non-Native group to reach Puget Sound from a southern route. A few years later the HBC traveled up the Cowlitz River from the Columbia River to near what is today Toledo and continued overland to the mouth of the Nisqually River. This route was known as the Cowlitz Trail, it became one of the primary travel routes into Puget Sound.

The HBC brought Hawaiian employees (Kanakas) to the Pacific Northwest, along with Scottish, English, Metis, and French Canadian descendants via its York Factory Express from northeastern Manitoba on Hudson's Bay to Fort Vancouver. From 1824 until 1846 "The Express" was the main overland connection to move correspondence and new-hires across Prince Rupert's Land, 2600 miles on foot through some of the toughest and most inhospitable terrain in North America, by canoe when possible, and by foot, when necessary, to their Columbia District in Oregon Territory.

The first major outpost was Fort Vancouver, established in 1824 on the north side of the Columbia River at the present site of Vancouver, Washington. It was followed by Fort Langley in 1827, on the Fraser River in British Columbia, Fort Stikine at what is now Wrangell, Alaska, in 1839 and Fort Durham in 1840 near present day Juneau. These forts were beyond the very edge of civilization, the most remote outposts in some of the harshest climates in North America, and the problems with getting and maintaining labor at them were constant. Gradually, without it ever being a matter of official policy, the northwest forts became filled with the worst that the HBC had to offer — convicts on the run, chronic drunks, and reprobates and bastards who could not be condoned anywhere else, would become indispensable in the Northwest. Stikine was one of the furthest north of the forts and became commensurately the worst of them — built on a swampy malodorous spit of leased land in the Russian America wilderness, only the men who could be tolerated nowhere else found a home there.

The original Fort Nisqually was the first white settlement on Puget Sound, established in 1833: lying 250 feet above sea level, north of the Nisqually River Delta, and 150 yards from a deep-water moorage. The dirt path from that anchorage to the fort was the region's first wagon road. The second Fort Nisqually was much larger than the first and erected in 1839 near today's Toledo, Washington, by Sequalitchew Creek and Edmonds Marsh, to be closer to abundant fresh water and more timber.

Fort Nisqually gradually developed from an obscure frontier fort and trading post into an international establishment that specialized in the export of beaver, muskrat and raccoon pelts. It also served as a vital communications and financial center, providing cash loans to businesses in the early settlements of Steilacoom, Tumwater and Olympia.

In 1840 the HBC expanded its operation by forming the Puget Sound Agricultural Company (PSAC) for vegetable farming and the breeding of herd livestock to sell to local settlers coming west. By 1841 Fort Nisqually had 200 acres of land under cultivation, with 3,000 head of sheep and 1,500 cattle. But 10 years later, they had 1,500 acres of active farmland with 12,000 sheep, and 10,000 head of cattle, plus 600 horses and oxen. They were all tended to on 161,000 acres of procured land which included everything between the Nisqually and Puyallup Rivers, including Tacoma (except Point Defiance), Fife, and Puyallup, a total of 252 square miles, all belonging to the HBC and the PSAC.

Owing to the remoteness of the territory, the lack of mineral riches, and the relative sparseness of native inhabitation, the European colonization here was remarkably conflict free — the HBC mostly stuck to their forts and their immediate surroundings and the Indians came and went as they pleased, happy to exchange their pelts for tobacco, sugar, candles, tools, and blankets. The HBC never waged war with any Native people it conducted business with, and because of this fair treatment an agent for the HBC was usually welcomed within their villages.

The London Convention of 1818 allowed the joint occupation and settlement of the Oregon Territory, which was known to Britain at that time as the Columbia District of the HBC. The treaty opened the new Oregon lands to joint occupancy by citizens of both nations and forced the HBC to align their business practices with British foreign policy, while at the same time paving the way for the peaceful colonization for all settlers.

The Oregon Treaty of 1846 between the United States and the United Kingdom ended the joint occupation of Oregon Territory with the British and made the Oregonians below the 49th parallel American citizens. As part of the treaty, the HBC was to be paid $650,000, but those monies were not allotted until 1870 when the HBC finally gave up control of their lands.

Unlike on the east coast, or in the rich bottom lands of the American south, there was, in the 1820s and 1830s, almost no European demand for land in the Pacific Northwest. The only thing of interest to the Old World were the rich furs of its untouched wilderness, and with the expense of bringing men and supplies into the area by far the most competitive route to those furs was through the Natives. Thousands of miles from home, on the remotest edge of the world, with the thinnest possible detachments of employees who were often not even fluent in each other's languages, much less that of the Natives', the best these forts could do was trade at set prices with the Indians and maintain enough inter-fort discipline to prevent any drunken mutinies from breaking out.

The Donation Land Claim Act (DLCA), was signed by President Millard Fillmore and took effect on Sept. 27, 1850, allowing settlers to claim land in the **Oregon Territory**, which at that time included Washington, Oregon, Idaho and parts of today's Wyoming. Settlers were able to claim 320 acres if single, or 640 acres if married for free until December 1st of 1850, when the claimable amount of land was cut in half. The Homestead Act, which opened up nearly all of the western territories, was signed by President Lincoln on May 20, 1862. It covered 160 million acres of public lands, 10 percent of the United States at that time, and allowed those who had never taken up arms against the USA, so as to exclude the soldiery of the then ablaze Confederacy, to claim 160 or 320 acres of land under the same requirements as the

DLCA as long as they made improvements, lived on the land, and could afford the $34 filing fee.

In the 1850s the earliest settlers arrived in Puget Sound, but by the 1860s newcomers hurtled into the region — which every year included hundreds of Europeans and Easterners making the long, rigorous trip via tall ship around Cape Horn, or to Panama and overland across the Isthmus. They then traveled north to Fort Vancouver and up the Cowlitz Trail, or sailed to the first Customs District at Olympia which was established in 1851 or to the second district at Port Townsend beginning in 1854.

The 1870 census of Washington Territory showed a total population of 18,231 people, comprised of 14,064 Native Americans and 4,167 Whites. The bulk of those individuals lived on or near Puget Sound and its tributary rivers for transportation and access to the abundance of salmon and natural food sources.

The settlers came in search of land, in search of farms they could tear out of the earth themselves with their own hands. They came looking for a life without rents, without taxes, and sometimes for a life without the need to look over their shoulders. And so, in this ancient land torn by glaciers and breathing heavy beneath the fog, the old world crashed once more into the new; all contributing to the folklore and legend of Whulge.

Part One

Bitter Water
Wusi áax'w Héen
April 16, 1842

Chief Trader John McLoughlin Jr. was gone from Fort Stikine, traveling north 130 miles by swift canoe for a few days up the Russian America coast to Fort Durham. Hudson's Bay Company Administrator George Simpson had given the order to close Durham so McLoughlin needed to deal with the ensuing circumstances and confer with officials there. Knowing when an opportunity presented itself, the Chief Trader's assistant, Thomas McPherson, and his two allies planned to take full advantage of his absence.

After the heavy front gate of the fort bolted behind him, McPherson made his way down to the dock through the crisp early morning air of what looked to be a fine day. The golden glow of the sunrise back-lit the snow-capped peaks of the Coastal Range to the east and the moon was still setting to the west. Carrying his musket on his back, he walked across the thick wharf planking to where his two rough Metis comrades, Antoine Kawannassé and Pierre Kannaquassé, were waiting.

Loaded in the dugout canoe was a cargo of trade goods for the Natives: a cast-iron kettle, bolts of calico cloth, tin boxes of tobacco, big bags of sugar, and molasses, candles, Hudson's Bay blankets, a small cask of gunpowder, and a medium-sized leather satchel of heavy musket balls were all lying in the canoe haphazardly, having been thrown in without regard for shape or weight.

"*Tout questions?*" Antoine asked, seated at his forward position in the dugout, and scratching at his ratty fur hat tilted sideways on his head. He cut a shabby figure in his filthy Hudson's Bay capote, the characteristic garb of the far north — a rough coat made from a striped Hudson's Bay wool blanket that had become treasured by the Tlingit.

"No," McPherson answered, handing Antoine his muzzle-loaded long gun to stow away. He climbed aboard, keeping one hand on his black tricorne hat. With a sly smirk the Metis added, "I changed the trade docket, so this trip is now on the schedule. Mr. John didn't notice before he left."

"Ah, *bien*," Pierre replied, pushing them off with the end of his paddle against a dock pier.

They plied their way north, towards the mouth of the Stikine River, past heavily forested islands with granite cliffs then turned east into the delta estuary. It was a wide expanse of separately threaded channels that wove through multiple sandy islands, they teemed with wildlife. Hundreds of shorebirds littered the tidelands, blue herons fished the shallow waters, a lone wolf stood on a far bank and watched them travel by.

As they cleaved their way up one of the shallower channels, they stayed away from the swifter currents in the various deeper channels, keeping to calm waters. Past marshlands and small silt-made islands of various sizes, braided and shaped by the glacial runoff from the Stikine Icefield, they paddled hard and fell into a rhythm, beating out the miles in silence.

The delta portion of the trip soon changed to a thickly timbered region where the river turned to the southeast. In the far-off distance, the snow-capped jagged peak Devil's Thumb stood guard over the vast and unbridled wilderness, a raw and savage land that deceived one with its solitude, a place where any measure of misfortune could pass undetected. After two hours of travel, they came to a wide segment of the channel where the current slowed and the river turned north.

"So, tell me Thomas, if Mr. John can keep a country wife, then why can't I have a woman at the fort?" Pierre asked. "I have my own cabin inside the stockade just like him, there is no reason!"

McPherson stopped paddling and fixed one eye on Pierre, a small ferret of a man with pock-marked cheeks and a sharp nose, then spat, "Yes, but he still thinks it was you that shot at him last fall, remember?" McPherson started paddling again, his hawk-like snout pointed into the wind.

"Ah, *monami*, I remember. But he had no proof and you convinced him it was a Kake Indian. *Oui*?"

"Yes, I did," McPherson replied.

"Then there's no reason that —"

"You two need to paddle more, and talk less," Antoine snapped, a lazy, tub-bellied lout with ruddy cheeks, who added, "We still have a way to go and I'm already worn out."

Thirty minutes later Antoine pointed his paddle towards the shore where there was a nubbin of beach, the two roughs began to paddle on the starboard side while McPherson used his paddle as a rudder, turning them into a small cove with a brushy low bank that would hide the dugout. As soon as they slid up on the sand the trader started barking orders.

"Alright, let's be lively, we don't have much time," McPherson commanded, leaping from the boat into the cold, shallow water. He dropped his paddle in the canoe and they pulled the bark up onto the shore. Then he picked up a bundle of blankets and headed inland.

"Pierre, you grab the musket balls and Antoine, you bring that keg of gunpowder. We still have to get up to the village and back to the fort today."

One-hundred yards into the woods they came to a stout but small windowless log structure, with its moss-covered roof and rock foundation it looked like it grew right up out of the forest. McPherson pulled a small ring of keys from his breeches and unlocked the crude door. Natural light flooded the interior showing stacks of Hudson's Bay Company supplies and trading goods, a small sleeping area of blankets was in one corner. Pierre sat the heavy satchel on the floor then stepped over to the rock fireplace and held his hand over the burnt pieces of wood.

"Cold," he said. "I don't think Frenchy has been living here."

"Maybe, but you know he doesn't like being called that," McPherson replied, setting the blankets down on top of a bundle of beaver pelts.

"I'll call him anything I like!" Pierre said, "There are worse things I could call him by."

"That's fine, it's your hide," McPherson retorted, being a man who relished in chiding his subordinates, standing tall with a rigid, resentful posture.

Antoine put the keg of gunpowder down next to the musket balls and then moaned, "What about the rest? Are we making another trip?"

"You two are! I need to write a note to leave for him. Hustle back down there and bring the rest of the blankets except three, grab two rungs of calico but leave the rest in the canoe. We're trading that with the Indians," McPherson said.

Once they were out of sight he got down on his knees, took off his tricorne hat, exposing his matted dark hair, and sat it on the floor next to him. Then he loosened a floorboard with the tip of his knife and removed it. Reaching blindly with his right hand into the secret compartment, he felt through the many hidden small tin boxes, pulled one out of the darkness and sat it on the floor next to him.

Opening it he found everything was still there: rings, a handful of tiny emeralds, nuggets of gold, a single sapphire, a few silver pieces, and a neat pile of shillings and pence. It was a frontier fortune, enough to get out of the far north and quickly, without anyone asking any questions along the way. He yanked a small leather pouch from his breeches and emptied its contents into the tin, closed it, and then returned the box of valuables back to its secure place. Standing up he searched inside of his jerkin vest for the pre-written letter and set it on top of the keg of gunpowder. He snatched his hat up off the floor just as his two cohorts returned.

Breathing hard, Antoine set the blankets down on the rest of them, "There we are . . . *monami*." Pierre dropped the bolts of calico in the corner. Both men glanced at the folded paper on the keg. McPherson noticed them.

"We need to move out! The day's a wasting!" McPherson spat, reaching into his pocket for the cabin key. Once the door was secure, they headed back down to the canoe and set off again.

They continued north. As the sun rose, the living warmth of it shone on their faces, its glare reflecting off the shimmering water. An hour later, on the opposite side of the river, a young Tlingit boy in a deerskin shirt and leggings ran out from the trees. The three men saw him right away. When their eyes met McPherson set down his paddle and raised the iron kettle over his head. The boy smiled broadly and motioned for them to continue upriver.

The men paddled in silence, save for the soft lapping of water against the hull of the dugout and the dipping of their paddles as they glided through the gentle current of the river. Coming to an island, they navigated a narrow channel that opened up into a small bay where the village came into view through the river mist. It rested on a hill at the base of a mountain with a long sandy shoreline where dozens of cedar dugout canoes of various lengths were beached. At the edge of the riverbank, tall totems of carved eagle and raven heads with jutting wings and beaks, bear, otter, black fish, and salmon figures lined the shore, dozens of them, each a monument documenting the stories and spirit quests of the clan. The fingers of fog that hung in the thick, moss-covered cedar trees above the village shrouded the camp with a degree of mystery to their domain.

McPherson once again raised the kettle over his head as whoops and cries rang out from the Natives, welcoming the traders. Soon everyone in the village was rushing to the riverbank, excited to see the men and the goods they'd brought.

McPherson scanned the shoreline until he saw Peter Goutre, standing with his Tlingit woman, holding hands, grinning ear to ear. Looking healthy and strong, Peter had a well-knit frame, a big full chest and a long thin dark beard that tapered to a point at his chest. Wearing black breeches and fringed seal skin moccasins with leggings, he had a wide blue waistband wrapped around his white Boston shirt and midsection, a black knit cap was tilted on his head. He raised his right fist, followed by his left, then opened both hands, lowered them and bowed in a sweeping movement of welcome as the traders' canoe slid up onto the sandy shore.

The children of the village instantly swept down on them like a hungry flock of gulls, touching and pecking at the three men then running back up to their parents. Peter finally walked down to them while the elders of the tribe watched from the bank.

"Ah, my friends," he said with a slight Quebecois accent, smiling. "It is good to see you today! You can attend my wedding!"

"Your wedding!" McPherson exclaimed. "What in the —"

"Careful, Thomas, the whole tribe is watching you," Peter replied, grinning.

"You're getting married? Today? This was not expected. Why wasn't I told last month?" McPherson asked, his voice harsh and suspicious, his eyes searching Peter's face.

"Nothing in the company charter says that I need approval. I do not need permission from anyone but Little Rain's parents, and they have agreed," Peter firmly replied.

McPherson looked hard at Peter, spat in the mud, then said, "Fine but don't let it get in the way of our trading here today, the company comes first."

"*Oui*, you can still trade. The ceremony is not until the sun is much higher. But tell me, how are things at the fort?"

"There are difficulties with some of the men. But we're here today because Mr. John is up north at Fort Durham for a few days," Thomas replied.

"Did you stop by the cabin?" Peter asked, glancing at his bride, still up on the bank, and then back to McPherson.

"Oh, yes. I left a fresh keg of gunpowder and more valuables for us. Our quest for bonanza is nearly complete. Soon we will be living like Kings," McPherson whispered back. Peter turned to the other men.

"Antoine! Pierre! You are both looking healthy, are you anxious to see your women?"

"Ah, *oui*," Pierre replied. Antoine opened his mouth to say something but McPherson cut him off.

"That's enough, we've got trading to do!" he said, motioning back to the canoe for Pierre and Antoine to start bringing up the goods.

Peter and Little Rain led the three men carrying their trade items through the village. They followed a trail that climbed a hill up to the biggest plank house where Chief Taneidi lived. As the men walked towards the longhouse, tribal members lined both sides of the rock stepped pathway. Some of the young warriors stood in deerskin clothing, others wore HBC hickory shirts and watched with hard faces, while a few smiled and rattled the strings of shell and bead necklaces that hung from their necks. Many of the women, most wearing deerskin dresses and moccasins with their black hair pinned in braids, smiled and pointed at the trade items, saying, "*kinguchwāan*" or "*toow s'eenāa*" as they walked by with their blankets, sugar, box of candles, kettle and other items.

There was one final staircase to climb of rock and earth that ended on a large cedar platform in front of the chief's home. Totem poles stood at each corner of the thick wedge split deck and lined the front. In the middle the planking had been cut-out, and a large round firepit of stones had been built-up from the ground underneath. They stopped in front of the chief's plank house, decorated with paintings of native animal artwork, where McPherson laid a blanket down and began to set the various trade goods on it as the villagers gathered around, but he left the other blankets and calico behind themselves. Once the main items were displayed the four men stepped back and McPherson called out, "Chief Taneidi *ne-si'ka yuk'-wa ko'pa mahkook!*" They waited for the chief to appear.

After a quiet pause, the door of the longhouse opened and a figure emerged wrapped in a white robe with a Raven made of beadwork with herringbone weavings on the back. The villagers all began to call, "*Aakáawu Taneidi!*" in loud, shrill voices while rattling their beads and loudly stomping their feet on the platform. The old chief looked out to his tribe with deep-set eyes and a determined jutting jaw, holding a carved walking stick of cedar, he raised his arms, then opened them up and his people's cries of "*Aakáawu!*" grew louder. His black hair was long and flowing but held to his head with a cedar bark band. Underneath his robe, he wore a white linen Boston shirt that he'd previously traded for. Standing with his carved wooden walking stick held in his right hand, his face was lined and weathered, he smiled broadly and nodded at the traders, who he had dealt with many times in the past.

Two women came out from the plank house — one was an old crone, wearing a fringed deerskin dress with beaded seams; she laid down a blanket for the chief to sit on and the other, heavy set and younger, placed a bowl filled with pieces of salmon pemmican and two clay jugs of fresh water. The chief motioned for them all to sit down. McPherson sat with his three men on either side of him, while Little Rain stood close by. McPherson pulled a small muslin pouch of tobacco from his jerkin vest, held it up, and then set it down in front of the chief. The chief rubbed his eyes and looked blankly at it then turned to the old crone and held out his hand. She in turn handed him a pair of spectacles, the chief slowly opened the thin wire arms of the glasses and put them on. Seeing the pouch of tobacco clearly, he smiled and turned his gaze back to the trader.

"*Klahowya*! *Klosche kinoose* for Chief Taneidi," McPherson said in Chinook Jargon, a guttural, sputtering language known to most tribes. The chief smiled, nodded, and picked up the tobacco. He held it up to his nose and smelled the pleasant aroma, then handed it to one of the women behind him. She took it into his home and returned. McPherson pointed at the box of candles.

"*Ocook gleese-stick*," he said, and held up four fingers, "*Lakit* for *ee'-na* pelts." But the chief shook his head and took a piece of pemmican from the bowl. He bit it off like it was a piece of plug tobacco and then chewed it slowly with an open mouth, grimacing from his broken and missing teeth that were fully exposed. He swallowed and looked blank-faced at the trader.

"*Wake*," he grunted in objection, holding up two fingers.

McPherson sighed, knowing how shrewd a negotiator Taneidi could be. He held up three fingers with one hand and took a piece of pemmican with the other but just held it in his fingers.

"*Klone ee'-na* pelts," McPherson said, pointing at the box full of candles. But Taneidi crossed his arms and frowned. He glanced at one of the braves near him then looked at McPherson.

"*Wake,*" the chief grunted again, still objecting. So McPherson held up two fingers and reluctantly agreed.

"*Ah-ha; e-éh,*" Taneidi said, grinning. The chief snatched up the small box of candles and handed it to the heavy-set woman who took it inside his longhouse and returned with two beaver pelts. McPherson bit into the fishy, fat laced pemmican and nodded.

They continued to haggle and trade for the other items while eating pemmican and slurping water until just the cast-iron kettle was left, the blankets and calico remained behind the traders. At that point McPherson looked to Peter knowing they were just about done.

Taneidi and Peter knew each other well, he had spent as much time as he could up at the village since he had first arrived at the fort over a year earlier and had now been living with the tribe. Strong and energetic, Peter was always eager to help however he could — chopping wood, bringing in the fish, tanning hides — and knew the jargon and even picked up a minimal amount of basic Tlingit to make his intentions known to any one of them, provided they gave him enough time and room to use sign-language with his hands. Over that period of time, Peter had become infatuated with their way of life and by now was smitten with and was to marry a young woman of the village.

McPherson held up all his fingers on both hands and said, "*Táht-lelum ee'-na* pelts for the *ket-ling,*" pointing at the cast iron kettle. But the 31-year-old trader was rejected.

"Wake, wake," Taneidi grumbled, shaking his head then crossing his arms again. But McPherson considered himself a veteran bush ranger and master of the bluff, so he picked the heavy kettle up off the blanket and set it behind Peter. It caused the chief, who prided himself on his ability to read fear in other men's eyes, to bite his lip and grind the few teeth he had left involuntarily. Taneidi stared coldly at McPherson and then looked at Peter.

The chief held up five fingers and said, *"Kwin'-num ee'-na!"* He pushed out his chin and tightened his jaw. Seeing the chief's reaction McPherson shook his head and glanced over at Peter.

Thinking the tribe probably needed the kettle, Pierre opened his mouth to say something but the proud chief would have nothing to do with having a subordinate speak to him. Taneidi held up his right hand.

"Cul'-tus wau'-wau'!" he scoffed, glaring at Pierre.

Knowing exactly what just happened, and in an act of friendship and keen understanding, Peter reached behind himself for the kettle and set it in front of the chief. The 38-year-old French Canadian picked through the bowl of pemmican carefully, choosing the best piece he could find, and held it up for Taneidi. The chief stared blankly at the offering. After a long, nervous pause he accepted the pemmican, and began to chew the mixture of salmon, dried berries and bear-fat.

For minutes this went on, both of them staring each other down, and slowly, deliberately eating pemmican while Peter stroked and pulled his long beard, until the chief threw up his hands and slapped them together. He pointed at the kettle and held up six fingers.

"O'-kok!" the old man exclaimed, waving both hands showing his

fingers to McPherson. At that point McPherson nudged Peter with his elbow in an effort to regain control of the negotiations.

"*Kloshe!*" McPherson replied. He set the iron kettle closer to the chief, signaling that the trade was complete.

The Tlingit Chief stood, picked up the kettle, then raised it above his head while his clan all called out, "*Aakáawu Taneidi!*" and pointed at the kettle with joyful smiles. In the celebration that ensued from the successful securing of the prized kettle, the three Hudson's Bay blankets and calico cloth were un-traded for and completely over-looked. McPherson knew exactly how to put them to use.

"Take those," he whispered discreetly to Peter, his hand over his mouth, "over to your woman's for now and give them to the parents of the girls who are coming to the fort tonight, then meet me down at the canoe."

Peter nodded and picked up the items, without the chief noticing, then walked off. The three men picked up the beaver pelts they'd traded for and made their way back down to the river. Halfway there McPherson pushed Pierre in the back. Pierre stopped and turned around.

"You ignorant bastard!" McPherson cursed, stabbing him in the chest with a stiff finger. "Opening up your mouth in front of Taneidi like that. Bloody hell, I should fire you right now!"

"I was trying to help," Pierre retorted, then turned around and started walking once more. At the river Antoine tripped and fell into the sandy muck, the pelts spilling out of his hands and into the soggy dirt.

"Some help you are!" The main trader scoffed, standing over Antoine while he picked himself up off the ground. He glared at the two as they loaded the canoe. "I'm sick of looking at the both of you. Get out of my sight! You've got twenty-minutes to find your quim and get back, so bugger off . . . but we're leaving soon! You got that?" McPherson growled.

The two men didn't say a word, they both headed up the bank and into the crowd, knowing exactly where they were going. Once they were out of ear-shot Antoine quietly remarked, "Sometimes I think that Nancy-boy can go bugger himself, but soon we'll be rich and can leave this place. Then we'll live a life of luxury and never have to work again."

Pierre looked at Antoine, "Ah, *oui*. Someday soon we will leave and live the life of Kings."

McPherson began to distribute the pelts in the canoe for balance and then covered them with a canvas tarp. He looked up at the sky. *There's more than enough daylight to get back*, he thought to himself, *with the current in our favor*.

The children of the village had followed them to the river. Once McPherson was done with his tasks some of them started running up to touch him, then dart away, laughing and giggling. Peter walked up, smiling at the scene before him.

"These young ones are the life-blood and future of this tribe. Someday Little Rain and I will have sons and daughters just like these," Peter said, pointing at all the smiling faces. But McPherson didn't care.

"I want three women at the fort tonight for those blankets and calico, understand?" McPherson said.

"Three?" Peter replied. "How am I supposed to manage that on my wedding day?"

"I don't care how you do it! And I don't give a damn about your wedding!" Thomas barked, "The last time you only brought one woman, remember how that went over," he said, raising an eyebrow. "You've got three blankets and two bolts of calico, so that will more than suffice for three girls."

"But I'm to be married today. It's quite a thing to ask a man, on the verge of matrimony, to put that aside in order to procure a passel of loose women for you!" Peter replied, glaring at McPherson.

"Listen to me, Mr. John is gone, and the men are expecting you to be there tonight. I guess you and your bride are just going to spend your wedding night at the fort if you have to."

"Damn it, man!"

"Don't you damn me! We have an agreement and you need to keep to it," McPherson bellowed, his voice fierce and rough. Peter shook his head and reminded himself of their corrupt arrangement.

"We didn't share any of the shillings or gems the men paid for that girl the last time I did this for you, nothing went to her or her parents. She saw the men pay you that night, and the whole tribe knows."

McPherson turned and stepped towards Peter with his eyes aflame, "This partnership is going to end in a hurry if you don't keep your end of the bargain!"

"But this kind of treatment —" Peter started to say but abruptly stopped talking when he noticed McPherson put his hand on his belted knife.

"They're savages! You need to change your ways," McPherson shrieked. "You're supposed to be up here working as an agent of the company, and for us, your comrades, not falling in love with some Tlingit girl and getting married!" McPherson glanced around then continued, "You just be at the fort tonight with three women. We still need to capitalize on our situation while we can, understand?"

Peter nodded, stroked his beard and quietly said, "*Oui*," realizing that if he ever wanted to leave this place with enough money so he could set himself up in a new life, he had to toe the line. "I'll be there."

"Good," McPherson replied, "we're in agreement then."

Peter nodded once more, turned and started to walk away but McPherson said to his back, "And, just so you know, I've been talking with Urbain Heroux how Mr. John has been having some late-night liaisons with his wife."

Peter spun around, lowered his head and eyed McPherson. He slowly stepped back to him.

"What did you just say? Mr. John and Urbain's wife? That's absurd. Why do you say that?"

"Because my plan to overthrow the fort is working. The men hate McLoughlin and are going to kill him," McPherson said quietly. Peter looked upward and thought about his boss's comment and what to do about it.

"If you're lying, and Urbain does kill Mr. John, then —"

"Then you should know not to ask any more questions unless you want to see any of those pretty little kids you were talkin' about grow up."

"Kill McLoughlin? If you do that and the Haida and the Kake find out, they'll raid the fort! What's been going on down there all winter?"

"Mr. John has been tormenting the men for months. He's got us buildin' his stupid barracks day and night for men that the company will never send, he never gives us enough to eat and besides all that, he's cut off the rum! A man can't get through a week of this soggy hell without rum, it's not civilized. Plus, he's got men in irons in his jailhouse and those he gets along with he won't even let them see their women. Benoni still can't walk for the beating he gave him, and all for nothing! Like no one has ever fallen asleep on watch before. The men believe he deserves to die."

"But you cannot kill, anyone. That is a sin."

"I'm not killing anyone! I'm advising my friend Urbain of the state of his spouse, and from there — he will do what needs to be done! Haul off with that!"

"He'll do it only because of your lies and treachery," Peter howled, his own face reddening. He pointed a finger at him, "Don't you do this thing. It's *not* right."

"Dammit, Goutre! This is what they've decided, it is done and you are part of it. So, I don't want to hear another word. You just be there tonight with the women!"

Peter stared at McPherson for a few moments, shook his head and then walked away, looking at the ground, thinking to himself, *I'm not going to be part of killing Mr. John. How am I going to convince any parent to trust him, or me, with their daughter for the night?* Growing more upset with the situation with every step, he began to hate what he had just agreed to do.

"Ah, Frenchy! Will you be bringing your quim tonight to share?"

Peter looked up — it was Pierre walking towards him, grinning like a schoolboy. A fire ignited inside of Peter that burned like lava in his veins. He took two more steps, grabbed Pierre by the throat and squeezed so hard that he started gasping for air, his eyes and face turning pale with fear. Peter pushed him backwards, towards a row of plank houses, shoving him up against the side of one.

"Don't you ever call me that, EVER!" Peter snarled. He slammed Pierre's head up against the building, and then lifted him up higher. He stared into his beady little eyes, grinned a devilish grin, threw him down on the ground and pounced on him, hitting him repeatedly in the face, hard enough to open up a gash under his left eye. Finally, before he knocked the life out of him, Peter got up, turned and walked away.

Pierre didn't move a muscle, and stayed there for a few moments, bleeding, until he rolled over on his side and pushed himself up off the ground. He started to make his way back down to the river, dazed, feeling his face to try and stop the bleeding and rubbing his jaw. Then he stopped, turned around and yelled, shaking his fist in the air. "I'll get you, *enculer,* you *bâtard*! You're gonna pay for this! Mr. John's gonna get it then you're gonna pay!"

Peter heard what Pierre hollered but he kept walking and told himself, *I'll never be part of McPherson's scheme. Killing means doom and prison and the end of freedom, for me and everyone at the fort. I'm still young and have a long life to live. I'll have nothing to do with McPherson, but I can't stay here, there'll be too much of a price to pay after he's murdered.*

II

Little Rain
K Sēew Sōow
SHAA' wuduwasháa

When the first traders from Fort Stikine came up the river to her village, the whole tribe was fascinated at the goods they brought. Axes, hatchets, cookware, candles, sugar, molasses and beautiful warm 3-point woolen blankets, but when Little Rain first held a pair of scissors in her hand and then used them to trim her mother's long hair, it hit her like nothing she'd ever experienced. She realized that their world was changing. However, during the previous summer, when Chief Trader John McLoughlin Jr. brought the gift of a pair of wire-rimmed spectacles to Chief Taneidi, with their magic of better eyesight, the whole village was endeared to him and forever grateful to Mr. John. At that point, Little Rain was even more curious of the changing world she'd never seen.

Soon, *K Sēew Sōow*, Little Rain, found herself dreaming about all these wonderful things — the kind of people that could make such things, that could bring them across the land to them. And then a new trader arrived. He was a tall, sinewy fellow with a black ponytail that went down his back, a long beard, brown eyes and a wide, white smile that he flashed easily and often when trading with them. She instantly took a liking to this fellow the traders called Peter, and began to look for him every time they would arrive. And finally, when their eyes met one spring day in 1841, she beamed at him until he returned her look with one of his wide, bright smiles.

On the traders' next trip he sought her out, introduced himself and then gave her an ivory hair comb and a small, hand mirror. Previously, she'd only seen herself in the reflection of calm water when the sun was right, but now, she could comb her hair and dream of the world where the mirror was made and what that place was like.

The following winter Little Rain made it her task to learn the guttural jargon mishmash of Northwest Indian dialects and English that the traders used so she could talk with Peter, who she was so smitten with, and learn about things beyond her home. Everything about the world outside of her village, and now too, Peter, was intriguing to her, both had been pulling daily at her heart since she had first laid hold on those steel scissors.

By the time Peter returned to Little Rain's home, she was sitting in front of the small, flat-front cedar plank house waiting with the blankets and calico beside her. When their eyes met, they both beamed. She sprang up and started to run to him but her calf-length deerskin dress hindered her stride, she pulled the dress up, exposing more of her bronze legs. They embraced until Peter pulled back and took another look at her; she was the most beautiful girl in the whole tribe and he was in love with her.

"*Ne-si'ka mal-i-éh ko'-pasun ko'-pa sun*," Peter said to her.

Instantly she smiled like summer sunshine, her warm eyes, blushing round face and dimpled chin melted his heart. She hugged him again. He looked her intently in the eyes and said, "But after, *kim'-ta*, we marry, *mal-i-êh*, we must leave, *mahsh,* right away. There are bad things happening at the fort, understand? We have no choice." She nodded, knowing most of what he said, then looked into his eyes, smiled, and took him by the hand to her parent's front door but before they went inside Peter picked up the blankets and bolts of calico and held them in both arms in front of himself. *To hell with McPherson, these will make perfect parental wedding gifts.*

Little Rain burst through the door talking faster than ever, first in Tlingit, then saying, "*Ne-si'-ka mal-i-éh, al-ta'*," in the jargon so Peter could understand. The excited seventeen-year-old had been in love with the Frenchman since he had arrived and dreamt of today for months, and because she didn't have any cross-cousin males to marry in her family, Little Rain had been allowed to wed outside of the clan. She didn't care about what some of them would say; her heart was set on Peter and she would marry him that day.

Inside the small earthen floor home, there were cedar platforms around the perimeter for sleeping and sitting. The main support poles and beams were hand-carved with images of fish, beaver, raven, and other creatures of the forest and river, all of them painted with the red of salmonberry juice. A central fire pit was dug into the dirt floor with a gaping hole above it in the roof — the dank smell of rotten wood and smoke permeated the air. Little Rain's parents and younger brother, *Yées Wāat Ǥooch*, Young Wolf, were huddled together on one of the bench platforms. Her father, *Dēix Ch'áak*, Two Eagles, stood up and smiled at his daughter and then Peter.

Two Eagles was a venerated elder of the Bitter Water tribe. He was a large man, with a big belly and a big face, adorned in his best finery for the wedding; strings of glass bead necklaces around his neck, a deerskin shirt knitted together with sinew and his prized deerskin leggings. Two Eagles knew that his daughter was infatuated with the lean Frenchman who'd been living amongst them, and he liked him, but he demanded the cold respect he was due at all times.

Peter stepped over to him with the blankets and calico. "Today Little Rain and I shall *mal-i-éh*. But there are bad things, *me-sáh-chie* at the fort, the men are going to make Mr. John *mem'-a-loost*. Little Rain and I must leave, *mahsh* the village after we marry, *mal-i-éh*."

The color drained from Two Eagle's face, he stared at Peter for a long time then he said, "Mr. John *mem'a-loost? De-láte?*"

"*Áh-ha*, yes, it is true, *de-láte*. I think the *ki'-wa*, crooked men at the fort are going to say, *wau'-wau* I did it. So Little Rain and I must leave, *mahsh, al'-ta*."

Two Eagles turned to his daughter, she nodded and said in her most sincere voice, "*Ni-ka tik-égh* Pee-ter *pe tik-égh nan'-itsh il'-la-hie*." Then she stepped over and gave her father a hug, saying, "*Youtl*."

He looked to his wife, *Aawal'éx Guwakaan*, Dancing Deer, a small woman with a thin face and dark eyes and motioned for her to follow him across the room to converse. For what seemed like hours, they quietly talked over the situation then came back and stood in front of Peter and their daughter.

Little Rain's father eyed the valuable blankets and calico cloth and looked over at his wife, she smiled and nodded in agreement. They'd decided to let their daughter leave the village and see the world.

Two Eagles turned back to Peter and held out his arms in acceptance of the wedding gifts. Peter placed them in his arms and said, "*Máh-sie, máh-sie,* thank you. Your *mal-i-éh* blessing is still strong, *skoo'-kum?*"

"*Áh-ha,*" Two Eagles replied.

Dancing Deer took the gifts from her husband, Little Rain stepped over to her father and embraced him. Then she began talking very quickly of how they had to depart right away after the ceremony and leave the region.

Two Eagles nodded and motioned for his son, giving him instructions to take to Chief Taneidi and sent him out the door. Then he looked at Peter and Little Rain and asked, "*Ik'-tah kah me-si'-ka klat'-a-wa?*"

Peter thought about how to say where they would go in the jargon but he didn't know the right words, so he said, "We will go south to Oregon Territory. It is safe there."

Two Eagles recognized the word Oregon and knew that it was where all the trading goods came from. He nodded at his daughter and then reminded her of the route to go, "*Me-si'-ka klat'-a-wa Kitschk-hin e'-lip. Pish pish Tsimshian clan.*"

Little Rain thought for a moment about what her father had just said and tried to remember the fish camp she'd gone to with her family years before. Then she smiled and nodded.

"*Áh-ha, áh-ha, Tsimshian Tlingit! Ni-ka kum'-tuks!*" Little Rain said, remembering her family traveling to the seasonal village.

An hour later the sun was high in the sky and it was time — when the wedding couple and her family arrived at the main longhouse they and the whole village were on and around the platform in front of Chief Taneidi's house. A large fire of dry cedar blocks was snapping with heat in the pit.

After escaping the claws of a grizzly bear, *Yeech Shoox'*, Soaring Bird, who was also the son of his recently deceased tribal Shaman father, had been elevated to be the current Shaman and re-named *Táakw Xōots*, Winter Bear. Wearing a cedar-carved Raven headdress with a jutting beak and square eyes he was cloaked in a flowing beaded robe and adornments to conduct the ceremony. He stood in high regalia with the Chief and his wife, the old crone, behind him, and the couple to be married in front, Little Rain's family by her side.

A large clay bowl of water sat on a Hudson's Bay blanket that was draped over a bench between them served as an altar. To the sides of the earthenware bowl there were scattered objects of spiritual power — Raven feathers, agates, bits of quartz, obsidian, and then other, smaller clay bowls with smoldering sticks of cedar and hemlock in them, giving the altar a fragrance of northwest incense. The assembled spiritual objects gave the ceremony power, and were only brought out on special occasions by the Shaman.

Winter Bear called for silence then began to chant sage reverent words. Peter could not pick out the specifics, but he could tell that the chant was very heavy with spiritual import — the joining of souls beneath the canopy of the Sky Father and how the Great Spirit of The Raven, who set free the sun, moon, and stars, would fly with and watch over them, in their travels on the tides across the *Tlein Heén*.

Next, the Shaman lifted the clay bowl of water over his head and blessed it. He set the bowl back down on the bench and began to wash his hands in it while reciting more spiritual words. He picked the bowl up again then held it out in front of Little Rain and Peter, they washed their hands to cleanse their spirits and wipe away their past lives. Then the crowd opened up and the couple stepped over to the fire where Peter took seven steps around it while reciting the wedding vow that Little Rain and her mother had taught him in the days before. Little Rain did the same and stopped in front of Peter where he handed her one of two six-inch long cylindrical message sticks of soapstone that he'd carved with braided sinew necklaces hanging from them. Over the winter Peter had discovered the tribe's spiritual signs of union, good health and prosperity, and had inscribed those symbols onto the message sticks, which would represent their unbreakable marriage bond. The couple held their marriage sticks out in front of the Shaman — he took the sticks and carefully cleansed each one in the bowl of water. When that was done, he lifted them up for the Sky Father to bless. The Shaman brought them down, held both to his chest then touched the beak of his Raven headdress with them and lifted both up again to the Sky Father, sanctifying the marriage sticks. Winter Bear slowly lowered them as Little Rain and Peter bowed, then he hung each other's marriage stick on their necks.

They turned and walked back to the altar and kneeled. The Shaman placed a hand on each of their heads to bless them and with that, they were married. Both stood, embraced and kissed and turned to face the gathered clan.

After hugging her parents, the new couple made their way down the plank and river rock path lined by the members of the tribe who bestowed upon Peter and Little Rain gifts of dried salmon wrapped in cloth, bowls of pemmican, and a few beaver pelts. The couple carried their wedding gifts to Peter's twenty-foot canoe, which he'd recently traded a double bit ax and two tin cups for. Hidden under a canvas tarp with a few pieces of driftwood on top of it was Peter's smoothbore musket, flintlock pistol and powder horn, his rucksack, a map of the Stikine area, compass, hatchet, some clothes, an HBC blanket, water bottle, a coil of sturdy hemp rope, ball of jute, and bailing pail.

Little Rain's family walked up to see them off. She hugged her parents and brother then spoke a few parting words to them. Her mother placed a bearskin blanket over her shoulders to keep her warm and gave her a freshly crafted pair of deerskin moccasins. They both hugged goodbye and Little Rain stepped into the bark and moved to the forward prow. Peter turned around and waved at the whole tribe, who were now standing at the edge of the river bank to see them off. He bowed to the clan members who he'd grown fond of and blew them a kiss to say goodbye and wish them well. Peter pushed the canoe into the water, hopped in the back, and paddled a few strokes to get out in the current where they both turned to wave goodbye again — he saw a few soft tears roll down his new wife's cheek, but he paddled on.

Peter's mind began to fill with thoughts of the next steps to free himself of Thomas McPherson and the Hudson's Bay Company. *If they kill Mr. John and then rid themselves of Fort Stikine and become rich deserters, then so can Little Rain and myself.* But first, he needed to calmly explain to his wife, in small bits and pieces of information, just what they had to do.

"I love you, Little Rain, and I want to take care of you forever," he said. She stopped paddling, turned around unsure of his words, then turned back and began stroking the water again. "I think we should start speaking English from now on. The word *love* means *tik-égh* in jargon."

Little Rain turned around in between strokes and smiled widely. She already knew a few words of her husband's language, including his name.

"Love Pee-ter!" she yelled to the sky, and then looked to see his reaction with a grin.

Traveling with the current, the dugout moved fast over the water. At the lookout spot a few boys of the village ran out from the woods and waved at them as they paddled by. Soon they were well past the home that Little Rain had known all her life and were approaching the nubbin of beach where the secret cabin was.

"We are going to *ko-pet* up ahead."

"*Ko-pet? Káh-ta?*"

Peter's mind started to reel, *you need to start your marriage off right, with the truth.* "I have a cabin, a *house*, over in the woods, the *sticks*. We need to *ko-pet* for supplies, *ik'-tah*."

Trusting her husband, Little Rain took her right hand off her paddle and raised it in acknowledgement but wondered what was going on, since Peter never mentioned a *house* downriver before.

For the last mile he'd been steering them to the correct side of the river that the cabin was on and after one last bend, when he could see the eddy up ahead and the timing was right, he called out, "Turn into the shore." Little Rain caught his meaning and paddled for the eddy.

From his rear position Peter steered the canoe towards the brushy bank just as the sun was beginning to fall low on the horizon. They both hopped out and pulled the bark up onto the sand where it was out of sight and he grabbed the tarp, exposing his musket, pistol and a glass bottle of water. Little Rain was aware of guns, many in her tribe had them. She didn't like them, but knew that Peter and the traders always had to be armed in case of trouble. He led them up the trail.

"*Ne-si'-ka mit'-lite yuk'-wa p o'-laklie?*" Little Rain asked.

Peter stopped and turned around, "*Wake,* no, we're not staying here tonight. We just need to get some things. *Ik'-tah.*"

As they hiked the short trail, Peter thought, *I have to explain to her what's going to happen at the fort and what the next two months will be like.*

"Like I told your parents and you there are some men at the fort who are going to kill Mr. John." Little Rain stopped and turned around with a look of bewilderment on her face.

"Make Mr. John *mem'-a-loost,*" Peter explained again. She nodded her head up and down, showing that she understood.

"*Káh-ta* Mr. John *mem'-a-loost?*" she quietly said.

"The men no like, *wake káh-kwa,* Mr. John, he's bad to the men at the fort, *me-sáh-chie; pe-shuk.*"

Little Rain looked at her husband, her eyes darted back and forth, searching his eyes for meaning, understanding, and safety. She started to shake her head.

"*Wake, wake*, when the men kill Mr. John, the Haida or the Kake will surely attack and overthrow the fort, I think that's what McPherson wants so he can leave with all his ill-gotten gain. When they kill Mr. John, we need to be well on our way to Oregon," Peter said, looking directly into his wife's eyes and using sign language to get his point across. Little Rain turned around, and started walking the trail again.

At the cabin Peter pulled a key from his breeches and unlocked the door. Inside it was dark, but everything was in its place. Little Rain's eyes grew wide when she walked in, seeing the many bundles of beaver pelts, blankets, the keg of gunpowder, and then the rock fireplace and sleeping area in the corner where she stood and kept an inquisitive eye on her new husband.

First, Peter picked up the letter on the keg that McPherson had left and shoved it in his pocket then he spread out the tarp on the floor. He got down on his knees, pulled his knife from its sheath, and, using its sharp tip, wedged open the small trap door in the floor. He reached inside and pulled out three tin boxes and glanced inside of each one. The money, the gems, rings, everything was still there, he set the boxes on the tarp. Next, he stood up and placed as many Hudson's Bay blankets on the tarp that he thought they could carry and wrapped it all up.

"*Ik'-tah yáh-ka kon'-a-way?*"

"This is going to make our new life, *ne-si'-ka chee kloshe*, good."

Little Rain looked at him, clearly confused. Peter smiled and, his voice loving but hurried, explained, "We've been squirreling all this away for months now — anytime any of us has been able to trade for something on the side or steal something from the company, every little thing of any value from me and McPherson and his allies that they were able to pick up or grab in their time here — it's all in these tins. The other men, the Metis, the Sandwich Islanders, they're all running from something — a wife, a father, someone else's husband — they've all got something they're getting away from, and then they spend everything they get on women and drink to try and forget why they came up here and then the fact that now they are here. But I'm different . . . we're different. We've been saving all this up for a rainy day, and this is it. This is my rainy day, *our* rainy day, between McPherson and that damned fool Heroux, so we're takin' the money and running, okay?"

Still looking disoriented but willing to believe what her husband was telling her, she nodded her head in agreement.

"I'll carry the keg and satchel, can you carry the tarp?" Peter asked, throwing the heavy leather bag over his shoulder. By his actions and tone of voice Little Rain knew what he wanted her to do, so she picked up the tarp and they carried the items back down to the river and the waiting canoe.

Peter set the keg in the dugout, saying, "I need to make one more trip," pointing up the trail and motioning like he was carrying something. Little Rain nodded her head and began to load the bark. "I'll be right back."

Back at the cabin, he opened the letter and read it. It was a fresh accounting of the items McPherson had left on his trip upriver earlier that day and how many pelts he needed to bring back to the fort to cover his theft from the company. Peter crumpled it up and dropped it on the floor, then he began to toss outside as many bundles of beaver pelts that he thought he could carry.

Beside the fireplace on the floor was a whale oil lamp, next to that was a flint with a rod and some tinder rope. Peter got down on one knee and with nervous, shaking hands, he began to strike the flint and rod together over a piece of tinder. As soon as it took to flame, he lifted the glass chimney on the lamp and in turn lit it. Then he put the flint, rod and tinder rope in his breeches, and looked around the cabin. His eyes settled on his tiny sleeping area of dirty blankets. He stood up and threw the lamp against the wall right above it, shattering it. It instantly burst into flames and, after watching it for a moment to make sure that the fire was going to take, he ran outside. In no time the cabin was fully engulfed.

At the river, Peter tossed the bundles of pelts into the canoe and pushed them off just as darkness was coming over them. Finally, once they were out in the current and moving swiftly downstream, Peter grabbed his flintlock and placed it next to him between the hull of the dugout and some pelts, then began to speak.

"McPherson wanted me to bring women down to the fort for the men tonight but I decided not to. It was the wrong thing to do and I'm obviously not going to work for him or the company any longer. So, we'll slip by them in the darkness and paddle all night to put as much distance between us and them, forever."

Little Rain turned her head back towards Peter and asked, her voice quavering, "*Káh-ta? Kah ne-si'-ka klat'-a-wa?*"

"We are going south to Oregon, like I told your father, to where it's safe, far from the fort and trouble there," Peter replied. He was relieved to see her move her head up and down so he knew she understood what was happening and that they were going to stick to the plan.

Listening to the sound and tone of her husband's voice and

47

traveling in a loaded canoe of stolen valuables, Little Rain believed she understood what was going on and that they were headed for a new life. She turned around again but this time to smile at her husband, and say goodbye to her life with the Tlingit Bitter Water tribe but instead, she saw a climbing tower of flames and black smoke. Wordlessly, she slowly turned back to the front of the canoe and resumed paddling.

When they got close to the mouth of the Stikine River, near the estuary, Peter steered the bark to the north to stay above the series of islands that dotted the delta. With only the stars to light the way they stayed on a westerly course and soon came to see the glow of the fort in the night. He could see Little Rain's silhouette in front of him, she kept turning her head, glancing in the direction of the fort but said nothing. They kept the numerous islands that filled the Sound to the south to block any chance of being sighted. For hours they fought the tide and finally, just before dawn, they'd gotten to the southeastern portion of an island where they headed for the shoreline. The fort was now behind them.

III

Zarembo Island
S'é X'áat'
April 17, 1842

After skirting past Fort Stikine under the cover of darkness, screened by the many small islands that littered the Sound, Peter and Little Rain paddled along the eastern side of Zarembo Island. Just before dawn they were still days to the north of Fort Simpson at Lax Kw'alaams, a place that Peter was wary of but he also knew that to trade their beaver pelts for food and other essential supplies he would eventually have to enter a Hudson's Bay Fort for an exchange.

Peter knew there was a very long journey before them and that they could run into a Haida war or slave taking party at any time, so he felt it would be best if they slept during the day and traveled in darkness for the time being. As the first light of dawn approached, he quietly said, "I think it's best we head for that island and sleep, *moo'-sum*."

Barely able to paddle any further, Little Rain was pleased to hear the word 'sleep.' She stopped paddling and turned around slowly, glanced at her husband and forced a smile, too tired to talk. Once Peter spied a suitable location where a creek spilled off a mountainside with enough brush along the waterline, he trailed his paddle in the water, steered the dugout towards the shore and they landed.

"We'll need to hide the canoe and stay here all day, *mit'-lite yuk'-wa*, till dark, *po'-lak-lie*."

"*Tum' klas'-ka cháh-ko kim'-ta ne-si'-ka?*" Little Rain asked about his former cohorts.

"They might come after us but I'm more concerned about the Haida raiders," Peter explained. He found the gifted beaver pelts and laid a few on the ground for Little Rain to sleep on with the bearskin robe and his HBC blanket. Then he got the empty water bottle and pemmican, set them next to the make-shift bed, and started cutting branches to cover the dugout. Once done he picked up the glass bottle.

"I'll be right back with some water, *chuk*."

When he returned from the creek, Little Rain was sitting on the pelts with the furry bear blanket wrapped around herself and a piece of pemmican in her hand, staring off into the forest, mute. Peter held out the vessel of fresh, cold water for her. She grabbed it, drank the whole thing, then handed it back with a weak smile. Peter returned to the creek and filled it again.

By the time he got back she'd eaten a good portion of the pemmican and was asleep, snoring. He took another pelt to use for his bed and laid down to get some rest. Before he could even think about it, Peter was asleep, sleeping the deep, deep sleep of a man who has just paddled for twelve-hours.

Later, when the sun was high in the sky, Peter awoke to find Little Rain already sitting upright. She turned and frowned at him, picked up the empty water bottle and held it up. But Peter, cold and still tired, scowled at the outstretched bottle, which Little Rain helpfully shook a little to emphasize that it was empty. Standing up from the damp ground he waved his hand, indicating 'no' and then motioned for his new wife to get up and follow him.

They hiked the trail that Peter had plotted earlier to the creek, filled the bottle together then he led them up to a cliff where they sat and kept lookout. After taking a drink, he said, "We're going to work on your Boston language," and began to point and talk about all the flora of the forest, in English, naming each kind of tree, pointing at rocks, bushes, the saltwater, himself and herself, until in what he thought was a soft wonderful moment he leaned in to kiss her but she pushed him away, hard . . . and then she slapped him across his face.

"*WAKE*!" Little Rain yelled, tears welling up in her eyes. She began to snap off dozens of words in Tlingit, each one as cold as an iceberg, her arms flailing. Peter caught her meaning as he rubbed his jaw, shame and remorse overtaking him and moving through his body. He realized the gravity of their situation had caught up with her, and now them. He looked deep into her eyes.

"I know this is painful for you to leave your family and clan but where we are going it is so much better, Oregon Territory is paradise," he said, pointing south. But from the look of bewilderment on Little Rain's face he knew she wasn't understanding. He searched his mind for the right words in jargon.

"Down there is a place they call Puget Sound, and it is heaven, *ságh-il-lie il'-la-hie*. There is everything you, *me-si'-ka*, could wish, *tik-égh*, for. I saw it after we left Fort Nisqually and steamed north to come up here. Not as much rain, *snass*, and it's warmer with plenty of salmon and food, *muck'-a-muck*, to be had," he said in a positive tone, moving his fingers in a downward motion to

51

show rain and then rubbing his stomach for food. But Little Rain's expression didn't change, she glared at him and then turned away. At that point he knew he had to tell her more.

"I told you that the men at the fort are going to kill, make dead, *mem'-a-loost*, Mr. John."

Little Rain jerked her head around like it was yanked by a string. The look of fear swept over her face. She covered her mouth with her hands, moaned softly and turned away for a moment.

"Mick-fear-son," she said, clumsily, "*mem'-a-loost*, Mr. John?"

"Yes, *áh-ha; e-éh*. When Mr. John is killed, there will be big, *hy-as'*, trouble, *kull*, difficulty, for *ne-si'-ka*, us. They were going to blame me, cheat, *la-láh* me," he said, pointing at himself. "I know it. And they might have killed me too."

Little Rain looked off in the distance, she wiped the tears from her cheeks then leapt to her feet and held her hand out. Peter grabbed hold, squeezed it tight, and she helped him up off the ground. Then she gave him a quick kiss on the cheek and said in a mixture of jargon and English, "*Ne-si'-ka*, we, *klat'-a-wa*, go," and pointed to the south. Peter smiled broadly.

"But first we have work, *mam'-ook*, on the canoe, *boat*, to do."

Little Rain led the way back down to the dugout. Peter was pleased to see that his wife understood the gravity of what was going to happen at Fort Stikine, along with its consequences, and even more pleased to have both of them together, as full partners with plans to make a better life for themselves.

At the canoe Peter dug through the cargo until he located the small tin boxes of valuables. Opening one, he held it out for her to look into. There were many different kinds of coins, the small red sapphire, gold rings, and shillings that the Stikine men had paid for a night with a Tlingit girl.

Little Rain picked up the sapphire with the look of wonderment on her face and weighed it in her hand, then said, *"Klose chik'-a-min,"* with a grin and placed it back in the box.

"Yes, its good money, *chik'-a-min*, for us," Peter replied, "and we need to hide it, *ip'-soot*, in the *boat*, somehow."

He paused to think for a minute, then began to unload all the cargo onto the shore, some of the pelts and gear wet from the nights travel. Little Rain watched at first and then understood what he was doing and helped. Once the bark was empty Peter scanned the inside, looking for any clue as to how and where he could hide the valuables.

He turned the canoe on its side to dump out the small amount of water and then examined the inside carefully and slowly, he finally spied three knot holes. "If I could cut out the center of those knots and bore into the wood, I could hide them in the cavity and then whittle up some new limbs to shove back in . . . perfect!" he said to himself.

Peter pulled his knife from its sheath just as a raven flew up and landed on a limb above him. It watched as he began to dig out the remaining wood in the knots. Once that was done, Peter started searching the forest floor until he found a few dead and dried out limbs close to or a little bigger than the knot holes, he began to strip the bark and whittle them down. While Peter worked, Little Rain laid down on the beaver pelts with the bearskin robe and took a nap.

Hours later, the red late-day sun was dipping towards the horizon and Peter had fashioned the exact sized plugs for the knot holes. He placed the sapphire into the smallest hole and shoved the plug into it then whacked the top of it with the butt end of his hatchet, it wedged itself deeper into the hole. He kept hitting it until it was tight. Satisfied with his ad-hoc hiding spot he went to work on the next one.

When he was finished, they were only big enough for the emeralds and too small for the gold and silver coins. "*Merde!*" he spat out, angry that he had to come up with another hiding place. He said it so loud that Little Rain woke up at his cursing, and, sleepily, she stood and walked over to watch him.

Peter held out the handful of coins and said, "We still need to hide these." Little Rain understood and nodded. She said, "*O'-pit-sah* wood," motioning with her hand flat, slashing her hand upward and pointing at the cross-brace seats.

He looked at the hand-cut seats and sides of the canoe, the multiple gashes in the wood showing different angles of cuts. *If I slice out some of the wood under the seats where they fit in the notches, I could wedge the coins under them.*

"*Sacre Bleu!*" Peter said, leaping up and hugging his wife. "That's it! That'll work!" and he went back to his task.

He placed the canoe on its side and began to carefully carve out tiny slots under one side of a seat with his buck knife, while the raven still watched. He held a coin up to the notch to check the sizing and worked some more. Once he was sure the coin would tightly fit, he pressed it into the slot and pushed with his fingers as hard as he could, then found a small rock to push with and finished the job. It was perfect, but it had taken too long and now dusk was coming upon them.

"I'll finish hiding the coins at our next stop," he said. Peter pulled a small leather pouch from his breeches and dumped the rest of the money inside of it, then started to reload the canoe. Little Rain understood and started to help.

"We should sleep, *moo'-sum*, for an hour and then start traveling again."

"Yes, sleep," Little Rain replied in Boston. Peter looked at her and smiled, happy to hear that his wife was beginning to learn the language she'd soon need to survive.

Turning to Little Rain and giving her a soft smile, he said, "I came up here on the Hudson's Bay ship *Beaver,* and tried my best to remember the coastline and the channels we traveled but we've got a long, long way to go and the map I have is only of the Stikine River. Are you sure when you left, *mahsh*, your village, your people, *til'i-cum*, go, *klat'a-wa*, south to the *pish* camp that you can find it again?" he said, pointing in the direction. Little Rain paused to think about the words he used and then smiled.

"Yes, I . . . *kum'-tuks*."

"So, you know the way south?"

"Yes," she repeated, pointing south, adding, "*Tsimshian Tlingit Kitschk-hin, pish, pish.*"

"How many days, *suns,* to get there?" Peter asked, his heart beginning to pound. Little Rain looked up to the sky to try and recall when she was little and her family took her and her brother to the fishing camp. She looked down at her fingers, counted them off, then looked up.

"*Klone suns*," she answered, holding up three fingers.

"Three," Peter said, showing his fingers, "days?"

"Yes," she replied again.

"*Merveilleuse!*" Peter exclaimed with joy just as the raven flew off. They watched it until it was out of sight, then he added, "Let's get some rest and we'll set out after dark."

Little Rain smiled and nodded.

IV

Etolin Island
HAA du éet yann X̄ōots
April 18, 1842

Before heading out, Peter and Little Rain each ate a small portion of their dwindling supply of pemmican and salmon, filled their bottle at the creek and they were ready. Peter pushed the canoe off and jumped in, taking his seat at the back of the dugout. They started paddling together and, after a few strokes, he looked up at the sky and was pleased to see the stars. First, they had to cross the narrow channel that drained the inland Sound and cross over to Etolin Island. Luck was with them, they rode an ebb tide on a diagonal course across the passage and got to the other side.

They then turned south, hugging the shore of Etolin, and headed down the strait. With the stars to keep them company they fell into a rhythm and made good time. But a third of the way down the island the wind came up and the stars disappeared — soon a windstorm was upon them, the tide changed and white caps crashed over the bow, soaking Little Rain to the bone.

"We've got to take cover!" Peter yelled into the wind, the cold waves splashing over the gunwales. "Turn, turn towards the shore! We'll never make any headway in this! It's going to get worse!"

Little Rain took his meaning and they both furiously paddled towards the island as it began to rain. Just a dozen yards from the beach, a wave grabbed the canoe and, carrying it high above the water, brought it back down onto the shore with a terrific crash! The newly married couple were both drenched by the spray and Peter watched helplessly as, bracing himself against the canoe, three of the beaver pelt bundles flew out of the dugout and into the foaming sea.

Jumping out they pulled the bark as far as they could up onto the beach, where Peter took the bowline and tied it off on the end of a drift log. Then the rain, which had been coming straight down, started coming at them sideways. Peter dug through the canoe's jumbled cargo and found an extra canvas tarp, they ran up to the edge of the forest where they took refuge under the limbs of a towering fir tree and huddled together, shivering, watching in cold, exhausted silence for hours as the rain and the wind battered the land and the sea, the surf roaring in outrage as it was pelted and shoved by the storm. As the dim light of day began to unfold, Peter and Little Rain, drenched and exhausted, finally faded off to sleep beneath the tarp, leaning against each other.

When they woke the skies were gray and sea had calmed, the tide was in and the canoe was floating. Peter walked down to the bow-line, pulled the bark to the shore, found the pemmican and water bottle and retied the dugout.

Handing the water and food to Little Rain, he said, "I don't think we can stay here. The boat can be seen so we need to head farther down the beach where we can hide it and us for the day."

His wife didn't say a word, she just looked at him, pouted, and then nodded her head up and down. She drank some of the water and ate a tiny portion of what was left of the now waterlogged pemmican.

Peter walked out on the beach and looked over the saltwater, then scanned up and down the shoreline. There was a small island to the west and another to the east just south of a point, the main big island they were on then turned to the south. *If we headed east, near that small island, there's got to be cover and we'd be closer to that shore to follow tonight. But what are we going to do about food?* He stepped back over to Little Rain.

"If we head up the beach towards that island," he said, pointing, "we should be able to find cover." His wife looked at him and held out the pemmican.

"You go ahead and eat it, *muck'-a muck*. We need to get going."

They got back in the canoe and paddled east along the shoreline, both of them still wet from the night's rainstorm and bone-tired. Feeling she'd made the biggest mistake in her life, Little Rain felt hopeless and lost. *Why did I do this? Is this what love is? I wish I was back home with my family, laughing and playing in my village*, when she saw something up ahead, splashing and moving across the water.

"*Nan'-itsh nah!*" she hollered, then turned around to see if Peter saw the same thing. "*Ik'-tah yáh-ka?*"

Little Rain bent down so Peter could see over and past her. He scanned the surface until he saw the same thing. Up ahead, just east of the canoe, there were three deer in the water, one stag with an enormous set of antlers and two does, swimming from the small island over to where Peter and Little Rain were headed.

"Deer! Paddle! Paddle as fast as you can!" Peter hollered. "We need to get that male before he gets to the shore!"

With their mouths instantly watering at the prospect of fresh venison, Peter and Little Rain paddled frantically towards the slowly swimming animals. Once they got close, Peter pointed at the lead stag with his paddle and happily cried, "We need to get right next to that buck so that I can grab him by his antlers!"

They swiftly closed on the animals and brought the canoe right up beside the big male, his coal black eyes darting back and forth, breathing hard and snorting through his nostrils. Peter closed his eyes, took a few deep breaths, addressed a quick prayer to Mother Mary that he be safe, and, bracing his legs against the side of the rough canoe, lunged for the deer and grabbed onto its slick antlers as hard as he could.

The stag bellowed and began to flail its front legs, the water splashing and churning around them. Seized by both Peter and terror, the deer began to jerk its head ferociously from side to side, desperate to knock the human away, trying to hit Peter with his horns but he held on and reached for the stern line, wrapping it around the great beast's antler just as the two does made it to shore. The animal bellowed in agony and Peter jerked even harder — its eyes rolled in fury as, exhausted already from the swim, he mustered the last of his strength to slash at Peter and at being lassoed and fastened to the bark while knocking the side of the canoe. Peter pulled his knife from its sheath and slashed the deer's throat — the stag pulled away at the last moment, stretching the lasso almost to breaking, and then, with a shattering blow, the line contracted and the beast threw itself against the canoe.

Little Rain screamed as the dugout rocked, and Peter's blood ran cold, time seemed to freeze as he lost his balance and slid on the slick floor of the dugout, falling below the gunwale. But the line held, and, suddenly recovering, Peter found he had not dropped his knife — looking back to make sure that Little Rain was okay, he jabbed again — the great stag had not been able to break the rope, so his reprieve had done him no good. Peter's Montreal-made steel knife cut through the thick, wet hide of the deer and spilled blood into the Sound. It shrieked and bellowed as the saltwater poured into him and his life poured out. The spasms of its death agony began, violent and wild, and as the animal splashed and reared in the water for all it was worth, Peter ducked back below the rear prow of the canoe and covered his head. He smiled at Little Rain, whose eyes were wild with fear and panic as she also crouched in the floor of the boat.

"It's okay," Peter said with a smile, almost inaudible over the shrieking of the dying stag, "This is the end, in a few minutes it will be over."

He beamed at her, knowing that, although the great majority of the work was still ahead of him, the dangerous part was done. Little Rain did not seem to share his enthusiasm, as they lay in the pooled saltwater in the bottom of their canoe, but he knew her mood would change once she had some roasted venison in her empty stomach. Finally, all the deer's blood had spilled into the saltwater, its cries silent, its life ended.

Peter, panting hard, looked to his wife — Little Rain was now smiling the biggest smile he'd seen since they got married because finally, they would feast.

Glancing around to see if any Haidas had heard the commotion, Peter saw no one on the shore or on the water in the distance but the beach looked too steep and there was no cover. Turning to the east, it appeared that there was an inlet where they could hide and butcher the deer.

"We need to go around that point so we're hidden," he remarked. Little Rain understood the words, turned around on her bench-like seat and began to paddle. *There should be some bit of beach with cover where we can carve this animal up, some backstrap will take care of the rumble in our bellies.*

Peter grabbed hold of his paddle and began to stroke with earnest, a twisted trail of slowly sinking blood following behind them. Once around the point a deep, narrow bay lay before them with brushy banks. A quarter mile into it Peter saw a suitable location with a shallow, sandy beach.

"There," he said, pointing with his paddle.

At the shore they had great difficulty struggling to handle the great beast, getting it untied, pulling and dragging it up to the shallows. Peter immediately gutted it and removed the intestines, letting them slosh into the water, the stink of the opened carcass fowling the air. Next, he began to skin the animal while Little Rain started to unload the canoe and carry the wet cargo into the close-by brush. She took a walk into the woods to empty her bladder and spotted a blown-down cedar tree, the dry splinters of wood jutting up from the stump. Little Rain snapped off a good number of small pieces and carried them back to the cargo area and dropped them on the ground. She walked back down to the canoe for another load.

Two-hours later, Peter had skinned the stag and was in the process of butchering a hind quarter. Little Rain had finished unloading the dugout and was cutting sticks with Peter's pocketknife at the campsite, whittling them up with sharp points at each end. When she was done, she went back to the cedar stump and got more pieces of kindling for the fire that night. She walked down to her husband to check on the butchering. He'd stripped off all the backstrap and had a good pile of the bloody stuff laying on the rocks next to him. Peter looked up and grinned at her.

"I think we'll need to cook as much of it as we can today. That way it will keep better. I wish we had some salt," he said, sweat dripping off his brow.

"Yes," Little Rain answered, "I make sticks *mam'-ook pi'-ah*."

"Good, thank you."

She picked up a handful of backstrap and carried it to the camp and began to mount each long piece on a stick for cooking then leaned them up against a near-by tree. Next, she searched the beach, looking for large flat stones she could cook venison steaks on. Soon she'd found a cache of them and a small freshwater stream trickling through the rocks and into the bay. She carried a few flat stones back to camp and arranged them in a circle. Then, using Peter's pocket knife, she cut out the forest floor duff and removed it all, exposing the rocky earthen soil for a fire pit. After that was done, she started whittling one of the cedar stump kindling pieces, running the blade perpendicular to the wood to create curly bits of tipsoo starter material for later. She walked back down to Peter, he was just about finished and dusk was coming on.

"We need to find a water, *chuk*, source," he said, looking up and down the beach.

"Yes," Little Rain replied, then pointed towards the little trickle of water she'd found earlier. "I *klap chuk*."

An hour later it was dark, and they were cooking backstrap beside a warm cedar fire that was snapping and bursting with energy, filling them with hopefulness and soon, much needed protein. They both lounged on dried beaver pelts and delighted in the aroma of charring venison, it filled their heads and soothed their souls. With her marital impulses aroused, Little Rain leaned over and kissed Peter, long and hard. Then she kicked off her moccasins, stood up while lifting her deerskin dress above her head and took it off, letting it fall to the forest floor, exposing her bosom and naked body. She lay on top of her husband and they made love for the first time, consummating their marriage.

At dawn Little Rain sat up with a start. She could hear rocks moving down on the beach and heavy breathing. Standing up her eyes bulged out of their sockets; an adult grizzly bear was rummaging around where some of the butchered carcass of the deer remained, licking and pushing it and the bloody rocks around. Instantly dropping down next to her soundly sleeping husband she placed her hand over his mouth.

"*Its 'woot si-am'*," she whispered, her expression burning with fear. Peter slowly opened his bleary eyes, confused at first, but then he grabbed Little Rain by the arm and pulled her down next to him. He quietly crept on his belly to catch a glimpse of the hungry animal. Once he saw the grizzly, twenty-yards away chomping on the carcass, he glanced around the camp. Cooked and still raw deer meat littered the encampment in piles. They didn't have much time, the bear would smell them out soon, they'd need to scramble to leave and silently, but he wasn't about to let that beast reward himself with their newfound gain.

Trying to stay as quiet as possible, almost not to even breathe, the two padded quietly around the camp, staying low, to gather their things. The knives, Peter's pistol, and the best but not all of the cooked steaks and backstrap went into Peter's rucksack, and then the two crept, low and slow, out of the camp and into the forest. The grizzly, if he noticed them, did not seem very interested — it was not every day that half a deer carcass showed up on your beach, still fresh, and you certainly never wasted such an opportunity to go chase around some skinny little humans.

When they were fifty-yards up the bay Peter stopped and looked back through the foliage. The bear was making his way towards their camp, his nose to the ground, sniffing his way right to their cache of life saving meat. *Do we make a run for the dugout and escape? Or do we wait the bear out and let him just have a feast of our food? Should I get my musket from the boat and shoot him? No, I can't do that, it would alarm any near-by hostile Haidas. Or do we make a run for the canoe, paddle across the bay and wait for him to leave? Maybe we should just watch him from here and see what he does?* Peter turned and looked at Little Rain.

"I think we should wait and watch, *tik'-tik*, the *its'woot si-am'*," he whispered. She nodded in agreement. They both turned back to the bear but he'd made his way up the bank and into the camp, the thick forest blocked their view. Peter put his nose to the wind, a slight breeze was coming into the bay from the strait. Thankfully they were downwind of the animal. Then Peter pointed uphill, above the camp, to where they would get a better viewing angle.

Silently they crept upward through the forest, glancing back and forth from the camp to the placement of each step they took. Soon they were above it and watched as the bear made fast work of their spoils, swallowing huge chunks of meat with an unlimited appetite, grunting in delight at such a hearty and easily found meal.

Twenty minutes later, the grizzly must have gotten its fill but was thinking in advance of future hunger, it sunk its teeth into one of the quarter sections and started dragging it away. Walking backwards with a hind section in its mouth, the bear made its way to the beach and north, back to its den.

"*Merde,*" Peter whispered. "If we go back to the camp or the canoe, we'll be upwind and the bear will smell us." Little Rain caught his meaning and looked at her husband.

"We *nan-itsh',*" she whispered, then shifted her eyes back to the grizzly.

In what seemed like no time the bear was a good way up the shoreline. Peter knew it would return but he also knew it would be a good thing to be able to see the animal at all times too. Staying as quiet as they could they went back to the camp to retrieve the rest of the deer meat and few belongings. Peter immediately went to the edge of the beach and looked up the bay but the bear had disappeared!

"HURRY! *Howh; Hy-ak'*! He's gone, it might have caught wind of us and taken the meat to the forest!"

Little Rain snatched the beaver pelt bedding, blanket and valuable water bottle up off the ground and Peter, still lugging the rucksack full of backstrap and deer meat, started to drag a hindquarter away. Little Rain saw his action and bundled everything under one arm and tip-toed over to Peter to help pull. Just as they got close to the canoe the crashing sound of tree limbs breaking and the rumbling noise of something big and angry came crashing through the trees. Their hearts racing, they tossed the hindquarter and rucksack into the boat and with both of them on either side of the canoe they pushed the heavy dugout into the water, jumped aboard and paddled as rapidly as they could.

A deep guttural ROAR! blasted from the shoreline. Turning around, they saw the grizzly, standing on its hind legs, it took a swing through the air with its giant paw, as if it was taking a swipe at them. Then it dropped down on all fours, growled, barring its teeth and after another deep, bass roar for good measure, the bear slowly, and lazily, made its way back to the meat still in the camp.

"*Ah ha!*" Peter exclaimed, nervously laughing with the relief of their getaway. "*Nous vivons pour voir un autre jour!*"

Little Rain threw her head back, laughing at her husband's joy, and sudden burst of French. She smiled at him and asked, "*Ik'-tah wau'-wau?*"

Peter searched his mind for the right words in jargon and then said, "We live to see another day! *Ne-si'-ka nan'-itsh to-mol'-la.*"

As they paddled south, both knew they couldn't just go across the bay where the bear could search them out, and Peter reminded himself that they shouldn't be traveling in daylight. *Where can we get away and be safe from that bear and not be sighted by any Haidas? The island! The island that the deer were swimming from!*

"We should head for that island," Peter said, he stopped paddling and pointed at the now in sight piece of land. Little Rain turned around and saw where he was aiming, she grinned and nodded in agreement.

Once there, they found a wide enough notch in the boulders that lined the island where they could hide and tie-off the dugout. For the rest of the day, they slept in the shaded forest, happy for both the respite and the fact that, once again, their stomachs and their packs were filled with food.

By dusk they'd nearly exhausted their water supply but still had plenty to eat. Each of them munched on charred backstrap until Peter said, "If we can get to the south end of *that* island by dawn," pointing at the large piece of ground across the channel in the distance, "we'll be in good shape."

Little Rain nodded, understanding the basic meaning of his words, she picked up their bedding and headed for the canoe and Peter followed. Night was coming on and it was time to get moving again.

Ketch-ih-kan
Kichx̱áan
April 22, 1842

After a night of traveling, and with the golden light of a new day cresting over the snowy peaks of the coastal range to the east, fanning out over the cold, calm waters of Clarence Strait, Peter and Little Rain had found their way to the southernmost point of the island. They ached from paddling and needed to rest. Twice they had stopped during the night when they could hear the cascade of fresh water emptying into the sea, to replenish their water supply. Across the narrow channel before them was a grouping of small islands and a large body of water beyond that they'd need to eventually cross.

We're a long way from that bear, there's probably just more down here at this end though, maybe we should head for that small group of islands? But there's no water out there. I think it's worth the risk to stay here, we need water.

"We should take cover over there," Peter said, pointing with his paddle at the shore. Once they found a brushy location at a shallow cove, they beached the canoe and went ashore where they found a small open clearing with perfect cover for a day camp. Little Rain went back to the bark to begin the process of unloading while Peter hiked up the beach with the bottle in search of fresh water.

A good ten minutes later he returned.

"How many more *suns* to the *pish*, camp?" he asked, taking off his knit cap and using it to wipe the sweat off his brow before putting it back on his head.

Little Rain stopped what she was doing, put her hands on her hips and thought. She looked at her fingers and was about to count them off but didn't.

"*Mokst, suns*, two," she said, smiling at the thought of knowing the right number in Boston language.

"*Merde*, still two days," Peter swore, knowing full well they'd lost a day or more with the deer and bear. "That means two more nights which means we're really going to take three days to traverse, what, forty miles? Forty-five? Any voyageur worth his salt back home would be going triple our speed! At least!" Little Rain watched him silently as he raged. When he had settled down, she padded over and gave him a soft hug. Peter smiled, "You know, considering everything that's happened . . . our pace really hasn't been that bad. We'll be okay."

They spent the rest of the day reclining under the evergreens wrapped in their beaver pelts and bear robe, quietly eating and napping and watching the soft sun gradually rise above and then gradually sink back into the horizon, bathing the water and the land in the warm reds and purples of evening. At one point in the late afternoon, they climbed to a high point where they could view the large body of water that they'd need to cross that night, and the strait beyond, past a peninsula. Little Rain pointed at the wide channel.

"*Yah-wa Tsimshiam Kitschk-hin*," she said.

"Will anyone be there?" he asked, "*til'-i-kum yah-wa; ko-pah?*"

Little Rain shook her head 'no' and then said, "*Wake pish, wake til'-i-kum.*"

"It's a summer fishing camp then?"

"Yes, two *moons pish.*"

"Right, the fish start running in June. So, we should get back and get ready to go," Peter said, standing, then helping his young bride to her feet. They hiked down the mountain to camp and began again to reload the canoe for another night of travel.

Ten-hours of arduous, but uneventful paddling later, they'd crossed the big expanse, riding with the tide over smooth, flat water and had made excellent time. At dawn they were at the southern tip of the peninsula that they'd viewed from the mountain lookout the day before. They were finally beginning to put some distance between them and Fort Stikine. *I wonder if McPherson discovered the burned down cabin yet? Did they even search for us or go to the Bitter Water village looking for me? Well, that's all in the past now.*

As the first light of day kissed the shore of the peninsula Peter began to scan in earnest for another resting spot — he espied a shrubby creek coming down the rocks of an island into the Sound and gestured for Little Rain to paddle towards it. They pulled ashore right as the sun was beginning to shine in earnest, and before the dispelling of the gray mists of dawn they had dragged everything ashore and were well on their way to making camp.

Six hours later a rain front moved in, the cold water on their faces waking both of them up. Peter grabbed the tarp and draped it over a low-hanging limb of a nearby hemlock tree to make them a lean-to where they stayed the rest of the day napping, eating deer meat and drinking water from the narrow stream.

At dusk they began the loading routine again and were soon paddling south, across a wide strait towards the narrow channel that would lead them to the fish camp location. Halfway across in the darkness Peter felt his feet getting cold. He reached down and discovered more water than there usually was in the bottom of the dugout. He instantly remembered the hard landing a few nights before during the storm — the canoe must have cracked then and he hadn't noticed, and had only been getting worse.

"We're taking on water! There's lots of water in the canoe! *Chuk ko'-pa boat!*" Peter cried, reaching for the bailing pail. Little Rain turned around with a confused and frightened look on her face.

"*Ni-ka mam'-ook,*" she replied, motioning for the bucket. Peter tossed it forward and Little Rain began bailing. She'd bail as much as she could and then paddle a little bit until the bark needed bailing again.

Three hours later, exhausted, they completed the hard crossing and had entered the channel but a stiff breeze came up, the narrow waterway turned into a wind tunnel, the breeze brought with it cloud cover taking away the night stars and the small amount of vision they had. They beached the canoe on the north side of the passage, dragging it up the shore as far as they could to keep the water from seeping in, and staggering to the tree line, laid down and tried to get some sleep.

In the morning the skies were clear and the water was calm once again. Peter unloaded the canoe and checked the condition of the bark, he found a thin four-foot-long crack in the hull but he didn't have the tools or materials to fix it. Cursing, he re-loaded the dugout knowing that he'd have to paddle while Little Rain bailed.

In the meantime, Little Rain had scanned the immediate area. She recognized a high cliff that jutted straight up out of the water and knew they were very close to the summer fish camp she'd visited with her parent's years before. Little Rain recollected playing with distant friends and relished in thoughts and memories dear to her heart. The reminder of those days bubbled up inside of her and she began to load the dugout with excitement. But Peter had different ideas.

"We can't travel in the daylight, there's too much danger with the threat of Haidas still. Plus, we need to plug that leak somehow," he mused.

"*Wake, wake* Haidas. *Tsimshian Tlingit pish camp*," she said, putting her hands to her heart. "My *til'-i-kum*."

"Those are your people?"

"Yes, my pee-pull," she said clumsily.

"And you think it's safe," he replied, then searched for a better word and said, "*kwass*?"

"Yes, yes!" she exclaimed, smiling and stomping her right foot to get her point across. "*Ne-si'-ka mam'-ook boat kloshe ko'-pa pish camp*."

"*Ayez votre chemin*!" Peter said in French. But his wife looked at him with an odd sideways grin.

"Yes, yes, have it your way! We can go and try to fix the boat at the fish camp."

Little Rain ran over to her husband, jumped into his arms, and hugged him tight. Then pulled back and kissed him hard on the lips. Peter smiled at seeing his wife so happy.

"*D'accord, d'accord.* Okay, okay, let's load the canoe and head out."

Little Rain was so happy she did a quick Tlingit dance, light on her feet with her arms held out like wings as she skip-hopped in a circle, full of joy. She eagerly loaded the dugout and was ready in no time.

Roughly ten-miles later, and four slow hours of one person paddling and one bailing, they came into view of a ramshackle camp next to a large creek with a good number of flat-front plank houses along the shore similar to her own village, but there wasn't a soul in sight — no men out fishing or repairing nets, no children at play, no women cooking over fires.

"Yep, no one here, wrong month for fish," Peter said, as they approached.

But Little Rain didn't say anything. Right when they landed, she leapt out of the dugout and ran up the bank to the deserted village. She immediately studied the buildings, settled on one she recognized, and bounded over to it, pushing the door open and going inside. A moment later she heard the caw of the raven and came back out. It had just landed in a near-by tree and was walking back and forth on a long limb, bobbing its head and cackling. She took it as a good sign even though the village was empty.

"I *kum'-tuks o'-koke*," she said, with a somber look.

"You remember that one, huh?" Peter asked, walking up to her nodding.

"Yes," Little Rain answered. She started walking around, gazing at other plank houses built of weathered cedar with shallow pitched shed roofs, peeking into them while Peter got his bearings and took a good look at their surroundings. There were piles of sharpened hemlock sticks used for drying salmon lying about and lots of fire pits ringed with rocks, nothing immediately useful. Then he turned his attention to the water and noticed that the channel they just traveled through was between two islands with a narrow southernly passage between them. Bulging mountains rose up to the east with glaciers and snowcapped peaks. He could see it was a fine spot for a fishing camp, being built right next to the wide, rushing creek and somewhat sheltered, when his heart skipped a beat.

Out there, on the clear, calm waters of the south passage, he could see a canoe paddling towards the village. Fast, coming on with a purpose, cutting and churning up the water violently as it approached. Although they were still far off, Peter felt that, looking at the silhouettes of the figures in it, they were men.

He glanced over at Little Rain, she was smiling and waving at them, next he looked down to the dugout, then at the oncoming canoe again. Believing that his wife was correct in her earlier statement of her people, but still a bit wary, he slowly made his way over to the dugout and found his pistol. Turning his back to the men in the canoe, he shoved the flintlock into his wide belt and walked up the bank and over to a still smiling and waving Little Rain.

"They're not Haidas?"

"*Wake*, no Haida. *Ni'-ka* pee-pull," she said, pointing at the shape of the canoe. "*Hul-o'-i-ma boat. Hul-o'-i-ma o-pitl-kegh.*"

As they got closer Peter understood what she was talking about, he remembered learning about how the Haidas built and sculpted the bows of their canoes with a large, sweeping upward turn. This boat's bow had a low attitude, but as they approached the two Indians had hard looks on their faces. It didn't deter his wife.

"*Ni-ka Tlingit. Aakáawu Taneidi. Shtax'héen!*" she yelled. Little Rain ran down to the water's edge and began speaking in her native tongue to them just as they landed. Peter listened carefully, trying to understand what they were saying, but more importantly, he wanted to get a feel for the tone of their words.

Both Indians bounded out of the canoe and stood talking with Little Rain. Each were wearing loincloths and had strings of shell and bead necklaces dangling from their necks, and long, bone knives sheathed in deer hide at their sides hanging from thin leather belts, black tattoos covered their upper heavy-set bodies. One wore a wicker hat of woven spruce root; each were barefoot and had long stringy black hair. Their voices, as they responded to Little Rain's babbling, were calm and smooth.

"*Tsimshian Tlingit,*" one of them said, bobbing his head up and down.

"*Taquan Maxlakxaala,*" the other said, pointing down the passage they'd just come from. All three continued to converse in the Tlingit dialect for another few minutes. Little Rain pointed at their leaky canoe a number of times but when Peter heard Little Rain say, *Mister John*, he knew he should try and stop her from saying anything more.

"A-hem!" Peter coughed, clearing his throat loudly. The three of them turned and looked at him. Little Rain pointed at Peter and said, "*Ni'ka man. Kloshe.*" She motioned for him to come over to them, which he did.

"*Klas'-ka tik-égh ne-si'-ka ko'-pa chah-ko ko'-pa,*" Little Rain said to Peter, her eyes bright and eager.

Peter glanced back and forth between his wife and the two Tlingit, then inside their canoe and back at them. They had sincere looks on their faces but there were five or six spears in their dugout. Then one of them started talking to Peter and pointing at his canoe. From the jargon he knew and the limited amount of Tlingit he'd picked up Peter soon came to realize that they were inviting them to their village and wanted to help fix the leak in their dugout. Peter nodded his head, looked at Little Rain and grinned.

"Maybe we could trade with them for some pemmican, and cook, *mam'-ook pi-ah*, the rest of the deer, *mow'-itsh*," he said, smiling at his wife. She returned his smile brightly, beaming with affection.

Little Rain turned to the two men and began speaking to them with great vigor while motioning with her hands. She latched onto Peter's arm and began to pull him towards their dugout just as the two Tlingit shoved off and jumped into their bark.

After another quarter of a day of paddling and bailing, they could see the welcome sight of smoke from campfires curling into the air. The weight that had been oppressing Peter's heart instantly disappeared as they rounded the rocky point of the oncoming island and, at the far end of a small bay, sighted on a lovely little stretch of level ground along the shore, above which he saw children playing, the adults bustling about their daily business, and the ever-present cedar plank houses and totems of the village. The canoe was going to be repaired, they would be able to restore their lost supplies, they were going to be okay.

The two Tlingit had gotten ahead of them and were already onshore, gathering a welcoming party for the visitors. Children rushed to the beach while other tribal members dropped their daily tasks and followed them to the beach to catch a glimpse of what was happening.

When they finally landed, Little Rain jumped from her bow position smiling and waving then helped Peter pull the bark up onto the sand. Peter took the tarp off the cargo and grabbed the hind quarter of deer. He raised the heavy piece of meat over his head and two young warriors walked over to him and carried it away for cooking, while children ran down to touch them, smiling and giggling.

The two Tlingit stood on the bank with an older man, who Peter took for the chief. He wore a red robe with artful weavings sewn on it depicting a black and gray sea lion while the tribe members called out, "*Aakáawu Taanta Kwaan!*" They motioned for the two of them to come up and into the village. Soon they were surrounded by Natives, smiling and talking happily in Tlingit, and led to the center of the encampment where there was a large circular firepit. The two youths who had taken the quarter section of deer already had it suspended over the pit on a rotisserie and were in the process of stoking the existing hot coals to cook it. Blankets were placed on the ground and the two guests sat down with Chief Taanta Kwaan next to them, women brought clay jugs of drinking water and bowls of shredded dried salmon.

Once they were settled, the Chief looked to Little Rain and they began to converse. For the next hour they talked, going back and forth, sometimes laughing and throwing their arms in the air, at other times the conversations seemed serious and heavy. The words '*Lax Kw'alaans*' and '*Or-e-gon*' came up a number of times, and the Chief also said, "*Tlëil Haida*," and he mentioned, "*Fort Sim-pah-son*," over and over. Peter's ears perked up whenever he heard either of them mention '*Tleil Haida*,' but whatever the context was or the direction of their meaning, Peter was not able to pick it up

Then the Chief called out over his people with a loud voice and three adult men emerged from the crowd surrounding them. He gave the three long, rambling instructions and they disappeared back into the village. The Chief looked at Peter, pointed a bony old finger at his chest and said, "*Xát yéi awsinei yee yaakw.*"

Peter had no idea what the Tyee had said, but the tone of his voice sounded like he was saying something good. Little Rain was smiling at him and nodding like he should agree. So Peter moved his head up and down, grinned, and said, "*Máh-sie*. Thank you." Then Little Rain leaned over to him and said, "*Haida mahsh*," and Peter took her comment to mean that the raiders had left the area and Chief Taanta Kwaan felt that they could travel during the day.

Next a group of young women appeared, wearing traditional deerskin dresses and bark headbands, and started dancing around the fire pit and singing. They raised their heads to the sky and sang songs that filled the air as the deer meat sizzled over the fire and good feelings came over the village.

That evening, as they watched the red sun sink into the Sound, barely able to move as they reclined on blankets on the sandy beach, stuffed to bursting from the welcoming feast of salmon, clams, crab, muscles, camas root cakes and venison, Peter and Little Rain saw men working on the canoe, carrying tools and clay

79

bowls over to the damaged bark. Groaning with effort, reluctant but responsible, the two levered themselves off their warm blankets and plodded over to the canoe to inspect their work.

The men had unloaded the canoe's cargo and covered it with their tarp further up the beach, to protect it from the ever-possible rain and the ever-present tide, and had begun to repair the crack the boat had suffered.

Using steel knives and cedar mallets, the men carefully, arduously cut out the crack in the hull of the canoe and then pounded in long strips of whittled cedar that had been soaked in pitch. The pitch grabbed on to the hull of the canoe, and after a night of drying Peter knew the craft would be ready to sail again, good as new. The men were skilled in their work, they'd done it a hundred times before and would do it a hundred times again, canoes were the lifeblood of every coastal tribe and the work of their maintenance was a critical constant of life.

Peter stepped closer to inspect the work, it was finely crafted, far better than anything he could do.

"*Máh-sie, máh-sie,*" Peter said, smiling appreciatively at the workers. They looked up from their work and grinned and nodded at him.

"*Gunalchéesh!*" Little Rain said, thanking them in Tlingit. They immediately smiled broadly and started talking to her, explaining and pointing out what they had done. The three of them then picked up the dugout, turned it right side up and set it down on a series of small logs next to them that would work to roll the boat back into the water in the morning. Then they reloaded the bark, smiled, and walked back to the village.

After spending the night in a small plank house provided just for them, they awoke to clear, sunny skies and a low tide. A group of young children were waiting for them outside when they emerged and led them down to their awaiting dugout canoe. It was filled with sewn deerskin bags of water, baskets of berries, pemmican, a huge basket of dried salmon fillets and even some deer meat from the night before. The Chief and some of the elders of the tribe arrived to see them off, waving and smiling.

Then Chief Taanta Kwaan walked down to them, he handed Little Rain a large rolled-up piece of deerskin. The Chief motioned for her to open it which she did. It was a hand-drawn map in dark dried berry juice of all the islands and straits that they had made especially for them. Peter grinned at Little Rain widely, saying, "It's a map!"

Taanta Kwaan pointed at the ground where they stood and then put his finger on the map, showing them where they were. Then he placed his finger on a different spot on the map and said, "*Sim-pah-son.*" Peter was elated.

"*Máh-sie, Máh-sie!*" Peter said, thanking him in jargon. The Chief smiled and gave Little Rain a hug. He nodded his head at Peter, then walked back up to his people.

Little Rain and Peter waved back and then began to push the canoe over the logs while a few young boys picked up the logs they'd just rolled over and carried them to the front of the canoe to roll on down to the waterline.

Before they began paddling, Peter stowed the new valuable

deerskin map with his Stikine map and wedged them between some cargo and the inside hull of the dugout where they'd be safe.

His chore done, Peter luxuriated in the dry canoe — never had it felt so good to put down his feet into something that wasn't filling with water. They paddled away smoothly, easily, the water was calm and glass-like, they would make good time to Fort Simpson, especially now that they had a map to follow. As they paddled, every so often reaching into one of their gift baskets for a breakfast of pemmican or dried salmon, they came upon a small canoe manned by two of the local Tlingit girls. As they approached, Peter could see that one was pulling up a thickly braided sinew line, the other was holding a crude net fashioned from a 'Y' shaped tree limb with woven bark netting, she was looking down at the water. When the girl holding the net raised her hand the other stopped pulling the line, the net went into the water and scooped up a crab!

Peter drifted closer and saw that they had a piece of deer meat on the end of the line that the crab must have clawed onto and did not let go of all the way to the top. He marveled at the simple, but ingenious method to catch fresh crab.

"We'll have to try that on our way to Fort Simpson," Peter said, as they began to paddle south.

"*Ne-si'-ka klat-a'-wa Sim-pah-sum!*" Little Rain exclaimed, happy to be headed towards the supply destination.

"Yes, we'll be able to trade for flour, *sap'-o-lill*, and some sugar, *shu'-gah*, maybe we could even get some *kau'-py!*"

They made good time on the ebb tide and traveled all day in the sunlight, which was a welcome change. At the southern tip of

Annette Island, they turned southeast towards the next island. Along the way Peter tried to remember his stop at Fort Simpson two years before on his way to Stikine and ruminated silently about their situation.

We were only there for one day, unloading supplies, and I spent most of the time on the Beaver, but I did go into the provision's depot. What was the name of that fellow that ran it? John Work? But what if McPherson and Kannaquassé and Heroux killed McLoughlin? If they did, would word of it have already reached Fort Simpson? That's not possible. But if word did, would they try to implicate Little Rain and I, or just me, or my theft of the HBC goods? And if we're going to trade a few beaver pelts for supplies then we'll need to re-band them with something different than the way they are now, they need to look like we trapped them.

Ten-hours later they were at the southwestern side of Duke Island and came upon a deep inlet that had a sheltered cove at its entrance where they decided to camp. After a meal of more pemmican and dried salmon they unpacked the beaver pelts and re-banded them with Peter's old hemp rope in different sized bundles loosely thrown together and then got some rest.

The next morning they pushed off to begin crossing the miles wide Revillagigedo Channel and headed due east, towards the mainland, then south along the shoreline. After two-hours of paddling the sound of pounding engine pistons rippled across the water and black smoke appeared on the horizon. Soon, the unmistakable silhouette of a steamer came into view and as it got closer the high-pitched wane of bagpipes pierced the air. *What's this?*

It was the paddle steamer *Cowlitz,* the head administrator of Hudson's Bay Company George Simpson's personal watercraft, traveling north! *It's headed for Stikine! Did McPherson and Heroux murder John McLoughlin? But how could he know, we haven't seen any other steamers on the water to bring word back. Or is he just on one of his fort inspections? This can't be good.*

Little Rain turned around to Peter with a startled look on her face. "It's alright," he replied, trying to smile. "No danger."

As he watched it ply the waters a half-mile away, its large circular paddles slapping the water and churning up a great white tide behind it, its boiler chimney belching wood smoke, he could see a few crewmen working the deck and wondered again about just what McPherson, Pierre or Urbain Heroux would say to Simpson when he got there. He told himself, *they'll never say a thing about the stolen goods, it would just expose themselves as thieves, and if that rotten little bastard Pierre squealed it would just bring more trouble on him and them. But they'll still have to account for me missing, so, I guess McPherson will report me in as a deserter at best, and a murderer at worst.*

Confident he was going to get away with his plunder, but definitely not his absence, Peter tried to put those thoughts out of his head. But then he wondered what, if any impact George Simpson's visit to Fort Simpson would have on his stop at the fort, since the *Cowlitz* was in all probability coming from there.

VI

Mister John
Aankáawu Ḡaatāa yēi Noow Shtax héen
April 21, 1842

Just past midnight, the alarm bell sounded at Fort Stikine with numerous clangs. Moments later gunshots rang out, thundering against the night. Men sprang from their bunks while sentries on the fort's upper gallery fired into the darkness at an unseen enemy. Once the smoke cleared, the acrid smell of burnt gunpowder heavy in the air, the alarm bell began to quiet and then, suddenly, ceased to toll through the black night.

Thirty-year old Urbain Heroux, his red worsted hat pushed up on his brow, stood in the darkness with his musket near the crumpled body of Chief Trader John McLoughlin Jr. who was lying face down on the platform in front of the men's barracks. With his own musket pinned beneath him, Mr. John labored to breath as blood filled his lungs.

Pandemonium broke out within the fort as McLoughlin's death struggle deepened. Undetected, Heroux crept closer to the Chief Trader, smiling a tight smile. He placed his back against the building wall, then set his moccasined foot on McLoughlin's neck to finish him off, but Mr. John kept breathing. Looking down, Heroux noticed John's gun underneath him. He pulled the musket out from under him and then struck McLoughlin in the back of his head with it, breaking the stock of the gun apart on his skull with a sharp smack.

"Try and get up, you bastard," Heroux whispered, tossing aside the pieces of the musket, his face flush with hate. "Now see if you can strike the men with your stick."

From the gangway on the fort's upper gallery Heroux's allies, Antoine Kawannassé, in his filthy capote, and Pierre Kannaquassé, the ugly gash under his eye that Peter Goutre had given him a week before now a festering scab, watched the whole affair unfold. Satisfied with Urbain's work, Pierre raised his musket in an evil display of victory and hollered out over the fort, "Hurrah for my gun! I stopped the attack! I stopped them!"

Elias Cole, a new Hawaiian Kanakas recruit at the fort, hid in his bed until the sound of the alarm and the loud report of guns being fired had stopped, then stood at the barracks door. Once the smoke cleared, he watched as Heroux ripped the master keys from McLoughlin's vest as some of the men ran up to him from other parts of the stockade. Urbain started barking orders to free the men locked in the jailhouse.

Next, he pushed past Cole and walked into the men's barracks then turned and asked, "How did Mr. John get shot?" Fearful of his own life Elias replied, "I do not know."

"I think we were just attacked by the Kanakas workers from Fort Durham!" Heroux said to the room. But William Lasserte, who had been on the receiving end of previous beatings by Mr. John replied, "No, I took all their guns earlier and they are all passed out drunk in the new bunkhouse."

"Then it must have been the Tlingit," Heroux quickly said.

Metis employee Francois Pressé, who had been dismissed from the HBC Moose Factory on James Bay in Ontario two years earlier for shooting at a man, ran past McLoughlin's dead body into the room from the jailhouse, freshly released from his chains for drunken brawling, and unaware of what had just transpired.

He looked at Heroux and asked, "Why is Mr. John lying on the ground? What's going on?"

"We were just attacked and someone killed him. Whoever it was placed himself near enough not to miss," was Urbain's cryptic reply, walking back outside while the men followed.

Finding some courage, Elias Cole pointed his finger at Heroux and taunted, "You're the one that killed him!"

Urbain spun around with the look of menace in his eyes and stepped towards Elias. Heroux pushed his worsted cap down on his brow then opened his mouth and said, "No, it was not I. We were attacked and this was Peter Goutre's work. He is aligned with the Tlingit, and the Kake. It was he who killed Mr. John."

"Goutre?" Lasserte questioned. "He's been living up at Bitter Water all winter and spring. Peter hasn't been here for months."

"And that is exactly why he is aligned with them! He is the one who wanted this. He planned to overthrow the fort."

"How do you know that?"

"He wanted us to help and we refused."

"And did you report it?"

Heroux didn't reply for a moment, then he glared at Lasserte and said, "I reported it right away but Mr. John didn't believe me, and now because of Goutre he is dead." Heroux turned and stood over the lifeless body of Mr. John, he shook his head and muttered, "Poor John, poor, poor Mr. John."

From his hiding place in the barracks, the fort's cook, Nahua, a Hawaiian Kanaka, crawled over to Mr. John and knelt beside his commander with tears in his eyes. He looked up at the men encircling him and asked Heroux if he had killed Mr. John. But Urbain would have nothing of it. He lunged at Nahua, striking the young cook with his fist, hollering, "I did not do it! You better take care of how you speak to me! This is Peter Goutre's work!"

Heroux then stared down every man that surrounded him who soon found themselves casting their eyes to the ground. A moment later, once their submission was clear, Urbain looked up to the gallery where Antoine waited and Pierre still stood with his musket over his head. They made eye contact and his ally slowly lowered it. Both climbed down the ladder and walked over to where Mr. John's body lay.

The three Iroquois stood over their kill in satisfied, arrogant silence as the new leaders of Fort Stikine while the men slowly stepped back. Seeing their withdrawal, Pierre Kawannassé looked down on Mr. John's body and, without a word, spat on him.

"I'm glad the attackers killed him, he deserved to die," Pierre grunted.

Elias Cole resigned himself to do the last thing they could for their former commander. "Somebody, help me carry him to the barracks to get the body cleaned up so we can bury him."

But Heroux scoffed, "Help? Ha! Pierre is right, we're better off without him."

The three allies skulked off while the rest of the men stood over the body, mute, lost and confused, as if they were waiting for Mr. John to spring back to life and start giving orders again.

Above them, on the runway of the fort's upper gallery, John McLoughlin Jr.'s assistant, Thomas McPherson, had stood quietly in the shadows the whole time. As he walked off, he lit a lantern and held it high scanning the aftermath. Its light illuminated the inner grounds below and clearly showed his unholstered, unfired pistols. McPherson's plan of a fake attack on the fort had worked, it was the cover he needed to eliminate Mr. John and take control of Fort Stikine and its inventory of wealth. All he needed now was for George Simpson to promote him to Chief Trader.

VII

Fort Simpson
Lax Kw'alaams
April 28, 1842

The first sign of the fort were the columns, too many to count, of black billowing smoke that rose in the distance. As they paddled closer, Peter realized there was a small city of Tsimshian camped out around the outside of the wooden walls. *It wasn't like this when I was here last.* Crude, haphazard plank houses, flimsy mat huts and lean-tos lined the shore and surrounded the stockade with multitudes of Natives milling about. One-hundred yards from the dock Peter stopped paddling. *This might be risky. I wonder if I should use a different name? We probably shouldn't stick around longer than we have to especially if they're already looking for a Stikine deserter, or worse yet, someone who might be implicated in the murder of Mr. John. And if I do use someone else's name* — when Peter's deceased uncle on his mother's side, Louis Comeau, instantly came to mind.

"I don't think we should stay long. *Wake mite'-lite youtl'-kut,*" Peter said to Little Rain. She turned to her husband with a quizzical look.

"We need to be careful, they might know about Mr. John, *mem'-a-loost.* And we can't take any risks with my deserting the company without notice or reason." Little Rain seemed to

91

understand and nodded. "I'll go into the fort but I think you should stay with the canoe. *Ne'-ka klat'-a-wa, me-si'-ka mit'-lite boat.*" She smiled in agreement and they paddled slowly up to the wharf.

When they landed at the dock a swarthy Metis with a massive square jaw and bent nose walked up. He was dressed in filthy buckskins, wearing a fur hat and had a beard that looked like the back side of a black bear, he came up to them with a stern look on his face.

"War' ya' comin' from?" he asked, smirking, his hand resting on the handle of his belted bowie knife.

"We've been trapping up north and wanted to trade for some flour and a few other things," Peter replied.

"Have ya' now."

"All over, up the Stikine, and Craig, but the Unuk most recently," Peter answered, lying.

"Well, I ain't never seen ya' before and I know all the trappers. Why's that?" he asked, staring down Peter then glancing back and forth to Little Rain.

"Couldn't tell you why. I guess you just haven't noticed me."

"Notice you? Ha! The only white person to visit this dock in weeks was the little emperor himself George Simpson! Why you should've seen him walking around here like some bonnie prince with his frilly clothes and bagpipes whining away," he said, eyeing him and Little Rain again. "And who's this squaw with ya'?"

"She's my wife . . . Little . . . Wing and I'm Louis Comeau," Peter said. He waited for the man to tell him his name but he didn't, so Peter continued. "If it's all right by you we'd like to trade a few of our pelts for some supplies and be on our way."

"And which way would that be?" the man asked, taking a square of tobacco out of his trousers and biting off a plug.

"We're going south, down to Oregon Territory," Peter answered. The man burst out laughing, nearly choking on his tobacco.

"Ha! Oregon Territory! That's a pretty big place. Just where do you think yer' gonna go there?"

"We're headed for Puget Sound," Peter replied, smiling.

"What are you, a fool? Yer' telling me that youse is gonna paddle that bark all the way down to what, Nisqually? In that thing?"

"I don't see why not."

"Puget Sound must be a thousand miles away, and you're gonna do it in that little floater?"

"The Indians must have done it at some point, I don't —"

"Ha! Maybe in one of them big war canoes the Haidas got, twenty men all pullin' together in one a' them big fifty-foot trees they hollow out — but hell, I'm sure you're as good as ten strong braves, right?" The man couldn't contain himself anymore, he started laughing as he continued, "I may have only been here for two months, but never have I heard of anything like this. Why I bet your little lady is good for, oh, what, twenty-miles a day, so actually you should do a sight better than any war party! Ha! Hell, youse is gonna need enough bacon and flour ta' feed 25 men! That little girl is gonna be pullin' hard on her paddle and you'll never be able to carry enough food!"

Peter, stone faced, thanked the man for his consideration and, after waiting a minute for him to recollect himself he latched onto the man's statement.

"So! You've been here two months, 'eh," Peter replied, stroking his beard and thinking it was his chance to take his one and only risk, asking, "is Chief Trader John Work around? I haven't seen him since last fall."

The look on the man's face instantly changed — he smirked, rubbed the black stubble on his chin and then said, "Chief Work is around and, in fact, I'm sure he'd be pleased to have old man Coogan bargain with ya' for them low quality, mangy pelts you got there," he said, pointing at the furs in the canoe. "Go on ahead." And with that he motioned for them to come ashore, turned around and went back to the fort.

The lanky Frenchman hopped up on the dock and tied the dugout off while Little Rain, without saying a word, tossed a bundle of three pelts up on the landing. Peter looked anxiously at his wife and quietly said, "Do not leave the canoe, *wake mahsh boat, mit'-lite.*"

Peter made his way up to the fort past a dozen Tsimshian and frontiersman camps. When, CRACK! a gun somewhere went off — Peter looked around and saw where it came from. On the edge of the forest a few trappers and traders were wasting the day's work and in the middle of a marksmanship contest, trying to shoot the limbs off a hemlock tree, laughing and carrying on, passing a bottle. Discipline did not seem to be in order at the fort that day.

Peter walked in through the fifteen-foot-high palisade at the front gate, lugging his pelts under his arm. Indians and Metis trading roughs, all in various degrees of frowziness in dress filled the stockade, a few drunks lay passed out in the mud.

The interior of the fort was similar to Stikine: a hand dug wooden well was in the center of it all, and rough-board buildings lined the perimeter. Barracks, mess hall and kitchen, blacksmith and carpentry sheds lined the walls, and, at some distance from the rest of the buildings sat a low, stone building that Peter recognized would be the magazine, where the shot and powder for the fort was stored. Stairs at each end climbed up to the elevated bastion and gangway galleries. Most of it was built of log and the rest shipped in lumber. Peter figured the trader's building was the one that was built on the side of a large storehouse and walked over to it.

He ducked his head below the low door-frame to enter the provisions depot — having been out in the open for so long, the smell of the place instantly attacked him with a power. The bad ventilation, combined with it being perennially stocked high with liquor and wet furs, as well as their combined form — drunk unwashed trappers and Natives dressed in filthy deerskins — meant that the building reeked to high heaven with the smell of frontier living. He did his best to steel himself against it all and set his bundle of three beaver pelts down on the trader's bench and cleared his throat. A balding man in his 50s, looking tired with a small ledger in his hand, walked out of a backroom. He had on a wrinkled Boston shirt and there was a pencil behind his right ear, the skin on his face was mealy white, a tuft of grey whiskers grew from his chin.

"Ah! Another trapper are ya'? More furs of the castor canadensis, the item of the aristocracy and the world's desire? Well, let's save us both a passel of time and consider that, before you tell me, I'm already very impressed about all the bad weather you had to battle and the bears you had to wrassle to get these poor little pelts," he said with the air of an eccentric old warehouseman. "War'd ya' trap these?"

"Oh, these?" Peter responded in a friendly tone, "I think it was up the Craig River, do you know it?"

"Aye, many a pelt from the Craig. What's the name ya' go by, boy?" he asked, raising an eyebrow, pulling the pencil from his ear.

"Louis Comeau."

"And how do you spell that last name of yer's? C-o-m-o?"

"No, *monsieur*, C-o-m-e-a-u. And your name would be?" Peter asked the man.

"I'm Coogan, and we're paying twelve shillings value in trade for a parchment pelt like this," he said, rubbing the fur of one of the pelts between his fingers, feeling the quality. Then he scribbled Peter's false name on his ledger sheet.

"Parchment pelts? *Monsieur*, I believe these to be coat beaver, and worth a few shillings more. They pay much more for such pelts like these up at Stikine, I know it for a fact," Peter protested. Coogan gave him a rueful look.

"Yes, well, Administrator Simpson was just here and he decreed twelve shillings value parchment and fifteen shillings for coat beaver, that goes for all trappers. Shipping costs are up, not to mention that he'll be up to Stikine next to change their payment schedules."

"*Oui*, I understand, but on the quality, I believe these to be of the best in the area."

The clerk set down his leger and gave him a dour look, saying, "Mister Comeau, I am only paying twelve shillings value on trades per pelt for these, and I do not have time to quibble. Are we doing business today or not?"

Desperately needing the supplies and not wanting to raise a commotion, Peter decided to not make any further of a fuss. "Fine, twelve shillings each if you throw in a map of the southern coast for free! I need five pounds flour, one pound sugar, a quart of molasses, one side of cured bacon, a half-pound of salt, and like I just asked, have you a map of a route south with the Inside Passage and Oregon Territory?"

"A map? What do you need a map for?" the clerk asked, completing Peter's order ticket and ripping it from his ledger pad.

"Well, *Monsieur* Coogan, I am working my way as far south as the trapping takes me."

"Then I guess this is your lucky day. I've got maps and charts galore that will get you as far south as Fort Langley, but why don't you just hire an Indian for a guide?"

But Peter shook his head 'no' in reply so Coogan hollered over his shoulder, "Hobbs!" and a dark-hued, low-browed clerk walked out of the storeroom and snatched the slip of paper from his hand.

"Retrieve these items for Mr. Comeau here, and get him a map of the waters south while I store his pelts," he ordered his employee.

97

The man silently turned and went back into the storeroom when two disheveled looking Tsimshian came in, shuffling their feet carrying a few beaver pelts. The clerk glared at them.

"No rum! *Wake lum!*" he barked, motioning at them to leave. They instantly began to shake their fists at Coogan and yell insults at him.

"Banned by the master-general of the Red River, the high king of the HBC George Simpson himself!" he hollered at them as they slowly ambled away. Coogan looked at Peter and grunted, "I think he wants to keep it all for himself!" Laughing at his own joke, Coogan left the room and went to store Peter's pelts.

Soon the extra clerk returned with a large wooden box of Peter's supplies and a rolled-up map, setting them all down on the long trading bench with a thud. Coogan returned and began itemizing them.

"This all looks in order," he said, "and worth your three pelts."

Peter eyed the supplies and picked up the sack of flour, weighing it in his hand, asking, "This is five pounds?"

"Aye, it is. Five-pound regulation."

Peter nodded his head up and down, then set it back in the box and unrolled the map. He eyed it for a moment and said, "So all this is worth thirty-six-shillings?"

"That map is a good one and normally costs two shillings, but I'll let you have it. Wouldn't want ya' to get lost," Coogan said, laughing, "because if you do, you'll need it to find your way back." Peter grinned and picked up the box.

"*Au revoir Monsieur* Coogan," he said, carrying his trade out the door and making his way through the fort. Just as he was walking out the main gate someone called out.

"Goutre! Peter Goutre?"

Peter clenched his teeth and, putting his head down, picked up his pace. Ducking behind one of the wood-plank buildings he slipped out the gate and, almost jogging now, went straight for the canoe. When Peter passed the dock-master he plodded after him.

"What's next? Is this lumber ark bound fer' Campbell Island and Bella Bella?" he asked, spitting a wad of brown chewing tobacco onto the dock planking.

"Maybe," Peter answered, handing the box of supplies to a smiling Little Rain, then hopped in the canoe.

"Ha!" the man laughed wolfishly, "that's about two-hundred miles of maybe, but ya' better hurry because George Simpson is closing it and shutting the whole operation down!" Pushing off from the dock, Peter was about to reply to him just as his name was called out again.

"Goutre! Hold on, is that you?!" a trapper dressed in buckskins hollered from the land's end of the dock. "It's me, Harvey Higgs!"

But Peter kept his eyes forward, leaned from his rear position in the bark and whispered to his wife, "Start paddling."

Then he turned his head and said over his shoulder, "*Adieu mon-amie!* I am sorry sir, we have never met but may we meet again someday!"

"When his excellency comes back south, I'll tell him to keep an eye out for you!" the dock guard yelled, "or maybe he'll just pick up yer' remains after a grizzly bear slices you up on some beach!"

Peter's heart skipped a beat, knowing that George Simpson very well could be informed of his absence and who knows what else could happen in the wake of John McLoughlin Jr.'s murder. Plus, Bella Bella was closing. He rolled the new map up with the others, stowed them against the cargo and the hull and paddled a few strokes.

Not replying, Peter doffed his knit cap, held it high in the air, and then spun it around in his hand, waving goodbye, just as a raven flew low above their heads, counting coup.

VIII

Bella Bella
Waglisla
May 11, 1842

Peter and Little Rain spent the next two weeks paddling hard, always south. They were both much less familiar with the territory, even with the map, so they had to travel by the light of day and just trust to luck and to God that they wouldn't be sighted by anyone bloody minded. They camped wherever they could find a creek along the coast at night, ate well but sparingly of the dried salmon and flour johnny cakes with molasses cooked in bacon grease, and Peter constantly wished for, but never gave voice to, a perennial desire, sometimes even rising to frustrated necessity, for rum, but found only creek water instead, which was at least cool and clear if not intoxicating. The rain was regular but soft, the fogs were thick but not freezing, and the spring strengthened as the days wore on, warming them up and encouraging them as they went on their journey.

They made good time but were anxious about getting to Fort McLoughlin as soon as possible on Campbell Island, near the mouth of the Nass River, where they could rest and replenish their supplies. When they came around a bend there was an ominous totem pole, blackened from weather and wood smoke, just above the high tide mark on a rocky point that faced the water. An encampment of Heiltsuk Indians were cooking and doing tasks around a campfire as the two of them paddled by.

Then finally, the fort came into view and the Hudson's Bay oak-built steamer *Beaver* was at the dock with a stream of men coming to and fro, loading it with goods. Along the rails and on the dock, men stood guard with muskets and pistols. Tribal members, who were living around the fort, and a good number of HBC employees were everywhere, commotion seemed to be ruling the day. They floated up to the one-hundred-foot steamship and Peter called out to a deckhand.

"Hey! You there! What's going on?" he yelled.

"We're loading for the trip south," a young fellow replied.

"Where south?"

"South Vancouver Island, at Camosun. Gonna build a new fort there by decree of George Simpson!"

"What's with all the guns?"

"We're worried that the Indians might try to take over the fort for everything in the warehouse before we leave!"

"Holy Christ!" Peter said, looking concerned. "Are you still trading for provisions?"

"Only if you've got sterling. The trading's all shut down."

"Who do I see about the purchase of supplies?"

"You'd want John Dunn or Charlie Ross, but I think both of them are busy right now. I don't know, there should be someone around here to help you."

"Very good," Peter responded, then added, "We'll land the canoe and find them onboard or in the fort, thank you."

They paddled away from the ship and over to the beach where the bow of the canoe ran up on the shore. Peter jumped out into the water then bent over the side of the bark and found his small leather drawstring pouch with their few shillings and pence in it, he was pleased that he didn't have to dig out any coins from under the seats. He also knew that they desperately needed to rest but with all the commotion going on around the fort he didn't think this was the place to do so.

"Can you stay, *mit'-lite*, with the canoe," Peter said to his wife. "I won't be long." She got out of the boat and stood on the beach.

"Yes, I stay," Little Rain replied, her eyes unfocused and tired.

Peter stepped over to his wife and wrapped his arms around her, then whispered in her ear, "I'm sorry, soon we'll be safe in Puget Sound."

Little Rain pulled away. The weak smile on her face seemed to say that she understood his words. She leaned up against the bow of the canoe and flipped her hand at the steamship. Peter understood her meaning and left for the *Beaver*.

Peter made his way up the bank and over to the path from the fort to the dock making his way through a line of men carrying wooden boxes and crates to the pier then up a gangway and onto the vessel. Figuring his chances were better on the ship than the fort he joined in the procession to blend in and went aboard. Peter scanned the busy scene and, picking out the only man whose hands weren't full of sacks or who wasn't barking at a man who was, made a beeline over to him and greeted him with a wave.

"Would you be John Dunn?" he asked.

"John's over at the fort," the man answered. "Who's askin'?"

"Louis Comeau. I'd like to get some flour and some —"

"No more trades fella," he said with a sour look on his unshaven face. "We've got to get outta here."

"Whaddya mean no trades? Listen, I have sterling, good, solid sterling and one of your deckhands said I needed to see John Dunn or Charlie Ross to buy some goods."

"Well," the man replied, glancing fore and aft, then rising on his toes and looking towards the stockade. "I'm Charlie," the fellow said, "and can sell you some goods. You got a list?"

"No list my friend, all in my head. I need five pounds of flour, bacon, salt, one pound of sugar or a jar of molasses, some salted pork or beef if you've —"

"Yes, yes, I understand. Follow me," Charlie said, turning and walking down some hatchway stairs and into the hold of the ship.

"Wait here," the man said at the foot of the staircase. He disappeared down a make-shift aisle of stacked boxes to each side. Peter stood amongst the loaded supplies, watching the men come

104

and go, each of them looking at him long and hard, identifying him as a stranger. Peter coughed and stepped back behind a particularly tall crate, deeply uncomfortable. A few moments later the man returned and handed Peter a slab of cured bacon wrapped in linen, winked, and disappeared again. He came back with a wooden box with sacks of flour, sugar, salt, and even some smoking tobacco that Peter hadn't asked for.

"There," Charlie said with a smile, "that should do ya'."

"How much do I owe you?"

"Oh, I'd say that'll be 30 shillings worth of goods," Charlie said in response, holding out his hand. Peter pulled the leather pouch out of his breeches and dumped some coins into his own hand and counted, then dropped the correct coins into the man's waiting palm.

"Thirty shillings, exact," Peter said, nodding with a grin.

Charlie closed his fist around the money, shoved the handful into his pants pocket, spun around, and walked up the stairs without another word.

With some difficulty, Peter got the goods under his arm and then trudged back to the beach, moving hurriedly with the many men rushing about with loads of their own. Approaching the canoe, Peter heard the commotion before he saw it — a few Heiltsuk braves had come to see the newcomers, and were having, as far as he could tell, an unwanted conversation with Little Rain. As he got closer, Peter could see that the three braves interrogating her had also started boldly rifling through the canoe's cargo, smelling and taking idle bites from their salmon, inspecting the quality of their remaining pelts and giving Little Rain threatening looks. He quickened his pace to get to her aid.

"*Pourquoi ta petite tête de merde éloigne-toi de mon bateau!* Get away from our canoe!" Peter hollered as he strode down from the bank, putting down his load as he approached. But they had no idea what he said so he tried some trade jargon.

"*Ik'-tah o'-koke? Klat'-a-wa!*" he shrieked, walking into the surf and looking at each of them. Peter glanced at their belts and saw that none of them had knives.

But the teenage boys didn't understand or weren't interested in his trade jargon, they didn't reply, staring back at Peter with tight mouths and thin eyes. Peter picked up the box and set it in the canoe then flipped his hand at them, motioning for them to leave.

"*Klat'-a-wa!*" Peter warned again, staring down the boys.

The three whispered amongst each other, casting glances at Peter and Little Rain. Seeming to come to some agreement their quiet conversation ended, and the two on Peter's right moved towards Little Rain, the other staying near the canoe. Saying something quickly, too quick for Peter or Little Rain to understand, the two suddenly shoved her down — she landed on the soft, wet sand, more angry than hurt. She jumped up to her feet and tried to slap one boy. Peter dodged instantly into the fray, throwing the first boy to the ground as the other danced away, laughing at Peter and his wife. The third, meanwhile, began pulling dried fish from their basket, inspecting each piece. Picking out a particularly old dried fillet the boy laughed, smelled it, took a small bite, then made a gagging sound for the benefit of his comrades and tossed the fish over his shoulder into the surf. Looking back, Peter saw what was up and, hurtling over the first boy, who was still in the sand, landed next to the one with the fish and threw him, in turn, down onto the beach. Before he was finished though the other two were back up and pushing Little Rain again, but they were no longer laughing at their game. Peter took his eyes off the little fish thief and advanced, planting himself firmly in the sand between his wife and the other two braves. The fish thief, seeing his chance with Peter's back turned, went to the canoe and, finding the maps, snatched them, then tucked them into his deerskin leggings. Seeing that the game had become serious, he popped over the canoe and approached the rest of the group with his chest pushed out.

"*Hàkglim qsú xàlà?*" he growled, glancing back and forth between them with a menacing look. But Peter wasn't threatened, he shoved him again towards the beach, the youth stumbled backwards and fell down. He jumped to his feet yelling and stepping towards Peter, but his two friends held him back.

"*Láláqila gvúlílm hlxa qsú wa!*" he screamed, spittle flying from his mouth, his black eyes on fire.

"Get in the canoe . . . *Ne-si'-ka klat'-a-wa!*" Peter ordered, pushing the dugout off the beach and into the water as Little Rain jumped aboard. A crowd of tribal elders had gathered at the top of the tree-lined bank, looking on while the three young braves heckled them as they paddled away.

"They were sure full of themselves and looking for trouble, *kull si-wash*," Peter said, relieved to be leaving. They paddled hard until they were out of sight of the fort.

Bone-tired from the day and sore from paddling for what seemed like forever Peter said, "We need to rest, *moo'-sum*." Little Rain turned around and weakly smiled. Peter pointed at an island up ahead and both paddled towards it.

They found a tiny beach on the western side of the rock-lined island where they landed the canoe and began to make camp. Peter laid down the bear blanket and beaver pelts for Little Rain to sleep on while he searched the immediate area for some fire starter material.

Minutes later, when he returned with some cedar twigs and dry moss, he could already hear the soft, rhythmic snoring of an exhausted young woman. Smiling, Peter began to prepare, as quietly as he could, their camp. With the help of his flint and tinder kit and a sudden stilling of the wind, he had a merry little fire going. As the campfire warmed and with the canoe beached, Peter tore off a piece of the pemmican and, chewing, looked south, across the water, and thought. *We need to conserve as much food as we can, getting that flour was important and will last but we'll need something more substantial to sustain us.*

Peter began searching the trees for a 'Y' piece of limb that he could fashion into a net. Once found, he severed it from the trunk with his buck knife and then peeled some strips of bark off a cedar tree. He weaved the bark back and forth on the 'V' part of the limb and soon had himself a net to crab with. Next, he found the ball of jute in the canoe and then sliced off a piece of bacon from the slab. He tied the bacon to the end of the jute, as he had seen the Tlingit girls do before, walked out to a rocky point where there was a drop-off, tossed it into the water and watched it slowly sink then sat down.

Fifteen-minutes later he began to retrieve the baited jute. As it came to the surface there were two large Dungeness crabs clinging to the bacon. Peter stopped pulling the line, and smiling, reached down with his ad-hoc net and scooped up the crustaceans with a wide grin. Not exactly sure how to clean them but with the built-in instincts of a trapper he dropped both crabs on the rocks and stepped on them before they could scramble away. He ripped their backs off, pulled the knife from his belt and cut them in half.

Little Rain woke to the smell of freshly cooked crab on an open fire and biscuits. She sat up, let out a long, lazy yawn, stretched her arms and enjoyed the slow process of gradually waking up from her nap.

"Umm, *kloshe*," she cooed, smiling. Peter held out a tin plate with a steaming half crab and two biscuits on it for her.

After they devoured their meal some cloud cover was coming in from the west so Peter used the tarp to build a lean-to, then assembled two sleeping areas for them with the pelts and stoked the fire. There was still a long way to go, but as Peter laid down alongside his wife, in that moment he was happy. Things were working out, they were going to make it.

IX

Inside Passage
A yík A góon
May 1842

Peter woke gradually — the organic waking up of a rested and happy man, someone who knows his plan and is eager to follow through with it. Softly squeezing Little Rain's shoulder, Peter rubbed the sleep from his eyes and looked out over the water, surveying the scene, his good mood instantly vanishing. The weather had deteriorated, sideways rain slashed the island and the lean-to flapped in the breeze. He sat up and stared out to the Sound, whitecaps rolled through the strait and pounded the beachfront. It would be useless to try and travel today, if they could even get the canoe going, they'd be swamped in moments by the steep waves and swells. But they were low on water so Peter set out all their cups and bowls outside the lean-to in a bid to catch as much rainfall as possible. He knew they had no choice but to wait out the storm so he went back to bed, curled up next to his wife and tried to get some more sleep.

Hours later, Peter woke again and found that the surf had died down and all of the receptacles he'd set out had a little water in each one but not enough to sustain them for even a day. Little Rain rose from her sleep and looked out over the saline sea. Peter brought her a tin cup with some water in it.

"The storm has moved through and we have very little, *ten'-as*, water, *chuk*. We need to head for the mainland or a larger island where we can find some, *ne-si'-ka is'-kum chuk*."

Little Rain reached for the metal cup nodding, she drank from it and said, "Yes, we *klat'-a-wa*." She got up and went to work tearing down the camp and loading the canoe. In minutes they were shoving off and traveling on an ebb tide through the inland passage that Peter had taken on the *Beaver* years ago.

But shortly after they set out the landscapes, islands and inlets all looked the same, there was nothing that stood out so Peter reached for his valuable maps. His hand finding nothing but an empty space up against the hull, Peter kept himself calm as he asked Little Rain.

"Did you move the maps?"

"*Wake*, map. No," Little Rain replied. Peter dug through more cargo but couldn't find them. *What happened? Where did they go? Wait! Those Heiltsuk at Bella Bella! They must have stolen them*!

"I think those Heiltsuk braves stole our maps! Should we go back?"

Little Rain shook her head 'no' and said, "*Wake, kull, wake*."

"*Merde*!" Peter spat.

As the day went on, they kept going, and kept their southerly course, but the further they traveled the more distressed Peter became. Everything looked the same, just rocky island after rocky island, stand of fir trees after stand of fir trees. He thought about his trip north on the *Beaver* and tried to remember its course but began to have doubts, a wrong-way-feeling came over him.

At one point he said, "I'm trying my best to find the right way," yet every rock-lined island they came to, every shoal, and reef they passed through the archipelago was exactly the same as the last, it was starting to be a never-ending maze.

"Do you know *yuk'-wa?*" Little Rain asked as they paddled smoothly through the gray, unsettled water.

"Well, you know . . . yes. Yes, absolutely," Peter said, gradually finding his determination.

"Did Mr. John send you here?" she asked clumsily.

"Ah, your Boston is getting better! However no, no we never operated this far south. I never worked down here, just the Stikine area. The company thinks the less fraternization between the traders and the locals the better. Which is generally true, but with an exception in our case, of course." Peter said, flashing a sly smile at his wife.

"If never came down here, then how you know?"

"Excuse me?"

"If never come, then how you know?"

Peter laughed uncomfortably. "Well, when I came up here originally it was on the mighty *Beaver*, the big HBC steamer! And we came right through here."

"Oh," Little Rain replied quietly. Peter smiled as the silence between them returned, and listened contently to the lap of the waves and the distant cry of gulls.

"If that was last time you here," Little Rain suddenly started again. Peter frowned out at the waves, feeling what was about to come.

"Was not *ikt cole* ago?" she continued.

"I mean . . . well . . . yes, yes it was. But hey, my memory is superb! I remember every rock and tree that I've ever seen, I know exactly where we are going."

"What is that?" asked Little Rain, pointing at a small island off their south-eastern bow.

"What is what?"

"That island! What name?"

"That island? Well . . . you know . . . it's . . ." Peter trailed off gradually, thinking as hard as he could. The silence returned, but it was not the happy one of earlier.

"You've been through here too you know! Why blame me when you're also at fault?" Peter suddenly started, angry at being shown up.

"Me?"

"You!"

"What?"

"Your fishing trips! You said your tribe came down here to fish all the time!"

"I no say that! Little Rain never go fish with men, that stupid. Stay home."

"Well then, you should have gone and are to blame for that! And besides, I do know where we're going, I just don't know every dumb little island . . . half of these things are too small for names

114

anyway, you just happened to pick one of 'em, but I know all the real ones, the ones with real names. And we're goin' south! That's all! We just keep the sun in our —" Peter pointed up towards the sun, at which point he noticed that the cloud cover had grown so thick that the sun could not be seen, not even a hint of light piercing through to show where it might be. The sky was a totally overwhelming, all-encompassing grey, and the sea was a dark and darkening, choppy grey in reflection. They both stopped paddling as they realized that they, actually, genuinely, did not know where they were or where they were going. Neither wanted to break the silence — Peter because he would have to admit he was wrong, and Little Rain because all she could say was that he was wrong, which in this moment was absolutely the worst thing that could be done. Their canoe bobbed up and down listlessly in the surf, pointlessly twisting one way and then the other. So, Peter started paddling again and Little Rain silently joined in.

Three hours later they came to the northern head of what Peter remembered as a very large and long island that split the waterway in half. But he couldn't recall if the waterway to the east was a continuous channel or a dead-end inlet, whereas he was fairly certain that the channel to the west would eventually lead to the open ocean but in all probability would also lead to a link up with the inside passage. He decided to take the channel to the west.

They followed the waterway but soon came to another island that split the channel once more in half. The only difference, as far as he could tell was, the passage to the west had two large islands at its opening. *Which way now? This is like a puzzle that no compass or map, even if we had one, would ever help with.* Peter stopped paddling and looked up to the sky to try and measure how much more time there was in the day, Little Rain could feel the canoe slowing. She stopped paddling and turned around.

"*Kah klat'a-wah?*" she asked. Peter raised his free hand and waved it back and forth in an unknowing motion. Then he pointed at the southeastern channel.

"That way looks more protected," he replied, still unsure but not wanting to show doubt. "It heads more south, so we should go that way."

Soon the sun's glow could be seen through the cloud cover, it was lower in the sky. They came to find themselves traveling down a narrow channel with a small waterfall cascading down a rocky hillside, it was the perfect place to stop for the night.

They landed the canoe and began to make camp. Little Rain collected some driftwood from the beach and built a fire for biscuits and Peter found his make-shift net and went to catch some crab. In what seemed like no time they were feasting once more on nature's bounty: open-fire cooked crab, biscuits, and cool creek water.

After their meal the skies cleared, the sun warmed the air and the tension of the day was far behind them. Soon they were relaxing on the beach, watching a red sun begin to set when Little Rain stood up and raised her deerskin dress over her head, exposing herself to Peter, her marriage stick hanging between her subtle breasts. She smiled a wide and bright smile, turned and ran towards the water and dove in, the cold clear saltwater rushing over her naked body. Peter immediately ripped off his clothes and dove in after her, the chilly water was overwhelmingly refreshing, he rose to the surface with a joyful yelp. They embraced and kissed.

Little Rain grabbed him by the hand and led him ashore and to the bed of beaver pelts where they made mad, passionate love as the sun set on their clean glistening bodies.

In the morning they awoke to beautiful blue skies, sunshine, and a high tide of flat water. During their breakfast of bacon and biscuits the raven flew up and landed on a beach log right in front of them, it began to walk up and down the log with two-footed hops between steps and cackling while bobbing its head. Each time it turned around it did so with a swift flap of its wings then it repeated its back-and-forth skip-hop dance. Finally, it took off and flew across the channel, cawing loudly and landing in the shady grove of some cedars in a small, somewhat hidden cove.

Little Rain watched it until Peter said, "Let's get the canoe loaded." Once that was done, they set forth on a southern course down the long, narrow channel. Three hours later there was a small island in the middle of the waterway. The views of snow-capped mountains to the east were breathtakingly beautiful, it invigorated Peter; he loved the vast, wide-open untouched wilderness and being a part of it, especially with Little Rain.

Soon they found themselves in a large Sound and the open ocean was to the west. Peter knew they were no longer following the inside passage, but far ahead of them there was another passage between what looked like a huge island and the mainland.

"We should head for that opening straight ahead, *klat'-a-wa de-làte,*" Peter suggested. Little Rain stopped paddling, turned around and beamed at her husband.

"Yes," she said. Peter smiled back, broadly.

In that moment Peter had never been so happy. Contentment moved through his body and the warm living sun shone on his face. The love he felt for Little Rain was immense, bigger than anything he'd ever known, bigger than himself, and bigger than the wilderness that surrounded them. For minutes Peter lost himself to a world of pure joy and happiness as he stroked the water. He gazed at the backside of his beautiful wife, paddling towards their new life, he thought about the family they would someday have, and wondered if she would be pregnant soon. In his mind's eye he pictured the home they would build: a cottage with a covered porch and their children playing in the yard with a pet dog. How wonderful it will all be once we're all settled in Puget Sound. *I can smell the food on the stove and feel the heat of a roaring fire in a rock fireplace.* Peter snapped out of his daydream and looked past Little Rain.

He squinted in the sunlight reflecting off the water. On the horizon, a pod of orcas, had just come around the point of an island up ahead. They were traveling rapidly across the water, the splashing from their fins seemed to make the water dance all around them and Peter delighted in spotting them. As they came closer it looked like a smaller pod than what they seemed to be when they first appeared. Now it looked to be a pod of only three, but with the glare of the sun in his eyes and the quickness by which they swam around the point and moved towards them, they were hard to make out. It was invigorating to see such a wild and free species of animal in their element, with tall dorsal fins running high off the water. The closer they came the more Peter squinted in the bright rays of the afternoon sun, its reflection bouncing off the surf was nearly blinding him, then Little Rain stopped paddling. She turned around, all the blood had drained from her face and the look of fear was in her eyes.

"HAIDAS!"

Peter rose from his seat and stared at what became clear to him. Three large black war canoes with the distinct raised bows of Haida design were full of raiders and bearing down on them, moving fast over the water. There must have been twenty warriors in each one, all of them paddling furiously. Peter scanned his escape options. What looked like the mainland side of the channel seemed closer.

"Turn to the land!" Peter screamed. Instantly they both were straining as hard as they could on the rough handles of their paddles, trying to put absolutely every drop of energy and strength in their bodies with each stroke. Peter looked over his shoulder and saw it — the Haidas had changed course to cut across their line, they were moving to intercept them.

"Faster! Faster!" Peter hollered. But they were no match for the swift raiders.

BOOM! The Haidas started throwing large stones that had holes in them where the end of a long rope was tied, they were like cannon balls landing next to them. One hit the side of their dugout, cracking it, it was instantly retrieved to be thrown again. Little Rain began yelling at them in Tlingit, her words coming sharp. Peter had no idea what she was saying but whatever it was seemed to have no effect on the raiders.

In no time they were trapped but close to shore. One boat had cut across their bow, stopping their travel while another came to rest near their stern, the third circled them.

Clearly outnumbered, Peter wasn't sure if they'd take everything and leave, or do something worse, then he got a look at what each war canoe contained. Plenty of warriors but also a good number of newly taken slaves: four Salish women and three children, two boys and a girl. All of them with their hands tied and mouths gagged, the look of terror in each of their eyes. *They're coming back early after a raid in the south!*

The warriors' bodies were heavily tattooed with symbols of salmon and eagles and other creatures of the forest and sea, all of them had painted faces, strings of shells hung from their necks and one, who was in the circling war boat and apparently the Tyee wore a bone breastplate. He started barking orders and pointing at Little Rain.

"Take all our pelts, everything we have, just let us go! We're no threat to you!" Peter hollered, looking at who he thought was their leader.

But the main Haida had already decided his course. The closest canoe came up next to their bow, Peter started digging for his pistol when one nasty looking warrior grabbed Little Rain by her arm and jerked her from their dugout. She began screaming, slapping and kicking the Haida but she was no match, he struck her with a wooden war club then threw her down out of sight in the longboat.

"LITTLE RAIN! Peter screamed, finally seizing his old flintlock. He raised it, aimed at the Haida who was manhandling her, took half a second to exhale and try to steady the gun in his wet, shaking hand, and squeezed the brass trigger. The flint clicked down onto the lock when what felt like the biggest stone in creation smashed into the back of his neck, toppling him overboard, causing him to momentarily lose consciousness and his grip on the gun, the shot missing its intended target. In a flash two raiders jumped aboard their dugout and began ransacking it, flinging pelt after pelt, the gunpowder and shot, and all their supplies across the water and into the waiting, eager hands of their comrades.

120

Stunned and sinking, the cold water brought Peter back to life. He swam to the surface at the stern of the closest Haida canoe and breathed as quietly as he could. He pulled the knife from his sheath, reached up and grabbed hold of the top rail of the boat, kicked his legs, pulled himself up and stabbed a Haida, cutting deep into his thigh.

Instantly tethered stones began raining down on him, some missing but one hitting him square in the back of his shoulder, knocking the wind out of him, and causing him to fall back into the surf and let go of his buck knife.

Disoriented, Peter held his breath and dove, then turned and made his way towards his canoe to surface and take a breath. He heard lots of yelling and what sounded like commands from the Tyee, a few paddles started to hit the water. *They think they killed me with those big rocks.* When Boom! Boom! More stones started to pound his canoe — *they're trying to sink it!*

Getting his bearings he dove again, then swam through the crystal-clear water towards the one longboat with Little Rain in it thinking he could grab hold and save her when the canoes started to move away fast. Peter surfaced.

Horror moved through his body. *Non, non, non, this can't be! I can't live without Little Rain, I don't care if I die, she's my life, my world. How can I live without her?*

Peter started screaming at the top of his lungs, "*Je vais vous tuer tous les bâtards!* I'll fight every single one of you! Come back here you cowards! Come and kill me!" Then he frantically started to hit the water with both hands, swinging and splashing and yelling. But they were gone.

He swam over to and grabbed hold of his sinking canoe then wailed with a pain so deep he wished his heart would stop beating. His mind told him to let go, sink and end his life but the words of his long-gone mother began to echo in his mind. He could hear her telling him as a young boy after his uncle had taken his own life, saying, *'Not wanting to live is a sin,'* over and over.

He held on.

After an hour of drifting on an incoming tide the canoe ground to a halt on a sandy shore. Peter woke from his stupor and found himself stranded on a beach, his canoe half full of water and weighted down with rocks. He pulled himself up, more dead than alive, and not caring if he lived or died, he crawled up onto the beach and dropped onto the sandy muck.

Hours later, near sunset, he came to. The tide was going out and his heavy, empty canoe sat high and dry on the shore. He sat up and gazed into a golden sunset. *If I had my pistol, I'd just shoot myself and be done with it.* But then the voice of his mother began again, *'No Peter, to not want to live is a sin.'* He dropped his head in his hands and began to moan and weep, then he gripped tight to the marriage stick still around his neck, until he fell over on his side and passed out.

In the morning, when the tide came up to his feet, his eyes opened. *Damn it, why am I still here?* He closed his eyes for the darkness he craved while fighting with the ghost of his mother and grabbing his soapstone marriage stick. Soon he was in a coma-like state, dreaming of past days with Little Rain, her warm eyes, dimpled chin, and smile beaming at him. He longed for those days again and ached for her love and spirit.

Deep in chimera sleep he saw her standing with her parents and brother. He saw her standing next to him on their wedding day.

He saw her young and beautiful, and then he saw her pulled into the Haida war boat and clubbed. In a flash she was kicking him in the legs and feet. He felt her touch his face and then she slapped him!

"Hey?! Are you alive?" she asked.

"Little Rain! You're alive! Are you okay? Did they hurt you?" Peter asked, opening his eyes to a fuzzy, unfocused world. But she wasn't there. A man with a long beard stood over him. He reached down and shook Peter's face.

"How'd you get here fella?" the beard asked. "What happened to you?"

Peter slowly sat up and rubbed his aching, sore shoulder and neck. There were three men, all of them gaping at him like he was a revenant left for dead. Peter squinted at the light — as his senses slowly returned, he could make out the low rhythm of a steam engine somewhere nearby. Peter glanced out to the water. The *Beaver* was anchored just off shore and a rowboat was beached near his canoe.

"No, go away," Peter said, waving them off with a weak motion of his good hand.

"We ain't goin' anywhere without you, fella. The deck watchman spotted you and we stopped to save yer' ass," the same fellow said.

Peter laid back down and rolled over on his side, he said, "I'm dead, you hear me, dead. Now take off."

With that two of the men picked him up, he screamed in pain from his injury but they didn't care. They began to drag him to their rowboat, but Peter continued to object.

"I said I'm not leaving. I'm staying, my life is over!"

"Nope, not as long as I have a say in this, and I say your comin' with us. Besides, I've seen worse, you're not so bad, fella. We'll get some soup in you on the ship and you'll be fine." Two of them muscled him back to walking again. Finally coming to his senses, Peter dug in his heels.

"Wait! Just give me a minute. I need to get something from my canoe," he hollered, shaking off the two of them. The company men eased up and let Peter stumble over to his ruined boat. Along the way he picked up a good-sized rock and then broke the bench seats in the dugout, exposing all the copper and silver coins he'd hidden weeks before. He grabbed them before they could see what he was doing and shoved them in the pocket of his tattered breeches, knowing he'd need the small amount of money eventually. Peter weakly walked back to the men, his clothes, hair, and beard covered in sand, muck, and seaweed, and got in their skiff.

He kept his head down and eyes closed as they paddled him out to the sidewheeler. He ached with pain at the loss of his wife and blamed himself for missing his one and only gun shot and with it, a chance to kill the Haida who clubbed her.

"So who are ya'?" one of the men asked. But Peter didn't answer, and didn't look up. "Damn it, man! Talk to me! What happened?"

Peter raised his head and opened his eyes, he glared at his rescuer and grunted, "Haidas."

Fort Langley
Snaqʷaməx
May 1842

Fifteen miles up the vast, lowland valley of the Fraser River, Peter stepped out on the starboard side-deck of the *Beaver* and leaned against the railing — it was late morning, the throbbing of the massive pistons rumbling deep in the ship's hull caused the deck to reverberate under his feet and slowly wake him up to a new reality. He stood alone in the fog that had settled upon the water like a thick blanket and looked glumly at the ghostly shapes of the tall evergreens and shoreline banks which did their best to break through their grey cover. None of it registered for Peter, who just stood at the rail and looked out, not seeing or feeling anything. He watched the riverbank for miles until the fog broke and the fort came into view. Docked on the up-river side of the wharf was a sharp-lined clipper ship with three masts, the wide red, white, and blue vertical stripes of its flag flapping in the wind. A steady line of men walked up and down the hill from the fort, loading the ship with bundles of beaver pelts and barrels of salted salmon. Across the river a line of Kwantlen Indian plank houses dotted the bank, dozens of rough-cut canoes were beached on the shore.

After days of staying below deck huddled in a tiny bunk, the knot in Peter's stomach hadn't left, nor had the pain in his heart. Not knowing where his life would lead or what he would do next, he looked at the tall palisade with a shallow, but unwavering gaze. He didn't really see anything, as there was nothing on earth that he needed or wanted to look at. Peter just stood staring at the fort and tried to contemplate his future, and wondered even if he wanted to live it.

"I see you found the clothes and hat we left at yer' bunk," a voice said from behind him. "You feel any better after all that sleep?" Before he turned around to look at the man Peter determined that he should be careful with what he said since he was a company deserter.

"Yes, thank you," he replied. Peter looked down at his new white and black striped hickory shirt, black trousers, and then adjusted the knit hat on his head. He turned to look at the fellow, it was the same bearded man from the beach.

"And I take it you found the galley during the last few days?"

"I did, thank you."

"So, um, the Haida trouble you had. I just want to say that I'm sorry you had to go through something like that. I wouldn't wish that on anyone. But, you're still alive," the man offered.

Peter looked at the fellow and nodded his head in thanks.

"Have ya' got a name?" the man asked. He had dark sunken eyes but there was a friendly tone to his voice.

"Louis — Louis Comeau."

"Well, Louis, if you're looking for work, we've got plenty here. But if you choose to go your own way you will need to reimburse the company for your new duds and pay for your passage south."

Peter nodded his head up and down. "I see, give me a day to think about it. And your name is?"

"Charlie Ross."

"Charlie Ross? You're —" Peter started but then stopped himself. He looked the man up and down — he bore no resemblance at all to the fellow at Bella Bella who had sold him his supplies. Peter smiled involuntarily as he suddenly understood why the man at Fort McLoughlin had given him things he hadn't asked for, and didn't fill out a supply order.

Still smiling, Peter said, "Good to meet you, Charlie. How long will the *Beaver* be docked here?"

"Just a day or two. We've got to deliver and pick up, then we're off to Camosun to start building a new fort for Administrator Simpson. After that the ship heads to Nisqually."

"Camosun, huh?"

"Yep. Great harbor there." Just then the *Beaver's* steam whistle blew. "Well, time to dock this thing. Good talking to you, Louis. You can sleep onboard until we shove off or you can take lodging over in the servant's quarters at the fort, just tell them I said it was okay. I sleep and stay on the ship most of the time, except when I visit the alehouse, but not tonight, too much work to do," Charlie said, walking away.

As the steamer eased up to the wharf Peter took notice of the big square-rigged ship on the opposite side and its French speaking crew. Their language triggered his upbringing outside of Montreal. He was suddenly seized with interest and his torpor vanished — the men in their bright, red and blue striped shirts, with their jolly faces, and above all he recognized the hearty language they were speaking and laughing in — French! They were Frenchmen, speaking French! It'd been years since Peter had spoken cordial French with anyone, in that moment he flew through time from the current walking purgatory he found himself in and back to Montreal, sledding in winter with his friends, Mass in their old stone church on Sundays, his mother cooking roast duck and singing to him — he was overwhelmed with feeling, his knees almost buckled under the weight of it.

As the gangplank hit the dock, Peter found himself drifting unconsciously away — along the deck, down the gangplank, and across the wharf, without thinking. He headed up the pier, climbed the short hill up to the front gate where two men armed with muskets stepped in front of him.

"Who are you and what's your business?" one of the guards said.

"Charlie Ross said I could stay here," Peter replied flatly. The two guards eyed him up and down and then glanced out at the steamer.

"That's fine, just no fights or we'll put you in the lockup and Charlie will have to pay your fine," one shot back. Then both of them stepped aside and Peter walked into Fort Langley.

Inside the palisade walls he found a more orderly community, one completely different than Fort Stikine or Simpson. A big two-story white house built of finished lumber stood at the top of a gently sloped hill that traveled the length of the fort. Outside of a cooperage, men pounded barrels together, the blaze of a blacksmith shop forge could be felt when Peter walked by outside of it. Across the way carpenters worked on the cedar shingle siding of a new storehouse and a line of men came and went from the supply depot building.

When Peter saw a trapper in buckskins walk out of what looked like an alehouse with a bottle of rum in his hand, he saw the answer for the knot in his stomach and the pain in his heart. He stepped inside and found a dimly lit room, empty of patrons, with candles on rough-cut tables and a bar built of planks resting on top of barrels along the far wall. Peter went over to it, pulled a few shillings from his trousers and slapped them on the bar. Behind it the tender was wiping the inside of a pewter mug with a filthy rag.

"A bottle of rum," he said to the fellow. The man eyed the shillings.

"Aye, that'll be eight shillings for a full jug," he grunted with an Irish accent. Peter didn't argue, he pulled out five more.

"Here," he said, placing the silver coins on the bar. The tender swept them up then set a bottle and mug in front of him. Peter grabbed the bottle by its neck but left the mug and went over to a table and sat down.

Pulling the cork out, he set it on the table where it promptly rolled off as he took a long, hard pull of liquor. Peter wiped his mouth with the sleeve of his shirt, glanced at the bartender, and then took another swig. The sting of the rum burned his gullet, warmed him from his insides out. It felt good. He took another and let his chin drop on his chest. *Now that my life is ruined maybe I'll just drink myself to death.*

"And where would yee be comin' from, lad?" the barkeeper asked from across the room. Peter slowly raised his head.

"Nowhere," he quietly answered. The bartender shrugged.

"Well, then, where yee be goin'?"

But Peter didn't reply.

"That yee name too? Mr. Nowhere?"

Peter ignored him. He drew another pull off the bottle and savored the fiery taste on his tongue. He swished the liquor around in his mouth and then swallowed.

"Well, I've got a name and it's Kilgore. If yee need anything else just give me a holler." He dropped his grungy rag on the bar and went into a backroom. In his absence Peter continued to sip from his bottle while contemplating his future. When Kilgore returned the only future Peter had planned out was wondering about his next meal.

"Where can . . . where's a guy get some food around, here?"

Kilgore pointed at the wall and said, "Over at the servant's quarters is the mess hall. Six pence will get yee a plate of whatever they be cookin' this day."

Peter answered by grunting with a nod. Knowing there was a cheap meal nearby he continued to drink for the next two hours while watching men come and go from the establishment. Finally, he stood up, found the cork on the floor and then headed for the door, the corked jug of rum in his hand.

With a good portion of the bottle in him, Peter found himself significantly more active. His limbs moved more easily, his eyes moved more quickly — he was more alert, if not more alive.

Outside Peter followed his nose to a log structure with cordwood piled up in front of it. Three sets of stairs rose to three different doors. With significant difficulty, Peter staggered up the end set of stairs, although it constantly tried to dodge away from him, and then laid hands upon the doorknob, although it tried to do the same.

Inside, the warm aroma of meat and potatoes filled the air. He walked through a series of bunk rooms to the kitchen at the far end and was surprised to find two women cooking, a few men were sitting at tables. One of the women, dressed in a long blue work dress with her hair pinned in a bun, noticed him and his jug.

"No alcohol in the mess," she ordered, putting her hands on her hips. Peter looked down at his half-full bottle.

"Oh, a . . . where can I put it for now?"

"Since I don't recognize you, uh . . . Are you a new hire or just spending the night?" she asked. Peter thought for a moment.

"So, ah, the man said I could . . . Charlie Ross says it's okay if I stay in the servant's —"

"Okay, then go back in the middle bunkroom, far right upper bunk. Made it this mornin' and no one's touched it since, use it," she said, pointing, "unless someone's got their gear on it, but I don't think so."

Peter did what he was told and hid the bottle under a bunk blanket and returned, finding six pence in his new trouser pocket along the way. The same lady saw him coming and held her hand out over the counter. Peter dropped the coins into her palm and she handed him a linen napkin and some cutlery.

"And don't be walkin' off with my silverware," she chided, casting him a wary eye while nodding at the knife and fork. She turned to the stove, saying, "We've got baked pork loin, mashed potatoes with gravy, and stewed carrots today." She piled the heavy food on a plate and handed it to Peter over the counter, adding, "clam chowder too if you want it."

"Yes," Peter mumbled and then nodded a thank you. He went over to a table, set the plate down, which seemed far too liquid to him, then returned for his clam chowder and spoon, went back to his table and began to wolf down his greasy food. A few moments later three men walked in. One was in buckskins and a jerkin vest, the other two wore black trousers, hickory shirts and wool coats.

"The *Cowlitz* just landed at the dock!" one said to the room.

"They rafted up beside the *Beaver*!" another added.

"Not Simpson again," a man at another table replied, "he was just here a couple of weeks ago."

"Yep, he's back."

Peter nearly choked on his last bite. He coughed and looked up at the men, unfocused and drunk, he wanted to ask them if there was any news from Stikine but decided against it. Instead, as gracefully as he could manage, he slowly walked his empty plate and bowl over to the end of the counter and quietly set them in a wash tub, then went back to retrieve his jug.

Outside, dusk was beginning to come over the fort. He took a long pull from the bottle and stumbled down to the main gate where he could view the *Cowlitz* tied up beside the other steamer.

Sure enough, there it was, looking fine and shipshape. George Simpson was out on the deck about to come ashore with his bagpiper. Dressed impeccably for the northern-frontier, Simpson was not a tall man but had an aura of command about him that seemed to make him as towering as the big cedars of the Salish Sea. In a tailored wool suit, with an ascot tie, a pair of black leather gloves, and a fine satin top-hat over his flaming red hair, he held a leather-bound accounting book in his right hand. Simpson seemed a man from another world amongst the rough laborers and bedraggled workers of Prince Rupert's Land as he stepped from the *Cowlitz* onto the *Beaver*. When Simpson walked imperiously down the gangway and onto the wharf Peter noticed a tall dark-skinned Metis in a black tricorne hat and a shorter fellow with a knit cap on his head walking close behind him. After a few, sozzled seconds to consider what he was seeing, it hit Peter in a flash — it was Thomas McPherson and Pierre Kannaquassé, from Fort Stikine just twenty-yards away from him! *What're they doing here? Are they looking for me? Did they talk Simpson into believing that I killed Mr. John?*

Peter's heart jumped into his throat. He stepped back from the gate and hid behind the crowd that lined the path. Then he went over behind the tall palisade wall and peered through a gap between two log uprights.

Looking like an arrogant peacock, Simpson strutted up the dock behind the blaring, high pitched wail of bagpipes, signaling his arrival. He climbed the mud rutted hill in polished boots up to the fort with a stern sullen look. Directly behind him the unreadable faces of McPherson and Pierre followed, both of their heads were constantly turning, looking at all the faces, searching the crowd. Behind them a few deckhands followed. He heard one say, "John McLoughlin's been murdered by his own men at Fort Stikine," to someone lining the path.

Fear seized Peter's body. *So they did it! They killed him. Those dumb bastards! Should I turn myself in and implicate McPherson? Tell Simpson the truth? But what if all the men at the fort lied and pinned me for the murder? Merde!*

He turned and watched from his hiding place as Simpson and his two Stikine cohorts walked by up the hill to the big house and went inside. Peter took a pull off his bottle and did his best to think about his options, he decided to go back to the ale house for a few minutes to see if he could learn anything more.

It was now full of men, talk, and pipe smoke. He spied a single chair up against the wall and sat down. Next to him a table of men were babbling away.

"I heard two of them are locked up at Sitka right now in the Russian jail," one said.

"No, not true. Only one is," another said in response. "They're looking for one more."

"Will they go to trial or just be shot?"

"Not sure, but they should be shot, and probably will."

"I wonder who they are?"

"Haven't heard any names yet."

134

"So, why is Simpson here then?"

"He's probably investigating the whole thing."

Peter's swimming mind raced with thoughts. *What should I do? Where can I go? I'd rather die than go to prison!*

This new development shocked him sober. He took a long pull of rum, thinking about his situation, and set the bottle on his knee, racking his brain about what to do.

"John McLoughlin Senior ain't gonna stand for this. He'll go to the gates of hell to bury the killer of his son and anyone else involved."

As the men spoke, two newcomers shoved open the doors of the tavern and went straight to the bar, instantly receiving pewter mugs and a bottle from the knowing bartender. Both were muscular and clean shaven, looking trim and fit in their striped shirts. Mugs and bottle in hand they made their way over near Peter where they sat down at a table. One poured the liquor and they began to drink, murmuring amongst each other in what Peter recognized right away as French. He stood up, then inched his way along the wall closer to them and listened to them talk. Even in his morose state of mind their conversation began to pull at his heart, it made him think of his mother and father, it made him long for those days when they were alive. He inched closer, fortified by over a half a bottle of rum, then finally spoke up.

"Bonjour les amis. Je n'ai pas pu m'empêcher d'entendre votre Francis. Puis-je m'assoir?" Peter said, asking if he could sit and drink with them.

But they ignored him and kept talking, so Peter stated, "*Mon pére est de Calais et a immigré dans le province du Bas-Canada il y a de nombreuses années.*"

Instantly, their expressions changed to bright smiles, both of them replied with a joyful, "*Calias*?!"

"*Ma mére est de Calais!*" one of them exclaimed. "*S'il te plaít sit down*, join us my new friend. What is your name?"

"My name . . . don't matter. I just heard you talking French," he slurred. He poured a slurp of rum into each of their mugs and asked, "Are you, from . . . the ship?"

"*Oui*, this is Francois and I am Marque," the older looking one of the two said.

Peter took another drink, set the bottle on the table and looked at it glumly. His eyes rolled upward and his head fell back, then he started to fall off his chair, but the two men caught Peter and laughed as they righted him.

"My friend, you have been washing your throat with too much rum!" Francois said, putting his hand on Peter's arm. "You are already half-seas over with liquor —"

"Ha!" Marque exclaimed. "Our new friend is full-seas over."

"I'm fine! I can drink this watered-down grog all night!" Peter croaked, closing his eyes and letting his chin drop down on his chest.

"I can see that," Francois said, laughing. He placed his hand at the base of Peter's bottle and slowly pushed it away from him.

136

"Do you work for Hudson's Bay?" Francois asked. Peter laughed, lolling his head to the side and drooling as he prepared to speak.

"I used to work for them, farther north . . . at Fort Stick-keen," he slurred. "But Mr. John, the Chief Trader got killed . . . murdered by his own men."

"Ah, yes," Marque said warily, "we have just heard about this terrible thing."

"The killers said it was me . . . but it wasn't. I outsmarted 'em! And now they're here looking for me," Peter confided.

"They are here now? Who? Where? They are looking for you?"

"Here! They're here, up in the big house, I saw 'em! I outsmarted 'em but . . . they found . . ." Peter trailed off for a while, trying hard to focus but failing. "It doesn't matter, let 'em find me. My canoe, the Haida . . . my wife." Peter did not realize it, but the two Frenchmen saw him start to cry, very softly.

Peter's two new friends looked around the room, then one asked, "Is your wife with your canoe?"

"No . . . We were ambushed by Haidas, on our way south . . . she was clubbed and . . . done away with — the steamer found me, brought me here."

"Clubbed and done away! Oh, my friend, we are so sorry to hear that. That is awful. But why are the killers of Mr. John blaming you?" Marque asked.

Peter leveled his eyes on his two new acquaintances and commenced to tell them all about what had really been going on at Fort Stikine and the plot that Thomas McPherson, Heroux, and Pierre Kannaquassé had hatched to kill Mr. John while they listened intently, believing him. "You see, I have nowhere to run, nowhere to hide, and I do not care about living anymore without my wife because my life is over."

"Ah, but your life is not over, you must pick yourself up and go on living, you are still young!" Francois said with an encouraging voice, patting him on the shoulder.

Peter looked at him and nodded just as the door opened, bringing a cold wind in off the river. Two men with hard faces walked through the open door and then stopped just inside the building — Peter sensed them before they saw him, the nerves on the back of his neck began to burn. It was McPherson and Pierre; they scanned the room and saw Peter then began to push their way through the crowded bar. As they did a hush fell over the room so Peter turned. When he saw them, his heart raced and jumped into his throat, he turned back to his two new friends and whispered in French, *"Those are the real men who killed Mr. John . . . they are here to take me away and have me shot for their sins."*

"I knew we'd catch up with you! We're taking you! NOW!" McPherson screamed, his face turned flush with hate and his voice menacing. "Pierre, grab him!"

Suddenly rising from his chair, Peter smashed his still quarter full bottle on the table, laughing, a wild look in his eye. Francois and Marque stood up and took a step backwards while the room went silent, some patrons backed away while others kept seated and watched, used to the common fracas that occurred in the alehouse.

"So, Frenchy, we meet again! I will be taking you to prison just as soon as I pay you back!" Pierre snarled, his eyes sparking — the object of his quest finally before him. Pierre drew a long, glittering knife from the sheath on his belt and stepped towards Peter. "You couldn't run forever, you low-down *bâtard*! And that little broken bottle won't save you. You're coming with us."

Pierre moved on Peter, his knife low in his right hand. The leathery Iroquois, smiling, held his left hand high — ready to catch anything that came at him. Suddenly face to face, Peter's courage failed him for just a moment — all he wanted was to rush forward, to bash Pierre's evil face in, but he couldn't. He was back in the canoe, fumbling with his pistol, the Haidas closing in. He could almost feel the cold waters enveloping him as he fell out of the boat as Francois, having stepped away when the ruckus started, brought his pewter mug straight down onto the back of Pierre's head, instantly dropping him to the floor. The tavern, which had been rendered mute by Pierre's accusation, erupted into gasps and cacophony, chair legs screeched as they scraped across the floor when the Iroquois went down. His comrade McPherson, reacting fast, went straight for Francois but Peter dropped the jagged bottle, tossed the table out of the way and threw himself at McPherson, his fists flying while everyone stepped back to make room for the melee.

First Peter hit McPherson square in the nose, breaking it sideways as blood splattered both of them. But McPherson tackled him to the floor, getting on top of him and hitting him in the face. Peter blocked the third swing and on the fourth Peter grabbed his fist with his left hand and stopped him, then hit him soundly on the jaw three times, finally knocking him into a dazed and semiconscious state. He slumped over on top of Peter.

In a flash, Pierre was on his feet and back in the fight, he shoved McPherson out of the way and pounced on Peter, hitting him repeatedly all about his face and neck. He pinned Peter's right arm under one leg and then his left. Pierre grabbed Peter by his long beard and jerked his head to the side and pummeled his left eye.

"You see, you see how it feels!" Pierre screamed, his eyes blazing, showing the emotion of a depraved madman, a grotesque bent on revenge, his pock-marked face dripping with sweat. He hit Peter over and over trying to scar him the same way he'd been. But Peter was so drunk he didn't feel a thing and the blows didn't break the skin under his eye. Then Peter began laughing at him so Pierre pulled at his beard even harder, trying to rip it right off his face.

Peter got his right arm free and grabbed Pierre by the throat, squeezing it as tight as he could until Pierre let go of his beard and with both hands began to choke Peter, each of them choking the other, determined to kill their nemesis.

"I'll be dancing . . . on your grave . . . tomorrow," Pierre said, his broken words barely audible as Peter tightened his grip on Pierre's neck.

"Nev . . . er," Peter spit out from the side of his mouth.

"You owe me —"

"Go. To. Hell."

It was then that Peter brought his right leg up high and around to the front of Pierre, got it under his chin and with all his might he levered him backwards. When his head hit the wooden floor, Pierre gave out a groan and rolled over. He saw the knife and started to crawl towards it but Peter beat him to it, grabbed it with his right hand and they began to struggle, rolling back and forth across the alehouse floor while patrons moved aside. Somehow, in their wrestling and hitting Peter stabbed Pierre in the leg, he let out a ghastly cry and stopped fighting, curled up in a ball and held his leg, moaning, "You son of a bitch . . . I'll get you for this."

Peter slowly pushed himself up off the floor, wavering, drunk, and breathing hard but still holding the knife, he worked to catch his breath then stepped over Pierre, stood over him and spat, "You're the son of a bitch, not me. And as for you, McPherson," Peter snarled, turning around.

Francois and Marque had picked McPherson up off the floor and Marque was standing behind him, holding him in a reverse headlock. Peter glared at his old partner in crime, stumbled over to him, trapped and struggling in Marque's tight headlock with his arms up in the air, but he stopped moving when Peter put the knife up to his throat.

"You see, this is what happens when you lie and cheat . . . and sell young girls to animals," Peter sneered, his voice quavering, his body full of alcohol and his knees about to give out. He pressed the blade into McPherson's skin until a trickle of blood began to slide down his neck.

"Where's my money?" McPherson snarled.

"You'll never see it again."

"I'll see it again," he sneered, "because you're no killer — just a greedy bastard like me. I'll find you someday and get back all of that sterling and gold — so bugger off."

Peter glared at him, thinking, *He's right. I've never killed a man and never will.* McPherson started to struggle again so Marque clamped down harder on his overbearing hold. Peter pulled the knife away, dropped it on the floor, stepped back and punched him in the face with all the strength he could muster, and then again and again, until blood began to coat McPherson's teeth and lips. Exhausted, Peter slammed his right hand into his face one last time. McPherson's head fell to his chest and Marque let go. He dropped to the floor, unconscious, and Peter, breathing hard and fully intoxicated, lost all the strength in his legs and crumpled down on his knees. He looked up blank-faced at Marque, his eyes blood-shot and he began to wretch, then tipped over, hitting the floor with a thud, and he puked.

Marque stared at him dumbfounded for a moment then glanced at Francois who tilted his head towards the door and they both bolted before anyone could react.

They ran halfway down to the fort gate when Francois grabbed his cohort by the shoulder, "Wait, we should wait and see what happens."

They stopped and caught their breath, both looking up and down the way. "They're going to kill him if they can. We need to do something," Francois said.

"Like what?"

"Save him, maybe."

"Save him?"

"I think we should. I believed him."

"Me too. I thought he was telling the truth."

"Well, let's hide and wait, see what happens." They crept over to the side of the blacksmith shop and crouched in the shadows.

Inside the alehouse, murmur and talk began to fill the room. Kilgore hollered, "That's it!" He walked around from the bar, adding, "you're done buster. Anyone know who this bloke is?"

"I saw him over in the mess hall earlier," one trader said.

"You talk to him? He tell you his name?" Kilgore asked. But the trader shook his head 'no'.

"Anyone else?" Kilgore said, standing over a bloodied Peter and his vomit.

"Nobody? . . . Okay," he said to the room. He pointed at two men, "Calhoun and Godfrey, haul this piece of shite out of my alehouse! NOW!" Then he turned his attention to McPherson and Pierre while shaking his head as the two men picked up Peter's feet and dragged him out the door to the main road.

"Anyone know these two?"

"I think they work for the company," one man replied.

"Well, we need to get them over to Doc Watermire's. That one's leg is bleeding pretty bad. So, you two," Kilgore said, pointing at a couple of men. "Take these fella's up to the Doc's quarters and the rest of you, help me pick up these tables and chairs and clean this joint up!"

XI

The Bourtange
Pa-si'-ooks La Piége

Outside, darkness had fallen thick on the fort, the pale sliver of the moon trying in vain to pierce the grey clouds above. The fight had been loud but typical, so no alarms had been rung, no emergencies called. Francois and Marque watched as Peter was dragged out of the alehouse by his feet and left in the road for whatever fate had in store for him. The two Frenchmen hiding in the shadows saw their chance. They ran as fast as they could over to Peter, his knit cap was lying next to him so Francois shoved it down on his head, then they lifted him up and started to walk on either side of him with his arms draped over their shoulders.

As Peter drifted gradually in and out of consciousness, the conversation between his two would-be saviors landed easily on his ears, and he knew that he understood the words being said individually, but the meaning was totally beyond his drunken self.

"You idiot, look at what you've done now! The captain said no more fights!"

"What should we have done, let him get killed?"

"They were going to arrest him, not kill him!"

"If you think those men were deputies, you're dumber than you look. Besides, he's French!"

"Barely! He's French Canadian."

"It doesn't matter, what's done is done! He's our responsibility now."

"Responsibility? He is not! We should leave him in the ditch and get back to the ship."

"No! I won't do that!"

"Then what?"

The pleasant melody of argumentative French was briefly interrupted by the last thing Peter heard at Fort Langley, which was the two burly Frenchmen trying to save him from his doom.

"We should stick him in a canoe, push him downstream."

"No, we shall take him to the ship, we're short of men right now and he speaks okay French, he'll do fine."

"But those men are going to come after him, and when they do the captain will turn him over."

"No, the one he stabbed in the leg will not be walking soon and the other, well, he knocked him out good, so who knows. I think we should smuggle him on board and hide him. He got so drunk he'll never remember what happened or even remember us, and was probably blind from drink the whole time. But your idea about the canoe has given me a thought."

Up ahead at the fort's gate, only one man stood guard. Francois whispered, "Start singing, we will make him think that we're drunk on our last night so, follow along."

Alouette, gentille alouette,
Alouette, je te plumerai.

Je te plumerai la tête,
Et la tête!
Alouette!
A-a-a-ah

Je te plumerai le bec.
Et le bec!
Et la tête!
Alouette!
A-a-a-ah

The guard paid them no mind. Once past the gate Francois steered them off the path and over into the shadows of the trees.

"Stay here out of sight, I'll be right back," Francois whispered, sneaking off underneath the wharf where he untied a canoe and pushed it downriver. He crept back into the woods where he softly said, "Now they'll think he left on his own, start singing again."

With Peter's head hanging down and the two Frenchman singing at the top of their lungs, their free arms moving in unison to the song, they stumbled onto the wharf. Francois quietly said, "Let's hide him in the sail room, let him sleep it off till tomorrow. By then we'll be well under way."

They made their way up the gangway and onto the ship, no one was around, all were below deck sleeping in their hammocks and with Peter's cap pulled down over his eyes he was unrecognizable. The sentry standing watch was at the far end so Francois raised his free arm to acknowledge him.

"Celui-ci avait trop de rum," he said. The guard just waved and laughed, saying, *"Souhaite que ce soit moi!"*

Silently, they crept through the shadows of the ship and down the main staircase to a passageway, barely lit by a small amount of lantern light at the far end. They found the door to the sail room and opened it. At the entrance were large pieces of sailcloth hanging from the ceiling beams, a maze of material. They carried Peter to the back of the room where there was a large bin of smaller, saved pieces of cloth. Francois and Marque rolled him into it, so he was hidden from sight, and then left the room.

The next morning, Peter awoke to the sound of the ship's bell and the bustle of shuffling feet on the deck above. His head pounded with the worst hangover of his life, and as he grasped uselessly at his temples the door of the room crashed open.

"Aller! Aller! Le vent est levé, nous partons!" a voice called out, barking departure orders. Peter raised his gaze then rubbed his eyes and blinked. *Where am I?* Then the ships bell clanged again and he realized: *I'm on The Bourtange! How did I get here?* He peeked through a gap in the side of the bin. Sailors had come into the room, a few men, plus a young boy, one started lighting lamps, others were gathering sails for departure.

Overwhelmed and disoriented by the activity, Peter surrendered to the pounding behind his eyes and laid his head back down, quickly covered himself in white cloth, and instantly passed out once more.

Peter woke unhappily an hour later, the ship began to creak, then it lurched, as the footsteps of men pounded the deck above. Muffled orders were made and slowly the ship began to pull away from the dock. Peter could feel the movement of the clipper as the capstan was wound with the thick warping line that was attached to a small anchor dropped in the river by the crew in a rowboat. As the capstan was hand-turned the *Bourtange* slowly, but surely, moved away from the wharf.

Peter was happy to be leaving, but confused. He would soon be gone from the trouble of Mr. John's murder but then fear and dread filled his emotions as hunger pinched his stomach. *Should I turn myself in or just wait until a sailor finds me? I think I was with some Frenchmen last night; were they part of the crew?*

In mid-afternoon Peter could feel the big ship heave up and down over the waves and hear the spray of saltwater against the hull. The vessel heeled over a strake to larboard and he knew they were well underway. Peter could almost feel the hum of the wind through the rigging. Emotion moved through his body with the fact that the Hudson's Bay Company was now behind him, he fell back into the deep reverie of sleep.

"*Philippe! Philippe!*" a voice yelled over Peter. Alarmed, he opened his eyes to see the same young boy standing over the bin.

"*Viens vite! Il y a un passage clandestine!*" the apprentice hollered, then ran out of the sail room. Seconds later two sailmakers had rushed over, pitching the sails hanging from the ceiling out of their way. Wearing gansey shirts and white cloth breeches, they both had small marlin spikes hanging on lanyards from their necks. The two stood over Peter and glared, then reached down and grabbed him.

"*Qui êtes vous? Pourquoi es-tu ici?*" they asked, pulling him from the bin. Peter didn't resist as his mind raced.

"*Je suis un francais et je m'appelle Louis Comeau,*" he explained, tripping along as the two sailmakers dragged him from the room and up a hatchway.

On deck, Peter glanced around, the wind felt good in his face and the sun was well up in the sky, it cast a brilliant pattern of light across the deck between the shadows of the sails as the ship moved west and the land fell away from it. The breeze was abaft the ships beam and she was heeling two strakes now. Peter smelled the fresh, astringent spice of saltwater, they were headed through the Strait of Juan De Fuca, her hull sang through the waves.

Most of the sailors stopped their tasks, all of them tanned with weather-beaten faces, most in brightly colored shirts, stained white cotton breeches cutoff at the calf, scars showing on every surface of skin, some barefooted but all of them with knives and spikes on their wide black leather belts. Their looks told Peter that they'd been all across the seas and traveled round many stormy capes. They knew what it was like to be thrown beyond the safety of land, into the void of the ocean.

Inside the captain's cabin, the smell of smoldering tobacco filled the air. Dressed in a pale blue waistcoat and white frilled shirt, the captain sat behind a desk covered in dockets, vouchers, logs and journals with smoke floating around him. Behind him, the curving white and gold painted woodwork surrounding the window panes offered a seaman's view to the east. Through a haze of sweet pipe smoke the captain looked up when his cabin door was rapped upon.

"*Capitaine Delahaye, nous avons trouvé un passage clandestine dans la salle à voile*," said one of the men, his hand on the iron latch, waiting to hear a reply.

"*Entrez si'-vous-plaît*," Delahaye answered, taking the long-stemmed pipe from his mouth and setting it carefully in an ashtray. He looked to the doorway and watched as his men brought Peter into his quarters. There was another man sitting across the room who Peter took to be the first mate.

Wearing a filthy, blue and white stripped Breton shirt the first mate glanced up at Peter through long curly brown hair with a sly twisted smirk, his forearms covered with tattoos. There was a knife on his belt and a string of golden rings running up his ear.

"*Et qu'est ce que c'est? Do we have* ourselves a stowaway?" the Capitaine asked, looking a squalid Peter up and down. His hair was by now matted and greasy, his clothes bloodied from the night before.

"*Oui Capitaine*, we found him in the sail room, hiding in a bin," one of the men offered.

"I see," the Capitaine responded, his wig of white hair dangling to the sides of his thin face. "You may leave now," he said to the sailmakers. Once they closed the door behind them the commander turned to Peter.

"Why are you on my ship?"

"*Capitaine,* I do not know how I got here."

"The punishment is twenty lashes for stowaways. Do you understand?"

151

"*Oui, Capitaine*," Peter answered, lowering his head.

"Are you the one that the Hudson's Bay fellow, what was his name . . . Mick-fear-son, yes, that was him. Was he looking for you this morning?"

Peter raised his head and stood straight, his arms at his side and thought, *this is your last chance so you'd better tell him the truth.* "I will never lie to you. My name is Peter Goutre and yes, he was looking for me, but I have no idea how I ended up on your ship. However, I am a good worker. I have worked many years as a fur trapper and trader. I can —"

"But what about Mick-fear-son? He had a nasty black-eye and a bandaged nose, he said he was looking for a murderer . . . and because I wish to continue to do business with Hudson's Bay, I allowed him and his men to search my vessel but, it is obvious he did not find you. So! What do you have to say for yourself?"

"*Capitaine*," Peter said, taking off his knit cap, "I am not a murderer, McPherson is trying to blame me for the killing of John McLoughlin Jr."

"My ship is no place for criminals."

"I am not a criminal, *Capitaine*. I swear to you."

"I'll be the judge of that," the Capitaine quipped. "Mick-fear-son said there was a canoe missing this morning and he thought you might have stolen it to escape. Did you do that to throw him off?"

"I know nothing of a canoe *Capitaine*, do not know about it. I drank too much rum last night and passed out, I do not know how I got here."

"You sound like a Frenchman."

"Yes, I am from Montreal but my parents immigrated from Calais. I used to be a trader for Hudson's Bay, farther north at Stikine."

"Used to be? So, you are a deserter then, maybe you are a murderer or a thief, and you think my vessel shall shield you from your pursuers."

Without hesitation Peter said, "*Non capitaine*. I murdered no one. The men at Stikine plotted to kill McLoughlin because they despised him and wanted to overthrow the fort. I had no part and left, and because I left, I was the easy one to blame. You see, I had recently married a Tlingit woman and left the company after ten years. We planned to take land in the new territory but on our travels south we were ambushed by Haida raiders and my wife was . . . killed. All our possessions —"

"But what is that to me? Why should I care about some stowaway who thinks I should grant them a new life?" he asked, picking up his pipe.

"No, I mean yes, *capitaine*," Peter said, nodding his head. "I am a good worker and I will be loyal to you, and this ship. Please, give me a chance. I will not disappoint you."

Delahaye nodded, striking a friction match and holding the flame over the bowl of his pipe, saying, "I have taken on land-lubbers — but my ship is already full of worthless landsmen. I am not needing another bumbler to get caught in the rigging lines. Can you reef and steer? Can you work the deck and trim a sail?"

Peter's mind raced; *reef and steer, trim, what does that mean?* "No, I have never worked a tall ship before."

"Then what good are you to me?!" he challenged, the tenor of his voice rising. "Maybe I should just toss you overboard? Or *maybee* let you fall by accident over the rail at Tierra del Fuego? Hmmm?" he said, putting flame to his bowl and puffing his pipe. The captain looked up at the ceiling and blew a smoke ring. Then he put his feet up on the desk, grinned and said, "Or perhaps I shall enjoy watching you puke your meals every day when we round the Horn?"

Peter began to get nervous. "I am a fast learner, *capitaine*. I will learn to do the work without getting sick, I never get sick," he replied, glancing down at his vomit-stained shirt. "And . . . I know beaver pelts! You have a hold full of them. I can get you a good price anywhere you are going," Peter said, assuredly. But the captain sat quiet, smoking, so Peter added, "I have a strong back. I will work as hard as anyone. And, surely you could use more hands."

The captain snapped his head around like it was jerked by a rigging line. His grin disappeared, he glared at Peter, then said, "Why would you think that? Do you think sailors jump my ship all the time?"

"No, no, I just thought you may be in need of help."

"But you are not a seaman, *Monsieur Goutre*."

"Yes, *capitaine*. I am not," Peter answered, looking at the floor, the sinking feeling in his empty stomach worsening.

After a short pause, Delahaye began to puff on his pipe again. He glanced at his first mate and then at all the work on his desk, moving a few papers around. He looked back at his mate in contemplation then to Peter. "I have heard of the Haidas and been warned of them. You say your wife was killed?"

"Ah, yes, *capitaine*," Peter said, holding his knit cap in front of him. "They bore down on us as we tried to paddle to safety. There were three war-boats full, maybe fifty or sixty of them." Delahaye nodded as Peter spoke, he seemed to believe him. "I aimed my pistol to shoot and try and save my wife but I was bombarded by stones that they threw, knocked me nearly unconscious and out of my boat. I rose to the surface and stabbed a raider but they pulled my wife into one of the canoes where they clubbed her," he said, grabbing the marriage stick hanging from his neck under his shirt. Peter kissed and crossed himself with it. "They took everything in ten seconds and were gone."

Delahaye sat for a moment, he tapped the mouthpiece of his long-stemmed pipe on the top of his desk, thinking, then pushed back his chair and stood up. "Alright," he said, motioning with a hand, "I am *Capitaine Étienne Delahaye* and I will allow you to stay on my ship. I will save your life but I will not pay you. You will work for nothing until I am confident in you and, you will serve me and this ship for a three-year term and only then we shall discuss payment . . . *Matisse*! Take *Monsieur Goutre* to the galley, then send the ship's boy to the bosun's mate and have him work the deck. But keep a sharp eye on this one at all times."

Matisse sprang from his chair to attention and said, "*Á vos ordres, capitaine*." He strode over to Peter and pointed at the door, smirking.

"*Merci, merci, Capitaine Delahaye*," Peter smiled, heading for the passageway.

As soon as the door closed behind them Matisse laughing, pushed him in the back, causing him to trip forward but he caught himself before falling. Peter turned around and glared at the first mate. He wanted to pick him up and slam him to the ground, the same way he did to Pierre at Bitter Water, but he knew better.

"Get going," Matisse rasped, his hand on the handle of his belted knife. "The *capitaine* may have saved you but you answer to me now," he said at Peter's back.

They descended a hatchway into the bowels of the clipper and through reeking wooden passageways, the whole way Matisse was pushing and prodding Peter every time he needed to turn down a hallway. Peter began to feel like an inmate on a floating prison.

In the galley, Matisse pointed at a shabby make-shift wooden work bench mounted against the hull timbers where a young boy was chopping onions. He was the same one that Peter had seen earlier.

"There is the new life you are looking for," he said to Peter, his voice dripping with malice. "Boy!" he barked at the cook's apprentice, "Report to the bosun immediately. You work the deck now."

The young fellow smiled widely and took off his over-sized food-stained apron and handed it to Peter, quietly saying, "I was looking for old sail cloth to make a new apron from when I uncovered you."

"Marcel!" Matisse loudly said to the balding, slovenly cook, "This is your new assistant. Work him like a dog . . . He is to bring me my lobscouse, hot, every day and my biscuits, without weevils!"

The cook nodded in agreement, stirring a large cauldron of stew, and Matisse left. The cook stopped his task and looked at Peter, he ran his fingers across his thin-haired head, asking, "Have you a name?"

"I am Peter — Goutre," he replied, wrapping the greasy apron around his waist and stepping over to his station. He picked up the long wide blade, it felt like it weighed twenty pounds, and started chopping onions while the cook began to go over the daily routine.

"Each man every day gets one pound of biscuit hard-tack, one and a half pounds of salt pork or salt beef, the men call it salt junk so when they say it to you, you'll know what they mean. They all get one cup of coffee or tea with sugar each meal and three quarts of water for drinking and washing. Try your best to keep the cockroaches and the weevils out of the food . . . And they'll want more tea to soak the hard-tack in so they can eat it but don't pour them extra. Keep to my orders and we'll have no trouble."

That night, exhausted, Peter lay weeping in his canvas hammock hanging from the beams in the crammed quarters between decks, with loudly snoring men close enough on either side to elbow him whenever they rolled over. The thought of Little Rain gone forever and them never having a family tore his heart apart. *Please forgive me dear Lord.*

For the next ten years Peter sailed the trade winds on the Seven Seas and found himself in many exotic ports. First, they sailed to Canton, China, where the beaver pelts and salted salmon were traded for silk, tea, and porcelain. Those goods were then carried back to the *Bourtange's* home port of Brest, France, where they were sold to merchants who then transported the goods to Paris.

Peter worked his way out of the galley and onto the deck, where he learned the sea fairing life. He finally earned seamanship and was eventually paid on every voyage. He went around the Horn eight times on five different ships, was wrecked and stranded, half foundered and dismasted. Peter sailed on all variations of clippers and barques all across the world; timber ships, tea and spice brigs, copper and coal carriers, and wool ketches, all of them under the French flag until he was able to work a one-way passage on a new clipper bound for the western coast of Prince Rupert's Land.

Part Two

XII

Fort Victoria
Camosun
May 1853

Under overcast skies, Peter stood at the port side rail taking in the sights as the 80-ton brigantine *Madeleine* eased through James Bay and into the inner harbor. To the west, on the edge of an Esquimalt Indian village, a half dozen Natives were out digging up camas roots in meadows lined with oak trees, and to the east, Songhees Indians lived and worked, downing and carving whole cedar trees into canoes on the beach. At the head of the harbor a long empty wharf waited for the merchant ship to land. Beyond the wharf lay the fort and a frontier collection of living arrangements and wooden buildings — cabins, workshops, and tents — it all made for a color picture painting of a northwest crown colony.

Once the ship was tied off and secured, Peter headed straight to the paymaster and collected his earnings in French gold, then he went below deck to gather up his savings of more gold and various coins from the sea chest he'd been using. Over the last seven-years he'd managed to save close to one gold piece each month, more than enough for a fresh start. He unlocked his barrel top chest, inside, most of the gold was hidden in socks, rolled up in clothing or in small tin boxes with his other monies from around the world. Peter put all of it into the leather rucksack that he got in Málaga,

161

slung it over his shoulder, then turned in his sea chest key to the bosun's mate and went ashore.

He stepped from the gangway, pleased to be back in the Pacific Northwest and finally free from ten years as a sailor. Peter took a long deep breath, and walked up the pier and into the fort while looking all around. The first to catch his interest was the Hudson's Bay Company store. He strolled in and went slack-jawed. Not only was he amazed that it was as big as a barn inside but how much inventory there was, everything imaginable under one roof; clothes, hardware, fresh food and baked goods, dry goods and sundries. Handsaws and planers, axes and tools, firearms, gunpowder and shot, books, tables and chairs, kitchenware, bake kettles, and canned fruit. He stopped and looked at a can of peaches then grabbed it, imagining how they tasted. Peter headed towards the front counter but a Bailey wood cookstove caught his eye. It had a hinged oven door with glass in it and two burning chambers; one for wood and one coal. *Someday I'm gonna have one of those.*

When he saw two women wearing floor-length dresses and plaid bonnets with baskets on their arms admiring a new charcoal clothes iron that opened up so hot coals could be put inside of it, he grinned. *What else could the modern world come up with?*

He walked away, shaking his head in disbelief, down another aisle and came upon a foot-powered sewing machine that was mounted on its own table one could sit at. He read a small advertisement sign on it; 'This Singer Sewing Machine Can Produce a Shirt in One Hour!' *Now I've seen everything! I've been at sea for far too long.*

Peter began to pile up a number of goods and items to buy on the twenty-foot-long purchase counter: a new musket, pistols, gunpowder and lead, iron kettle, cookware, map, compass, spyglass, hunting knives with leather sheaths, pocket knives, a metal container of friction matches, a bucksaw, hammer and nails, chisel, shovel, lamp and coal oil, blankets, trinkets, and a dozen bottles of rum and corkscrews to trade with. Plus, flour, bacon, coffee, sugar, his can of peaches, and everything he could possibly eat and need for his travel south. He decided to rid himself of his breeches and seafaring clothes and get new frontier clothing: black canvas trousers, leather boots, a grey work shirt, wool coat, a brown vest and he added a new navy blue knit cap to his pile. In no time he'd taken up a good portion of the counter with all his gear.

The clerk, a tall, pale man with a brown handlebar mustache, eyed him cautiously as he bustled about the shop. Finally, with a sigh, he bent over the counter and started filling out a purchase ticket.

Peter picked up the can of peaches and held it out, saying, "How does a fellow open one of these?"

"Easy," the man said, glancing at Peter's pile of goods, "it looks like you've got the right tools to do it, just read the directions."

Peter looked at the label, 'Cut round the top near the outer edge with a chisel and hammer.' He picked up the two items from his pile and started to tap on the metal top with the chisel, thinking, *somebody has got to invent something better to do this*, while the clerk watched him open and then peel back the jagged lid without cutting himself. Peter slurped some of the thick sweet juice.

"Oh, *monami,* that's good!"

"Where ya' headed?" the clerk asked, going through everything.

"Going south, Puget Sound in Oregon Territory. I'm planning on claiming some land," Peter answered, stabbing a thick piece of peach with a pocketknife he was buying and then taking a bite.

"Ah, a new homesteader huh. So, um, I guess you haven't heard then. Puget Sound's not in Oregon Territory anymore."

"What? Did they move it?" Peter replied, laughing.

"No, no, they just moved the boundary line. It's a new territory. Everything north of the Columbia is Washington Territory, and Fillmore is finally gone. Pierce is in the White House now! Just got himself inaugurated two months ago, but from all this gear it looks like you're gonna have a boat load."

"Well I'll be, a new territory huh? But speaking of a boat load, how much do the Natives usually want for their canoes?"

"What do ya' mean?"

"I am asking, *monsieur,* how much do they want in trade for one?"

"Good question, cause they ain't givin' 'em away and they're some damn good negotiators. It depends on how many of 'em work on each one cause normally, each one wants something."

"Oh, I know a thing or two about haggling. I was hoping to trade a jug of rum for a twenty-footer," Peter remarked, drinking from the peach can.

"That's a possibility, since we don't trade liquor with the Natives. But you'll have to find a boat that only one of 'em worked on then. I'd guess that you'll be givin' up two or three jugs to two or three Indians, plus a little more."

"Oh, I'll get the price down. I need to keep most of that for myself!" Peter exclaimed, motioning at the liquor.

The clerk laughed and asked, "Which route are you taking?"

"Haven't looked at my new map yet. Why?"

"Because we've got some treacherous waters around here so you need to exercise some caution. You've got two choices, you can either stay on the outside of Whidbey Island in the big rough water or you can go the Deception Pass route. If you take Deception, which I highly encourage you to do, it'll take you down the east side of Whidbey in calmer water and if you wait for the ebb tide to go slack outside of the pass then you'll be able to navigate it on the flood with ease. That route gets you to the best part of northern Puget Sound much faster. Once yer' through Deception stick to the west side of the waterway and find Penn Cove, I hear there's some white settlers there."

"That's some good advice, thank you," Peter said, smiling, and eating a peach.

"Alright, so, you've got an awful lot of equipment and food here, sir. I've added it all up and it comes out to be £30 pounds sterling," the clerk said, ripping the ticket out of his small pad.

Peter snatched the ticket and looked at it, then stated, "I will be making payment with French gold." He set the empty peach can on the counter and took off his rucksack then opened it.

"French gold? What's a fella doing here with French gold?"

"I've been at sea for 10 years on French merchant ships *monami*. I just landed on the *Madeleine* and was paid in gold," Peter said, pulling out one round gold piece from his rucksack and showing it to him. Then he shoved it in an empty front pocket in case he needed it for canoe trading.

"Well, let's see, French gold for British sterling value. Let me check the weights for you."

He went into a back-office room and returned a moment later.

"The manager is not very interested in your gold but he will trade in sterling value for the gold that you have. So! You're in luck. We can give you your goods for 33 of your gold pieces."

Peter nodded and counted out the small coins of gold and handed them over, then asked, "And how much would each of my gold pieces be worth in American dollars?"

The clerk shrugged and walked to the back office again and soon returned, "Your gold pieces weigh in at 1/5th of an ounce and an ounce of gold right now is valued at twenty American dollars. So, each gold piece of yours, assuming 90% purity, is worth four American dollars. If you'd like to convert them now then I would have to check with the manager."

"No thank you, *monsieur*. I think I will hold onto most of my gold for the time being but I would like to change one piece into American money," Peter said, reaching into his rucksack for another gold coin. He handed it to the fellow and asked, "Could I get American silver for that? And would it be possible for you to hold my goods in storage until I have purchased a canoe? I plan to do that today."

"Certainly," the clerk said. "I'll get you four silver dollars and store everything in the backroom for you."

"*Ah bien, merci, monsieur,*" Peter replied, grabbing one bottle of rum and a hunting knife that he put in his back pocket. He opened the rum with a corkscrew then put the cork back in the bottle. While Peter was doing that the clerk went and got his money for him and brought it back. He handed the coins to Peter.

"I'll be back soon," he said, taking and then storing the silver dollars in his rucksack.

Peter walked out of the building and strolled over to the east side of the harbor, where he found a beautiful new western red cedar dugout canoe resting on log rollers. When he started inspecting it four Songhees in blackened buckskins walked over to him from two dugouts under construction, smiling and murmuring amongst themselves.

Two close-by canoe builders were in the process of steaming the inside of a dugout so they could widen it. One of them was carrying hot rocks with a shovel from a large beach fire and dropping them in the boat which had water in it. When the steam increased, the other builder covered the canoe with mats to hold the heat in.

As they worked Peter bent over and checked to see how straight the keel was on the finished canoe, while the four Songhees, who were anxious for a sale, watched and followed him around the canoe, eyeing his bottle. Satisfied with the keel, Peter began to run his fingers over the hull to see if the curvature was uniform, then he pushed on each seat to check for strength. Two hand-carved cedar paddles were also inside of it, a handsome bonus. At the raised bow there was a mouth-like notch and the stern had a graceful upward tapering. *This is exactly what I need, it's perfect!*

"*Kloshe sun. Huy-huy, huihui?*" Peter asked in trade jargon.

167

"*Nawitka!*" the oldest looking one said in jargon.

"*Káh-ta hy-iu chik'-a-min?*" Peter asked, holding up his free hand and rubbing his fingers together.

"*Lakit la-boo-ti' lum,*" the same one answered, holding up four fingers and then pointing at his bottle.

"Hah!" Peter scoffed, shaking his head. "That's too high, too high. *Wake, ko'-pa ságh-a-lie!*"

The Songhees looked at each other and frowned. They huddled together and whispered a few words of their own dialect. After a moment they turned back to Peter and the same one said, "*Klone la-boo-ti' lum.*"

"*Wake, klone lums ko'-pa ságh-a-lie,*" Peter responded. "Still too high, but," he said, reaching into his back pocket. He pulled out the new hunting knife and held it and the jug of rum up, he offered, "*O'-koke.*"

One of the Songhees smiled while the others shrugged. They huddled in council again then countered, "*Mokst la-boo-ti' lum pe o'-pit-sah.*"

"Hmm, two jugs and the knife," Peter replied, thinking about it. He walked around the canoe again, inspecting it as the Songhees followed on his heels. After crouching and looking at the hull again, he stood up and said, "*Wake,* too high!"

All of them let out a collective sigh, then threw up their hands and stared at Peter. He shoved the knife back in his pocket and pulled the cork from the bottle and took a swig. They all let out a groan and huddled again while Peter waited for their reply.

Suddenly, two of the four stomped off angrily, their discussion over. The other two stepped over to Peter smiling, the older one looked at the rum and the other pointed at Peter's backside pocket, then he raised his right hand and rubbed his fingers together, saying, "*chik'-a-min.*"

"*Ne-si'-ka is'-kum ikt lum pe o'-pit-sah pe chik'-a-min,*" the older one added, both of them holding out their hands, grinning.

"And you want money too?!" Peter exclaimed. He shrugged his shoulders and pulled out the single gold piece, he held it up for them. "Here, one piece of gold. *Kloshe chik'-a-min.*"

"*Wake, mokst chik'-a-min,*" the older one said.

"I've only got one, *ikt chik'-a-min,*" Peter grinned, pulling the insides of his pockets out so the two canoe builders could see that they were empty and hoping they would think he was broke.

The two Songhees turned away from Peter and whispered to each other then turned around. The older of the two stepped over to the canoe and took one of the hand-carved paddles out, grinned and pointed at the three trade items Peter had and said, "*Al'ta kloshe.*"

"Oh I bet you're all good with it now. Okay, alright," Peter said, holding out the gold piece, rum and hunting knife.

He saw their acceptance as an acknowledgement that they were the only two who had worked on the canoe, and that each of them got something, plus a gold piece.

They snatched the items from Peter and then motioned that they were going to help him get the canoe in the water over the log rollers. Peter pushed the dugout while the other two carried each roller from the back to the front until it was in the bay.

"*Kloshe*," Peter said, hopping in. He picked up the remaining paddle and made his way across the water and next to the wharf where he beached his new craft and went back into the Hudson's Bay store to retrieve his goods and buy a spool of line to tie off his new craft.

He slept that night on the beach next to his dugout then spent the following day strolling about the town that was springing up around the outside of the fort: a haphazard array of tents surrounded by ankle-deep, mud rutted pathways. Peter took notice of the several sawmills, cutting and selling lumber as fast as they could. He marveled at how the steam driven mills were laid out and how the men skidded the logs into place with oxen and loaded the carriage to mill the timbers. One sawmill he witnessed ran by the waterpower from a rushing creek. It was a method he believed he could duplicate, with some help.

Then he set his sights to where Little Rain and he had set their dreams for years before, Puget Sound and a new-found life, liberated from any HBC constraints or difficulties, and free of clipper ship first mates. For once and all he would be unshackled from the murder of John McLoughlin Jr.

In the morning, Peter was bursting with vigor and eager to get out on the water. He cut a fine pioneer image when he left Fort Victoria, he had reinvented himself and more importantly, saved himself. On his first day of paddling, he headed east below cloudy skies across Haro Strait towards the southern tip of San Juan Island, Peter felt more alive than he had in many years. He was an independent man, and the world was a wide-open place. Land was for the taking and he was bound to get his share.

Using his new map, his plan was to follow the southern ends of San Juan and Lopez Islands and then skirt across Rosario Strait and find Deception Pass. Once there he'd paddle through the narrow opening during low slack water and head south by way of Saratoga Passage. From there he didn't care where he landed, just as long as he could find a suitable place to homestead — enough land for a cabin, and a garden, an orchard, maybe even some pigs and cows! All along the water too, for easy access and so he could fish and crab — and hell, if there was a stream too then all the better, maybe he could even get one of those mills going like he'd seen.

After two days of hard paddling amid calm seas, Peter was thrilled to reach the western end of Deception Pass — he was right on time and dead-on course. He spent the night at a crescent-shaped cove just to the north with a small island in front of it, camping out beneath the stars on a thick bear pelt he'd brought just for the purpose, chewing fresh pemmican he'd bought from the Songhees and rejoicing in the silence and solemnity of the night amongst the tall evergreens.

Peter woke to a stellar blue sky the next day, and while the tide was still ebbing, he readied his canoe then stood and looked out over the strait. A river of saltwater could clearly be seen streaming out from the narrow pass and into the greater calm of the bay, like a vein of flowing life. As the strait welcomed the flowing tide, he could see the immense body of water heave and sway, the low rolling swells moving to and fro. It was in that trice of time, when he saw the Sound as a living, breathing entity, full of vitality, its rhythmic pattern of life in constant motion. He relished in the moment until the tide slowed and ultimately ceased. Smiling, Peter pushed off his canoe and began to paddle in earnest.

He hugged the northern shoreline, traveling past rocky

outcroppings, tide pools and small inlets. Around the corner of a point, he came into sight of an island on the left side of the pass, a granite pillar of solid rock carved thousands of years ago by retreating glaciers. It jutted two-hundred feet straight up, with a slender passage between it and the north side. He headed towards it.

As Peter approached the western portal, the quietness of the day came over him, he stopped paddling and floated on the calm slack water for a while with only the faint sound of water dripping from the end of his paddle blade to accompany him. Gazing up at the time weathered rock walls Peter felt like he was traveling through a secret passageway to his future, but it reminded him of his past, sitting in the cathedral of the old stone church in Montreal with his mother and father on Sundays, praying and singing hymns. A rush of emotion surged through him, his body tingled with spirituality, time and tide had stopped and the world was all his in a life-affirming moment.

Basking in the glory and beauty of the wilderness, the miracle of God's creation touched his soul. Peter reached down outside of his canoe and brushed the cold salty water with his fingers, brought the moisture up to his face and rubbed his forehead then crossed himself, anointing himself with the saline waters of Puget Sound. Elation moved through his system, he let his body fall backwards against the stern, then looked up to the brilliant cobalt sky and reveled in the experience.

A moment later the incoming current turned the thin channel into a liquid conduit of rushing waves, the rapids and his paddling pushed his twenty-foot canoe through the canyon-walled notch and out the other end. He emerged from the eastern portal of the waterway where it turned south and widened into a hidden inland saltwater sea.

The warm sun shone down on Peter, to the northeast a bulging volcano shaped mountain covered in snow and glaciers stood out on the horizon. He stopped paddling and drifted with the fast-moving current on a golden day in a golden land. Three deer were on the shore of a close-in beach taking in the sunshine and, above them, a bald eagle stood guard perched in an old-growth snag while a red-tailed hawk circled above. The unspoiled world lay wild and free before him. He felt like an argonaut that had just found the golden fleece in a wide-open pristine land that was all there for him. But then he looked at the empty seat in the front of the canoe and his mood instantly swung to melancholy. *Little Rain should be here. Dear God I wish she was here. I'm so sorry. I never should have taken her away from her family. It's all my fault she's gone. Please God, forgive me.*

Peter paddled on easily, slowly — the joy of the world around him tempered by his memories. He was surrounded by resplendence the likes few breathing white men had ever seen. But the pain of Little Rain's loss bore down on him with the weight of his still being alive, he knew he'd be burdened with it for the rest of his days, gnawing away at him, causing despair.

Peter reached forward and grabbed a bottle of rum, pulled the cork and drank deeply. For the rest of the day, he rode the incoming tide, most of the time using his paddle as a rudder and letting the water push him along. When he came to the edge of a wide, deep bay that opened to the east towards a mountain range, he decided to make camp on the eastern shore of Whidbey Island.

After he got a driftwood fire going, he didn't feel like cooking anything and continued to drink, his past was beginning to talk to him. Peter stared at the flames and felt he could die of sadness. *It's my fault Little Rain's not here, I'm so ashamed. I should never have let myself get caught up in McPherson's thieving ways.*

Maybe I should have stayed in Montreal all those years ago.

Torn between the past and wanting to be part of this new frontier, the push and pull of Peter's inner demons was only eased by the burning taste of rum. He tossed another piece of driftwood on the fire and looked up.

In the distance, the same volcano shaped, snow covered mountain stood like a sentry over the territory, and as the sun began to set it glowed with a pinkish luster that tried its best to warm Peter's heart like the coals of his evening campfire, but he couldn't stop blaming himself. *How am I going to walk this earth without her?* The loss of his beautiful wife tore at him but he knew coming to Puget Sound was the right thing to do. *I need to honor her by keeping to our original plan. I'll do it for her.*

XIII

Penn Cove
Tscha-kole-chy
May 1853

In the morning Peter broke camp and set forth, promising himself to leave the gloom of his previous day behind. Staying on the western side of the passage, he scanned the shoreline and banks with his spyglass every mile or two hoping to spot a potential creek to power a sawmill but saw nothing promising. However, along the way he did see numerous Native encampments on many different beaches, the people fishing, digging clams and gathering food. When he came to a wide, deep inlet that cut into Whidbey Island, he saw more smoke. As he turned into the large bay, there was a Lower Skagit Indian longhouse on the north shore with a few canoes on the beach and some women cooking over open fires, directly across the entrance to the cove was another Skagit village.

Once he paddled farther, the undeniable pioneering sound of a hammer pounding nails echoed across the water. Peter began to see a few interspersed frontier dwellings dotting both sides of the cove. Then he spotted a good-sized cabin with smoke pouring out from its chimney. A white man and woman were carrying wooden boxes and brown paper packages wrapped in twine from a jumbled pile of goods into the structure, a few chickens scratched about, there was a pen of pigs and split-rail corrals holding horses and cattle behind it. Nearby, but closer to the head of the cove, there was a building under construction that had an open fire in front of it.

"Hello!" Peter hollered to them. They hadn't seen him approach and turned at the sound of his voice. When they saw him, they waved.

"Yes, hello!" the man said. Peter paddled up to the beach, got out of his boat and walked over to them. The fellow working on the other building stopped hammering on his porch and began to walk over.

"Good afternoon," Peter offered to the homesteaders.

"Hello there," the man replied. "Good to see a fellow settler, still not too many of us 'round these parts! What brings you out here?"

"Just passing through."

"Passing through to where?"

"Oh, I'm just a settler like you. Looking for land to homestead."

"Well, I'm John Alexander and this is my wife Frances," he said. Peter shook hands with him while his wife nodded her welcome, looking him up and down, casting him a wary eye.

"Good to meet you. I'm Peter Goutre."

"That there is Benjamin Barstow," John said, motioning at the gentleman walking towards them. "Benjamin is just about finished building a trading post and we've opened a general store

176

in our cabin," John related.

"That's good to know. As you can see my canoe is fully loaded but I'll be needing supplies sometime in the future," Peter said as the neighbor walked up. "Pleased to meet you, Benjamin," Peter said, shaking his hand.

"Are you here like the rest of the bunch? Eager for land and looking to file a claim?" he asked. "Cause if you are there's not much good farming ground left and just about everything around the cove is taken. Lansdale and Holbrook are over past me and Davis is on my other side to the south. Plus, there's all the Ebey's and Crockett's and everyone else."

"Well," Peter commented, glancing around, thinking they may not want more settlers there, "I will eventually, but probably over on the mainland where I can find a good-sized creek and enough timber to support a sawmill." When he said mainland the three of them smiled.

"We could use a mill here, that's for sure. But there's not many creeks on the island. We hand dug our wells, but for the first few months we carried our water from the spring out by the point," John said. "And we had to ship in the lumber, same for our livestock."

"That we did," Benjamin replied. Once Frances learned that Peter wasn't there for land she warmed up.

"I bet you're hungry, I've got some venison stew on the stove," she offered.

"M*agnifique*!" Peter exclaimed.

"Ha! I knew you didn't sound regular. Are you from France?" she asked, her eyes brightening.

"No, no, *madame*. I grew up near Montreal, in Canada, and came out with the Hudson's Bay. But I am now an independent man."

"Well good! Welcome to Whidbey Island. Come on in the cabin and we'll have some supper. You can tell us all about your travels."

The home held a table in one corner, there was a wood cookstove next to one wall and a long rough-cut counter ran the length of another with metal washbasins on it and a calico curtain underneath, above, under the rafters was a sleeping loft. The rest of the home was filled with shelving covered with canned goods and casks of flour, salt, sugar and dry goods all stacked about.

"It's not easy living in a general store," Frances said with a sweeping movement of her arm. "Please, have a seat."

"We've been in business now for nearly a year," John remarked, sitting down. Peter and Benjamin took a seat. "So! You're looking for some ground to settle on the mainland, are you? It's too bad Mr. Ebey isn't around today," John said.

"Yes, you could have met Isaac. He and his wife have a claim of 640 acres of fine prairie farmland just southwest of here, the best soil on the island," Benjamin added. "He's got a fine valley of crops over there."

"Is he working off the farm today?" Peter asked. Frances set a bowl in front of him. Peter lowered his head and smelled the pleasing aroma. "This is wonderful, thank you."

"You're welcome, Peter," she answered.

"I believe Isaac is down in Olympia for another day then he'll be back, he represents us in territorial affairs and does legal work. He's also over in Port Townsend a lot, paddles the strait from his side of the island," John said, pointing to the west, "across Admiralty Inlet. And, he helps the locals with their claims." Frances set a full bowl in front of the other two men.

"Well, I'd like to meet him someday," Peter responded, he dipped his spoon into the stew and tasted it. "This is *excellent!*"

"Glad to hear it," Frances answered. "So! You need to know we've been having some difficulties with the Indians. The first white man here, Glasgow I think his name was, filed on what is now the Ebey claim. But he came home one day to find thousands of Indians there having a sit down about what to do about him and the other settlers and that was after he took up with the Chief's daughter! Imagine that, a white man and an Indian woman felt so threatened by her own people they left for Olympia and never came back. Isaac filed on all of that beautiful prairie land. Not to worry you though, the Indians have gotten more used to us. But enough about us, will you be staying long?"

"Oh, I've had plenty of dealings with Indians, but as far as staying I'll travel a few more miles today and find a beach to camp on down Saratoga Passage. Then I'm headed farther south. I'm planning on building a water powered sawmill. I saw one up at Fort Victoria and I'll need a good running creek to do it. Gonna mill enough timber for everyone on Puget Sound!"

"A lumber mill that runs on water power?" John asked.

"Yes," Peter replied, taking in another spoonful of stew. "I was on the lookout for a good creek as I made my way here, but didn't see anything."

"That's interesting because I plan to build a gristmill someday. But tell me more about your sawmill idea," John requested.

"It's simple really. Instead of a steam powered mill I'll build a waterwheel over a creek, just like on a sidewheeler steamship, the paddles turn an axle that's geared to run a sawblade and cut timber," Peter answered, finishing his stew. "Would it be alright if I filled my water jugs before I head out?"

"Why that sounds like quite the idea you have, and of course, you can load up on as much of our good Whidbey water as you need!" John offered.

For the next hour they continued to chat until it was time for Peter to continue traveling. After he'd filled his jugs with well water Peter shook hands with his new friends and said goodbye.

"Thank you for the hospitality, I sure appreciate it," he said to the three of them.

"Good to meet you, Peter," Benjamin said. "My trading post will be opened as soon as the ship gets here and I'll have all kinds of hard goods available, hand tools, shovels, picks, axes, cross-cut saws and everything else to cut timber with. Plus, whatever the Indians bring to trade."

"And if you need to file a homestead claim, then come back and see Isaac," John offered. "Because if you're single you can claim 160 acres, but once you've found a claim site, you'll need to draw a detailed map of it and stake some approximate corners, then have a witness sign the map, and after that you'll need to bring it back for Isaac."

"Thank you, John and Frances. Thank you, Benjamin. That's all good to know. I'll be back for one reason or another," Peter replied.

"You're welcome, Peter, and we'll be pleased to sell you whatever you need," John said, chuckling, then added, "did you know that you can get twice as much land if you're married? You should get hitched as soon as possible! Not too many white women around yet of course, but there's plenty of squaws if you think that'd suit you. A man needs a woman anyway, doesn't he?"

Peter's shoulders stiffened. *I don't think I could ever love another woman like I did Little Rain and I don't need that much land.* He quickly decided to be cordial. "I guess you're right but first I've got to get a cabin built, and plant the farm, and then get the big mill going like we talked about! You'll be seeing me again though after I stake out a claim, real soon I hope!"

XIV

Tulalip Bay
dxʷlilap
May 1853

After two days of hard paddling and no sign of any suitable creek for his mill plans, Peter came to find himself in a large Sound with what looked like a mile-long island in the middle of it, he pulled out his map to get his bearings. *That flat-topped island straight ahead must be Gedney and all around it is Possession Sound, so Tulalip Bay must be right over there to the east.*

In the distance, a crown of jagged mountains rose out of the mist — the snow shining in the spring sun brilliantly atop them, the highest of them triangular at its peak, a perfect natural pyramid amongst God's creation. To the south, the hazy particulate of woodsmoke hung in the air where the water met the land. *Is that an Indian camp down there?* Peter looked at the map again. *That ribbon of water curling around that finger of land and then heading inland looks like a river delta so, I bet there's a village down there.* And to the east, at water level, he squinted at the opening to Tulalip, surrounded by a thick forest of evergreens. It looked like a potential homestead location and just the thing he was looking for.

He paddled towards the entrance and found a long, narrow

peninsula with a hook-shaped spit of sandy ground that curled from the end of it and into the small, protected bay. After he cleaved his way farther, he spied a single canoe beached at a cove, but there wasn't any campfire smoke or other sign of life. He paddled on by.

Peter turned south, hugging the eastern shore, and discovered a small finger-shaped inlet with a creek spilling off a hill. His body tingled with excitement. He beached his canoe and climbed the bank.

A fast-moving stream that he thought might be large enough for a waterwheel lay before him. He turned around and gazed at the tree covered peninsula that sheltered the bays entrance, turned around again and saw nothing but the pristine wilderness of the Pacific Northwest: Douglas-fir and hemlock, bigleaf maple and groves of western red cedar trees, large graceful ferns dotted the moss-covered forest floor along with salmon and huckleberry bushes. *A good mix of soft and hardwoods, a suitable creek, easy access to the Sound and protected from the wind . . . It's perfect —*

Ka-POW! A shotgun blast reverberated through the forest! Peter about jumped out of his new boots as he dove behind an old-growth tree almost before he even registered the sound. *I guess there's someone already living here!*

"Raise yer' hands and come out whar' I can see ya'!" a rough voice called out. Peter scanned the woods from behind his hiding place but couldn't see anyone, it might as well have been the trees themselves shooting at him.

"Okay, okay, *monsieur*," Peter hollered, "but don't shoot!"
He stepped out from his hiding place with his hands over his head.

A grungy looking old hermit in a felt hat, bent upward at his forehead, wearing filthy dungarees held up by only an old rope and a prayer, emerged from behind an old growth cedar tree with a shotgun leveled on him.

"Nobody's ever called me *monsieur*! Who are ya' and what'd ya' want?" the fellow said through a grey-black, chest-length beard.

"Just traveling through, looking for some timberland to homestead and maybe build a sawmill," Peter replied.

"Yeah, well, yer' best to keep on movin' fella," he said, motioning with the end of his shotgun, "ain't nothin' left here! I got it all, ya' hear! Perfectly legal, I filed my claim and done everythin' right, so ya' know what that makes you?" Peter did not respond — with every word the man thrust his gun forward and then back, while Peter's mind was wholly absorbed in prayers that the workmanship of that shotgun's trigger be as sturdy and heavy as possible. "What're ya', slow? It makes you a trespasser! Yer' trespassin' on my land!"

Peter's mind raced. *He can't own all of this, there's too much of it and this creek is exactly what I'm after. I need to think fast.*

"You even own that peninsula of land out there?" Peter asked, pointing across the small bay towards the entrance.

"What? The point? Hell no, that's Indian burial grounds. No need to be out there with all them ghosts! Not me!"

"Oh," Peter answered. *Indian burial grounds? Out there?* "What about the creek and waterfall? You own that?" he asked, motioning at the rushing water.

185

"I do, and you need to get outta here right now!"

"Alright, okay! But I think I'm going to file a claim on that point and we're gonna be neighbors, soon."

"Are you tellin' me, in your fancy foreign accent, that youse is gonna live over there on Skayu Point with all them dead souls? What are you some kind-a fool?"

"No, no my friend. I am not a fool, but I am French Canadian. How about if we talk this over since we shall be neighbors?"

There was a long nervous pause while the hermit scratched his chin and thought things over. "What's a Frenchman doing here at Tulalip Bay? You still ain't told me who ya' are."

"My name is Peter Goutre and I have been a merchant sailor for the last ten years, before that I was a trader for Hudson's Bay. And who am I speaking with?"

"Ah, came out here with Hudson's Bay did ya'? Well, you're talkin' to Jehiel Hall, and my daddy and his daddy before him were the far-famed Hall's o' Hartford County, Connecticut, and we answer to no man, no matter how big he is or how French he may be! I come round the Horn nearly two years ago and landed in Olympia, ended up here. And here I'm a gonna stay!"

"Good to meet you Jehiel. How about if we get ourselves acquainted? *May-bee* sit down and be neighborly, neighbor," Peter suggested, slowly putting down his hands.

Another long pause ensued until Jehiel let the barrel of his shotgun fall and he motioned with a hand, "Okay, come on up to the cabin then," and he started to turn around.

"You like rum?" Peter asked. Jehiel jerked his body around and his eyes widened.

"You got a bottle?"

"I sure do! Hold on and I'll be right back," Peter said. He ran back down to the beach, pulled a jug out of the wooden box, and then ran back up to Jehiel waving it in the air.

Jehiel saw him approach and grinned. He turned around and headed into the woods along the creek while Peter followed behind him.

They came to a crude bridge of two cedar logs side-by-side that they crossed where a trail took off. It headed through the forest and ended at a small log hut that had a shed roof porch on the front of it with a pile of cordwood. A brood of chickens were scratching around, two fat hogs and some piglets lay in the deep mud of a paddock, there was a freshly planted vegetable garden nearby.

"Nice place," Peter said, looking around, then seeing the peek-a-boo view through the trees out to the bay.

"Oh, it ain't much but it's home. Go ahead, sit down, take a load off," he offered, pointing at the floor of the porch with the barrel of his shotgun. He went inside his cabin and returned with two mugs, handing Peter one then held his own out.

Peter poured them both a drink and sat down on the hand-hewn timbers while Jehiel took a seat in his rocking chair, setting the shotgun across his lap. Both of them took a sip.

"Boy howdy," Jehiel said, "that sure burns good. Whar'd ya' get it?"

"Up at Fort Victoria. So, Jehiel, how do you like living here at Tulalip Bay?" Peter asked, getting the conversation started. Jehiel nodded.

"Been here awhile now, like it quite a bit."

"You build this place all by yourself?"

"Yep."

"You know, I was looking around earlier and I think your creek is perfect for a water powered sawmill," Peter stated.

"Water powered sawmills is common back east."

"Is that so?"

"Yep, water powers lots a' stuff."

"You've got the perfect creek for it."

"Oh, I know," Jehiel said, taking another drink. He held out his mug and Peter poured a larger portion.

Peter nodded at the reply but he wanted to get down to business. "I'd like to own a sawmill, how about us being partners? You bring the land and some timber to mill and I'll get the mill built."

"Ha!" Jehiel laughed, "that's a good one. How's one-man gonna build a sawmill all by himself?"

"We could build it together, share in the profits."

"Oh, no thanks. I'm not much for hard labor these days."

"But we could sell lumber to all of Puget Sound. We could be rich!"

"Aw, what do I need money for, huh? I've got everything I need right here."

"Everything? Really? Have you seen what they've got at the Fort Victoria store?"

"Can't say as I have," Jehiel replied, taking a sip.

"They've got wood cookstoves now with a window in the oven door so you can see what's baking, and sewing machines that make shirts, and they sell leather boots like these," he said, pointing at his feet, "all kinds of great new things."

"Aw come on, I don't need any of that crap."

"*Oui*, but soon the trading will go away and money will take its place."

"Maybe so, we'll see," Jehiel said, taking a drink. He wiped his mouth with his forearm and added, "That's sure some fine liquor."

"It is . . . but if we start a sawmill and get rich before everyone else, we'll get a head start on this new world. I stopped at Penn Cove and settlers are building stores, and will soon have a grist-mill. We could do the same thing here."

"Oh, I know all about Penn Cove," Jehiel said, downing the contents of his mug. He held it out again and Peter filled it.

"I might be interested in some kind of arrangement, but if I were, then I'd expect my fair share in any kind of profit."

189

"But of course."

"And what sort of arrangement would we make?"

"How about if I rent five acres from you?"

"Hmm, rent five acres down there by the creek. But I'd want a healthy share in the project too, you see," he contended, raising an eyebrow.

"Then we should be partners, *monami*."

"Well," Jehiel started to ruminate, "how about if I rent you five acres for say, ten dollars now, today, for a down payment and I'll give you until the end of say, August, or the first of September at the latest to get started on a mill and be up and running soon after that?" Peter opened his mouth to speak but Jehiel kept talking. "And once yer' up and running I get twenty-five percent ownership, meaning, I get one quarter of the income of any lumber you sell but, I want five dollars a month rent until yer' up and running. After that I get my twenty-five percent . . . take it or leave it."

Ten American dollars! And five-dollars a month! That's a huge amount of money! But I don't think I have a choice. Peter looked off towards the potential mill site and said, "The five acres would be down on the bay where the creek drains?"

"Yep."

"And the timber? It would be included to be used for the building and anything else, like lumber to sell from the extra trees? And the rent goes away after you get your percentage . . . Right?"

"Yep, I'll do that, for ten dollars cash money. Right now, to show some good faith and so's you got some skin in the game! And, don't forget, five dollars a month rent until you are up and running. After that I'll make it easy on ya' and won't charge rent . . . you can think of it as a gracious donation from my heart, but not one tree is cut or shovel put in the ground until you got a plan and a crew that's got some wits about 'em and the machinery and tools to build it all! You got that?"

Peter's brow furrowed. *I didn't see any other potential creeks for a sawmill on my way here so I need to make a deal right now.* He started to nod his head. "I agree to not cut any trees until I have the men and a plan. I will do as you say, however *monsieur*, I only have a few dollars right now, but I have plenty of gold."

Jehiel's eyes lit up. "You have gold!?"

"Yes, *monsieur*, French gold."

"French gold?"

"It is good currency. Solid, pure and unclipped."

"Well then let's see it!" Jehiel demanded.

Peter stood up and started walking. "I'll be right back!" he hollered over his shoulder. At the two-log bridge he practically skipped across it and then danced his way down to his canoe and rucksack. He dug two gold pieces and two silver dollars out of it, shoved them in his pocket and ran back the way he came with the rucksack over his shoulder. Jehiel was still on the porch when he returned, pouring himself another mug-full of Peter's bottle.

Breathing hard, Peter held out one of the gold pieces for his potential partner to see.

"French gold, huh?" Jehiel said, rocking forward and reaching out with an open palm. Peter dropped the small gold piece in his hand, smiling. Jehiel placed it between his front teeth and tried to bite into it, then looked at the stamped portrait of Napoleon.

"Is this ten-dollars' worth?" he asked, warily.

"*Monsieur,* every partnership must be based on truth and honesty, after all, truth is the coin of the realm, *capiche?*" Peter said, grinning. "I will tell you now that last week I checked with an official at Fort Victoria, and that gold coin in your hand is worth four American dollars. So, I brought one more and two silver dollars to equal ten," he said, reaching into his pocket again and pulling out the extra money. He held it all out for Jehiel to see.

Jehiel gazed at the money in Peter's hand and then glanced at the gold piece in his. He held the gold up in his own hand and weighed it, saying, "Boy oh boy, I can't wait to tell Doc Cherry about this."

"So! Are we in basic agreement on the five acres and the timber rights, and everything we have talked about then?"

"You know, a fella just never knows what the day will bring. Here I got some Frenchman floated in on the tide that's now sitting on my porch pourin' me rum and ready to give me money that I don't really have to do anything for, right?"

"That is correct, *monsieur,* you don't have to do anything, except rent me the land and watch me build a mill."

"You are rather ambitious, aren't ya'?"

"*Oui*, my friend, I have great dreams and I will do what I say."

"Well then, yes, I do believe that we have the makings of an agreement," Jehiel replied, smiling.

"Very good. I will pay you the money if we sign an agreement in writing that gives me the right to use the five acres on the terms we spoke of. The timber rights to cut and mill the trees on that piece of ground while you in turn receive one-quarter of the profits, but you must also agree to sign over the water rights and have the land surveyed so we know what trees we can cut. And, I will need you to sign my claim map as a witness."

Jehiel started rocking back and forth while he thought the proposal over. At the same time Peter held the rest of the money tight in his hand. Jehiel finished his mug in one big gulp so Peter filled it again.

"Ah, thank you," Jehiel said, nodding. "It'll be years before any kind of government survey will take place here but we could do our own and pace off the measurements, stake some corners. But no cuttin' trees until you prove up on a crew with tools and machinery. How's that sound?"

"That would be fine," Peter agreed.

After a few moments Jehiel stood up, leaned the shotgun against his cabin and set down his mug, then turned to Peter, spit in his hand, and stuck it out.

"Alright, Goo-tray. I guess we got ourselves a deal! My friends call me Jake," he said, shaking Peter's hand.

"Alright! Then how about a toast?" Peter offered, raising his mug and handing over the gold and silver. Jake shoved the coins in his pocket and raised his mug. Peter said, "Here's to getting rich on Tulalip Bay!" They both smiled, clinked their cups, and drank the liquor.

For the next few days Peter hiked the sandy beaches and rocky shorelines, and the hilly, varied terrain of the forested peninsula. He discovered a fairly level area with a commanding view of the Sound, but close to the inside bay, it was an excellent location for a homesite. Farther to the north, out on the peninsula, he found multiple elevated Indian burial canoes. Most of them supported between the forks of trees while others were propped up with chopped limbs and split wood, like legs. Some of the canoes were covered by planking, others open with the skeletal remains wrapped or covered in blankets. Many held baskets with bowls of shells, skins, pieces of cloth, deerskin bags of trinkets, and small bones; they looked like offerings of friendship or affection. A few of them had broken arrows and bows in them which Peter imagined held warriors, strings of beads and shells hung from most of the dugouts. Peter understood the burial ground was a sacred place and as he walked through the relics a deep sense of connection came over him, he felt closer to Little Rain's spirit. Feeling peaceful, he sat down next to one with his legs crossed and thought deeply. *I can feel your presence, Little Rain. It feels like I should be here, closer to you, it feels like home. This is such a beautiful place. There's no reason why I couldn't live here with your spirit, but I will live farther down, away from these grounds.*

Peter pulled out his marriage stick, closed his eyes and crossed himself with it. He opened them, then rose to his feet, placed his hands in prayer and bowed to the grave in front of him, when a lone raven landed on the rail of the canoe, it stared at him and he stared back.

"I would like to live here, among these people," Peter said to the raven, raising his arms. "I mean no harm and was married to a beautiful Tlingit woman once."

The raven started walking along the rail of the dugout, bobbing its head as if it was considering what Peter had said. Then it hopped back and forth from rail to rail and stopped, it looked at Peter again.

"May I have your blessing?" Peter asked, placing his hands in prayer.

To that the raven opened its beak and cawed, then flapped its wings and flew off due west, out over the water.

Peter watched it turn to the south and follow the coastline until it was out of sight. He nodded his head, smiling, and slowly walked away with his head down. Once he was a good distance from the graves, back down the hill and between the Sound and the bay he pulled his knife from its sheath on his belt and began to carve 'PG' in the bark of many trees at what would be a potential cabin site. Then he carved his name on a piece of cedar he split stating: Peter Goutre Claim, and hung it on a tree.

Next, he drew a map of the land with the bay and peninsula and wrote a description that he could take back to Isaac Ebey and file a claim with. The following morning, after putting one silver dollar in his pocket, he buried the rest of his gold and monies at the base of an old growth tree. Peter had Jehiel underwrite the map as a witness and then he paddled to Penn Cove, eager to make his claim.

XV

Ebey's Landing
sqájət ulg̱ʷədxʷ
June 1853

The sun shone serenely down on Puget Sound as Peter paddled to shore at Penn Cove, his signed map and sawmill documents tucked carefully into his pocket. As he approached, Frances Alexander saw him and waved, smiling.

"*Bonjour, mademoiselle*! Do you know if Isaac is around today?"

"Is that you, Peter?" Frances asked, her hand up to her forehead to block the sun's rays.

"*Oui*, I mean, yes, it is."

"I don't think he's around until later this afternoon," she replied, "I believe he's over in Port Townsend today."

"That's fine, I'll wait. Can you tell me where his home is?" Peter asked, stepping onto the beach from his canoe. "I need his help to file a claim."

"Okay, but John is out with the horse and wagon today getting cordwood. I'll have Benjamin take you there." Frances turned and, cupping her hands to her mouth, she yelled towards her neighbor's building down the beach, "Peter Goutre is back and needs to file a claim!"

Walking out from inside of his trading post and wiping the sweat from his forehead with a shirt-sleeve, Benjamin shouted, "That's great for him — why're ya' tellin' me?"

"Because he needs a kind, Christian gentleman to show him the way to Isaac's is why!"

Benjamin stepped off his porch and spat in the dirt "Well, I hope he can find one, those are pretty scarce out here in the territory."

"Benjamin!"

"What!?"

"You! You're gonna show him the way!"

"But —"

"No arguments! Get your fanny over here and do it right now!" When there was no response, Frances smiled and turned back to Peter. "He'd be very happy to take you there, he'll be right over."

Smiling politely, Peter crouched down besides the cabin in the shade to wait, ten minutes later Benjamin walked up. "I found the perfect spot over on the mainland and need to see Isaac about a claim," Peter said, walking over to shake his hand. "Good to see you again."

"Yes, yes, you too," Benjamin returned. "I'll take you up there and introduce you to his wife, Rebecca. It's about a mile or so away."

The two men set to walking southwest on a worn-down dirt path, the warm sun and slight breeze making for a pleasant hike. Once they climbed the gentle slope that rose from Penn Cove, the views from the crest of the hill took in a mile-wide natural saddle-shaped prairie of colorful cultivated farmland: squared off fields formed various patterns of green interspersed with black soil, and past them, in the distance, the wide-open waters of the Strait of Juan de Fuca led to the Pacific. Soon they made their way past rows of potato, and vegetable plantings, early starts of corn, oats and wheat, a young apple orchard and small heard of dairy cows lined the road grazing in the warm spring air. It was a cradle of life in the wilderness and the essential beginnings of a new civilization. Peter was overtaken with the beauty of it and amazed at the progress and potential of the area, but he also knew that the entire territory would soon be overrun by newcomers like him. It was too beautiful to resist.

"We recently had our first Island County meeting and this path was voted on and approved for a county road project," Benjamin mentioned proudly, trying to impress the newcomer.

"Island County? You already have a government?"

"We do," Benjamin replied.

"And how will the road be paid for?"

"Once everyone proves up on their claims and is issued title a property tax will be assessed and those funds will go towards our support systems; roads, bridges, schools, those kinds of things. Things that the community will need as it grows. But I must admit that's way off."

"Those are some big plans! How big is this county even going to be?" Peter asked.

"All of this island, and across to the mainland down past Point Elliott, about twenty-five miles south of here. As for Isaac's place, he's found himself a fine deep-water harbor, such that all the big trading ships from the east coast can sail right up, anchor and unload," Benjamin said, "and with my trading post and the Alexander's general store on the east side of the island, and only about a mile away, we'll have the ability to trade and sell goods to everyone coming over from the mainland and up and down the island. Isaac will have all the business coming in and we will have all the business going out. I'll be in business as soon as the supply ship shows up, and that should be any day now."

"So between the three of you, you'll corner the market," Peter remarked.

"I suppose so, the supply will help bring the settlers, who'll have the need for goods, but they'll also bring to the community other skills and support systems and soon, we'll have a level of community greater than any other settlement in northern Puget Sound."

"Sounds like you've got a good plan."

"There's the Ebey cabins," Benjamin said, stopping and pointing at a small log home nestled amongst several smaller wooden outbuildings on the ridge to the north at the tree line. Peter looked and saw a cluster of low, rough log buildings, with two children playing with a border collie in front of the largest of them. The dog noticed them as they approached and charged them, barking fiercely.

"Hey, hey there boy! You're okay!" Benjamin called, laughing —

the dog, recognizing him, instantly changed moods, playfully biting at Benjamin's feet and then dodging away, towards the children, trying to lead them back to the cabin. "Good boy, Rover, good boy. Where's your Mama? Huh?"

A moment later a pregnant woman of average height emerged from the cabin with an apron tied around her midsection and a dish cloth in her hand. She was frail-looking with light brown hair and wore a green plaid ankle-length work dress and leather lace up shoes.

"Benjamin! How are you today?" she asked, wiping her brow and then coughing. "You caught me during lunch."

"I'm good, Mrs. Ebey!" Benjamin answered, "but the real question is how are you doing?"

"Oh I'm fine, but ready to have this child!" she replied, covering her mouth and starting to cough again. "And who is this . . ." She had started to say 'fine looking fellow' but then caught herself, "gentleman you have with you?"

"This is Peter Goutre. He's here to file a homestead claim over on the mainland." Peter stepped forward to introduce himself.

"It's a pleasure to meet you, *madame*," Peter said, nodding and bowing his head.

"Yes, hello Peter," Rebecca responded. "Your voice . . . you don't sound like you're from around here."

"*Oui*, I am French Canadian but I am working on my English now," Peter said, grinning and stroking his beard.

She laughed, then said, "I see, well good thing you came on a Saturday, Isaac will be home in a few hours and I've got housework to do. You're welcome to wait here on the porch or you can go down to the beach if you'd like to wait for him there."

"*Oui*, the beach," Peter said, glancing down the hill to the waves hitting the shore, "I will wait there, thank you."

Peter and Benjamin shook hands and departed in opposite directions. Peter walked away from the cabin and down the hill to the shore. A long sweep of curving beachfront ran north and south, terns and gulls scurried about on the shoreline, pecking at empty clam and crab shells. Shanks of beached logs and driftwood littered the high-water mark.

Peter sat down on a log and looked out to the vast open strait. A western breeze blew softly in his face. A couple of hours later after the tide switched a tiny spec on the water slowly grew into a man in a canoe. Peter waited to call out until he had landed.

"Hello there!" Peter hollered, once Isaac stepped from his wooden craft. He raised a hand then began to walk up the shore to tie off his boat. "Looks like this wind helped a little."

"Yes, these prevailing westerlies in the afternoon are a great help," Isaac answered, taking off his wide brimmed hat and looking up, seeing Peter.

"Are you here looking for me?"

"*Oui*, I mean yes, I need help filing a homestead claim," he replied, walking down to him. "My name is Peter Goutre."

"Ah, Goo-tray, sounds French. Don't think we have any French on the island yet," Isaac said with a deep resounding voice, walking over to Peter and extending his hand.

"It's a pleasure to meet you, *monsieur*," Peter said, shaking his hand with a firm grip.

Isaac Ebey was a barrel-chested man with dark, heavy eyebrows and a thick black beard. He wore a tight-fitting black vest, white shirt, black trousers, heavy brogan boots and he carried a weighted down brown leather satchel, spattered with seafoam.

"So you need help?" Isaac asked, beginning to walk towards the bank and up the trail to his home.

"I am told that you are the one that I should see about filing a homestead claim."

"That's true, I can help you," Isaac said, "and where on the island are you planning on settling?"

"Oh, no, *monsieur*. I will be homesteading over on the mainland. About twenty miles south."

"Hmm, twenty-miles south. Down near Possession Sound?"

"*Oui*, it is on Tulalip Bay. Do you know it?"

"I do," Isaac said curtly. He motioned towards the path to take and they began the long walk up the ridge. Isaac looked out over his fields and smiled. Peter noticed.

"You should be very proud of the work you've done here," Peter offered.

"Yes, the good Lord has been very generous to us," Isaac replied. When they got nearer to the home his dog came running up, wagging its tail. "Ah, Rover," Isaac said, petting the dog.

At Isaac and Rebecca's cabin, their two boys came out to greet their father. They ran up and both hugged his legs.

"There's my boys!" Isaac said, hugging them back. "Peter, this is Eason and Ellison. Kids say hello to Mr. Goo-tray."

"Hello Mr. Goo-tray," they clumsily said at the same time.

Rebecca walked out of the home and stood on the porch waving. "How was your day, Isaac?" she asked, catching her breath. "I see you've met Peter."

"Yes, I have," Isaac answered, glancing at the new homesteader. "Good day over at Port Townsend, very busy. Peter, how about if you have a seat here on the porch while I go get one of my maps and we can get started on your claim."

With that everyone else went inside where Isaac retrieved a rolled-up map from a shelf and a ledger book. The home was very modest. A kitchen with table and chairs on one side, fireplace across from it and a narrow hall that led to bedrooms. Isaac went back outside, sat down on the porch steps next to Peter and spread his map out on his lap.

"So! Where's this land you wish to claim?" Isaac asked. Peter scanned the well-used map and stabbed the location with his finger.

"There," he said, looking at Isaac who peered at the spot, considering it for a moment. "On the point there is an Indian burial ground, but I plan to build my homestead away from it."

"Oh, the point at Tulalip Bay," Isaac remarked, glancing at Peter. "I believe the Snohomish are a peaceful people but I don't think they'd like you claiming their burial grounds for a homestead."

Peter nodded his head, listening to Isaac then said, "I've had many dealings with Indians during earlier times and have always gotten along with them. I have certain reasons for wanting to be near their grounds and will respect them, keep my distance."

"Yes, I can understand that," Isaac replied, glancing at Peter, "and keeping your distance is one thing, but I don't think it's such a good idea laying claim to that land."

"It is okay *monsieur*. I will deal with the consequences and work to get along with the tribe. Like I said, I have my reasons to live close to their grounds and I mean no harm, whatsoever," Peter said in earnest.

"Well, I don't want to hear about you having difficulties with the Snohomish or any other tribe," Isaac countered, casting Peter a heedful eye.

"I promise you that if there is the slightest sign of trouble, I will correct it and if I can't then I will leave."

"Good! So, if anyone from the tribe comes to me or anyone else with a problem about you being there then you'll leave?"

"Yes, *monsieur*, I will. You have my word."

"Alright, but you need to live as far to the south as you can."

"Thank you, yes, I will do as you say."

"Okay! Very good then. If you're a single man you can claim 160 acres."

"That will be more than enough land. This area here, along the water," Peter said, placing his finger on the map south of the point, "it is steep but I like being near the water. Plus, the land is thick with timber."

"And what will you do with all that *thick* timber?"

"I hope to build a water powered sawmill, *monsieur*."

"A water powered sawmill? Why, I don't think one of those has been built in the area yet," Isaac remarked with interest.

"I saw one on Vancouver Island, outside Fort Victoria powered by a paddlewheel, just like a riverboat. I have entered into an agreement for five acres with Jake Hall, it is on a creek across the bay."

"Jake Hall?" Isaac asked, "I know of a Jehiel Hall there on the bay, I helped him with his claim."

"*Oui*, that is him. I'm sorry, he goes by Jake, too," Peter replied. "Jehiel was my witness for my claim map, but I understand that you do legal work so we have also made this agreement. I'd like you to look at it for me," Peter said, pulling two pieces of paper from his trouser pants pocket and unfolding them. "You see, I hope to find one or two partners who can claim more land around me and the bay to log because Jehiel is not going to do any work at the mill." He handed the papers to Isaac.

"Well, why didn't you say so in the first place? Let's have a look," Isaac said, taking the papers and reading. "This is quite good for a frontier contract."

"My father was very strict about my church attendance, it was where I learned to read and write."

"Funny, so was mine," Isaac responded. "I see you've got the description for the five acres, the ten-dollars that you have already paid, the rent and partnership terms, and water rights . . . but all surveys are preliminary so you'll have to pace off the land and stake your corners and flag your lines on your own for now. But you must accept the acreage amount of the government survey when it does occur. Your homestead map looks acceptable."

Isaac went inside and pulled down a piece of paper from a clean, well-organized shelf of books, along with an inkwell and a quill that looked like it hadn't been that long off the goose. He grabbed a bread board from the kitchen to write on and went back outside.

"Under the Donation Land Claim Act, you're required to live on the land and cultivate it for four years before clear title is patented. Do you understand?" Isaac said, sitting down next to Peter with the board on his lap.

"*Oui*, I mean yes, but what does clear title mean?" Peter asked.

"In other words, to get clear title for the acreage you'll need to build a home and plant a garden *and* you will need to pay for a notification survey once we have a Surveyor General for the state."

"I see . . . and there are no surveyors here yet?"

"Not yet. Once a land office is set up in Olympia then the surveyors will go to work, but for the time being we just have to make do without. It might be years before they get anyone official up here. Even though we just became a territory in March we still have to file our claims in Oregon City. I'll mail this claim I'm writing out for you from Port Townsend, it will get to Oregon City faster from there. But the stamp will cost you three-cents," Isaac said, opening his ledger book. "And I will write out a second claim notice that you can take with you."

"Thank you," Peter said. He pulled the silver dollar out of his trousers and showed to Isaac.

Isaac eyed the large coin, then asked, "Is that all you have?"

"Yes, I am sorry, *monsieur*."

"It's okay, I've got change in the house. But there is one more thing. I'm guessing that you're still a Canadian citizen so you'll need to file for citizenship in Olympia. To get the final title you'll have to prove that you're a U.S. citizen. Once you have that, and the claim certification clearly showing your right to the Tulalip Bay land, you will be a land-owning American," Isaac replied, writing Peter's name and claim location in his ledger.

Peter's destiny was before him and, signing where Isaac indicated on the document, he seized it.

XVI

Skayu Point
skayuʔqs
June 1853

The whole way back, Peter beamed with a gladness that he hadn't felt in a long time, but when he paddled into Tulalip Bay on a high tide as a proud official homesteader, he was shocked to see someone's canoe beached on the inside shore of his claim. He ran his canoe up onto the sand right next to it, hopped out of his craft and started calling, "Hello! Whose canoe is this on my land?!"

After twenty-minutes a short, stout man of about 30 years, wearing tan dungarees, a green flannel shirt and felt hat walked out from the trees and down the low bank over to Peter.

"Good afternoon," the fellow said, walking up. "This looks like an interesting place to homestead."

"It is," Peter replied, "and that's why I've already claimed it." He pulled his freshly written claim copy from his pocket, unfolded it and held it out for the man to see. "Here's my paper proving it."

The fellow looked at it. "And you'd be Peter . . . Goo-tree?" he asked.

"It is pronounced Gou-tray."

"Are you the one who put the sign up and carved those initials on them trees in the woods?" the stranger asked.

"I did, and you are?"

"I'm John Gould. I came out west prospecting for gold and silver like every other crazy man on the continent in search of El Dorado, but gave up. So, I came up the Cowlitz Trail. In Olympia I heard about Penn Cove, saw this bay on my way up there, thought I'd stop to see if there were any land possibilities. However, I understand that there's lots of opportunity up on Whidbey, fertile land for farming and homesteading."

"You better hurry then," Peter related. "Good luck!" He turned to walk away but the man continued to talk.

"What! Good luck? Why'd you say that?"

"I was just up there, filing this claim."

"Yeah, but why'd you tell me to hurry?"

"Because all the good farming land is taken. I saw for myself."

"It is already? Dang it!" he said, kicking some sand on the beach and stomping away. Peter watched, wordlessly, as he circled a few times, kicking as he went, then stopped, seemed to look all around the bay again as if for the first time, and walked back up to Peter. Gould took his hat off and scratching his head, he said, "So, tell me, whatcha got planned for this place?" He wiped his brow with a handkerchief then put his hat back on.

Peter contemplated his question for a moment then replied, "I'm going to build a sawmill across the bay on another man's land where there's a creek, I've made an agreement with him. But the land on the point and one-hundred acres to the south is going to be my homestead and the source of trees for the mill."

"Ah! A lumberman, are ya'? That's some dangerous work . . . where'd you log before here?"

Peter was stunned by the question and had always thought that anyone could run a sawmill or log timber.

"Well, I mean, I haven't," was his reply.

"You haven't been a logger or worked in a sawmill?"

"No, *monsieur*. I have not. But I know I can do it. I am still young and strong, it does not scare me."

"So, you don't know how to get one of these big things on the ground?" he asked, looking up a good-sized hemlock tree. "Do you even have a cross-cut saw or sledge and wedges?"

"I will get the right tools."

"But logging is difficult work and it takes experienced men," Gould said.

"*Oui, monsieur*, I will learn."

"Learn? More like learn how to kill yourself in the process. Do you even have a partner in this mill you're thinking about building?"

"Only with the man who owns the land. But he is not going to help build it."

"Looks to me like you're going to need someone to help you get your operation going."

"Oh, I guess I will," Peter remarked, looking down at the ground. After a short pause John took off his hat and scratched his head again.

"Well, I guess I better get going before it's too late," John said, putting his hat back on. He started walking towards his canoe and mentioned over his shoulder, "Gonna make my way up to Penn Cove anyway. My father owned a mercantile back home, so I guess instead of farming I'll start a trading post or a general store."

Peter looked up and replied, "A man by the name of Benjamin Barstow has already built a trading post at Penn Cove, and John Alexander has a general store opened."

"Dammit!" John spat, kicking at the ground. "I knew it! I had a feeling I'd be too late."

Thoughts about his agreement with Jake suddenly raced through Peter's mind. *I'm required to have a plan and soon! Should I offer a partnership to this man? Maybe this fellow should just claim more land around Jake and I, then I could charge him to mill his logs? But I don't know how to log, or mill, and I have to get a crew with, what did Jake call it? Some wits about them. And . . . I have to come up with a building plan!*

John started to untie his canoe line, muttering to himself with his head down.

"*Monsieur* Gould!" Peter said. John stopped and turned around. He looked at Peter with a hard, unreadable face. "I will be needing a partner or two to help me build the mill and log the timber. I cannot do it all by myself. Why don't you claim more land here? There's plenty for everyone," Peter said, holding out his arms and looking around. John grinned.

"Are you serious? Because I've fell many a tree in my day and know what to do in the woods."

"*Oui*, we can form a partnership."

"Are you serious?" John asked, stepping back over to Peter. "Because I'll be your partner. Should we shake on it?"

Peter stepped forward with an outreached hand, they both shook, and the partnership was made.

"We'll get that mill up and running!" John exclaimed, smiling. He glanced around, then added, "I'll tell you what. Today I walked everything from the point, and to the south up the hill, then a little to the east around the bay," he said, pointing back and forth. "How about if we draw us up a map showing your claim, with the point and all of your land, and tack on my 160 acres next to yours. I know what I want. Then you sign off as a witness for me and I'll skedaddle on up to Whidbey to file on it. While I'm there I'll get a load of supplies and scoot right on back."

"*Fantastique!*" Peter said, grinning ear to ear.

Weeks later, Peter had begun to build a small log cabin in the level area with the beginning of the hill towards the point to the north and his homestead land to the south, and in his mind, well away from the burial grounds. He started to clear a small patch of ground for a vegetable garden and hand dug a shallow water well close-by. Peter lugged up his lantern, guns, hand tools, and everything else he'd brought with him to the cabin site and stowed them under a tarp lean-to. A skinned deer carcass was strung by its hindlegs from a sturdy hemlock branch, drying in the soft wind, and Peter kept his small cookfire going at all times, fed by a steady diet of fragrant cedar and hemlock limbs.

Looking out from his bluff across the water one afternoon, Peter, exhausted from work but happy with his progress, closed his eyes and took a few deliberate, slow breaths of the Puget Sound air. It was cool and sweet, the purest and cleanest air in the world, and it was a fine luxury to just sit still and breathe it sometimes. Opening his eyes, he gradually, slowly, realized that there was movement below — two Indians, youths by the look of them, were landing a canoe on the sandy beach of the Sound. They got out of their bark and began climbing up the steep bank, approaching him.

Peter got to his feet and rummaged around in his lean-to, he found a blanket, not a prized Hudson's Bay blanket, but a blanket nonetheless. He held it at his side and waited for some kind of sign to see if there were upset with him being close to their relics. Peter knew he had to start with a gift, a friendly gesture, knowing that they'd go back to their village right away and talk to their elders about him and where he was.

He stood still and watched them carefully, thinking they'd come of their own accord and were curious about new smoke coming from near the tribal burial grounds. As they approached, both of them bare chested but wearing deerskin leggings and breechcloth, their eyes darted around at his workings: the campfire and kettle of venison with dumplings, the skinned and hanging carved up deer, and then at him. Peter grinned and held out the gift.

"*Kloshe sun pot'-latch*," Peter said, holding out the blanket. The two boys looked at each other. Peter wasn't sure if they spoke the jargon.

Instantly, with the quickness of a bobcat, the bigger of the two reached out and snatched the blanket. They both ran away and back down to their dugout. Peter chuckled to himself and, after he was sure they had departed, went about his business for the rest of the day.

The following afternoon they were back, but this time there were two dugouts with three young boys in each. Peter knew they were there to trade so he dug through his rucksack and found two pennies and a nickel from his stamp purchase change. He watched as they paddled on the high tide into the bay and beached their dugouts then walked up the slope towards him, talking to each other. But when they got to his camp, they went silent. All of them lined up on the other side of the fire away from him, their eyes scanning his belongings.

Finally, the oldest of them, who looked to be thirteen, stepped forward. He held out a string of blue-glass multifaceted trade beads with one hand and pointed at Peter's musket leaning up against a tree.

Peter took his meaning right away and scoffed, "My musket for that string of beads? Ha! It's too high, too high! Never! *Wake!*"

The boys understood his refusal. The same one glanced around his camp and spotted his hatchet, he pointed at it and nodded.

"My hatchet for those beads?" Peter scoffed again. "Too high!" With that the boys huddled up and conversed quietly, one of them holding his hand up to his mouth. Peter knew he had to be cordial with them, so he reached into his pocket and pulled out two pennies.

"Here," Peter said. He held out the tiny coins in an open palm to get their attention and added, "*kloshe chik'-a-min*, take it."

Once again, in a flash of movement the biggest boy tossed the string of trade beads at Peter's feet, then reached out and snatched the metal money. They turned to walk back to their dugouts, and as they did one of them yelled over his shoulder, "*Me-si'-ka moo'sum ko'-pa skoo'-kums! Dukwibal nan'-itsh me-si'-ka.*" They all took off running and made their way to the beach.

"I sleep with ghosts? *Dukwibal* sees me?!" Peter hollered at their backs, not recognizing at first what they had truly said. Then he realized what the Indian boy was yelling about. Peter hiked out to the burial grounds and stopped at the relic he had first sat at. He stood in front of it, crossed himself, then bowed and said, "I respect your God and I believe you respect my God. I am living here because I feel closer to my wife, who I lost years ago. Please, I want to be here because I want to live the rest of my days here, and die here, where I feel Little Rain's presence so strongly. I pray for us all." He stepped forward and touched one of the elevated canoes, then stepped back. He slowly walked through the rest of the relics, taking pause at many of them, paying his respects.

On his walk back to camp he noticed a huge blown over cedar tree down the hill towards the bay that he hadn't detected before. He went over to it, there was another much smaller cedar that the big one had taken down with it. The large stump had shanks of splintered wood jutting up, one of them caught his eye because of its intriguing shape. Peter stared at it, and in an instant, he saw right through to its true form, an overwhelming image was right in front of him.

Marriage stick! To honor Little Rain! I shall carve her a new marriage stick, a big one, that I can hang beads and shells on and carve all kinds of symbols into. I'll make my own memorial to her at the homestead — where I wish she was now. Peter grabbed hold of the marriage stick under his shirt, pulled it out and crossed himself with it and kissed it, then stood there mesmerized when another image came to him. *I will build her a totem pole that I can hang her marriage stick from*!

He went back and got his hatchet then returned, cut out the three-foot shank of cedar, and carried it home.

That evening, while sitting at his campfire, whittling and carving on the piece of cedar, the pleasant stillness of the full moon night was shattered by Jake Hall crying, "Hey French Peter! Where are ya', ya' filthy frog? Lemme see ya'!"

"French Peter? Filthy frog?" Peter muttered to himself. *Who does he think he is calling me French Peter! Damn Yankee!* He jumped to his feet and started to walk away from his camp and confront his neighbor, but after five steps he reminded himself about their partnership. *Calm down, you need to stay friends.* So, he hollered and waved. "Good to see you! Welcome!"

Jake walked up and glanced around his crude encampment. "Heck of a spot you've got here. Nice view too," he said, looking out to the moon lit Sound then sitting down next to the fire.

"*Oui*, it's not much yet but it will be."

"How've you been? Looks like yer' keepin' busy," Jehiel said, holding out a small metal flask with a grin. "Here ya' go, have some."

"I made my homestead claim," Peter said, smiling and taking it.

"You did! That's good news."

"Ah, *monami*, is it American whiskey?" Peter asked, smelling the flask's spout.

"Go on, give it a try," Jake said. Peter raised the vessel to his lips and took a pull.

"*Sacre bleu!*" Peter coughed, bringing his hand up to his mouth. "*Le démon!*" he exclaimed, handing it back to his neighbor.

"The devil you say!" Jake croaked. "That's American corn mash my friend, made it myself, too."

"That burns more than all the rum in Nassau," Peter said, handing the flask back.

"Ha! Of course it does, you lily-livered Frenchmen can't take the taste of *real* alcohol — this is the same recipe my pappy used, and his pappy and his pappy before him, going right on back to the first great Jehiel Hall who walked off'n the ark, I tell ya'!"

Peter looked at the man for a second before replying, "You mean Noah's Ark?"

"Course I do! What other Ark you know about?"

"N-none' Peter said, "I just . . . I mean . . ."

"Well, of course it ain't in *your* bible, French Peter, but that's just cuz yer' pope wants to cover it up." Peter's shoulders stiffened at the mention of Jake's new nick name for him but resolved himself to it, and to staying on good terms with his partner.

Jake took another swig, glanced across the bay and said, "How's things comin' along on yer' mill?"

"Good! Things are progressing and I already have one fellow interested in being a partner."

"Youse do! Who is it?"

"A man by the name of John Gould. I met him here a few days ago, but he's up at Penn Cove right now getting supplies. He'll be back soon."

"And this fellow's a woodsman?"

"Yep, says he can cut down trees all day long."

Jake nodded, took another swig and said, "That's good, sounds like you just might pull this sawmill thing off." Then he looked up the hill to the north and asked, "All them dead Indians up there? Don't it give you the creeps, livin' near 'em all?"

"The creeps? No, *non*. I am far enough away from them, their ghosts have not bothered me and I do not believe they will because there is plenty of room between us. This is a beautiful spot, though. Don't you agree?"

"I suppose, but I couldn't live over here on this side of the bay."

"I like being here above the water where I can see all that approach."

Jake looked out over the moonlit sparkling water and illuminated clouds hanging on the horizon, then held out the flask and said, "I guess I can see that. Here, have another belt."

"Ah, *oui,* I think I will," Peter said, grabbing it and taking a drink.

The next day, Peter watched from the top of the bluff as a canoe with two Snohomish Indian men and two boys made their way around the point during high tide and landed below his cabin site. He stood and waited while they climbed the trail and as they got closer, he recognized the two boys from their other encounters, it appeared they were with their fathers. All of them were barefoot, wearing buckskin leggings and breechcloth, but the men also wore deerskin capes and had knives that hung from thin deer hide belts, one was carrying a spear. Each had long black hair.

"*Klahowya,*" Peter offered, greeting them. The men nodded with hard faces while the boys kept their heads down. *Is there going to be some trouble?*

After a nervous pause one of the men replied, "*Klahowya,*" in the jargon. He held out in the palm of his hand the pennies the two boys had traded the beads for. He said, "*Kap-su-al-la ka-mo'-suk.*"

Peter thought for a moment. *Ah! They want those beads back. I need to comply.* He raised a finger and grinned, then went to find the string of tiny square blue beads.

"*Yuk'-wa*," Peter said, holding out the trade beads with one hand and extending an open palm with the other.

The man stepped forward, dropped the coins in Peter's hand and took back the glass beads.

"*Kloshe*," he said. Then he stared at Peter and asked why he was there, "*Káh-ta me-si'ka yuk'wa?*"

"*Ni-ka yuk'wa ikt cole*," Peter answered, saying he was going to live there.

"*Me-si'ka wau'-wau nan'-itsh Tyee*," the man said.

He wants me to go and see his Chief, talk with him. Without hesitation Peter nodded in agreement and said, "*Áh-ha*."

The man nodded back and seemed to be pleased that Peter had agreed to go and meet with his Tyee. His eyes brightened a little and he said, "*Cháh-ko potlatch klone suns ko'-pa . . . Hibuləb*."

He's inviting me to his village to trade in three days and meet the Chief. "*Kah potlatch?*" Peter asked.

"*Sdohobcs Chuk la boos wake si-áh*," the man answered, pointing south. *It's like I thought, at the mouth of the river.*

"*E-éh ni-ka tum'-tum ko-páh*," Peter replied, agreeing again to come.

Then the man put his right hand over his heart and said, "*Takhumkun*." He looked at Peter and nodded.

Oh, that's his name. "*Takhumkun*," Peter repeated, nodding back.

221

He placed his hand on his heart and said, "*Ni-ka*, Peter."

"Pee-ter," the man said, clumsily. Then he stepped back and looked around Peter's camp, the construction of his log cabin and the new fresh deer carcass hanging from the tree limb.

He turned to leave but the other man, who had the spear and was silent the whole time looked at Peter and pointed at the ground, he said, "*Skayuʔqs.*"

"Yes, *áh-ha*, Skayu Point," Peter agreed, nodding.

"*Ságh-a-lie ty-ee'*," Takhumkun added, turning around. Then he said, "*Dukwibal yuk'-wa tik'-tik me-si-ka.*"

Peter looked up the hill towards the burial grounds and thought; *Did he say that spirits live here or God lives here? Dukwibal is watching me? Dukwibal must be their God or worshipping spirit. That was the same thing that boy said.*

"I believe in your God, your Spirits," Peter replied. But he wasn't sure if the man meant their God was angry at him for choosing to live near their relics or if he meant something else.

"Are you trying to tell me that your God, *Dukwibal*, is watching me? Or is he just watching your burial grounds?" Peter asked.

They looked at him with blank faces so he added, "I'm here because I was married to a beautiful Tlingit woman once and feel closer to her here because she is gone now."

Takhumkun titled his head and gave Peter a sideways grin, not understanding any of his words. Then he pointed at Peter and the ground, the sky and the point. He finished and they all turned and

222

headed back to their canoes.

"Wait!" Peter hollered. "Am I damned or am I blessed?"

But they didn't turn around. Peter watched them paddle away and felt as if he'd been touched by their beliefs, but he wasn't sure in what way. His heart uncertain, Peter waited until their canoe disappeared before turning around and walking over to his unfinished cabin.

The next morning Peter awoke to the sound of finches chirping and the flute-like call of a wood thrush, the golden light of the sun was rising in the east. He sat up and glanced around his encampment, there was much work to do but he had other thoughts on his mind.

Picking up his bucksaw, Peter wandered down to the two downed cedar trees and started to cut the smaller one into two different lengths and then removed the limbs, he dragged them back to camp. Once that was done, he cut down a couple of near-by hemlock saplings at waist height and sawed-out a downward V-shape in the top of them, like a saddle. He picked up the longer cedar log, dragged it over to his ad-hoc sawhorse tree stumps and set one end on it and then the other.

Using his hunting knife, Peter stripped all the bark off and then picked up a cold piece of charcoal from the firepit. Then he set to work drawing the shapes of what he wanted to carve. For the next few days, he dedicated himself to this singular task.

Soon he'd carved a head and face at the top to symbolize Little

Rain, he even cut out a dimple on her chin. He notched and mounted the shorter cedar length for a cross-piece that he lashed to the main pole and carved an open hand on each end with the palms facing out. Next, he used some short hemp rope lengths and fashioned a wig for the top.

Once it was done, he hollowed out a hole at the top of his new cedar marriage stick with the point of his hunting knife, looped some rope through it like a necklace and hung it from the upper part, so it draped over the cross piece. Then he dragged it up the hill just above his homesite to the north and dug a three-foot hole. Peter stood it up facing the west so it could be seen from the water.

That evening, he sat with Little Rain's totem and watched a perfect golden orange sunset that lit up the sky when a lone raven flew up and landed on the cross-piece arm. After staring at Peter, it began to peck at the pole with its beak and cackle.

"*Klahowya*!" Peter said. "Do you like what I've done?"

The raven cawed and hopped along one cross piece arm while flapping its wings. Then it stopped and looked at Peter and cackled softly. It flapped its wings and hopped over to the other arm and danced along it, then it flew up and landed on the top — it opened its beak, cawed and then pecked just below the rope wig on Little Rain's forehead a few times and stopped. It flapped its wings once more, cackled again and flew off.

"Does that mean yes?" Peter hollered as he watched it fly away.

XVII

Hibulb
Hibuləb
The place where white doves live
July 1853

It was a fine day, not a cloud in the sky. After a breakfast of biscuits and fried venison steak Peter started loading his leather rucksack with trade goods: a cloth sack with about a pound of sugar, a jar of molasses, one bottle of rum, a pair of scissors, a pocketknife that he put in his trousers, one hunting knife, fry pan, and then he folded up a prized HBC blanket that he would hand carry. Peter slung his pack over his shoulder and headed to his cache of French gold. He dug it up, took one piece and put it in a trouser pocket before reburying it, then walked down the trail to his canoe where he pushed off, hopped in, and started paddling.

Once he was around Skayu Point then down to the sandy cliff and beach he looked up and saw Little Rain standing like a sentry over the Sound in the early morning sun, he stopped paddling and smiled broadly. There she stood with open arms, welcoming all, loving all, respecting all, high above the saline Salish Sea. Little Rain's totem, her image and spirit, was there for all.

Traveling on, he soon rounded another point and came to a wide estuary of river channels and deltas, he could feel the current of the incoming tide clash with the flow of the outgoing river, causing his canoe to jostle about. The wind coming downriver swirled with the westerly breeze from the bay, it spun circles all around him. In the not too far distance, plumes of campfire smoke rose in the sky.

To the east was an island: a mixture of sedge, cattail, dune grass, and wild berry bushes. Hooded mergansers, with narrow white stripes along their backs and reddish-brown crests extending from the back of their heads made their way across the water in groups. Gulls and terns patrolled the tide flats and a mature blue heron stood in ten inches of water waiting to spear breakfast. To the west, a squad of cormorants out in deeper water plied the surface then dove, making a little half-jump first to help propel them in their search for candlefish and herring.

As he approached, Peter was amazed at the size of the village fortifications. A palisade built of twenty-foot-high vertical cedar logs ran the length of the bank. People were everywhere, carrying woven baskets to and from open fires on the canoe lined beach.

At the water's edge, in front of the main palisade opening, stood a tribesman, dressed in a fine buckskin shirt, leggings and fringed breechcloth with strings of shells and beads hanging around his neck, he was beating a small hand drum.

Then upriver, coming around the bend, a sight for the ages: a longboat adorned in natural regalia, strings of white yarrow flowers were fastened along the rail with many paddlers cleaving the water, most of them bare chested, their muscular bronze bodies glistening with sweat. At the bow stood a Chieftain wearing a flat-top hat with tassels hanging from it and a double-breasted coat, looking proud and stoic. Behind and beside him were a multitude of canoes, full of elders and children, all of them smiling and waving. The Grand Hyas and his flotilla of the ancient ways was coming down from the Illahee to potlatch.

The lone drummer at the water's edge began to bang his drum faster and sing, bringing more people out of the village, they rushed to the water's edge to greet the Chief with spears doing a welcoming dance, as whoops and calls filled the air. When the Tyee stepped from the boat, the adoring crowd surrounded him, touching and greeting him while his warriors began unloading woven baskets of dried salmon, and elder and huckleberries. The Chieftain climbed the bank with his followers and they walked through the main gate.

Peter beached his canoe downriver from the others, hopped out and tied the bowline off on the end of a drift log then headed up towards the village. Tribespeople wearing woven conical hats, moccasins and clothes of shredded cedar bark were tending beach fires with iron kettles of steaming clams. Peter took notice of one man that was chopping firewood with a metal ax, another man stood next to him with a hatchet held behind his belt. *White traders have been through here.*

The two men looked at him with hard faces, both were wearing deerskin leggings and breechcloths, one put his hand on his belted hatchet and the other dropped his ax and started walking towards him.

"*Cheechako!*" he barked. Peter was familiar with the word and stopped walking. *He's calling me a fledgling . . . I might be a settler now, but I'm no fledgling!*

"*Klak'-sta me-si'-ka? Káh-ta me-si'-ka yuk'-wa,*" the man demanded, wanting to know who he was and why he was there.

"*Ni-ka,* Peter," the French Canadian said, looking him square in

227

the eye. He placed his hand on his heart and added, "*Skayu*," pointing north. Peter stared at the man blankly, and waited for a response, stroking his long beard. The fellow turned to the other tribesman and he started walking towards them with his hand still on his hatchet.

"*Ik'-tah me-si'-ka tik-égh?*" he grunted. Peter glanced around, unsure of his next move. *Stay calm*. He shoved his right hand into his pants pocket, grabbed hold of the pocketknife and was about to take it out thinking he could quell the situation by offering it to them, when a loud voice caused the three of them to turn their heads.

"*Klahowya!*"

It was Takhumkun, the man he'd met a few days before who had invited him. He was walking up to them.

"*Ɂəcá ƛ̕ákʷadi,*" he said in Lushootseed, a dialect that Peter was unfamiliar with. His two tribal members nodded and grunted, then returned to their tasks. Peter turned back to him, relieved.

"*Klahowya!*" Peter replied in jargon, happy to see him, "*kloshe ko'-pa nan'-itsh me-si'-ka.*"

"*Klahowyum ko'pa Sdoh-doh-hohbsh til'-i-kum,*" Takhumkun said, raising both arms. He nodded with a slight grin and motioned for him to follow.

They walked along the shore past more open fires. Women in fringed cedar bark skirts were boiling camas roots while an elderly woman in a deerskin dress sat on a drift log talking to a small group of children. She was motioning with her hands, her voice rising and falling. It looked like she was teaching or telling them

228

a story.

A few men were finishing different kinds and lengths of canoes. One twelve-foot dugout caught Peter's eye, he stopped to look at it. *I'd like to have a smaller, lighter canoe like that one, it would be a lot faster.* It had a raised bow like the other longer canoes and one seat in it. Peter got down on his knees and tried to check the keel for straightness, then ran his fingers along the hull and looked inside, there was a finely crafted cedar paddle with a tapered blade.

"*Me-si'-ka mahkook?*" Takhumkun asked.

"Ah, *oui, monami,*" Peter answered, standing up, "I mean, *é-eh mahkook,* I'd like to trade for it."

"*Kloshe,*" Takhumkun replied, then said, "*kim'-ta klat'-a-wa Patkanim.*" He motioned again for Peter to follow him and started walking.

Up ahead, a beautiful young woman carrying a baby wrapped in a white matted fur blanket was coming towards them. She was adorned in tooth shell jewelry; a wide choker of multiple dentalium shells held together by strips of deer hide with glass beads encircled her neck and her black hair was braided with wildflowers. From her ears hung thin white feathers and a white Boston shirt with colorful beadwork stitched onto it topped her deerskin dress. As she walked past, Peter took notice of her light bronze complexion and high cheekbones. He was so taken by her beauty that he turned around to watch her: she sat down on a beach log just above one of the canoe builders.

Inside the village a long row of cedar plank houses ran up and downriver, interspersed with a few longhouses and tents built out of woven cattail mats. Behind the plank homes a high bank rose to a forested peninsula. Peter saw two braves carrying a freshly killed stag down a trail between them hanging from its hooves on a tree limb. A small clearwater creek cascaded off the hill, cutting the village in half where it leveled out. Two women and some children were taking clams from a basket and cleaning the sand from them in the water while a few dogs barked and chased each other. Racks of dried fish were laid out beside fresh flounder and crab, clams and oysters. On split cedar plank tables sat clay bowls of light brown pheasant and white duck eggs, along with salmon and huckleberries, and boiled camas roots: all of it waiting to be added to for the afternoon feast.

The first longhouse they went inside was built of hand-split cedar timber framing with plank siding smoothed with an adze and shed-like roofing. Along the exterior walls were platforms for seating and rooms partitioned by woven mats where women were teaching children the legends of their people. One woman in a deerskin dress was acting out like she was climbing a ladder or a tree. Another woman held an ornate carved pole in both her hands and pushed it upward, calling out, "Ya-hoh," stabbing the air each time she did. The children, all of them with happy and healthy faces doing the same, following along, calling together, "Ya-hoh! Ya-hoh! Ya-hoh!" jumping up and down while pushing their open palms up to the sky, learning Creator stories.

Then Takhumkun took him to the biggest longhouse, the outside planking was decorated with colorful murals of salmon, raven, and whales. Inside the great hall, the smell of the salty waterfront rose up from the ground like the pillars of carved cedar that held the rafters up to the heavens. Many men sat in a large circle around an open fire like the ancients, dressed in the high regalia of deerskin, beads and shells, they beat their drums and sang, the sound reverberating off the walls. Peter stood and watched, then he

230

noticed the fire's smoke: instead of rising straight up from the flames, it spun upward in a circle, like a cycle of life. Peter was mesmerized, he stared at the fire to see if there was something causing it, but he saw nothing. He continued to watch the rotating smoke float up slowly to the roof where it broke into separate thin streams, like a serpentine, as it made its way along the roof planking and out the opening.

A palpable sense of spirituality welled up inside of Peter, the essence of life surrounded and embraced him. The chanting singers and thundering drums pounded into Peter's soul, like the rhythmic beat of tidal surge, combined with the circular wood smoke it took his soul to a new place. In that supreme moment he became untethered from the world, the experience triggered a transcendence that lifted him up to the sky.

At the far end of the lodge, the round-faced Chieftain, who Peter saw earlier, was seated on an elevated split cedar armchair talking with other elders next to him. More members and relatives sat on benches that lined the walls and were arranged around the great room. Peter stood with Takhumkun near the entrance, taking it all in. When the drums stopped the Chief stood and started talking in Lushootseed.

Peter was new to the dialect, but from all the nodding and grinning on the faces of the tribal members, who were listening intently, it felt like he was in the presence of a great leader. As he spoke, tribesmen occasionally would stand, wait to be acknowledged, and then ask him what sounded to be questions. The chief responded to each of their concerns at length and then, once the tribesman sat down, he would resume his speech, easily and quickly, showing no sign of hesitance. When the Chief was finally done a long line of tribal members formed in front of him. He greeted and spoke with each one as they exchanged gifts.

Takhumkun led Peter up to get in line to meet him.

Once they were at the front, Peter stood behind Takhumkun while he spoke to the Chief, who had by now taken off his double-breasted coat to reveal a clean but fraying white Boston shirt. Takhumkun pointed to the north and said, "*Skayuʔqs,*" then he pointed to the east and said, "*Chi-Cha-dee-a,*" and mentioned '*jargon*' a few times, each time Takhumkun turned around to look and motion at Peter. The Chief nodded politely as Takhumkun spoke, but his eyes wandered across the hall as more tribesmen formed behind them to greet the Tyee. When Takhumkun was done he turned to Peter and motioned for him to step forward, saying, "*Tyee Patkanim.*"

Peter stood in front of Chief Patkanim and nodded his head once, then held out the HBC blanket and said, "*Kloshe sun pot'-latch.*" Patkanim grinned and motioned down the line of benches that extended from each side of him. A woman came up and accepted the gift from Peter. Then Patkanim motioned down to the other end of the bench and said something, another woman walked up and handed Peter a loop of thin deer-hide with Dentalium shells strung on it. He immediately lifted it over his head and let it fall on his neck and chest, then looked at the Chief.

"*Máh-sie Tyee Patkanim,*" Peter said, thanking Patkanim for the gift.

"*Ságh-a-lie ty-ee' Dukwibal tik'-tik me-si-ka,*" the Chief replied.

Dukwibal is watching me. That's what Takhumkun said. Oh, he's asking me about Skayu Point.

"*E-éh, ni-ka káh-kwa Skayu,*" Peter affirmed, pulling on his beard.

232

"*Wake shem pel'-ton man ko-pa mem'-a-loost?*" Patkanim asked, staring at Peter's long facial hair.

Do you have shame living with our dead? I think he wants me to ask for permission to live near their burial grounds. I need to explain myself.

"*Ni-ka mal-éh Tlingit klootsh'-man yah-ka mem'-a-loost. Ni-ka tik-égh klootsh'-man. Ni-ka nan'itsh Skayu lak'it de-láte wau' wau kwanness. Yout Tyee Patkanim,* Peter *house ko-páh Skayu?*" Peter said, describing his marriage and love for Little Rain, her passing, and asking the Grand Hyas for permission to live near their burial grounds.

Patkanim nodded a few times then whispered something to the man sitting next him, who Peter took as a sub-chief. The sub-chief listened to his leader then Patkanim turned his gaze back to Peter, still stroking and pulling on his beard. The Chief looked at Peter and lifted his right forearm but kept his elbow on the cedar armrest of the chair, he pointed his right index finger upward and began to spin his arm as he spoke.

"*E-éh, house Skayu ko'-pa Dukwibal,*" the Tyee agreed but added, "*Dukwibal tum'-tum yáh-ka sé-áh-host me-si'-ka.*" Everyone around them nodded and spoke softly about what the great Tyee had just said, as he continued to spin his arm.

He just said that Dukwibal will keep his eyes on me.

Peter's heart started to pound, he glanced back to the swirling woodsmoke, then turned to the Chief who was staring at him with a somber, knowing look but still rotating his forearm, just like the smoke. Peter waited until the murmurs died down then said, "*Máh-sie Tyee Patkanim.*" The Chief slapped his hands together and nodded at Peter, then motioned for the next person in line to greet him.

With that, a grinning Peter walked back outside into the bright and warm sunshine with Takhumkun, more fires had been started. At one, women were cooking crab and clams in big iron kettles and at another, nettles were being boiled for tea. Feeling good about himself and the day, Peter wandered over to a table made of split-planks on top of log uprights where more food was being prepared. He took his rucksack off and pulled out the sack of sugar then gave it to one of the women working on the feast, saying in jargon, "*Le sook, tsee.*"

The older lady looked up into his eyes and then at his beard, she smiled a toothless smile and opened the sack. She licked a finger, stuck it in the sugar and took a taste. "*ʔadʷáləqəq,*" she replied in Lushootseed, smiling and setting the sugar down on the table, going back to her task.

Peter saw Takhumkun with some of his friends getting something to eat so he went over to them. There was a stack of carved cedar plates, he grabbed one and helped himself to half a crab, some clams, a bit of dried salmon and some berries. Takhumkun went off with his fellow tribe members so Peter took his meal out to the beach, sat down on a drift log, and pulled out his marriage stick. He crossed himself, kissed it and then put it back under his shirt. *Little Rain would've loved it here.*

Looking down the beach, he saw the same man working on the canoe he'd inspected earlier. The beautiful woman he'd seen was still sitting with her child watching him, who Peter took as her husband. *That's the best canoe of that size I've ever seen, it has some nice lines to it, sleek. I bet it would be swift going up to Penn Cove for supplies. I wonder what he'd take for it.*

234

By the time he had finished his meal, more members of the tribe had gathered to sit on the beach with plates of food. Peter set his plate down on the log and started to walk over to the canoe builder. He looked to be in his early twenties with a black ponytail down his back and was bare chested wearing a breechcloth and buckskin leggings, chiseling out grooves on the inside for a second seat. The man raised his head as Peter approached.

"*Cheechako*," he grunted.

"*Klahowya!* . . . *Mika boat?*" Peter asked, stroking his beard.

"*Áh-ha*," he answered, picking up a crude wooden mallet to hammer a second seat into place.

"*Mahkook?*" Peter asked.

"*Huy-huy, huihui!*" he answered, looking at Peter and then at his long pointy beard. "*Nika mahkook.*"

Good, he wants to trade. Peter took the bottle of rum out of his rucksack and the Barlow pocketknife from his trousers. He held them up for the man to see. Peter pointed at the canoe.

"*Wake, wake mahkook!*" the fellow snapped. He held up three fingers and stated, "*Klone la-boo-ti' lum pe chik'-a-min.*"

"Three bottles of rum and money! Ha! That's too high! Too high!" Peter replied. He got the scissors from the rucksack and offered it with the other two items.

"*O'-koke o'-pit-sah* see'-zo and *la-boo-ti*," Peter said, but the man wasn't about to take less.

"*Wake*," he grumbled and went back to work. His fellow tribal members on the beach started to laugh and snicker, one of them started to stroke his face like Peter did with his beard. Peter frowned at being made fun of but tried once more.

"*O'-koke le see'-zo and la-boo-ti*," Peter offered again, holding up everything and smiling.

The man glanced at the items, so Peter opened and closed the scissors to show him how well they worked.

"*Wake mahkook*," the man repeated, then said, "*Stu-hy.*" The people on the beach immediately started talking to each other, covering their mouths as they did, giggling and repeating, '*Stu-hy*,' to each other. A few started stroking their faces. Peter shoved the pocket knife back in his trousers.

But he was determined. He walked around the canoe again but this time trying to find any imperfection that he could use to get the price down. Peter leaned over to look at the keel again, however it was as straight as an arrow, so he stood back up and put his hands on his hips. *I'd really like to have this boat.*

He got the hunting knife with its fine bone handle and leather sheath from his rucksack and held it up with the scissors and bottle of rum.

"*Le see'-zo* and *la-boo-ti* and *skookum o'-pit-sah*!" he exclaimed, trying to get the man's attention.

When the canoe builder saw the hunting knife his eyes lit up. He stopped what he was doing and went over to Peter, looked at him earnestly and nodded, pointing at the knife.

Peter held it out for him. He took the hunting knife, held the sheath in his left hand and then pulled the knife out with his right and gazed at the curved top edge that came to a point. He felt its sharpness with his thumb.

"*Mmm, kloshe o'-pit-sah,*" he said, admiring the knife and its bone handle, then nodded his head. He looked over at his wife but she frowned. "*Wake mahkook,*" he said, rejecting the trade.

"What*? Ik-tah*? No trade? *Wake mahkook?*"

"*Wake,*" he grumbled. But then the man raised two fingers and thumb, rubbed them together and again said, "*Chik'-a-min.*"

Peter stroked his beard a few times then reached deep down into his front pocket and pulled out his one piece of French gold. He held it up and said, "*Ikt pe chik'-a-min* for *boat.*"

"*Wake kanawi,*" he simply stated, and kept tapping the seat into place.

"You want everything? By the Holy Christ! Alright, you win!" Peter said, handing over the gold piece to the grinning canoe builder with the rum, scissors and hunting knife. Peter nodded and asked, "*Kloshe?*"

"*Kloshe!*" the man replied grinning. He looked up at his wife and held up the gold for her. She beamed with delight. Seeing that everyone was happy, Peter put his hand over his heart and said, "Peter," and bowed his head.

The man in turn, did the same and said, "*Keokuk.*" Then he turned to the people sitting on the beach log, and said, "*kʷáxʷ*," motioning with a hand, and two men walked down to help them.

237

They started pushing the canoe over log rollers down to the shoreline where Peter pushed it into the water and jumped in. *At least I've still got the fry pan, jar of molasses and the pocketknife!*

Peter paddled his new canoe downstream to where his larger dugout was now floating on the in-coming tide. He landed and then pulled in the line that his big canoe was tied to and tied his new craft to its stern so he could tow it home.

He headed back up the beach to the village to find Takhumkun, but by the time he got back to where the canoe builder had been working, Peter found him with his wife and friends, sharing the rum. As he walked up to them Keokuk held out the bottle.

"Don't mind if I do," Peter said, then added, "*Nawitka, máh-sie.*" He latched onto the jug and took a swig and Keokuk asked him to sit and drink, "*Stu-hy Pee-ter mitlite tenas?*"

"*Non, non, monami,*" Peter answered, handing back the bottle, but then said, "*Klatawa nan'-itsh Takhumkun.*" He walked over to get his plate then headed back to the village where he found more tables of food.

The two braves who brought in the huge stag now had it hanging by its hooves from an upright hemlock pole rack, they'd already skinned it and were in the process of removing the prized back strap, a new fire was being built next to it.

Peter continued down the main passageway between the plank houses and palisade, people were sitting on benches eating and talking, grinning and laughing. Surrounded by the Lushootseed dialect, he marveled at the musical syntax that was resonating around him, he felt encircled by song birds. Peter stopped and took in the wonderful, melodious sounds for a moment. Smiling, he walked over to the same table he had left the sugar on and set his plate down when he was offered a clay vessel of nettle tea by an elderly woman.

"*Máh-sie,*" Peter said, thanking the woman and accepting the tea. As soon as she let go of the clay vessel, she looked at him and started to stroke her face like she had a beard, grinning. Peter chuckled and took a bitter sip of the tea but he didn't react to its earthy taste. He nodded a thank you and inched his way down the table to the sugar and added a few pinches of it when Takhumkun walked up.

"*Kahta maika,* Pee-ter?" he asked.

"*Ah bien. Kloshe mashie! Nika is'-kum boat!*" Peter remarked about his new canoe, smiling.

"*Kloshe, kloshe!*" Takhumkun exclaimed, happy for him. He raised two fingers and thumb then rubbed them together and asked, "*Chik'-a-min?*"

Takhumkun wants to know if I had to give up some metal money. Keokuk is going to tell him about the gold anyway so I might as well let him know that I did. Peter answered, "*Ah-ha, e-éh, ikt lum, o'-pit-sah, le see'-zo.*" Right when Peter replied a few braves close by turned and started to stare at him.

Takhumkun nodded. Peter thought back to when he traded the pennies to the teenagers for their beads just a short time before. *Takhumkun knew I had metal money then and now he knows I have gold and these fellows staring at me are making me nervous. Now everyone's going to know I have gold. Did I just make a mistake?* He started to stroke his beard and a tingle went up his spine, it felt like it was time to head home.

"Kloshe nanitch, me-si'-ka klat'-a-wa Skayu," Peter said.

Takhumkun grinned slyly and stated, *"Nawitka kloshe sun!"*

Peter nodded a goodbye to him, set his empty clay mug down on the table and headed to the beach. When he got there the canoe builder, his wife and their friends were already gone, so he untied his canoe and towed his new prize home behind him.

XVIII

The Mill
Tə Búlla
1853 - 1854

One late afternoon Peter was busy lashing down the purlins on the roof of his log cabin when he looked out over the Sound. He could see two approaching canoes that were running low in the water, coming across from Whidbey Island. Each was loaded down with supplies, both with one paddler. Peter climbed down off the roof and watched them go around the point and into the bay, so he headed to the waterline.

"Hello, Peter!" one of the men hollered. It was John Gould.

"John! Good to see you!" Peter replied as they landed.

"Peter, meet Charlie Phillips," John said, motioning towards the fellow in the other boat.

"Hello, Charlie, good to meet you. What brings you way out here?" Peter asked.

"Well, John told me all about your sawmill plans," Charlie answered, stepping from his dugout.

"Yes!" John remarked, "I met Charlie up at Penn Cove and he is very interested in becoming a partner with us on the mill."

"That I am," Charlie said, stepping over and shaking Peter's hand. "And I'm hoping you'll take me on. I'm a darn good carpenter and know exactly how to build your mill."

"You do?" Peter asked. "Where'd you learn that?"

"My dad was a carpenter and my uncle used to own a sawmill, and I worked for both of them in my younger days. When my uncle died, I inherited some of his sawmill equipment," Charlie said, motioning at his loaded canoe. "How about if we go over to the site, take a look around and get acquainted?"

"I guess that would be fine," Peter said.

"Okay," Charlie responded, "John mentioned you want to build a waterwheel to run the saw so I'd like to see the creek you had in mind too, see if it's gonna work and then figure out if we can build it."

"Aren't they all the same?" Peter asked.

"Well, the saw I've brought is my uncle's small old up-down Muley, but the water source and potential mill site is very important," Charlie answered.

"You brought a saw? Here?" Peter said, slack-jawed.

"But just the sawblade to show you how serious I am. I took it apart and left the mounting guides at home, so it easily fit in my canoe. It's a forty-two-inch blade and does a damn good job with medium sized timber."

"*Magnifique!*" Peter exclaimed. Charlie grinned at his French.

"I've always wanted to own a mill and could never find any partners who wanted to do the work, then I took a job carrying the mail from Olympia to Whatcom. A friend of mine is filling in for me for the time being but I will quit that job and go to work with you, that is, if you'll take me on as a partner."

"Very good," Peter replied. "But that sounds like a good job with a steady income."

"Aw, it wasn't bad, had to pay an Indian paddler to help on the route, but I want to get into the lumber trade. It's in my blood."

"Well, let's head over to the site," Peter offered. They climbed into his big canoe and paddled across the high-tide of the bay. As soon as they entered the small finger-shaped inlet Charlie's eyes widened.

"This will make for a perfect log pond," he said. Then Charlie looked up at the water spilling down off the short hill. "I can already see it with the mill building up there and a log ramp coming up from down here. Let's go and see the creek."

They beached the canoe and climbed the bank. Once they were standing next to the fast-moving brook Charlie found a stiff tree limb on the ground, he grabbed it and walked around upstream. He stuck it in the water to measure its depth.

"Looks like we're going to have to build a dam," he said, eyeing the water's mark on the limb. He turned and scanned the upstream area, then added, "With the banks shaped like that it'll be easy, it's a great site for a reservoir. We'll be fine."

Peter and John looked at each other and then both of them turned to Charlie. Peter said, "Well, if we have to build a dam, then we'll build a dam!"

"I'm ready, by golly," John added.

"That's the spirit!" Charlie exclaimed. "With a dam we'll have more than enough head to push an overshot wheel."

"An overshot wheel?" Peter asked. Charlie walked back over to them.

"That's where the water hits the wheel at the top, the flow and weight of the water pushes it. But we'll have to divert the creek and do a lot of digging. You see, we'll build the sawmill so that the axel from the waterwheel can come into the building underneath the saw to the gearbox. And with this hill to work with it will help us gain some drop. Follow?"

"I think so," Peter replied, trying very hard to mask his confusion.

"The saw," Charlie continued, "would be on the second level up above us. But the gearbox that runs it would need to be below where the axle drive comes into the building, I didn't bring the gearbox."

"Right," Peter answered, looking like he understood.

"That's a good plan," John said, nodding.

"We'll have to divert the creek so we can dry the ground out, then dig it out level. Then we'll build a penstock flume to bring the water to the wheel from the dam," Charlie added. He took some folded-up paper and a carpenter's pencil out of his pocket. He sharpened the end of it with a pocket knife then started drawing a design. In a few minutes he had the basic idea of the mill drawn then showed it to Peter and John.

"Take a look," he said, holding out the rendering.

"By-golly Charlie, yer' a genius!" John proclaimed.

"That's good," Peter added, gazing at the drawing of a two-story building with a waterwheel and flume.

That night, after a meal of fresh deer steaks, biscuits and coffee, the three men sat around the campfire and got down to brass tacks and began to hammer out a business agreement.

"So!" Peter began, "I have entered into a rental agreement for five acres on the creek to build the mill with Jake Hall, who owns the land, but he gets a quarter interest in the profits. We must factor that into our arrangement. If I have bargained for the mill site and paid rent, and now that Charlie is going to design and build the sawmill, then that brings us to the point of what're you going to offer, John?"

"I'm glad you finally asked me that," Gould replied. "In my canoe I've got cross-cut saws, a pit-saw, sledges and mallets, chains, a broad ax for hewing and double-bit axes to under-cut the trees. I also bought an auger and a block and tackle from the trading post at Penn Cove. Plus, I have other hand tools and my homestead claim will supply timber for the mill."

245

"*Fantastique!*" Peter exclaimed. "So, with Jake and us it will round out the partnership, all four of us will each have a one-quarter share in the mill and its profits. But what about all the other machinery and equipment for it? Where will we get that?"

"I've arranged for the shipment of my log carriage and gearbox by supply boat, it will be here as soon as I send for it," Charlie boasted.

"Then it's agreed!" Peter cried, hopping up from his seat.

"Partners!" The other men said, raising their tin cups of coffee.

Across the rest of the summer of 1853 the three men, faithful to their word, worked at the plan. First, with the pickaxe, heavy steel breaker bar, and good iron shovels that John had brought, they excavated the mill site, diverted the creek, and then prepared the foundation for the mill building. They squared up fir logs for the post and beam construction of the building with the double-handled pit-saw, fastened everything with hand carved-wooden pins in hand-drilled auger holes, and soon had the frame of the mill building erected. Next, they built a dam of rocks and gravel combined with an elevated wooden penstock to deliver the water to the top of the wheel, plus a gate valve to divert the water down a by-pass channel. Once that was done, they fabricated a rough but sturdy wooden waterwheel. Animated by the promise of a whole world to be built there, the promise of that world whose building would require untold board-feet of good Puget Sound lumber, the men worked diligently and without complaint at their project, working in the morning to assemble their breakfasts, sweating under the hot sun of the noon to build the mill, and then

246

working again in the evening to cook their suppers. Everything had to be torn out of the earth with a man's own hands and strength, and they constantly pushed themselves as hard as they could, knowing that their fortunes and their destinies were in their own control.

One fine late September afternoon, the natural quiet and calm of the land was shattered by the blowing of a steam whistle, it was the supply boat *H.C. Page* coming up from Olympia. The three partners turned their heads to listen from inside the now finished building. They went outside and grinned at the sight of the side-wheeler; it had all the parts and machinery to complete the mill. John Gould took off his wide-brimmed hat and waved it in the air. "Halleluiah boys, it's the *Page*! Now we're in business!" he hollered.

By the first part of October, the men had mounted the Muley-saw and its carriage, all the belts, pulleys, and chains to drive the sawblade, and built a ramp from the inlet up to the mill room. John and Peter went to work downing the first trees on John's claim. They fell hemlock and fir trees right on the edge of the bay at low-tide when they could top, buck and limb them. During high-tide they'd float them across the water to their log pond, then pull one length at a time up the ramp with John's block and tackle. They did all that while Charlie was putting the finishing touches on the penstock that delivered the water to the wheel and the bypass gate valve.

In a few months they had milled thousands of board feet of dimensional lumber and had it all drying, stickered and stacked outside the millhouse.

On a cold winter day in 1854, Peter was on the lower level of the building digging out the sawdust underneath the Muley saw when a man paddled up in a canoe down at the log pond.

"Anyone around?" the fellow yelled.

Peter stopped shoveling, walked over to a glassless window opening and stuck his head outside, the man saw him. "How can I help you?" Peter called.

"The name's John Izett and I'm looking to purchase some lumber for up at Utsaladdy, on Camano Island," he said.

"Good!" Peter replied, "we've got plenty. Beach your canoe and come on up."

The man landed his dugout and headed up the hill while Peter climbed out from the lower level. By the time he was out from the sawdust pit the fellow was already inspecting their stacks of lumber.

"I'm Peter Goutre," Peter said, approaching the fellow. He had on a pair of filthy canvas work pants, a black wool coat, and a salt and pepper flat cap on his head.

"Good to meet you, Mr. Goo-tray. John Alexander told me about your mill," Izett said.

"He did! How's he doing? I haven't been up there for a few months."

"He's good, business is picking up at the cove. So! My boss, Marshall Campbell, has got a contract to supply boatbuilders in England and France with masts and spars for their tall ships, got a spar camp to build. I'm Campbell's foreman. I need lumber for a bunkhouse, mess hall, storehouse, and maybe even a wharf."

"You do?! Well, what a small world! This is a great day. My father was from *Calais*!"

"Is that a town in Europe?" John asked.

"*Oui*, it is in France. He would have been seventy-five this year."

"He's no longer with us?"

"*Non, monsieur,* he died when I was quite young."

"Well, I'm sorry to hear that . . . but as far as business, it looks like you've got plenty of framing lumber. What about planking for floors and cedar for board and batten siding?" Izett asked.

"Ah, *oui*," Peter answered. "We can do an order for that . . . how much wood will you be needing?"

Mr. Izett turned to look at the lumber again and then back to Peter. He grinned and said, "All of it."

XIX

Treaty Day
Ki'-wa Péh-pah
January 22, 1855

"Hey Peter! French Peter! Where are ya'?" Jake yelled from down at the beach inside the bay, breaking the quiet stillness of the early morning. "Hurry up! This was your idea!"

A few moments later Peter came running down his trail, trying to put on his coat while shoving a cold biscuit in his mouth.

"*Oui, monami!*" Peter hollered, his mouth full of dough, still half asleep. He pushed them off, jumped in the canoe and started paddling. Overhead the winter sky was a dull gun-metal grey and a chilly breeze greeted them around the point, a small flock of cormorants flew past.

"You know, I still don't see why we gotta go all the way down there," Jake said, paddling slowly.

"Come on, it's historic! All the Tyees will be there, and Governor Stevens is gonna be there too!" Peter replied, paddling more enthusiastically and alternating sides with his paddle to keep the canoe on course since Jake was dragging.

"Pah, the Governor! Nobody voted for him. He was appointed you know."

"Well, I am not from your country, so excuse me if I am wrong, but since the Governor —"

"I knows the rules! Grandpappy Hall told me that we had a cousin at the constitutional convention, I'll have you know! But it don't mean I like 'em. Some fancy aristocrat from the east shows up and just 'cuz he's got a stamp with him from the pres-zee-dent that don't mean we all gotta' go listen!"

"Well, the treaty will be a good thing, once it's signed."

"Treaty shmeety! I wouldn't give a rotten cob a' corn for some piece a' paper no one's gonna respect the moment they don't need to!"

"Come now, Jake, my friend," Peter said slowly. He was trying very hard. "It is not a bad thing for people to come together and agree to live in peace with each other. There is plenty of land for everyone, we can work something out."

"Pah! Even if they do, us bein' there and losin' a day of you not working the mill isn't gonna influence it one way or the other. You got orders and that means we got orders, which means I make money, for still doin' nothin'! Youse got so much wood to mill that it's burnin' me up just thinkin' about all the money I'm losin' goin' on this stupid little tourist excursion a' yours!"

"Come now — everyone who is anyone in the territory will be there. Think of it as an opportunity to hob-knob with the big boys. We could meet our next customer!" Jake didn't respond. His eyes were unfocused, no longer looking at the canoe or the water. After

252

some time passed his paddling picked up speed and finally matched pace with Peter's.

All the tribes and their families had traveled in canoes from across northern Puget Sound and down the rivers to Point Elliot for the historic event. After thousands of years of living with and on the land, the Native tribes of the region were now going to be placed on reservations, forced to fully assimilate to the white man's culture and way of life, required to change where and how they lived, what they wore and what they learned. There were too many settlers coming into the region and they were bound to overwhelm the Native populations so as far as the government was concerned, treaties needed to be signed.

Once Peter and Jake were close, they could see the hundreds of canoes that lined the beach north of the point. The sailing schooner *Sarah Stone*, plus the 97-foot iron-hulled propeller steamer *Major Tomkins*, were anchored offshore, both of them looking like floating palaces to the First Nation People.

Onshore, nearly every northern mainland tribe was represented, from the Duwamish River in the south, north to the Canadian border. Most of the Tyees had been at Point Elliot for over a week, camping at the beach, in council with each other about the treaty they were to sign. The chiefs and elders of each tribe met daily, morning, noon, and night to discuss the ramifications and effects it would have on their people and way of life.

When they landed, Peter was pleased to see so many Natives in attendance, there were thousands. Women wearing side seam moccasins, woven conical reed hats and warm layered clothes made from the shredded inner bark of cedar trees held toddlers wrapped in white furry blankets with handmade dolls in their hands. The men wore buckskin shirts with leggings and moccasins with wool blankets or bearskin capes wrapped around themselves.

Once the canoe was secure, Peter and Jake walked up the beach and were greeted by a long line of Snohomish and Snoqualmie Indians on the bank, welcoming the newcomers. They went over to it and shook hands with them. Halfway through Peter saw Takhumkun and Keokuk, they all smiled at each other as they shook hands. Keokuk called him, "*Stu-hy.*" Peter grinned, stroked his beard and continued.

The first white person he saw was Isaac Ebey, standing with a companion with their eyes on the Sound like they were waiting for someone. Peter walked straight over to them.

"Hello Isaac, how've you been?" Peter asked. "How's the family?"

"Ah, yes," Isaac replied, turning and then recognizing him, "Peter Goutre! Good to see you. The family's good, home on the farm." Both men shook hands.

"*Oui*, good to see you too," Peter said. "This is my neighbor, Jake Hall, I mean, Jehiel Hall. He owns the land my sawmill is on."

"Hello, Jehiel, good to see you again. How's life at Tulalip Bay?" Isaac asked, shaking his hand.

"It's about as good as it could be, I guess. I just hope this little hootenanny was worth coming all this way for," he answered.

"And this is my cousin, George Beam," Isaac added, motioning towards his relative.

Peter and Jake both doffed their hats. "Good to meet you,

George," Peter offered, nodding at him.

"So you *did* build the mill, then? On Tulalip Bay?" Isaac asked, a touch of concern in his voice.

"I did," Peter answered, "with my partners John Gould and Charlie Phillips."

"You mean Charles Phillips that carries the mail?" Isaac asked.

"*Oui*, that's him," Peter answered.

"Oh, he'll be a good partner, and how are you getting along with the Snohomish?"

"We are on good terms, *monsieur*, with no troubles. How are things over on Whidbey?"

Isaac scratched the hair under his chin and then ruminated, "Good, but most of the Lower Skagit who live on Whidbey are not happy about the treaty. Chief Goliah of the Upper Skagit and Samish tribes is here representing them."

"If they want to stay on Whidbey, then they should be allowed to," Peter offered.

"Oh, Isaac Stevens won't let that happen," Ebey remarked sternly. "He's over there working on the wording of the treaty with George Gibbs right now," Isaac said, motioning at a large canvas tent with two tables, chairs and an American flag in front of it. "Stevens is a true believer in the advancement of the west, and a real patriot, so he's bound and determined to get them all settled on reservations. But, you see, the tribes need help, especially after getting hit so hard by smallpox and I do believe they want the treaty as much as Stevens does."

"This whole move the locals to a new place to live and then call it a reservation is nonsense. The government should just let them stay where they're all living now and make that a reservation," Peter remarked.

Isaac nodded his head up and down, he looked directly into Peter's eyes and said, "We've been here since Saturday, listening to the different tribes talk between themselves and, well, I'm not sure how to tell you this, so I'll just say it. The Tyees of the Snohomish, Snoqualmie and Skykomish tribes are planning on selecting Tulalip Bay and the land around it as their reservation."

Peter didn't reply right away. After a few seconds he blurted, "Tulalip? Our Tulalip?"

"Look, Peter, I didn't encourage —"

"*Non, non*, you couldn't mean our Tulalip, the land you yourself helped us with!"

"What?" Jake croaked. "But I claimed that land too. I own it! That can't be right. Are you sure?" Both men stared at Isaac and waited for a reply.

"Well," Ebey said, scratching his beard some more. "The Tyees have made their choice but I have no idea if that's where Governor Stevens is going to place them."

"*Merde*! *Je ne peux pas croire que cela arrive!*" Peter yelled, ripping off his knit cap and throwing it on the ground. His face was pale white, drained of color, he stood there for a moment shaking his head, finally, he picked his hat up and put it back on.

"Damn that Stevens' hide! This is the — Why I —" Jake hollered at Isaac.

"Listen, boys, it's not all bad — if the government decides to take your land and place the tribes out at Tulalip then they'll compensate both of you," Isaac said, trying to reassure them.

"Compensate?" Peter asked, looking at Isaac, exasperated.

"Yes, compensate you," Isaac replied. "They won't just steal your land. They'll pay you in dollars."

"Yer' tellin' me that I might get some money outta this deal?" Jake asked, his eyebrows raised.

"Yes," George Beam said, breaking into the conversation. "The government will appraise your land and improvements and then pay you for them, that is, after Congress ratifies the treaty."

"You know we've really improved Tulalip! The mill, and our cabins! I know you haven't seen it, but it's definitely worth a lot of money," Jake said.

"But we'll still have to find new claims and move," Peter complained, looking at Jake.

"There's still plenty of good land over on Whidbey," Isaac remarked. "Come on over and live with us. You could start another sawmill. We'll help you move."

But Peter and Jake just stood there blank-faced and mute, angry about the new development.

"So!" Isaac said, breaking the silence, "how about a cup of coffee before the signing starts? Come on over to our camp, I've got a fresh pot going."

"Fine," Peter mumbled, Jake spat in the dirt and then nodded in approval. They followed Isaac to his camp through a burgeoning crowd, walking past a huge military-style tent with crude wooden tables groaning under the weight of all the food provided by Governor Stevens' commissary: beef, elk, wild goose, duck, mutton, salmon, and clams, all cooked to perfection. Two-thousand native people were camped in small tule mat tents with campfires in front of them, they covered the grasslands north and south of the salt marsh lagoon, even up on the hillside and on the beach. Groups of men huddled in circles conversing in life-changing discussions everywhere while children played with new-found friends or tribal cousins, teenagers played stickgame.

"Here we are," Isaac said, motioning at a small white pup tent and the coals of a campfire with a coffee pot on a flat rock in the middle of it. Peter and Jake sat down on the ground.

"I'll get us something to drink from," George said, crawling into the canvas tent. Isaac stoked the fire and George came back and handed everyone a mug.

Peter glanced around, near to them Keokuk and his wife were camping, their little baby was a walking toddler now and she was cradling a new child wrapped in blankets in her arms. They had a black Labrador with two puppies with them. Peter noticed how happy they seemed, watching after their little one who was playing with the young pups. *I'll go over there and say hello in a bit.*

"The Snohomish Indians have used this place for centuries, they call it, 'Muk-wil-teo' which means narrow passage in Lushootseed," Isaac said, pouring a cup of hot black coffee for his guests. "It's sacred ground to them."

"So, um, how many tribes are here?" Jake asked.

"All of the northern ones from this side of the mountains!" George answered, speaking up. "From the Duwamish River down south all the way up to Whatcom at the border of the British Crown Colony."

"Except the Nooksack, they're all snowed in up at Mount Baker," Isaac said, looking at his cousin.

"Yes, yes," George responded. "Snowed in under big Koma Kulshan. But Chief Seathl's camp is right over there," George said, pointing to a group a few camps over. "He's the Duwamish Tyee, but when he was baptized, he took the name 'Noah.'"

"Ah, Noah," Peter said, "but he's also the one they call *Le Gros*, the Big Guy," Peter said, taking his eyes away from the puppies. "That's what they called him when I worked at Nisqually years ago." Standing up and looking towards the camp Peter saw a large group of Indians huddled around a campfire with a kettle of steaming clam chowder hung over it.

"Yes," Isaac heartily agreed, "he's widely respected between all the tribes and was a proud warrior in his day. But now he's known more as a diplomat than a fighter."

"He's sure got a lot of grey hair," Peter replied. "He must be getting pretty old. Who's that with him?"

Isaac looked over at the camp and said, "That's Doc Maynard, they're good friends. He helped arrange this council and built a store at the next settlement south that he's calling Seattle, he named it after Chief Seathl."

Just then a loud, clear voice called out over the multitudes, "Gather up! It's time to begin!" All heads in every camp turned in the direction of Stevens' white tent, people began walking towards the shoreline.

"It must be time for the dignitaries and the speeches," George said, standing up. All of them began to walk over to where the Governor was going to speak.

As the men approached, they could see the people thickening up significantly — everyone was crowding around the large white canvas tent that sat on a rough but sturdy wooden platform erected for the purpose. Important-looking white men in black frock coats were seated all along one side of the table with pens and ink, large sheafs of documents were set before them. One aide was standing near the edge of the platform and directing the crowd to let the Tyees sit closest to the document-covered table where the appointed Territorial Governor, who was also the Superintendent of Indian Affairs, Isaac Ingalls Stevens was standing.

Peter and Jake stood with Isaac and George on the perimeter waiting for the proceedings to begin. Peter turned his head towards Isaac and asked, "Where does this Governor come from?"

"He's from Massachusetts and a very accomplished man for his age. When he was nine years old his parents had a terrible carriage accident that fatally injured his mother, it left the family in a rough state. But he pulled himself up by the bootstraps and graduated from West Point at the top of his class."

At five feet three inches, Stevens was a short man but had a forceful presence that seemed to make him taller than he was, an innate sense of authority, earned or not. He was dressed in a rough but clean black wool coat with a red flannel shirt beneath it, a loose-fitting silk tie at his throat. Mud-spattered black linen trousers were tucked tightly into his leather boots, and above it all he wore a crushed black felt hat with a wooden pipe held firm in its headband. He patiently waited until the crowd was still. Governor Stevens walked around to the front of the table slowly, such that he was standing between it and the crowd. He stood silently until the crowd grew quiet and then began to speak in a loud, but thin voice to the masses with the main Tyee's sitting in several different semi-circles in front of him.

"My children! You are not my children because you are the fruit of my loins, but because you are children for whom I have the same feeling as if you were the fruit of my loins. You are my children for whom I will strenuously labor all the days of my life until I shall be taken hence."

"Yesterday, I saw among you the sign of the cross, which I think the most holy of all signs. I address you therefore mainly as Christians, who know that this life is a preparation for the life to come," he said, looking stoic with his hands on his coat lapels.

"The Great Father, our President Franklin Pierce, thinks you ought to have homes, and he wants you to have a school where your children can learn to read, and can be made farmers and taught trades. He is willing that you should catch fish in the waters, this paper," Stevens said, motioning at the treaty on the table, "secures your fish. The Great Father wishes you all to be virtuous and industrious, and to become a happy and prosperous community. Do you want this?" he said, looking out over the thousands.

After his interpreter, Benjamin Shaw, repeated his words in Chinook Jargon then John Taylor repeated them in Lushootseed, an enormous response erupted from the throng.

"*Čəł' huy! Čəł' huy!*" two-thousand voices cried out, agreeing.

With an approving nod of his head Stevens picked up the Treaty and began to read it out loud. At Article 3 he conveyed, "There is also reserved from the lands hereby ceded the amount of thirty-six sections, or one township of land, on the northeastern shore of Port Gardner, and north of the mouth of the Snohomish River, including Tulalip Bay and the before-mentioned Kwilt-seh-da Creek, for the purpose of establishing thereon an agricultural and industrial school, as hereinafter mentioned and agreed, and with a view of ultimately drawing thereto and settling thereon all the Indians living west of the Cascade Mountains in said Territory. Provided, however, that the President may establish the central agency and general reservation at such other point as he may deem for the benefit of the Indians."

Tulalip Bay. Isaac was right. Peter looked over at Jake for a reaction but his hard, frozen face was focused on Stevens, so he turned back to listen to the Governor as his heart began to sink.

"And finally, Article 15: This treaty shall be obligatory on the contracting parties as soon as the same shall be ratified by the President and Senate of the United States," Stevens said. Then he motioned for his translators, Ben Shaw and John Taylor. They again interpreted all fifteen articles for the crowd.

When they were finished Stevens called out, "I want Chief Seathl to give his will to me and speak to his people."

The revered leader of the Duwamish slowly stood up and, leaning heavily on an ornately-carved cedar staff, began to walk up to the

262

platform. The crowd was silent as he made his way forward, watching him carefully. Wearing a white Boston shirt and baggy tan trousers, he reached the front of the desk and gazed out at all the people. It was then he started to speak in a rich bass voice, diminished only slightly by age. His Lushootseed syntax and baritone vocalizations were like the low melodic notes of a song, the words and syllables similar to a deep resounding drum. Standing tall with his long, straight grey hair parted in the middle, he looked every part frontier royalty.

After the Chief was done, John Taylor came forward with his notes and stood next to him and translated his speech in English, at first looking at the Governor, then out to the crowd.

"I look upon you as my father. I and the rest regard you as such. All of the Indians have the same good feeling toward you and will send it on paper to the Great Father. All of them, men, women and children, rejoice that he has sent you to take care of them."

"The great white chief sends us word that he wants to buy our lands but is willing to allow us to reserve enough to live on comfortably. This indeed appears generous, for the red man no longer has rights that he need respect, and the offer may be wise, also, for we are no longer in need of a great country."

"Since King George has moved his boundaries to the north our great and good father says he will protect us. His brave armies will give us a wall of shelter and strength, and his great ships of war will fill our harbors so that our ancient enemies far to the north will no longer frighten our women and old men. Then he will be our father and we will be his children."

"But let us hope that hostilities between the red-man and his pale-face brothers may never return. We would have everything to lose and nothing to gain."

"Men come and go like the waves of the ocean. A tear, a Tomanawas, a dirge, and they are gone from our longing eyes forever. Even the white man, whose God walked and talked with him, as friend to friend, as a brother. We may be brothers after all. We shall see."

"Your proposition seems a just one, and my people will accept it and will retire to the reservation you offer them, and we will dwell apart and in peace, for the words of the great white chief seem to be the voice of nature speaking to my people out of the thick darkness that is fast gathering around them like a dense fog floating inward from a midnight sea. I will sign this paper today for all our people."

When the interpreter was finished the great Chief bowed to his people and then turned from the crowd to the table, picked up the pen, dipped it in an ink well and made an 'X' next to his name on the coarse paper, like a mark etched onto the page by the tip of a sharp knife.

Chief Patkanim of the Snoqualmie and Snohomish Tribes was next, wearing his fold-over breast top coat and flat top hat with tassel, then Chow-its-hoot of the Lummi, who had paddled all the way from his home on Portage Island far to the north, and after him Goliah of the Skagits. In total, eighty-two chiefs, sub-chiefs, headmen and delegates made their way up to the table and scribed their mark on the treaty. As the last of them walked away from the platform and rejoined their people in the crowd, Governor Stevens stood up and quietly thanked them. A polite round of applause and some cheers followed, and it was over, at least on paper. They had an agreement.

With the official activity done, the crowd came alive again with talk and movement, although less excited than before. Peter watched Governor Stevens gather up the signed treaty and begin to walk away. Thinking he was probably headed for the steamer, Peter ran through the crowd to him.

"*Monsieur* Stevens!" Peter said, catching his breath, trying to get the governor's attention. But when he got close, two of his aides stepped in front of him, blocking his way. "*Monsieur!*" Peter exclaimed, "I own Tulalip Bay! I have a homestead claim there and have built a sawmill!"

Stevens turned around at the mention of Tulalip Bay and, taking a moment to size Peter up, motioned for his aides to let him approach.

"Yes," he said, "and your name is?"

Peter doffed his knit hat and answered, "My name is Peter Goutre, sir, and I filed a legal homestead claim on Tulalip Bay two years ago. I have built a home and sawmill there with my partners."

"Are your partners here today?" Stevens asked, looking over his shoulder.

"One of them is. We have all worked very hard to build the mill and have many orders for lumber and that lumber is helping build and settle this frontier. We are needed."

"Well, you and your partners can rest assured that the federal government will appraise your claims and pay you fairly for the land and improvements."

"I will need full compensation, *monsieur*," Peter replied in earnest.

"As I just said, Mr. Goutre, rest assured, the government will compensate you at a fair and equitable rate. Now if you'll excuse me—"

"But what do my partners and I do for now? Can we keep working our mill until we are compensated?" Peter asked. Stevens gave him a stern look.

"Mr. Goutre, you will need to make plans to move. The Indians are going to own Tulalip. We'll contact you soon after the treaty is ratified by Congress. Now if you'll excuse me, my assistant and I need to work on the next treaty for Point No Point. Good day," Stevens said, turning around and walking away before Peter could respond.

Peter stood and watched him walk down the beach and get into a rowboat, then he turned around and walked back to his friends, but only Isaac Ebey was waiting for him.

"I still cannot believe this," Peter said to Isaac, shaking his head.

"I thought I'd give you a moment alone with the governor," he replied. "You see, you may be giving up your claim but think of all the land that these tribes are giving up. Everything from the eastern shore of Puget Sound from the Duwamish to the 49th parallel. That's got to be about five-million acres."

Peter stroked his beard and pondered his situation. "Stevens said something about the tribes moving to their reservations in a year. Did I hear that right?"

"One year from when Congress ratifies the treaty, not one year from now," Isaac answered. They started walking back to his camp.

"So how long before you think that will happen?" Peter asked.

"Hard to say my friend. But the way Congress operates these days, I don't think anything will happen for a while. They're all working on the coinage act right now, taking most of the silver out of our money."

Jake and George were already sitting at the campfire when they came up, eating plates of commissary food.

"This is great!" George said, his mouth full of elk meat and pointing at his plate with his fork. "You should get some."

"No thanks, I'm not hungry after all that," Peter remarked, sitting down. He glanced over at Jake, who was shoveling food into his mouth so rapidly that half of it had wound up in his beard.

"Well," George said, "that went better than I expected. I thought there'd be more protesting from the Lower Skagit."

"Yes, I thought the same thing," Isaac agreed, picking up his mug and pouring himself some coffee. "Anyone else?"

Peter and the two other men shook their heads just when a black Labrador puppy ran over to their camp. Its owner, Keokuk, quickly followed and picked it up.

"Keokuk! *Klahowya!*" Peter said.

"*Stu-hy,*" Keokuk replied, smiling. "*Klahowya.*"

"Keokuk built one of my canoes," Peter said to his friends, then he asked, "*Me-si'-ka kam'-ooks?*"

"*Ah-ha*," Keokuk answered, nodding, holding the pup against his chest, petting it.

Then Isaac started speaking in broken Lushootseed with Keokuk. After the conversation was done Isaac looked at George and then at Peter.

"Both of those puppies need a home. The family can't keep them. We've already got Rover but do you think you might?" Isaac asked, looking at his cousin.

"Oh gosh no," George answered. "I don't need a puppy to take care of."

"I'll take a puppy," Peter suddenly said, popping up from the ground. Everyone turned their heads.

"You want a puppy?" Jake asked, looking surprised.

"*Oui*, he will be a great companion!"

"Okay then," Isaac said, "let's go over and get you one."

The two men went over to their camp and Isaac introduced himself to Keokuk and his beautiful wife, who was sitting cross-legged on some beaver pelts with an HBC blanket wrapped around her next to the fire holding their baby. "Her name is Takua," Isaac said to Peter.

"*Klahowya*," Peter said, nodding at her with a smile. Isaac then spoke with the family as Peter looked on. After he was done,

Keokuk picked up a puppy and walked over to Peter and held it out, then he did the same with the other.

"They want you to choose one," Isaac relayed. Peter noticed that one was sleepy-eyed and lethargic, the other bright-eyed and restless, moving around in Keokuk's hands.

"I'll take this one," Peter said, reaching for the energetic pup. When Peter's hands touched the soft warm fur of the dog a jolt of energy shot through him that went straight to his heart.

"*Merci monami*," Peter gushed. "I will take excellent care of him, I promise." He accepted the pup and held it close to himself. Then Peter bowed to the family, smiled, took two steps backwards and returned to Isaac and George's camp. Peter held the puppy high in the air as he approached.

"Take a look at *le bébé-phoque*," he said to Jake.

"Why on this good earth would you want a dog? What're ya' gonna feed him?" he observed. "Huh? That things gotta eat you know! And when he runs away what're you gonna do to get him to come to ya'? Youse is gonna have to train him and give him a name too!"

Peter thought about his questions and knew right away he could train the dog and that table scraps and deer bones would keep him fed, but his young Lab needed a special name, one that meant something, a name that would be important to him and his life. When the memory of Little Rain and their short life on the Stikine loomed large in his mind. *I could call him Little Rain, but that's not really a name for a male puppy. I know . . . I'll name him after John McLoughlin. I never had any quarrels with him like the other men did. That's it, I'll name him John.*

"I will call him, John," Peter proclaimed. But Jake burst out laughing.

"John?! What kind of a name is that? John Gould ain't gonna like it," he said, slapping his thigh.

"I'm not naming him for John Gould, you old fool. I'm naming him in memory of Mr. John who ran Fort Stikine. John McLoughlin Jr."

"Alright, okay," Jake replied. "I shouldn't have laughed. John would be a fine name."

"He's the one who was killed by his men up there, right?" Isaac asked.

"*Oui,* I heard they did. I knew him and we got along fine," Peter said, looking away.

"Well, it's a good name. I like it," Isaac acknowledged.

"I think it's time we started back," Jehiel suggested, gazing up at the darkening sky.

"Yes, it's getting late," Peter said. Isaac walked with Peter down to the beach to see him off while Jake held back and talked with George for a moment.

"I'm planning on raising a militia for the county district in my area and putting myself forward for the colonel's position. Would you consider volunteering for your part of the county if we form a district here? That is, if there's trouble and you're needed?" Isaac asked.

270

Peter was honored by his request. It made him feel part of this new country and proud to be asked. He didn't hesitate.

"I care about this territory, so I will volunteer for you, if needed, *Monsieur* Ebey!" Peter proudly answered, holding his pup close to his chest and saluting with his free right hand.

"Excellent!" Isaac replied. "I was hoping you'd agree. Thank you."

"It would be my distinct privilege to stand with you. It was good to see you again, and I hope to see you soon. *Au revoir*, Isaac," Peter offered, doffing his knit cap then bowing slightly. Isaac smiled a bright and wide smile just as Jake walked up.

"God's speed . . . Peter Goutre," Isaac said, finishing their conversation and looking him square in the eye, stepping towards him. Both men shook hands with gratitude and respect for each other.

"And Jehiel," Isaac said, "glad to see that you're doing well. I'm going to be raising a militia soon and I'll need all the men I can get."

"Pah, no militia for me," Jake grumbled, shaking his head. "Why would I join some rag-tag army and then fight for a government that just stole my property!" Spitting in the dirt, Jake spun on his heel and marched off before Isaac, dumb-founded, could reply.

Trying to hide his laughter, Peter followed, they made their way down the beach in search of their canoe amongst the hundreds of others. Once found, Peter set his new pup on the floor of the bark. His dog immediately started sniffing and whimpering, putting its front paws up on the sides of the canoe.

Right after they pushed off and had paddled away, Jake said, "I ain't never fightin' fer' this country, not now, not after this! Take my land and cabin, will they! Well to hell with 'em! Just what are we supposed to do anyway?"

"That's what I asked Governor Stevens and he said we need to make plans to move. But I don't think we should move until the government buys our claims, be sure about that. Besides, I thought you liked the idea of being paid off?"

"Make plans to move? Ha! Get paid off? Ha! That'll be the day. I'm not moving a single teeny tiny inch until I get my money. And I suggest we all do the same!" Jake fumed.

Peter didn't reply. The two men were mostly silent during the trip home but Peter kept thinking about the future, what it would hold and where he would go. Halfway home he looked over at Gedney Island, in the middle of Possession Sound, and thought to himself, *I bet the government wouldn't care about that place.*

"Hey Jake, what about Gedney Island? It might be a good place to homestead!"

"Homestead on Gedney?" he replied, then stopped paddling and looked at Peter. "Why?"

"Well, why not?" Peter answered. "It'd be the same as living on the mainland and we'd have the whole place to ourselves. It'd be like owning our own country. So why not?"

"Well, I could see it if you had a woman or a partner to help with things."

"You could homestead the other half!"

272

"No thanks, too small and probably no fresh water over there. Once we get paid off, I think I'll head over to Whidbey. Stake another claim."

"But I hear that there's not so much good farming ground left on Whidbey."

"Pah! Whidbey Island's huge! I don't need that much ground for my livestock and vegetables. Plus, I'll be a whole lot closer to getting supplies."

"Okay, but Gedney might just suit me fine, that is, once I pull up stakes at Tulalip."

XX

Colonel Ebey
T'kope Hyas
August 1857

Peter was carrying an armload of freshly-cut lumber from the mill when he looked down at the log pond, someone in a canoe had just paddled into the inlet. He added his load to a pile outside in the yard and wondered if it was a customer coming over from Whidbey or down from Camano. Then the man in the boat stopped paddling and waved.

"Is that you Peter?" the fellow called out.

"Yes, it is," he hollered back, staring at the dugout with a hand above his brow to shadow the glare of the afternoon sun. "Who do I have the pleasure of addressing?"

"It's George Beam! From Whidbey!"

"*Bonjour*, George!" Peter yelled, happy to see him since his last trip to Penn Cove for supplies and mail months before. But George didn't reply. Peter watched as he landed and then waited for him to climb the bank trail up to the mill building.

"Peter," George said, sweating profusely from his trip and breathing hard. He took off his wide-brimmed hat and looked at Peter, sadness was in his eyes and he seemed to be shaking.

275

George pulled a handkerchief from his back pocket and wiped his brow.

"I wasn't sure if you'd be here, what with the reservation and all," George said, looking tired.

"Just like I mentioned to you back in May, we're still here and we've got orders to fill," Peter replied.

"Well, I'm glad you're here. Can we go and sit in the shade? Have you some water?"

"Yes, of course. What brings you all this way?" Peter asked, leading him inside the noisy mill. His dog John was over two-years old now, he sat up from his afternoon snooze on his blanket and looked at the new person. He got up and bounded over to him, sniffed the new fellow and then jumped up on him with his front paws, his tail wagging vigorously.

"Down Mr. John," Peter said, pushing him away, "Go lie down," and pointed at his blanket snapping his fingers. John returned to his spot and laid down.

"So, that's the same pup you got at the treaty signing that day?" George asked, looking at his dog.

"It is. Charlie! John! Shut it down," Peter hollered, "George Beam is here from Whidbey." Peter went to the water pail, picked it up by its handle and carried it over to George. He dipped the ladle in the water and handed it to him.

"Thank you," George said, drinking.

Peter pointed at some hand-made stools against a wall, saying,

"Let's go sit down."

"It's good to see you again," Charlie said, walking over and sitting on a stool. George wiped his face with the handkerchief and nodded a hello. "Good to see you too."

"George, meet my other partner, John Gould," Peter offered, pulling up a seat.

George nodded again then looked at the floor for a few moments. Finally, he raised his eyes to the rafters, then looked at Peter. His puffy, unshaven face was pale and his shoulders were hanging heavy.

"Have you heard the news?" he asked. They looked at him blank-faced and shrugged their shoulders. "So, uh, I don't really know how to say this but, well . . . Isaac Ebey is dead."

"Our Isaac? Dead?!" Peter exclaimed, looking into George's eyes. "How can that be?"

George leaned over and dipped the ladle again, then drank. He set the ladle back in the pail, raised his head and pushed back his shoulders to straighten his back, and then bent forward. He put his hands on his knees and shook his head.

"Indian raiders came down from the north, shot him, right in front of his cabin," he said at the floor.

"Haidas!" Peter cried, instantly going back in time to his loss of Little Rain fifteen years before. He jumped up and paced the floor with his hands on his hips, mumbling to himself in French.

"Why on God's green earth would the Haidas kill Colonel Ebey?"

Charlie asked, looking to George for answers. "We've got a treaty, all this is supposed to be over." Peter stopped pacing and sat down on his stool again.

"We're not sure if it was the Haidas," George said, looking up. His eyes now a touch watery. "Some think it was Tlingits in revenge for the two dozen of them that were killed by the *Massachusetts* over at Port Gamble last year."

"Tlingits?!" Peter snapped. "The Tlingits would have never done such a thing. It must have been the Haida!"

"There's been a lot of conjecture about that," George said, looking at Peter, "and we believe that the killing of a Tlingit Chief at Port Gamble was the motivation for them taking Isaac's life. Most believe it was done by the Kake."

Peter's mind raced with the past news of the Port Gamble trouble, he tried to remember what he'd been told at the time a year before. "Kake? I think they're a Tlingit clan," Peter replied, rubbing his chin. Then he thought about Isaac's family.

"What about his family? Are they —"

"The family's fine, they escaped out the rear window and into the forest," George answered. "They're safe with Isaac's parents and his brother, Winfield."

"They really killed him at his cabin?" John asked.

"Right in his own yard," George responded, "but that's not all." He paused for a moment and took another drink of water then looked up at the rafters again. "They shot him four times and killed him . . . and then they beheaded him."

278

"NO!" Peter screamed, standing up so fast that his stool fell over backwards. "They cut off his head?! Oh, no, no, no. This cannot be," he yelled. Peter crossed himself then placed his hands in prayer and closed his eyes.

George said, "The whole community has been stricken with grief for the last week and we are lost without him." He stared at the floor shaking his head while Peter dropped down on his knees and started to quietly pray. John stood up with a sigh and walked outside. Charlie dropped his head down into his hands and mumbled to himself. A moment later John came back with a bottle, he took a drink and handed it to George.

"But why would they kill Isaac?" John asked. "He didn't have anything to do with that Port Gamble mess."

"I know, I know," George answered, taking a swig of corn liquor. "Isaac had nothing to do with Port Gamble. From what Winfield has been able to determine the Kake were looking for a white Tyee to kill. You see, they lost over two-dozen warriors at Port Gamble plus their chief. In their thinking, it's an eye for an eye, and a life for a life."

When Peter heard George's comment he slowly stood up and walked back over to the group.

"*Pro Pelle Cutem*," Peter said, nodding his head and righting his stool.

"And what's that supposed to mean?" John asked.

"It's the Hudson's Bay motto," Peter replied. He sat back down and stared at him, and somberly said, "It means a skin for a skin."

"But why Isaac?" Charlie asked, before his two partners got into an argument. George took another drink and handed him the bottle.

"Well, Winfield claims that they'd heard about Dr. Kellogg and wanted to kill him. You see, a white doctor is like a shaman or witch doctor to them. Someone with healing power is big medicine in their world. We got a report that they went looking for him but he was away in his canoe tending to patients and they were determined to take their revenge out on a white Tyee."

"So, they paddled north, up the island from Kellogg's place and stopped at Ebey's Landing. They walked up to his cabin that very afternoon asking about buying provisions, you know, flour and sugar and such, but they were being spies, looking around. Isaac refused them and tried to send them off. Then they asked for a hammer and nails to work on what they claimed was a broken dugout. Isaac didn't believe them and told them to leave."

"From what Winfield told me, on their way back to the beach they walked down to Isaac's field where one of his workers was cutting grain, a fine young man by the name of Thomas Hastie, not sure if you know of him, but they asked him if the man in the cabin was the owner of the farm and he said, 'yes.' He didn't think anything of it, and they walked away, of course he had no idea of what they were up to."

"Okay," Peter said, "then what?" He took the bottle from Charlie and had a belt then passed it to George, but he refused and pointed at Charlie. Peter handed him the bottle.

"Well past midnight, Isaac's dog started barking. It woke them up, then they heard shouting and some banging on the door, so Isaac opened it thinking someone probably needed help. Anyway, he opened the door unarmed and stepped out on the porch and they shot at him, grazed him in the side of his head."

"You can't be serious — an old hand like Ebey answered the door at midnight for strangers and didn't even have his gun ready?" Charlie asked, wiping the residue of corn mash from his lips. He handed the jug to George.

"Nope, didn't have a pistol or musket in the house. Winfield thinks that all the guns were gone from the home, but he doesn't know why. Nothing, maybe because he didn't want his children around them. I guess when the shooting started, he stumbled around the corner on the porch and Mrs. Ebey took off the opposite way with the kids out the back window and into the woods. Thank God Almighty they did since the Indians probably would've scalped them too if they had the chance."

"There were three more shots and that was it. They killed him right in his own yard and then cut off his head . . . and they took it."

"*Sacre le bleu!*" Peter exclaimed, jumping up. He threw his knit hat on the floor and started pulling his hair. "*Sauvages!*" he said, walking back and forth. "*Is ne sont pas comme les Indiens que je connais!*"

"They took his head?" John said, standing up and ripping the bottle from George's hand. He took a long pull and then hollered, "Tlingits! I'll kill them all!"

"Tlingits?! You don't know it was them!" Peter yelled back.

"Knock it off, Peter," John hollered.

"The man said this and that, we do not know if it is true!" Peter replied, walking towards him and glaring.

"Hold on here!" Charlie said. "Nobody's gonna kill nobody! The Kake Tlingit ain't a local tribe, John. You two just sit your butts down and take a drink."

John walked back over with the bottle and sat on his stool, took a pull, then held it out for Charlie. The three mill partners looked at George.

"What else?" Charlie asked, taking a belt.

"Before they left, they ransacked the cabin, broke all the windows, and stole the clothing and bedding. Even took the crockery, cut up mattresses, broke open trunks and took everything in them," George related, looking at the floor again. Charlie handed him the bottle and put a hand on his shoulder.

"I'm so sorry for you and the family, George, we all are," Charlie said, his eyes watery and red. "What can we do? All you have to do is ask and we'll do it for you."

"Yes," Peter added, "what can we do for you and the family?"

George looked at Peter and then Charlie, saying, "Thank you, gentlemen, from the bottom of my heart. But there's not much you can do. We've laid him to rest but the community is still mourning and now scared. Some have decided to leave the island, others are building blockhouses to protect their families if there are more attacks."

"The killing of that lieutenant down near the White River last December didn't help," John remarked.

"The problems we have right now with our local Indians has nothing to do with these raiders from the north, John," George spat, taking a drink. "The federal government hasn't ratified the treaties here yet, so that means the Indians are all expecting a lot of money and supplies that haven't arrived. Things are bad and will keep gettin' worse until Congress gets off its ass, there is great frustration right now. They were promised a number of things and our government has not followed through for them."

"What about the militia?" Peter asked.

"Well," George said, scratching the side of his face, "Winfield told me that Marshall Corliss is going to convene a meeting about that soon so we can elect a new colonel. You should come Peter, Isaac thought highly of you." Peter didn't hesitate.

"I'll be there."

"Good," George replied, "it's in a week and a half on Saturday the 29th at 2:00 in the afternoon. When you land just ask anyone you see where it's at and they'll give you directions. We normally meet at Lawrence Grennan's store over at Coveland but I'm not sure. I'll tell you though, if they come back, we'll be ready this time. You know, you boys should consider building yourselves a blockhouse, keep yourself safe if things get worse. More are planned on the island."

The three partners looked at each other, George held out the bottle for someone to take. John did, he took a long pull and wiped his chin with his forearm. "Hell, we don't need to build a blockhouse. We've already got this place, it's built stout," he bragged, then pointed at the floor. "We'll fight off any hostiles right here."

After a pause George stood up. "Well, Isaac felt pretty safe in his house too, so I'll leave you with that . . . I need to start back. I thought it was important to get the news to you, and if you see anyone, please pass the word to be on the lookout for any Northern war canoes. Personally, I have a feeling that they got their white Tyee and things will quiet down, but you never know."

"Give the family and everyone our best, please," Peter said, standing up. "I'll walk you down to the beach."

With that the men shook hands and said their goodbyes. At the door, Peter said, "Come on boy," to Mr. John then took his pocket watch out of his vest, looked at it, turned around and said, "That's it for today. I'm taking the rest of the afternoon off."

Walking down the path with Mr. John in the lead, tail wagging, George said, "Isaac liked you, Peter. He told me when we were paddling home from the treaty signing that day that you'd agreed to volunteer for a militia if one was needed over here."

"He did?"

"Yes, well, it was funny to see him go on about it, but he said you could be our own Lafayette over here on the mainland, and help us like he did with Washington back east. He was pleased to have you available here at Tulalip."

The comment stunned Peter, he stopped in his tracks and felt a tingle go up his spine. He felt blessed to be thought of that way and proud to have known Isaac Ebey. He started walking again.

At the inlet George turned and said, "Of all the settlers for them to grab, Isaac was probably the most important one they could have. He did everything for us, he was our link to the federal government, to the outside world, and I do believe he would have been governor someday. It's a terrible blow to the territory, to say nothing of his family and the community over on Whidbey. But we'll persevere, they won't get rid of us that easily." George stuck out his hand. "It was good to see you again, Peter. Take care of yourself."

"You too, George," Peter replied, shaking his hand. He untied his bowline and they pushed the canoe down to the water's edge where George got in.

"*Au revoir*," Peter said, taking off his knit hat and waving.

George lifted his paddle in between strokes in acknowledgement. Peter walked farther down the beach, sat down on a log and watched with his faithful dog at his side until George was outside of the bay. Peter looked down at Mr. John, he was sitting up with a stick in his mouth.

"Always the fetching," Peter said, taking the piece of driftwood from his dog's mouth and tossing it into the water for his Lab to retrieve.

Later, at sunset, Peter and Mr. John were sitting on the bluff next to Little Rain's totem, looking to the west and watching the sun go down, the distant clouds on the horizon glowing red and orange. He pulled the soapstone marriage stick and string of shells out from under his shirt and crossed himself with the stick, then kissed it. Peter's thoughts turned to when he had first met Isaac at his landing, and meeting his family. He remembered how impressed he was with the man and what he'd accomplished during his time on earth, and wished that Little Rain and him could have had a family like Isaac, then he looked at John, lying next to him, his eyes closed, relaxed and calm. Peter turned back to the sunset. A cloud had partially moved in front of the sun, causing a golden spec of sunlight to shine on the water, he thought back to when Jake and he had left Isaac and were paddling back from the treaty that day. He leveled his eyes on Gedney Island.

"I think it's just about time to pull up stakes, Mr. John," he said, reaching over and petting his dog. "That's the place for us, as long as there's fresh water over there."

That Sunday, the tide was in and the water was flat. Peter tossed a shovel in the canoe and then snapped his fingers and pointed at the boat, looking at Mr. John. He jumped right in.

"Good boy," Peter said, pushing off the canoe. On the way over to Gedney a huge squad of cormorants were floating on the tide, sunning themselves, preening, and generally enjoying a peaceful morning on the water. Right when Mr. John saw them, he stood up and started barking and whining at them, ruining Peter's serene moment.

"*Arrête ca*, My Man! They do not need you barking at them. Leave them alone!"

Mr. John looked at his master and back at the birds, then whined a little more and sat on his haunches, watching them but staying quiet.

When they landed on the northeast point of the island, Mr. John leapt from the dugout and ran around on the beach, happy and free. Peter grabbed his shovel and headed up the shore. Driftwood debris and whole cedar trees, some with their roots systems still intact, lay in a jumbled pile at the high-water mark, all of them stripped of bark and battered by storms. He made his way over and around all the weather-worn logs and found a lovely level stretch of ground covered with natural foliage. Tufts of blue-grey dune grass with three-foot tall blades dotted the landscape interspersed with yellow flowered gumweed and clumps of purple lupine. It was a beautiful sight to behold. At the edge of the meadow the hill of the island rose up, it was covered with fir, hemlock and maple trees.

This looks promising. There's a lifetime's worth of cordwood on the beach and this level area is the perfect spot for a cabin. He called out, "Come on boy!" Mr. John looked up from the backside of a drift log and bolted towards Peter. "That's My Man."

Peter scanned the side of the hill again, there was a ravine that came down from the top of the island. *That looks like a good place to try.*

With the shovel on his shoulder, Peter, and Mr. John walked over to the ravine and then climbed up it through the underbrush. He came upon a swale in the ground with a tiny grove of tree saplings growing. *That low spot looks good.* He started digging.

An hour later he was standing in a three-foot hole with mud in the bottom. He stuck the blade in the uphill side of it, jumped up, landed with both feet on the shovel and then pulled out the blade. A trickle of fresh water flowed out from the bottom.

"Ah, *bien*," Peter said to his dog, who looked at him from the rim of the cavity in happy confusion, "That will do. John, welcome to our new home."

Part Three

XXI

Gedney Island
čəčəs
1859 - 1862

After years of waiting to be paid, and once the treaty was ratified by Congress, the government finally sent assessor Caleb Miller to inspect Peter's claim and the sawmill to determine a value. After a long day of walking all around Skayu Point and seeing the mill, Mr. Miller worked up some figures and handed a sheet of paper to Peter.

"Two-thousand dollars?" Peter asked, his eyes zeroing in on the bottom line.

The appraiser scratched his chin, glanced around the mill, and nodded. "Yep. Two-thousand."

Peter was quiet for a moment, lips shut tight. "And when would I get that?"

"By the power invested in me by Congress and Washington Territory, I can authorize an official voucher certificate now, which you can take to the land office in Olympia and they'll issue you greenback dollars."

"A certificate? You don't have the money on you?"

Miller smirked, "Are you serious? No one with a brain in their head travels through wild territory with money like that or a bunch of gold on 'em. The voucher is guaranteed by the power of the US government."

"But Olympia is a week to travel there in my canoe and a week back, maybe more if the weather turns bad."

"Not my problem. I've made my judgement, and unless you're going to file an appeal then I'll sign it over to you now and we'll shake hands." The appraiser withdrew a sheaf of documents from his tattered worn-out leather satchel, extracted a piece of yellowed parchment, and began writing on it on the bench in the mill he was sitting on. Peter sighed and looked away — he had been there for six years, this was supposed to be it. His final home near Little Rain's spirit, the promised land to the south. And now a stranger was going to give him a piece of paper and that would be it, his cabin and sawmill would all be gone.

"Did you look close enough at all this equipment?"

"Yes Mr. Goo-tray, I've seen everything —"

"I mean REALLY looked at it? We had the machinery brought in from —"

"The United States Government is not interested in your mill or its equipment! I have more traveling today, either you take it," the appraiser had finished writing the certificate, tore it from the parchment, and held it up with one hand, "or I leave and you get the distinct pleasure of taking suit against Uncle Sam . . . Well?"

"And two-thousand dollars is all you're going to give me? For everything?" Peter spat, his blood pressure rising. "One-hundred and sixty acres, my home and the only working sawmill in the area? This is a very successful business, *monsieur*!"

But the appraiser just held the certificate out in the air flimsily, almost as if he was going to drop it on the floor. Peter took off his knit cap and gripped it tightly in his hands. "Everyone else already took the money?"

"Oh yes. Your country cousin, Mr. Hall, actually took it from me before I had finished telling him his rights, told me that I had made him rich for the first time in his life, and danced away. You're the last private citizen at Tulalip."

Peter closed his eyes, breathed out, slowly, and then opened them again. "Okay. I won't fight you, it's yours. Give me a day or two to clear out and I won't cause any trouble."

The appraiser smiled for the first time since he'd arrived, gave Peter the piece of paper, put his documents back in his satchel and doffed his hat. "Thank you for making it easier on yourself. The Indians won't be here for months yet, so you're not under any serious time pressure, but be aware that, if you're still here when they arrive, there may be problems. So, tell me, where're you headed?"

"Where am I headed?"

"Yes, where are you moving to? Do you plan to stake another claim somewhere?"

He wants to know where I'm going next? Why? Is he going to just follow me around the countryside and let me make another claim so he can steal it from me again? Never!

Peter groaned, then looked at the certificate the government agent had just handed him and saw that it was official. He glared at the appraiser and said, "*Non, non, monsieur.* Where I am going you will never find me, no one will."

"Very well then, now if you'll excuse me," the appraiser turned around without waiting for Peter to respond and headed out of the building and down the trail to the log pond, where he jumped in his canoe and paddled away.

Peter watched him move across the water until he vanished, a distant dark dot being swallowed up by the Sound. He stood perfectly still for a long time, just breathing in the cool, sweet air of his surroundings and letting the soft wind gently blow by.

Finally, with long sigh, he smiled, looked down at Mr. John, who had waited very patiently through the whole negotiation, and said, "Well, that's it boy! We're officially homeless, me and you. Of course, you don't know what's going on, but it's a big world, and your man here already has done a good deal of work over at our new home. Come on," Peter ruffled the lab's black head and turned from the bay to walk the long way back to his cabin, "Let's get us some supper and visit Little Rain, then we need to start packing. We've got a lot of work to do."

That evening at sunset, Peter and Mr. John hiked up to Little Rain's totem. As they approached his dog stopped and started growling, there were three ravens standing on her arms and another dozen or so on the limbs of the trees surrounding her, bobbing their heads and softly cackling to each other.

"Would you look at that," Peter said, petting a still growling Mr. John. "It's alright, boy. They're friends."

Then he noticed something new: multiple necklaces of shell and blue glass trade bead jewelry covered Little Rain's arms and were hanging from her neck. Bits of prized pinto abalone shell tied to sinew and deer hide were draped over her hands and, around the lower circumference of the main upright a thick, multilayered skirt of cattail and bulrush reeds had been fastened, a mountain of clam shells, rocks, and dried starfish were piled up at the base. On top, her eyes had been carved out and black obsidian was placed in the sockets. Peter's wig of hemp rope was now decorated with a raven feathered headdress that hung down to her cross piece, providing the finishing touches to what was now, Little Rain's monument.

Peter was shocked and stood frozen for some time, considering the possibilities, and when he finally exhaled and began breathing again, he felt his heart beating more smoothly and calmly than it had in a long, long time. The Natives had been there, many times it looked like, and they'd been paying tribute as well. Peter stood with his hands at his side as a visceral organic feeling welled up through his soul because Little Rain had been accepted by the ancients. He instantly took the potlatch necklace that Chief Patkanim had given him from around his neck and hung it on Little Rain's left hand, offering the spiritual adornment to her as a goodbye gift for now.

Days later, Peter had tied a tow line between his two canoes and lashed the last load of his share of lumber from the sawmill into the twelve-foot dugout. He had his leather rucksack in the larger bark: it held two canning jars that he'd gotten in Penn Cove on his last supply trip, one was full of French gold and the other had the government certificate folded up in it. He got his now four-year-old Lab into the canoe then pushed them off and hopped in. It took him a good number of paddle strokes before he could get both of them to move, but once he got some momentum going, he was able to make good time towing his last load out to Gedney Island.

When he landed on the northeast shore, Mr. John bounded out from the dugout onto the beach like he always did and started running up and down the shoreline, barking at birds and waterfowl, wagging his tail proudly as he sauntered, immediately letting everything in sight know that he was the master of the place.

Peter threw his rucksack over his shoulder and headed up the beach with a bucket in his hand, walking over, around, and past shanks of driftwood. At the level area he stopped, turned around and took in the view — to the north he could see the enormous, glacier encrusted volcano — old Koma Kulshan. And from it a string of jagged, snowcapped peaks that ran to the south and east, culminating in the enormous, pyramid-shaped peak the Snohomish called Red Water. It was glorious. Peter smiled a smile so wide it made his face hurt. Mr. John ran over to him.

"It's ours boy, all ours," Peter quietly said to his faithful companion, petting him on the head. He turned around and strolled over to the base of the hill at the ravine then looked up the trail he'd opened up over the last year.

"Let's go," Peter said, and they both started climbing, Mr. John leaping and bounding about the trail in front of him. A short way up the path they came to the fresh water cistern that Peter had been building, he'd lined the walls with large beach rocks and built a lean-to over it with driftwood to keep falling leaves and tree sprigs out of it. Peter dipped his bucket into the clear, fresh water and set it in front of his dog. Mr. John lapped it up.

They continued up the way. At the northern top of the island was a large plateau, with a grove of wind-swept cedars and hemlock. At the edge of the hill near the trail was an enormous old-growth western red cedar, its large claw-like roots fanning out into the black earth at the bottom. He got down on his knees and took a small hand spade out of the rucksack.

Using his spade he peeled back the thick, carpet-like moss that covered two roots and folded it over to the side. Then he dug a deep hole between them and put the two watertight canning jars with all his gold and valuables in it. Peter covered the jars with dirt and carefully placed the moss back over the roots then stood up and nodded with satisfaction at his work. *Nobody will ever find that.*

Next, Peter walked south, away from his hiding spot and kicked his heel into the ground, upturning a small piece of ground. He got down on his knees, pulled the moss and duff back exposing the rich, black, moist soil beneath. Peter dug at the earth with his fingers, lifted a handful up to his face and breathed in the aroma of the healthy loam through his nostrils, his dog at his side.

"Ah, perfect," he said, then he looked at Mr. John and added, "There's too much sand and salt down below. This is where we'll plant our garden and orchard."

For most of the day Peter unloaded his canoes, exhausting bundle by exhausting bundle of the last lumber that had been cut at their mill. Then he built a crude lean-to out of driftwood and lumber at the top of the beach where he stowed his guns and various tools, the sacks of corn meal, salt and sugar, flour, pounds of salted venison, as well as cured bacon and coffee that represented enough food to cook over a beach fire to keep both of them alive for months yet. That evening he pulled the smaller canoe farther up the shoreline to a sandy spot where he tipped it over for Mr. John and him to sleep under.

During the next two months, Peter traveled to Olympia to collect his greenbacks from the land office, filed for citizenship, and mailed a livestock and supply order to the PSAC, then, once home, he worked around the clock to get ready for winter. First, on the level area back from the edge of the beach, he built a stout post and beam foundation with rough-cut dimension lumber from the mill and then nailed down a floor. For the walls he downed young cedar trees and left an opening for a window that looked out to the Sound, and for the roof he used more of his lumber. By the first of August, he'd built a small but sturdy home where he could see the water and the mountains to the east.

He built two paddocks up at the garden area, one very large and one small. For the large one he cut small trees to use for posts, planting them in between still standing trees, he nailed lumber cross pieces from post to tree to post for rails. Then he built a chicken coop, and finally started in on a woodshed and outhouse near his cabin.

A month later, on a sunny day in mid-September the low rumble of steam-driven pistons moved across Possession Sound. Peter drove a nail in his outhouse roof and turned his gaze to the south: a steamship was coming up the island.

"Look-it, boy, look-it!' Peter cried, pointing out to the water for Mr. John's benefit. "I know that ship! It's the *Otter* with our livestock!"

He crawled down from his outhouse roof and ran to the beach, waving at the Hudson's Bay steamer. The captain immediately blasted his loud whistle and Mr. John, running after him, began barking. As it slowly approached the shore, two deckhands started to ready the extralong gangplank, and the captain waved from his pilothouse.

"Good to see you!" Peter hollered, waving his greasy old knit cap in the air.

"You the one that ordered these cows?" one of the deckhands yelled, motioning at four calves, tied to the deck rail.

"*Oui, monami,*" Peter replied just as the captain had the engineer to go into reverse, causing the side paddles to churn up the water, stopping the vessel with its bow close to shore. The captain stuck his head out of the pilothouse window.

"I guess you'd be Peter Goo-tray?"

"That I am," Peter answered, putting his hat back on. The captain disappeared back into the pilothouse, then his head re-emerged in the window, a long-left arm following with a sheet of crumpled paper clenched in his hand.

"Says here I've got, two piglets, one sow and one boar, two Hereford beef cattle, little ones you can breed and two Jersey milk calves, same deal, and a dozen chickens for you. That right?"

"*Oui Capitaine*! And *monami,* you should have a Bailey cook-

299

stove and more! A glass window, plus flour, salt, sugar, yeast and two barrels of feed, one for the chickens and barley for the little piggies. And apple and vegetable seed for next spring, *oui*?"

"Yes, yes, I believe we do. Alright, so, it says here that you already paid half deposit, which means you still owe me one-hundred and fifteen dollars, and that includes our shipping charge."

"I will go get it right now! Oh, do you take dollars or gold?"

"No gold? None, my friend, only dollars. Guaranteed by the US government, redeemable at —"

"Okay, I'll be right back."

"Fine, sure, bring 'em here and we'll sign it all over."

Peter ran away towards his cabin with Mr. John close behind. He scurried up the hill, out of sight, to the upper plateau and his hiding place. Once there, he curled the moss over at the base of the cedar tree, dug out the dirt with his fingers and found his money jars while his dog started to dig a hole next to him. Peter spun open the lid of the greenback jar, inside were his dollars from selling Tulalip Bay to the government. He counted out the money owed, then returned the jar to its hiding place and carefully covered it with dirt and then the carpet of moss.

"Come on boy," Peter said, heading back down to the beach. Mr. John looked up from his diggings and followed.

While he was gone the deckhands had off-loaded everything and piled up his goods along the shore: his square four-pane window was leaned up against a drift log, two small casks of flour, his Baily cast iron cookstove, a beaten-up cage full to bursting with screaming chickens and his calves were tethered to drift log. The deckhands were waiting for him on the beach but the piglets were still onboard.

"Here you are," Peter said, walking up to them. Both were dressed in company garb, hickory shirts, tan trousers and brogan boots. He counted out the money and handed it to one with a swarthy complexion.

"Okay, so, um, them piglets," the dark-skinned one said, "we've got 'em harnessed with bridles but they're pretty slippery."

"Ah, *monami*, not to worry. I will handle them. But I do need a hand with that stove. Could you help me carry it over to my house, *si'l vous plait*?" Peter asked, clasping his hands together at his chest with his head slightly bowed.

They both turned to look at the captain. One of them yelled, "He wants us to help him carry the cookstove," pointing at it. The captain stuck his arm out the window and motioned at them with a flip of his hand.

"Ah, *bien, merci*," Peter said, walking over to where it was. The two men followed and they carried the heavy stove up the beach through the driftwood and over to the cabin while Mr. John followed. Once there they set it down.

"You live out here all by yer' lonesome?" one asked, trying to catch his breath.

"Yes. Mr. John and me," Peter said, reaching down and petting his dog.

"Okay, so, where do ya' want the stove?"

"Right here, in the house."

"House? This?" The man laughed and winked to his comrade, who began laughing as well. "This shed lookin-thing? You live here? In that?"

Peter's cheerful attitude disappeared, he glared at the fellow with a sour look on his face and seethed, "I left the Hudson's Bay Company because of assholes like you."

"Oh, sorry mister, I've just never —"

"Sorry mister? Ha! You'll never see the inside of my home, not ever, not after insulting me like that. Get off my island! Now!" Peter snarled.

"But what about your pigs?"

"I'll get them myself," Peter grunted and stormed down to the beach and the sidewheeler. Just then the captain blasted his steam whistle.

"Don't forget yer' piggies!" the captain hollered out his pilot house window.

"Oh, don't worry about my livestock! You should worry more about your employees and teach them how to respect customers — I'd fire all of you if it was up to me!"

Peter ran up the gangway to his piglets with a scowl and quickly untied them, both of them squealing and snorting. He led the two little ones down the ramp and a few steps up the beach. The two deckhands walked by him with their heads down and onto the steamer. Peter watched as the gangplank was raised and then lowered onto the vessel's side deck then he walked his pigs over to the rest of his livestock while Mr. John followed, growling and barking, not sure what to do about these new animals. Peter turned around to him and tried, with his blood boiling, to calm him down, "They will be living here with us, My Man, so you better get used to them. But those men from Hudson's Bay, we'll never see them again, *le connards*."

The steamer's side paddles began to slap the water as it backed up. They stopped for a moment, then they started slapping again as it turned forward and to the north, its tall black chimney belching thick smoke.

For the rest of the day Peter led each animal up the well-worn trail one-by-one, securing the cattle in the large paddock and the piglets in the other.

That evening Mr. John and Peter sat on the beach and watched as Koma Kulshan to the northeast glowed pink from the sunset. As he gazed at the majesty of the other peaks to the east, he contemplated the magnificence of the mountains and reflected on his past — his childhood in Montreal, his travels west, his work as a fur-trader and life at sea, and he felt that, without a doubt, his time with Little Rain was the best time of his life, and he thought . . . *She would have loved this place.*

Long thin curls of wood spun out from the blade of the jack plane and dropped to the sandy ground in front of the cabin, Peter was trying his hand at building a new door. The ad-hoc one that he'd built from rough-cut mill lumber sufficed, but it wasn't square, didn't close well, and had a gap at the floor wide enough for a rock crab to scurry through. Wiping the sweat from his brow he looked up, a square-rigged top sail schooner appeared out on the water. Peter stopped working and set the plane down.

He'd come to love the grace and beauty of the tall ships after spending so many years as a sailor, and this one caught his fancy. Gliding across the smooth water of a high tide, the fore-and-aft rigged white hulled ship with its black bowsprit and spars cut a fine image on a fine afternoon. Peter watched in wistful contentment as it cut across the Sound towards Tulalip Bay.

"Would you look at that," he said to Mr. John, sitting in the sandy dirt next to his sawhorses. "Maybe we should go take a closer look for fun. We've worked enough on this thing today and I don't know if it will ever get done, let's take a break. Come on boy!" he said to his faithful companion.

Peter headed for his smaller, swift canoe and his dog followed. He snapped his fingers at the dugout and Mr. John jumped in, Peter pushed them off.

When they got close the name on the ship's stern could be seen, it was the 160-ton *Jefferson Davis*, an armed customs service cutter.

"Maybe there's some commotion on the reservation," Peter said to his dog, standing on his hind legs with his front paws on the canoe rail. Mr. John barked at the big ship and then looked back proudly at his master. "You tell 'em, My Man!"

They watched as the schooner slowly slipped into Tulalip on the high tide with just enough water to get through the entrance. When it was in the center of the bay the great anchor was dropped and Peter paddled over near it.

There were a few sailors standing at the starboard rail with an eye on him. One of them called out.

"State your business!"

"I used to own this place and ran the mill over behind you!" Peter hollered, "I live across the way on that island now."

"You're gonna need to move along, mister," he replied.

"Alright, okay! Why are you here?"

"We're here with a detachment of troops to supervise the disposition of supplies to the Indians!"

Peter nodded and held up his paddle in acknowledgement, but didn't paddle away. He stayed for a minute, just watching the ship float gloriously on the water. Then, with a sigh, he turned the canoe around. "How about we stop by and see Little Rain," Peter said to Mr. John, his front paws up on the bow again, tail wagging. He turned around to see his master with his tongue hanging out and then lifted his head and barked at the world.

Once around the point and down at the sandy beach Peter looked up and there she was, standing tall and looking out over the Sound. The afternoon sun blazed down on her, and the abalone and glass bead jewelry she'd been given sparkled dazzlingly in the sunshine. She looked like a goddess draped in strings of diamonds.

For a few wonderful warm moments, Peter and John floated on the tide, basking in the pleasant countenance of Little Rain high on the bluff. As they drifted, Peter couldn't help but miss her gentle temperament, her graceful small frame and bronze skin, the dimple on her chin. He smiled a loving smile of remembrance as he gazed upward at her and in that trice of time, he realized that she had become something lofty and magnificent. The simple totem that he'd carved from a blown-down cedar tree years before, which then became a monument adorned in high regalia, had transformed into a symbol, an image, a glorious shimmering statue, and for him, she was now; the Princess of Possession Sound.

XXII

Fowler & Frost
Chako Mahkook
Fall 1862

In the years that followed Isaac Ebey's death, Peter continued to paddle north to Penn Cove for his mail and supplies and maybe visit with the few acquaintances he'd come to know. But after Peter's move to Gedney Island he decided to go to Point Elliot for his provisions, as it was much closer.

On his first trip he filled his canoe with woven baskets, ready to be filled with winter supplies. With every other stroke of his paddle, he'd tap the side rail of his slender wooden boat to keep a sense of rhythm and ward off any up-heaving orca whales surfacing from feeding on salmon, while Mr. John kept watch.

To the east, about a mile south of the Snohomish River, he noticed a new plume of smoke rising up from the trees just up the hill near the edge of the water. "*Incroyable*! More settlers coming to the area! You watch Mr. John, they'll ruin the whole country before you know it," Peter complained. He kept glancing at the smoke between paddle strokes and thought he saw a tiny spec on the water. *Is that a canoe?*

As Peter got closer to the outpost, he grinned at the sight of seeing so many Natives on the beach. It reminded him of the old days.

Once his canoe hit the shore he stepped from his dugout and some of the Tulalip men recognized him, calling out, "*Stu-hy!*"

Peter raised a hand to acknowledge them as Mr. John jumped out to chase shorebirds. The Natives sat in groups waiting for the tide to change as young girls played with hand-carved wooden dolls and mothers knitted socks. Peter smiled, knowing they were now fully moved out to the reservation and that the government was finally starting to make good on their promises.

Along the crest of the beach, a smattering of wooden structures dribbled along the bank, looking defiant, some of them already turning grey from the weather, all with pitched roofs of cedar. One stood tall against the gusts of the bay, its hastily installed glass windows rattling in the wind; the good-sized building battling the elements. Next to it another frame building rested comfortably above the highwater mark.

Peter grabbed onto the tangled bowline and tossed it onto the shore, then found the end and walked up the ebbing beach, scrunching over the smooth round rocks while shaking the line to pull it free from its entanglement. He looped it around the end of a beach log, stepped through the cutout log path and went over to the smaller structure. Mr. John ran up just as he did. On the porch Peter snapped his fingers and pointed at the wooden planking, his dog plopped down.

Inside, the air was a mixture of stale pipe smoke and the pleasant aroma of the daily meal. A few locals sat at tables and turned their heads when the door opened, they were nursing mugs of coffee, the low hum of palaver and gossip hung in the air.

"Good afternoon," the clean-shaven man behind the bar said. "How can I help you?" He looked to be in his mid-twenties, of medium height and had a white apron wrapped around his waist.

"Here to stock my winter larder," Peter replied, looking around.

"Welcome to the Exchange Saloon and Hotel, the finest purveyor of libations and rooms on the Sound! I'm the proprietor, Jacob Fowler, pleased to meetcha'. You can get all your winter goods in the building next door. Are you new to the area?" he asked with a jaunty smile, sticking out his hand.

"Peter Goutre's the name — I settled in the area just when Pierce got himself inaugurated, but I'll admit this is the first time I've been down here for supplies," Peter said, shaking hands. He tilted his head and stared at Jacob. After a moment he said, "You look familiar, have I seen you before?"

"Maybe so, my wife Mary and I operated a tavern and trading post over on Whidbey at Ebey's Landing prior to this."

"Ah, I've probably seen you up at Coupeville or Coveland then, maybe. I'm friends with George Beam and used to go there for my supplies. I owned part of Tulalip Bay before the reservation and now I'm over on Gedney Island, gonna file a claim soon."

"Peter Goutre, Peter Goutre . . . Say, you're not French Peter, are ya'?"

"French Peter?"

"Yeah. Everyone calls you French Peter, right?"

"Well, yes, but my friends don't call me that."

"Then that's you all right! Not many French around here, the men have talked about you. Why I heard you were one of the first to settle these parts," Jacob said, smiling. He wiped his hands off on his apron and pulled a bottle and shot glass out from under the bar. He filled the jigger with whiskey and pushed it in front of Peter.

"This one's on the house. Jehiel Hall told me when we first opened up that you helped start the sawmill out at Tulalip with French gold," Jacob said, grinning and running his fingers through his dark hair. Peter winched at the word 'gold' and glanced at the brown liquor, then at Jacob.

"Well, um, the gold's all gone, spent it on tools and supplies, but you know George, huh, and Jehiel?"

"Oh, yes. Known George for years, he's over on Protection Island now, and Jehiel told Morris just last fall that he was on his way to Seattle. I heard all about how you used to be a trader for Hudson's Bay and how you were here at the treaty signing and about the government buying you out so the Indians could have their reservation. All that." Jacob talked so fast it made Peter a little nervous.

"George is a good man," Peter replied, drinking the shot. "How's he doing?"

"Fine, as far as I know."

"But Jehiel told me he was headed to Whidbey to stake a new claim."

"Yeah, well," Jacob grinned, "I guess if he told Morris he was going to Seattle and you that he was going to Whidbey then that must mean he was headed to Olympia! He's a slippery one I tell ya'."

Just then the door opened and an older man with a grey beard and thick eyebrows wearing a white shirt and black tie walked in. Jacob motioned him over.

"Morris, this is French Peter," Jacob said, introducing him. "Peter, this is my partner, Morris Frost. Morris here handles the books but since I'm busy with customers he can help you next door."

"Happy to help and good to meet you, Peter," Morris said in a deep, gravelly voice.

"Morris," Peter replied, nodding.

"Peter's here to stock his winter larder," Jacob mentioned.

"Yes," Peter added. "The basic things you see: flour, sugar, salt, yeast, coffee, whiskey. I've got a list."

"How about some salted pork?" Morris suggested. "We've got lots of that right now, plus we have plenty of fresh huckleberries."

"Ah! I could make some pemmican!"

"The Tulalips just brought in five huge baskets of them today," Morris remarked. "Come on over and we'll get you some."

Peter touched the top of the shot glass and Jacob poured him another dram. He downed the shot and then set a quarter dollar piece on the bar.

Jacob swiped up the quarter and slapped down a dime, Peter picked it up. "*Merci*, Jacob," Peter said, nodding, then followed Morris towards the door.

311

"And if you've got anything to mail," Jacob added, "we've got a post office too, so we're on the route now."

"Very good! Put me on your general delivery list," Peter remarked, raising a hand in acknowledgement. "*Au revoir*!"

Mr. John got to his feet when Peter stepped from the Exchange and then tagged along behind the two men as they made their way next door. Once there, Peter snapped his fingers and pointed at the porch flooring again. His dog laid down and curled up, the tip of its tail faintly wagging.

"Good looking pup you got there," Morris remarked, opening the door of his business.

"Yes, I got him on Treaty Day. Mr. John is a fine companion."

"Mr. John?" Morris asked, walking inside and then closing the door behind Peter.

"He's named after an old boss."

"Oh, I see," Morris replied.

Inside, the building was filled with tools and hardware, bins of nails, plus clothes, hats, boots and shoes, tables, chairs, bedding, crockery, shelves of dry goods and baskets full of berries.

Morris walked behind the counter and held out a handful of them.

"The Tulalips trade us these, aren't they beautiful? We send them out all over, Seattle, Olympia, Whatcom."

Peter strolled over to the counter to look at them and nodded. He reached into his trousers, pulled out his list and handed it to Morris, who looked it over.

"Okay, we've got all of this. Are you buying or trading today?"

"Buying."

"Gold or cash?"

"What's with everyone around here? I don't have any more gold," Peter lied, "only silver and greenbacks."

"Very good, we like that. I'll be right back," he said, walking towards a backroom, swerving around stacked boxes and goods like a well-oiled weather vane.

Peter began to wander around the room, looking at the various items for sale and trade. Some shelving had used books, he ran his finger along the spines and stopped at one that was very wide, *Moby-Dick or, the Whale*. He pulled it from the shelf then sat down at a table by the front window and thumbed through it. *Looks like a lot of pages and words. I'll figure them out even if it takes me years.*

He set the book aside and noticed an old wrinkled copy of the *Washington Standard* newspaper on the table, there was an article on the lower part of the page that caught his eye about the Conscription Act. Peter stroked his beard as he started to read about how for $300 a man could buy his way out of the war by hiring a substitute. He scratched the side of his face then stroked his beard. *What's the world coming to when a rich man can buy his way out of fighting?*

Morris walked back into the front-room carrying a wooden box and set it on the counter just as a fellow walked in the door. Peter held up the paper and pointed at the article, "What's this I see now about the South letting their men pay for substitutes?"

"A Northerner can do the same! Oh, don't get me started about that!" Morris piped over his shoulder as he returned to the storage room.

"That whole payin' a substitute thing's a crock. Who's to stop some crook from posing as a substitute soldier and gettin' a payday, then deserting and doin' it all over again?" the fellow who just walked in remarked, joining the conversation.

"Ah, *oui monsieur.* You speak the truth!" Peter said, grinning.

The man looked at Peter and said, "Well, glad you agree." Then he glanced around, not seeing anyone else he asked, "You a newcomer?"

"No *monami,* just new to the place," Peter replied, taking in the surroundings. "This is good though, and so much closer than Penn Cove."

The man nodded at Peter's comment, he was middle-aged and medium sized with a bushy beard wearing a navy-blue frock coat and felt hat. "Well, I suppose so. The name's Dennis Brigham, just came out here from the east, got a claim started about four miles north of here. You?"

"Over on Gedney, got the far end of the island all to myself," Peter answered, standing up. "I'm Peter Goutre. Did I see your smoke on my way over?"

"Probably, I've got the roof on and stove installed, hope to have the kitchen done real soon."

"Log cabin?"

"Nope, frame lumber. Had it shipped up from Seattle, Yesler's Mill."

"Doors?" Peter asked, his eyes brightening.

"Doors and windows came up from Nisqually, even a wash basin with its own stand!"

Just then Morris walked back into the store with another box, Peter and Dennis went over to him and Peter set the book on the counter. He looked in the boxes, there were sacks of flour, a tin of lard and six quarts of Old Pepper. Morris grinned at the other customer.

"Dennis, how've you been? Got yer' place finished yet?"

"Just about," he replied.

"What can I do for you today?"

"Oh, I just needed to get a few things."

"Okay, let me finish up with Peter here and I'll be right with you."

"Great, thank you," Dennis said, walking over to the front table and sitting down.

"So, how much is a pound of flour going for these days?" Peter asked, holding a sack, weighing it in his hand.

"Three cents a pound," Morris said over his shoulder, just before he returned to the backroom.

"And lard?" Peter hollered, setting the flour back in its box.

A moment later Morris brushed past the curtained doorway with yet another box. He set it down and replied, "Lard is at thirteen cents a pound right now."

"Thirteen cents!" Peter blurted. "How can that be when a pound of flour is only three cents?"

Morris looked at Peter with a furrowed brow. "The wholesaler sets the prices, not Jacob and I, things are going up these days."

"*In-croy-able,*" Peter muttered, while shaking his head. *I'm not even going to ask how much the berries are*. He glanced at Morris and then motioned with a hand for him to continue.

Morris walked up and down a few isles of shelving to gather up the last items for Peter. Once he had everything from Peter's list on the counter, he picked up a paper pad and itemized all the provisions, including the book, and added up the bill. He handed the slip of paper to Peter. *Fourteen dollars and eighty-six cents!*

Peter wanted to spit but restrained himself, instead he reached into his pocket and pulled out some crumpled dollar bills. He counted the money off and handed it to Morris. *Don't say anything, you need to get along with this man.*

"*Merci monsieur,*" Peter said, forcing a smile. "This will get me through the cold winter months. Could you help me load it in my canoe?"

Morris picked up a crate, saying, "Absolutely."

On the way out the door Peter stopped and said to Dennis, "Sounds like you're a carpenter."

"All my life," Dennis answered, standing up.

"I've been struggling with my front door. Any chance I could get you over to the island for a little repair work? I've got fresh eggs to trade."

"Sure, no problem," Dennis answered. "I'll get over there as soon as I get my place weathered in."

"Great, see you then," Peter said, smiling.

Fifteen-minutes later they'd loaded the cargo into Peter's baskets in his dugout while Mr. John stood and watched. The tide had begun to come in and a few Tulalips were still straggling on the beach. As Peter finished loading his supplies, one of them, a tall, lean-looking man with long, straight black hair, came over.

"*Stu-hy! Ne-si'-ka keep' mam'ook ko'-pa la gwin moo' la,*" he said to Peter.

"Sounds like something broke at the sawmill," Peter remarked to Morris.

"Ah," Morris replied, "I'm impressed, you speak that chinook stuff pretty well."

"Since the '30s."

"*Me-si'-ka chah-ka?*" the man asked Peter.

"*Oui,* yes. I mean, *àh-ha,* I'll come and fix it, *mam'-ook chee,*"

Peter said to him. The Tulalip man nodded a thank you and walked back to the others. Peter turned to Morris.

"*Monsieur*, Mr. John and I shall see you in the spring."

"Yes, yes," Morris responded, "we'll be here."

Peter snapped his fingers twice and his dog leapt into the boat, taking his traditional spot in the prow of the canoe. With a wave and a final thank you, Peter pushed the dugout into the surf and then leapt in as well, grabbing his paddle and then pulling with the tide.

"Thanks for the business!" Morris hollered.

Peter waved then doffed his knit hat and spun it goodbye in the air.

XXIII

Island Chores
O'-le-man Mam'-ook
1862 - 1874

Peter stood at his cabin's single, small window, looking across the Sound. A disagreeable storm had moved in, sideways rain pelted the glass and, further out, he could see, through the thick mist of the storm, whitecaps crashing into each other and strafing the stony beach of the island. It was an ugly, ugly day for anyone who had to be out and about. For the man in a warm cabin, with a merry fire going in his stove and a good dog at his feet, the weather was no problem at all.

The constant dripping of rainwater into the two bowls on the floor was bothersome, but in a lonely way, it kept him company. Peter flipped over the eggs frying on the stove then stepped over to pick one of the full bowls up. He took it over to the door, opened it, and then tossed the rainwater out. Before he could do the same to the second, Mr. John lazily walked over and lapped some up.

"Hey! You've got your own right there," Peter said, pointing at the front corner. He picked the bowl up and tossed the water outside and returned to cooking breakfast.

When the eggs and fry bread were done, he walked over to the table and slid the eggs off onto two plates and sat down. Mr. John wandered over and sat on his haunches next to him, panting, his long tongue hanging out over his shaggy lips.

"I know, I know. As soon as it cools down it's all yours."

Peter sipped some coffee and took a bite of crispy hot bread then picked up his book and started to read. *Call me Ishmael. Some years ago — never mind how long precisely — having little or no money in my . . .*

Mr. John pushed Peter in the leg with his nose.

"Ah, my four-legged friend, did I forget about you?" he said, petting his dog. Peter got up with the other plate and scraped the eggs off into John's bowl and went back to his book and meal.

That afternoon, when the skies had cleared, Peter and Mr. John hiked up the trail to tend to the livestock. Once there, he noticed how the calves had eaten all the native grass in the extra-large paddock.

While Peter thought about his dilemma, he went over and fed his piglets some barley while Mr. John dug a new hole. *It will be another year or so before those cows are ready to breed so I should just let them roam free. After all, they're not about to swim away.*

He walked over to the paddock and opened the gate. The calves mosied out of the corral, but one stopped after a short way. It turned around and looked at Peter, confused as to what to do or what was going on. Then it dropped its head and started feeding on the untouched forest grass. Peter kept the gate open. Next, he unlatched the door of the coop so the chickens could eventually wander out and spend the day scratching and pecking.

"Here boy!" he called to Mr. John. Before the hens left the safety of their coop Peter and John headed back down the trail. He spent the rest of the day cleaning and polishing his guns while John slept on the floor, then Peter read his book until dinner time.

The next morning the sun was shining, the mountains were out, and the bay was as flat and reflective as a mirror. After breakfast Peter and John went down to the beach and hopped in the fast canoe. They headed straight for Tulalip Bay.

Once there, the same man who Peter had talked with at the trading post was waving from the top of the bank next to the mill building. He wore a white cotton shirt, black trousers and boots. Peter beached his canoe at the log pond and walked up the trail while Mr. John followed.

"*Klahowya!*" Peter said, approaching the man.

"*Klahowyum,*" the fellow replied, then motioned for Peter to follow him inside the old mill building.

"Something broke so you send for old Peter, is that it?"

Mr. John looked up at Peter and whined, not recognizing any of his words.

"It's fine old boy," Peter laughed while stepping inside, "I can help, I just —" Peter stopped speaking abruptly as his eyes adjusted to the dark of the old mill building and the man standing on the log carriage, hunched over the sawblade, who unmistakably wore the black frock of a Catholic priest, the first Peter had seen since Father Demers at Fort Nisqually in the 30s, was examining the mechanism. Recognizing his old home, Mr. John immediately went over to his former spot and laid down.

"*Bonjour*! Hello there!" the priest said with a French accent, turning around and smiling. "You must be the man everyone here calls, *Stu-hy*." Peter froze, trying hard to remember the last time he went to Mass and what one was supposed to do in the presence of a man of the cloth. Aware that everyone was looking at him, he eventually settled on taking off his hat, crossing himself, and bowing.

"*Oui*, the locals gave me that name a few years ago when we did more trading," Peter said. "I'm Peter Goutre."

The priest hopped down from the carriage, he was medium height and clean-shaven, his hair was neatly combed back, parted on the side, he looked to be in his mid-forties.

"And I'm Father Chirouse, it's a pleasure to meet you. I was sent here to help oversee the tribe and establish schools and a church."

"*Ah, oui*, that is a good thing and it is good to meet you, too," Peter replied.

"It's rare to meet a fellow Frenchman in these parts. Are you from the old country?" Chirouse asked.

"*Non*, Father, I am from Montreal. You?"

"Bourge-de-Peage in the southeastern region by the Isêre River. Have you heard of it?"

322

"I have not, Father," Peter answered.

"Well, Peter, I welcome you to the Tulalip Reservation. I understand you were the previous owner here."

"That is true. Three other men and myself built this mill and I lived over south of the point," Peter said. "But now I am out on Gedney Island."

"I see, I see. That is good? Living on the island, *oui*?"

"Oh, *oui*, Father. It is good. But what about the saw? I spoke with your man at the trading post and he said it needed fixing."

"Oh, the saw," Chirouse said, turning around and walking over to it, the floors still creaking like before. "It's jammed and I must admit I'm not familiar with mill machinery. I do enjoy carving wood but running a machine such as this, *non*."

"It's probably the saw guide — we never could get it working right, had to constantly keep putting it back in position. Are the wrenches still here we left for you?" Peter asked, stepping onto the carriage and examining the blade guides.

Father Chirouse set a small wooden box of various hand tools next to Peter. "I believe this is them."

Peter looked down at the box, nodded and then took off his wool coat. He draped it over the log on the carriage and then went to work.

For the next three hours Peter took apart the wooden guide assembly, cleaned it, greased it, and discovered that one guide had cracked and needed replacement. Using a hand saw and auger he fabricated a new part and rebuilt the whole apparatus.

"One guide was broken and I believe that's why it wouldn't run smooth and got jammed up. Let's test it," Peter suggested.

Chirouse said a few words combined of English and Lushootseed to the two workers to begin the procedure and start the saw. First, one man ran outside to the dam and opened the penstock to get the water flowing towards the wheel and closed off the gate valve at the bypass channel. He came back inside and the other man pulled the waterwheel lever to engage the gearbox, the Muley-saw sprang to life, smoothly moving up and down. The first fellow pulled the carriage lever causing the log to move forward into the blade, it cut through the wood perfectly. Both workers looked at Peter and smiled.

"Excellent work, Peter!" Chirouse exclaimed. "I can't thank you enough. Thank goodness it didn't do this last summer when we needed extra lumber."

"Happy to help. I'm glad to see that everything is going well here, but the day is late and I must get back."

"Thank you again, you should come by sometime so I can give you a tour of our new boy's school and dormitory. We are in the beginning stages of planning for a girl's school and dormitory but that is still a number of years off, I'm afraid."

"Well, at least now you can start stockpiling lumber for it. But I must say, you should probably think about junking this old Muley and converting to a circular saw."

Chirouse chuckled and said, "Ah, we shall think about that, *monami*. Thank you again for taking the time to come over. You are welcome at Mass anytime. Please come, won't you?"

"Thank you, your, ah . . . Grace," Peter replied. "I will try. But for now, I must be heading home. John, My Man," Peter said, giving a quick whistle, "come on boy. And, 'er . . . excuse me, Father.'"

"You are excused, my son," the priest said, smiling. "Go with God!"

Mr. John raised his head, then stood up and followed his master down to the log pond and canoe.

As they approached their island home, Peter laughed when he saw the two Hereford calves down by his cabin. Right when the canoe hit the shore Mr. John bolted from the boat and ran straight for the two animals, barking like mad.

"Mr. John!" Peter hollered. "*Arrête! Arrête!*" Peter ran from the canoe, forgetting to tie it up, and tried to get between a barking Mr. John and the two calves while waving his arms at his dog to stop. Soon, Mr. John got the idea of what his master was trying to do: he turned into a herd dog, barking, moving, and getting the two young cattle to go back up the trail. Peter looked at his dog, out of breath but now happy.

"Good job, boy," Peter said, petting Mr. John. Then he turned around and saw his dugout floating away from the shore!

"Agg!!" Peter groaned, running back down to the beach and into the cold water, to save his boat, cursing all the way.

One day the weather was perfect so Peter thought he'd take a break from chores for a change and go for a walk along the beach with Mr. John. He tossed sticks for his dog to fetch as a few gulls cawed and flew overhead, a bald eagle stood high on a tree snag just above a large nest watching them, and a lone harbor seal broke the surface of the calm water, on a mid-morning hunt to find breakfast. When they got to the sandy point at the middle of the island, Peter picked up a stick and tossed it out into the water. Mr. John gladly bounded into the small cove and brought it back. Peter was about to throw it again when he heard a voice come across the bay.

"Hello Peter!"

Peter looked out to the water as Mr. John started barking, but the sun's reflective glare blinded him momentarily, he rubbed his eyes then put his hands against his forehead.

"Who's that?"

"It's Dennis Brigham! I brought you something," he hollered, turning his canoe to the north.

"Oh, I couldn't see you in the glare," Peter said, reaching down to Mr. John, trying to calm him. "It's alright boy, he's a friend."

"I thought I'd come over and help you with that door of yours," Dennis said, paddling offshore, a long slab of wood sitting upright in his canoe.

"Took you long enough! What's that in your boat?"

"I built a door for you."

"You built a door? For me?"

"Sure, been building doors for years. Is your cabin farther up this way?"

"Up at the far beach!" Peter replied, pointing.

"See you there."

Twenty minutes later Brigham was carrying the new door up the shore and over to Peter's cabin where he set it down and leaned it against the exterior wall of the tiny hovel. Mr. John ran up ahead to Dennis, wagging his tail and panting.

"That's a good boy," Dennis said, kneeling down and scratching Mr. John behind the ears. Peter walked up with a smirk on his face.

"Wasn't planning on doing this today," he said, "But I guess it's good to see you again."

"Well, I guess it's good to see you too," Brigham retorted, standing up and extending his hand. After they greeted each other with a handshake Peter glanced at the new door.

"Nice work," he remarked, looking at it. "Will it fit?"

"I built it two-foot eight inches wide," Dennis answered, pulling a donut-shaped Chesterman tape from his pocket. He walked over to the cabin and measured the width and length of Peter's ad-hoc door.

"Good, the existing is a little bit bigger so I'll just build out the opening a touch and get it mounted for you," he said. "I've got all the tools and extra lumber I need in the canoe."

"Okay, what can I do?" Peter asked, following him down to the beach.

"Well, right now you can help carry a few things."

First, Dennis removed the leather-hinged existing door and built out the rough opening and a new jam. He chiseled away the wood on the edge of the door for the metal hinges he'd brought, mounted them, then they carried the door over to the cabin and placed it in the opening, it fit perfectly.

"*Merveilleuse!*" Peter exclaimed.

"That worked pretty good," Dennis said, "now if you could lift it up just a smidge, I'll put a shim under it. Then we'll attach the hinges, exterior handle, and a hasp for a padlock."

Thirty minutes later the door was mounted and Brigham was nailing some trim boards around it.

Both of them stood back and admired the new door on Peter's abode. "I think this calls for a toast! Come on in."

Dennis sat down in one of the two chairs at the table while Peter took a couple of mugs and a bottle of Old Pepper off the shelf and pulled the cork. He poured his guest a healthy mug full of whiskey and did the same for himself.

"Here's to the best carpenter on Gedney Island," Peter proclaimed, raising his mug.

"Thank you . . . and here's to looking up your old address!" Dennis said, answering his toast, and they drank down the brown liquor. He set his mug down and glanced around Peter's little habitat.

"Speaking to your old address, how long you been here?"

Peter didn't reply right away, he took another swig and said, "Oh, *monami*, I have been all around this world but it's three or four-years maybe that I've been on the island. But I first came out here in '29 on the York Express, by boat and foot to Fort Vancouver. Then I was at Nisqually for years and even lived with the Tlingit up the Stikine River back when the Tsar owned it. In those days I was working for Hudson's Bay. After that I traveled the world on merchant ships."

"Any children?"

"*Non*, my friend," Peter said with a touch of dejection. He poured more whiskey for the both of them and then looked out the open doorway for a few quiet moments then said, "I was married once, to a beautiful Tlingit girl."

"You were? When was that?"

"Oh, it was a very long time ago, back when I was up north."

"And where is she now?"

Peter paused and took another drink, then replied, stuttering with a sullen look, "She, ah, well, she passed away, right after we were married."

"Jeez, Peter, I'm sorry to hear that."

329

Goutre didn't say anything for a moment. He kept looking out the doorway and then he glanced at Dennis and said, "Thank you, she was a sweet girl. But enough about me, where do you hail from?"

"Waster, Massachusetts! That's where I learned carpentry. I didn't want to work in the mills like my dad so I went to work for my uncle building houses and such, worked with him and then on my own for 30 years. I finally got sick of all the growth and people, so I came out here." Dennis finished his whiskey and stood up.

"Well, I should get back. Thanks for the drink."

"How much do I owe you?"

"Nothing, I like helping my neighbors. Besides, I may need help with something someday."

"Oh, no," Peter said, standing up. He stepped over to his kitchen area and took a small basket of eggs off the shelf. "Here, fresh eggs for your efforts."

"Thank you, Peter," Dennis said. "I haven't had any eggs in months."

On the way to the beach Peter said, chuckling, "If you need anything just give me a shout across the bay."

Dennis laughed and remarked, "That's a pretty big shout. But you know, maybe we should come up with a way to signal each other if there's an accident or something, like smoke signals."

"That's a good idea," Peter replied. "How about bonfires?"

"I like that idea, but seeing one fire could mean that one of us is just doing chores, so we should light two fires, side by side and very big."

"Yes, I will make two bonfire piles right over there," he said, pointing at the big level area south of his cabin, "just above the beach, say twenty paces from each other so that they are ready when needed. How does that sound?"

"That's a capital idea, my friend," Brigham answered. "I'll do the same."

At the canoe Dennis carefully set his basket of eggs in it and they both pushed the dugout to the water's edge where he climbed in and Peter pushed him off.

"Thank you, Dennis. Come on over anytime!"

"Same to you," Brigham responded over his shoulder.

That afternoon Peter began building two driftwood piles for bonfires at the edge of the beach above the high-water line. Over the ensuing years he added tree limbs and anything else that floated up on the beach he could carry until both were about six-feet tall and a dozen feet around. His life became an existence of constant chores, day in and day out, to keep up with his growing herd of livestock, apple orchard, and the many other duties of island homestead living.

XXIV

Snohomish City
Sinnahamis
October 26, 1875

Dark rain clouds filled the sky, the current ran fast against the hull of the white box-like double level steamer *Zephyr* as it twisted and turned its way up the meandering Snohomish River. Captain Wright was constantly engaged in the endless search for safe water, dodging his craft this way and that, the rippling lines of the current charting his course, telling him a deep-water story — the ever-changing sandbars and silt-choked channels now covered by just enough muddy water to make upriver travel even more treacherous, the overhanging tree branches and bank snags still many.

At a sharp bend in the river, they came upon a long wooden landing built against the bank and the makings of a logging camp. There was a cluster of frame buildings with corrals of oxen and above it a stump-covered hillside. Then a rumble sounded, like a thunderstorm moving across the land: a massive log was barreling down the side of the same hill on a wooden chute. It slammed into the river, forcing a blast of water that shot upward a hundred feet

333

or more and then rained back to earth in a downpour.

A half-mile later the boat skirted past an island in the middle of the waterway with a log structure and flag pole, there were some ramparts on the upriver side, it looked like it had been a fortified stockade at one time.

When the *Zephyr* landed at Snohomish City the few passengers aboard slowly began to disembark down a wobbly gangplank, walking by numerous canoes tied up along the shore, then up the bank into town. Two newcomers followed behind and seemed to take their time glancing around, making themselves familiar with their fresh surroundings. Both looked to be in their 60s, one wearing the blue of a union jacket and the other the clothes of a hard traveler. Each with a wide brim felt hat on and a tattered and torn rucksack slung over their shoulders. The one in blue called out to a fellow passenger up ahead of them.

"Where can a guy get a drink in this place?"

"Right over there at the Blue Eagle," another traveler said, pointing.

The men walked over silently to the false-front, unpainted establishment of hand-split cedar shakes and hewn timbers, their eyes deliberately scanning the settlement. They pushed through the wooden doors, without hailing the man behind the bar, and sat down at an open table. Then waited for the proprietor to acknowledge them.

"Afternoon gents, what can I get you?" the barkeep asked from his station, wearing a long white apron tied around his waist and a bow-tie.

"We'll start with a bottle of whiskey and a couple of shot glasses but we're here to stake homesteads. We understand that around these parts this is where we can file a claim. Who do we see about that?" the stranger in military garb asked.

"You'll want see my brother, Emory Ferguson. He handles all the claims, and just about everything elsewise here in the county," the tender replied, walking over with a bottle and two shot glasses. "Where you gents from?" he asked, pouring the liquor. Both men downed their shots before answering.

"Oh, just about everywhere I guess," the same stranger answered, not looking at the bartender. "We served together in the war and now come west, lookin' to take out some timberland, start up a shake or sawmill."

"Well, ya' better hurry. There's not much left around town to claim, farther up the Pilchuck River there is. Just follow the north wagon road that came up near the landing. After the road and the mud goes away and it changes to a trail go another mile 'er more, it's pretty much wide-open and claimable after that."

"Ya' don't say. I guess we'll have to check that out," the man said, glancing over at his partner. "So where can we find, 'er, what was his name again?"

"Emory. He's got the cottage next door, just give him a knock and he'll take good care of you."

"And what about a room for the night?"

"I've got bachelor rooms down the back hall, a dollar a night and that gets you breakfast too."

"Any hotels in town?"

"The Exchange is a fine establishment, Isaac Cathcart runs that one. Then there's The Riverside, just down the way and the City Hotel over —"

"That's good, we got the picture," the talkative one said, cutting him off. "How much for the bottle?"

"That'll be a dollar-fifty."

"What! A dollar-fifty? In Portland and even Seattle we could get a bottle for a dollar at the most."

"Well, those are pretty civilized towns these days, you're up in the wilderness now."

"You mean to tell me that you boys haven't got yourselves a distillery going here yet? Hear that?" he said, looking at his cohort. "Why, we should start making corn whiskey in this town. We could finally get rich!" He slapped six quarter dollar coins on the table, glancing at the barman.

"So, my name's Clark," the bartender said, sweeping up the coins, then sticking out his hand, saying, "And who may I have the honor of meeting today?"

"McPherson," the fellow grumbled, standing up but not shaking his hand. He grabbed the bottle instead and added, "Maybe we'll see you around."

Once the two men were out of the building Pierre Kannaquassé's blood pressure began to boil with every limping step, after a half dozen he stopped.

"I am growing tired of this endless search on a bum leg. We checked the homestead records at Olympia and there was nothing, we went to Seattle and still nothing, and now you have brought me to this soggy place, and for what?" Kannaquassé complained, trying not to draw too much attention. "If we don't find him here then I'm done."

McPherson took the rucksack from his shoulder, placed the bottle in it and then said, "Do you not agree that Goutre stole our life and wealth from us? Goutre took as much from me as he did from you."

"I already know all of that and he needs to pay for it —"

"Pay for it? How? I am not, we are not doing away with anyone if that's what you mean. The two of us are only here to take back what is ours!" McPherson barked, he stopped talking and grabbed Kannaquassé by the collar, stepping in and shouting directly into his face "Money is everything! The lack of that money ruined my life! It ruined yours! We did the work, we planned it all out, we —"

McPherson stopped shouting and, aware that he was making a scene, lowered his voice to a whisper, "we took care of John McLoughlin, and then that Frog bastard just sails off with the gold and the sterling, the emeralds and safire, everything, and then he burned the rest."

McPherson released Kannaquassé's dirty collar and stepped back. "And if you don't want your half of that then go, just turn right around and go."

Kannaquassé eyed McPherson and said, "I said if we don't find him here, meaning in this county, then I am done, and I will never forget that Frenchy stole everything from us. Do I need to remind you once more of my life being ruined because of him? I had no way to gainfully support myself for thirty years besides doing hard labor with this rotten leg of mine that he sliced open."

"You'll get your revenge in glorious wealth my friend. Please remember, when we left Stikine all those years ago the dockmaster at Fort Simpson said a man that fit Goutre's description said he was bound for Puget Sound and I believe that we will find him here," McPherson said as he started to walk away.

At the small Ferguson cottage, McPherson went up the porch steps to the door and knocked while Pierre waited in the yard. A lady answered the door.

"You here to see Ferg?" the small woman asked.

"Yes, good afternoon, ma'am. We were told that this is where we can make a homestead claim," McPherson replied, doffing his blue felt hat and bowing his head of matted and greasy grey hair.

"I'm sorry, but he's out with a survey team. Should be back in two or three days, maybe more."

"Oh," McPherson said, turning to Pierre to see his response then back to the woman. "Two or three days, maybe more? No sooner?"

"I'm afraid so. He's out in the sticks and won't be back for a while."

"Well, is there any way we could view the homestead records? We'd like to get an idea of where most of the claims are being staked."

"Oh, no, only Ferg can help you with that. Please come back in a few days, he'll be back then. Now, if you'll excuse me —"

"Would it be possible to make a homestead application?" McPherson asked, just before the door closed. Mrs. Ferguson paused.

"Do you have your parcel picked out?"

"Why, no ma'am, we don't. Just arrived in town."

"Then I suggest you find one and return," she replied, closing the door on them.

McPherson turned to a red-faced Kannaquassé but he chose to stay silent. They left the residence and headed back towards the Blue Eagle. Not yet knowing his next move, McPherson said exactly what Pierre needed to hear.

"I'll keep paying for your room and board until we're able to look at those records. If Peter Goutre is not listed as being in the area, then I'll pay you what I owe and for your passage east."

Pierre nodded and said, "Then what is your plan until this *Monsieur* Fer-gus-son returns?" McPherson thought for a moment.

"Since we have presented ourselves as homesteaders then we will act as such and take in the countryside to find unclaimed tracts of land that will suit our purposes, and then return to make filings."

"And where do we start?"

"Well, that fellow Clark suggested we go north, so north is where we will search."

After posing as newcomers for far longer than they wanted to in the Pilchuck Valley, they'd finally staked out two parcels of unclaimed land along the river that they could use as a ploy to file a claim on. They returned to the Ferguson cottage and knocked on the door. This time a light-haired man with a stubbly beard, large frame and bright inquisitive eyes answered.

"Hello there," the man said, looking the two men up and down. "How can I help you fellas?"

"Good afternoon, Mr. Ferguson, is it?" McPherson asked in his friendliest tone. "We'd like to file a claim."

"Lucetta said somebody came by a while ago, would that be you?" Ferguson asked.

"Yes, we've found two parcels we'd like to file on up in the valley to the north, up the Pilchuck."

"Alright, come on in," Emory said, welcoming them into his two-room home. "Take a seat," he said, pointing at a couple of chairs. The two men sat down in front of his desk in the corner. The walls were covered with shelves full of ledgers and record books, maps, note pads, and piles of letters. Ferguson rolled out a map of the area on his desk for them to inspect.

"There's lots of good ground to be had over there," he commented. McPherson searched the map intently until he found what he thought were the two parcels.

"Yes, we'd like to stake two claims on the ground right there," McPherson said, placing his finger on the map at the location.

"Oh, I see. Right where that creek flows into the river, that's a good spot. Lots of bottom ground for livestock and crops and good timber on the hill. Did you put any stakes in the ground?"

"We did."

"And how much ground you boys fixin' on?"

"We understand that the Homestead Act allows us each to claim up to 160 acres each, so I believe that's what we'll both take," McPherson stated. Just then Mrs. Ferguson called out for her husband from the backdoor.

"Ferg? It's that darn laundry line again."

Emory sighed and looked at the men, "Duty calls. I'll be right back. Make yourselves comfortable."

The second that Ferguson was out of the room McPherson got up and started to scan the spines of the ledger books on the shelving while Pierre sat and kept watch.

He ran his finger across the ledgers and came across a large volume marked F through N, and took it from the shelf. Searching through the pages, McPherson's eyes scanned as many as he could knowing Ferguson would return any second. He ran a finger down each page until his eyes lit up and he grinned a wicked grin.

"There," he whispered, stabbing the page and then staring at Kannaquassé briefly. "Peter Goutre, 160 acres at north Gedney Island. Where the hell is that?" He carefully closed the ledger and returned it just in time. Right as he sat down a screen door slapped shut and Emory walked back into the room.

"Sorry about that. So!" he said, opening a desk drawer. He set two sheets of paper on the desktop, saying, "If you gents will write down your names, birthdates, and addresses, I'll add a legal description and then you'll each need to pay the thirty-four-dollar filing fee, and of course, you will have to live on those parcels and improve the land for five years. Once that's done, the land office will issue title and the claim will be proved up and yours."

McPherson picked a pencil up off the desk and stared blankly at the piece of paper. "How soon do you need payment?" he asked, pretending to write.

"Well, today, of course."

McPherson dropped the pencil. "Oh, today? I don't think we've got thirty-four-dollars between us, let alone double that," he said, trying to look surprised.

"Yep, that's the deal. No fee, no claim," Ferguson stated dourly.

McPherson looked at Kannaquassé and slightly tilted his head towards the door. He turned back to Emory.

"I guess we'll need to mail a couple of letters. I'm sure my brother will help fund me," McPherson said, glancing over at Pierre and nodding. "Once we've got our funds in order we'll come back by. Is there any way you could hold those two pieces for us?"

"I'm afraid not. County policy is first come first served, but you can write and mail your letters right here!"

Just then the front door opened and a tall man, barrel-chested sporting a wide girth walked in. He took his hat off and bellowed in a loud and hearty tone, "Afternoon Ferg, I hear you're looking for me."

"Sheriff!" Emory declared, welcoming the man, standing up and shaking his hand. McPherson and Kannaquassé slumped in their chairs.

"Gentlemen, this is our County Sheriff, Benjamin Stretch," Ferguson said, introducing the two men. Both stood and shook hands with the sheriff and said, "Hello," at the same time, then grimaced.

"Thank you for all your help, Mr. Ferguson, we need to talk this over and decide which relative we should mail for the money. Then we'll come back by to send our letters," McPherson offered, stepping towards the door. Pierre followed behind and they left.

"What'd those two want?" the sheriff asked.

"Oh, they were just a couple of broke newcomers looking to file on some homesteads for free," Ferguson replied. He picked up the two pieces of paper and looked at them, nothing had been written down.

"That's odd," Emory remarked, staring at the blank page. "They didn't write anything."

"Interesting," the sheriff noted, scratching the side of his face.

"Oh well, they'll come back when they're ready."

Once away from the Ferguson cottage the two of them stood at the edge of a thirty-foot deep gulch with a small creek at the bottom of it, the banks were covered with a thicket of wild berry bushes.

"Now what?" Pierre asked quietly.

"We need to find out where Gedney Island is and then make a plan for recompence."

"*Oui*, but how are we going to find that out? We just can't ask people and raise suspicion. People are going to remember us if we start asking questions."

McPherson agreed, "That's right, we've got to figure this out by ourselves without looking suspicious." He pointed away from the gulch towards the riverbank and a place to sit down.

"Not only do we need a plan for recompence, but first we have to find and get out to this Gedney Island place, plus come up with an escape plan as well. Let's think about this for a minute."

Both men sat down at the top of the riverbank just as bright warm sunshine broke through the clouds and watched as an Indian in a canoe paddled by, headed downstream.

"That sun sure feels good for a change," Pierre said.

"Yes, well, Gedney Island is obviously in this county and the only place an island would be is out there in the saltwater where we came from. And," McPherson ruminated, keeping his eyes focused on the dugout now past them, "the first thing I think we need to do is get us some more grub and supplies, then we need to get ourselves a canoe."

XXV

Mukilteo
bəqx̌tlyuʔ
October 30, 1875

On their way over to the trading post Mr. John gazed out across the Sound from his normal station at the bow of the fast canoe, his jowls hanging and grey snout pointed into the breeze. When a sea lion broke the surface of the water, John turned his head, but didn't bark. Instead, he weakly growled and went back to scanning the saline Sound and its surroundings.

"What was that? A seal?" Peter asked, coughing, his voice rough. Mr. John turned his head halfway towards his master but then turned back. "Oh, I see. It's the silent treatment today." He paddled a few more strokes and then asked, "Can you see the trading post over there? Because it just looks like a blurry green mess to me." The decades of staring into the glare off the water was finally taking its toll.

Peter ran his craft up on the shore and slowly got himself and Mr. John out of the dugout. At low tide the beach smelled of salt and muck, drained by the ebb, an underwater layer of raw, rocky earth exposed twice a day for a few hours. Seaweed and eel grass were scattered about on the rocky shore, the holdfast of a kelp root, its green slimy blades twisted and curled lay in wait for the flood to return it to its underwater forest, small crab crawled about. Gulls methodically pecked at clam shells and were soon joined by a few crows while shorebirds scurried around on the round rocks and pebbles. Once Peter got to the porch of the Exchange, he snapped his fingers then grabbed hold of the doorknob, Mr. John laid down.

"Well, well, well. Look what drifted in on the tide!" Jacob Fowler cried. "It's about time ya' got off that island of yours," he added, wiping his hands off on a bar towel and then slapping them together. "I figured you'd be over soon."

"Yes, but first a quick dram then I've got to get over next door," Peter replied, rubbing and blinking his eyes. He took off his filthy old tattered wool coat, covered in dog hair, and eased over to the bar and sat down. "On the way over, everything was fuzzy and out of focus, I was lucky to get here. My eyes are just gettin' worse and worse by the day, it's time to get some spectacles."

"Morris is the one to see about glasses. In the meantime, I've got some Irish whiskey, or, if you've got some time to kill, then Joe Butterfield is due any moment with a fresh batch of his beer."

"I guess I'll wait for a bottle of brew," Peter said with a sour look, slapping down a two-bit piece. Jacob looked at the quarter and picked it up.

"I thought you only dealt in gold," he remarked, grinning, dropping the coin in his cash box. He poured Peter a shot of whiskey and gave him back a dime.

"Ah, no," Peter grunted, raising an eyebrow just before he raised the shot to his lips, tasting it. "Haven't had any gold for a long time, spent it all. After all these years I guess that's still what people think."

"Most do."

Jacob Fowler regarded Peter silently for a second. Peter looked back at him over his whiskey, then said, "People can think what they want. Any news on the Seybert kid?"

"Nope, I guess he hasn't escaped from the asylum yet," Jacob said. Then he added, "But George Pickett died," nodding at the paper on the bar.

"George Pickett? You mean Captain Pickett, from the Pig War?" Peter remarked, sipping his whisky.

"I do — some kind of liver disease, died in his bed."

"I'll be dog-gone. He did good up in the islands, but after he switched sides they never should've pardoned him for what he did to those Yankee boys. He died a murderer, far as I'm concerned."

"Even still, the paper said liver disease," Jacob replied, shaking his head.

"Those boys weren't deserters —"

Just then the front door flew open and an oval-faced man with blue eyes that were half-covered by the overhanging brim of his felt hat walked in, it was Eagle Brewery owner Joe Butterfield and his friend Jack Wiggins, each carrying a wooden box of bottled beer.

"Gentlemen! Good to see you, you've saved us," Fowler said, "and just in time too!"

The two men set their boxes down on the bar, the top of each bottle sticking upward out of the case, all corked and wired down looking like soldiers in a box canyon ready to be picked off one by one.

"And there ya' go!" Butterfield exclaimed. "We'll be right back with two more."

"Is this that batch of lager you were talking about?" Fowler asked as Joe turned for the door.

"That's right, and this time you need to charge ten cents a bottle," Butterfield said over his shoulder.

Jack Wiggins tipped his hand over the beer and softly said with amused eyes, "Had one earlier, it's his best yet."

"And I'm sure you'll be havin' another," Fowler remarked as they walked out.

Peter glanced at Jacob, he pushed the dime towards the tender and glowered. "Sounds like robbery to me, but I'm thirsty."

Jacob pulled a bottle out from the box and twisted off the wire and popped the cork, a head of froth pushed its way up the neck and out of the bottle, it dribbled down the outside. Fowler set it in front of Peter and picked up the dime.

"Some fellas came in here a few days ago on their way to Snohomish City, saying they were looking for land to homestead and asking if there were any old Hudson's Bay people in these parts," Jacob said. Peter had lifted the bottle to his lips but stopped and jerked his head around and stared at him.

"Why would anyone be looking for old company men?"

"They didn't say, hopped off the mail boat when it landed. Came in and stayed a night then caught the *Zephyr* the next day after that big rain storm, headed upriver," Jacob said, motioning northward.

"What'd they have to say?" Peter asked, taking a drink of beer.

"Oh, one did most of the talkin', he flashed an easy smile and said they were old friends with a bunch of HBC men, named off some and even mentioned, get this, Peter Goutre."

"Hmmm, did he now?" Peter replied, his brow furrowing. He set his bottle down and stroked his grey beard, then asked, "What'd that one look like? You ask his name?"

"Well," Jacob answered, as Peter took another drink. Fowler looked up at the ceiling and then scratched the underside of his clean-shaven chin. "He was wearing an old blue union coat and looked to be a bit younger than you, maybe in his mid-60s. Called himself McPherson."

Peter's shoulder's instantly stiffened, he choked on his beer involuntarily, coughing as he set the bottle down on the bar.

"You okay there, old man?"

"Yeah," Peter said between hacks. "I'm fine, mind your own business. It just went down the wrong way."

"So, you know him?"

"Oh, I knew all the traders," Peter mumbled, his mind racing but trying to stay calm. "But McPherson. Never heard of him. What'd ya' tell him?"

"Oh hell, what'd you think I told 'em? I said there was no one around here like that. I wasn't born yesterday, I've been a barman long enough to know when to keep my mouth shut."

"And what about the other?"

"He was quiet the whole time, kind of a mousey-looking fella with a pointy nose and walked with a limp. But when I asked for his name the morning they left, he gave me a blank stare and mumbled something like he was the ghost of a hero."

"A hero?" Goutre asked, his heart skipping a beat knowing full well the name Urbain Heroux but then he said, "I know of no hero. Then what happened?"

"Nothing, they got on the *Zephyr* to Snohomish City and left."

"And the one was wearing a blue union coat ya' say?"

"Yep."

"They carrying Springfields or some other kind of sidearms?"

"Nope, not that I saw."

Peter didn't reply. He stared, silently at his beer for a long time, and Jacob silently watched him.

"Is . . . is there anything you want to tell me? Anything you need to talk about?" The barman finally asked.

Peter waited a long time before speaking. "No," he finally replied, saying it very carefully and slowly, but firmly. "No, I don't think there is." He lifted the bottle, drained it, and then put it softly back onto the counter. Peter stood up and put his ratty old coat back on, then started to take a step but stopped.

"There's a silver dollar in it for you if you get word to me next time they're around, okay?" Peter flatly stated.

Jacob nodded, then Peter turned around and left the bar, not saying another word.

When he went next door, Peter walked right past Mr. John without whistling or calling for him. After a confused split-second My Man John fell in behind his master regardless. When Peter opened the door, John laid down on the porch and his master went inside. The place had grown so much over the years with more inventory than ever before. It was packed to the rafters with goods: tools, saws, bins of nails, hammers and axes covered one side of the building. On the other some tables were up front, then shelves of dry goods, crates of fruit and vegetables, and even some baked goods.

"There's the man from Hat Island! How goes the battle over there?" Morris said, greeting his longtime customer.

"To hell with the battle and everything else. And how many times do I have to tell you to quit calling my island that! It's Gedney Island!" Peter grumbled, walking up to the counter, dropping his head and giving Morris a quick glare. After a pause Peter rubbed his eyes and said, "I need to get some spectacles for these damn eyes of mine."

"Sure, sure," Frost replied, "let me get the catalog."

Then the front door flew open and Jacob and Mary Fowler's 13-year-old daughter, Louisa, ran into the store, seeing Peter she burst

351

into a smile, ran to him, and hugged him around his midsection.

"Mr. Goutre! I thought that was your canoe on the beach. Can you tell me more about the Battle of 7 Oakes or the time when you were shipwrecked?" she pleaded, excitedly, looking up to him. "Please! I just love to hear your stories!"

"Not today young lady. I've got too many chores and things to deal with," Peter said.

Morris instantly rolled his eyes at him and said, "Okay Louisa, maybe your mom or dad have a few Saturday chores for you to do?" She pulled away from Peter, glanced over at Mr. Frost and then looked downward at her peach-colored fawn dress.

"Oh, yes, I suppose," she replied, twisting her feet on the floor. "I'll feed the chickens and then do the dishes over in the hotel, I guess. But I'll be back for a story, Mr. Goutre." Then she held out a few bright pebbles she'd found on the beach, saying, "Here, these are for you."

Peter opened his right palm and Louisa dropped them into his hand with a grin. He nodded at her, glanced at the colorful tiny rocks and shoved them in his front pocket. Peter watched her walk towards the door, then said, "I'll have a story and more time for you on my next trip over."

Louisa turned, smiled at French Peter and waved, saying, "Okay, see you then." And out the door she went.

Morris set a large catalog on the counter and started flipping through the pages. "Here we go," he said, stabbing the page, "are you near-sighted or far-sighted?"

Peter looked at the page, rubbed his eyes, and then quipped, "You tell me."

"Alright, I see. Got up on the wrong side of the bed today, huh," Morris said. But Peter just stared blankly at him. "Well, if you can see things close up then you're near-sighted and if you can only see things far away then you're far-sighted."

"Oh," Peter replied with a myopic look, "well, I guess I'm near-sighted then."

"Boy, you do need glasses. Those right there should help," Morris said, placing his finger on the catalog page, "I'll order them right away. Should be here in a week or two."

"Good, get them here. I need 'em."

After an uncomfortable pause Morris asked, "How's the harvest coming along?"

"I'll have around eighty bushels this year for you. Got most of them picked and ready to bring over next time I come across."

"Gosh, Peter, last week I was buying, but I'm all stocked now," the old customs officer remarked, pointing at a table filled with fruit.

"Damn it, Morris! You knew dang well I'd be looking for a sale! What am I gonna do with eighty bushels?"

Morris eyed the old trader. "I'm sorry, Peter. I didn't know when you'd be over and the *North Pacific* showed up last week with a bin of Red Delicious at a good price. So, I bought it."

Peter glared at the trading post owner, his jaw tightening, and said, "I thought I could depend on you but I guess not."

"Oh, I knew you'd need a sale and you *can* depend on me because I've got a buyer lined up. The new brewery owner Joe Butterfield has got some cash for your crop! He wants them for a batch of cider."

"Good, I was about to skin and tan your hide! Why didn't you say so right away?"

XXVI

Camano Head
xʷuyšəd
November 7, 1875

After days of unseasonably warm weather, Peter decided to give his sore back a Sunday afternoon break from carrying his apple harvest down from the orchard. He set his shovel, bucket, and a half-full bottle of Old Pepper in the fast canoe then called out, "Here John! Let's go My Man!" His dog's head appeared from behind a pile of drift logs on the beach, its tongue hanging out, his jowls and face grey from age.

"Come on boy, we've got clams to dig."

Mr. John slowly walked across the beach and over to Peter, his master picked him up and set him in the canoe at his regular spot at the bow where he could stick his nose in the wind. Peter pushed the dugout into the water and got in. The quiet lee of the island was a blessing that day, the Sound smooth as silk.

Once he was closer to his favorite clamming spot, he thought he could see the fuzzy outlines of a few dugouts on the shore of the beach and the movement of people. *Merde,* Peter muttered to himself, "I was hoping to have the place all to myself."

355

As Peter and his dog approached the exposed tide flat, My Man John made himself known to the family with a few barks of greeting, eager to jump out but too old to do so. Right when the hull of the canoe slid up on the sandy shore John barked again but waited for Peter to lift him out. After being set down, Peter's lab ambled over to the small group of folks unhurriedly, looking for affection and, if possible, something to eat.

Peter got his bucket and shovel then looked over to where Mr. John was. He squinted in the sunshine, trying to focus on the family of clam diggers working the sand when a voice hollered, "Hey *Stu-hy*! Beautiful day!"

Pretending not to hear him, Peter squished across the oozeful flat and watched for clam water to squirt up from muddy holes. With each step he muttered, "*Allez petits bâtards*," until he dropped his bucket and began to dig up littleneck clams all around him.

Two young men wandered over to where Peter was working, both dressed in white cotton shirts and black canvas trousers rolled up to their calves. They looked into his bucket to see his amount but Peter paid them no mind, he just kept digging.

"We're gonna steam ours on the fire," one said.

Peter glanced up at him and croaked, "a-huh."

"With lots of butter," the other replied, "and we've got an extra pot if you want to steam some of yours?"

Peter bristled at the invitation — he was hoping to spend a quiet day digging clams alone with his dog. He hesitated at first and then grunted, "maybe." The two fellows looked at each other and shrugged their shoulders, they walked back to their family.

356

While Peter worked, Mr. John slowly walked back and forth between the two groups, sniffing out clams and baby crab, drooling on the sand and seaweed, snapping at sand fleas. Peter kept glancing over at the middle-aged man as he worked his way across the beach, then the same gentleman called out.

"*Cheechako!*"

Peter jerked his head around, he hadn't heard the word for more than 20 years.

"Who's that?" Peter yelled, glaring at the fellow.

"You know who it is."

"No, I don't . . . and don't call me *Cheechako!*"

"But we are friends. Remember?"

Peter started walking towards the guy to confront him. When he was right next to him his eyes finally focused. *Is that the Snohomish Indian that built my canoe?*

"Keokuk?" Peter asked.

"It is," he answered with a grin. Then he bent over to continue his digging and said, "But I go by Samuel now."

"Well, I'll be damned. I was gonna come over there and give you hell," Peter said with a grin. He turned around and went back to his clam digging hole. Samuel was with his wife, Takua, and their two sons who were now adults, 20 and 22 years old. Another family, a husband and wife with a small child in her lap, were up at the high spot of the beach, tending a fire and setting up for a

357

picnic.

After Peter's pail was full, he walked his bucket of clams out to shallow water and cleaned them. Glancing up, he saw Samuel waving him over to their driftwood campfire. Mr. John was already there, tail wagging, so Peter knew he had to go and try to be somewhat friendly. He walked over to his bark, stowed his shovel, and took a long drink of Old Pepper; lately it had become his daily anthem and helped his spirit. But he left his jug in the dugout, then pulled the canoe farther up on the sand to ward off the incoming tide. He carried his bucket up to the impromptu clambake.

"Peter, how've you been?" Samuel asked. "Your dog's getting old."

Peter nodded and grinned at him; he was petting the pup he once owned. He set down his clams and glanced around at the small group, then out at his canoe. *This could end up being a long, uncomfortable afternoon. I should have brought that bottle.*

"Yeah, we're all getting older," Peter groused. "You're going by Samuel now, huh? And you're speaking pretty good English."

"Yes, we all have Christian names and speak English now. Takua's new name is Teresa and my boys are Luke and Nathan. But you can call me Sam, we chose to keep Keokuk for our last name. Say hello to Peter, boys."

"Hi Peter," both of them said at the same time, smiling.

Peter nodded at them and their mother. She was still like he remembered her: beautiful complexion, high cheekbones, dark eyes and long black hair but now with streaks of grey, however, she wasn't wearing any tooth shell jewelry.

No one spoke for a moment, after a protracted pause Sam pointed out to the water and asked, "Is that the same canoe?"

"It is," Peter replied, then frowned, "paid too much for it though."

"Aw, you still got a fine boat. It's lasted you all these years."

"Oh, I suppose," Peter groaned, his eyes cast downward.

"So! How's life on the island?"

Peter laughed hollowly. He eased down slowly on a log for some rest, then spat, "It's work! Nothin' but work! My back hurts, my hands hurt, my head hurts just thinkin' about all the chores I have to do every day — picking apples and hauling 'em down below to get to market, pruning the orchard, got piles of limbs all over up top. Got lots of burning to do. Too many things to do. The livestock. It never stops for an old man like me," he complained, hunched over and looking tired, the lines on his face now deep and many, his long beard solid grey.

After another uncomfortable lull Sam spoke up, "So, ah, Peter this is my oldest nephew, David, his wife Ann, and their daughter Catherine. David is my sister's son and grew up here but Ann grew up on Lummi Island."

Peter turned his head their way, the couple looked to be in their early thirties. He wasn't going to say anything but then remembered the few manners he still had and doffed his knit hat, exposing his balding head, and nodded a hello. When he looked towards the young toddler something about her caught his attention. Because of his poor eyesight he was compelled to get a closer look — when she came into focus, he saw the same round face, the same warm eyes and the same dimpled chin that Little Rain had. Even her bronze-colored skin was the same, but a touch lighter. Peter was stunned and immediately mesmerized, he couldn't take his eyes away from her.

"Catherine, you said?" Peter asked, staring at the toddler. For some inexplicable reason the child made him feel younger.

"Catherine Rose Reed," Sam answered, "she's almost three years old."

Peter looked at the parents, but this time with a smile, then he gazed again at the child in wonderment. She was dressed in colorful clothes and held a small figurine carved out of wood in her hand. He moved over to a log next to her mother and her, forgetting all about his bucket of clams, Mr. John and the bottle of Old Pepper.

"Would you like to hold her?" Ann asked. Peter's eyes brightened and he smiled wider than he had in decades.

"Yes. Could I?"

She stood up, stepped directly in front of Peter and held the child out for him. The old trader's body tingled with a sensation he hadn't felt for a very long time. He reached out and took hold of the toddler then set her on his knee facing him. Their eyes locked and Peter's world stood still. The child smiled at him.

A sharp sensation struck Peter like a bolt of lightning, his blood quickened and he felt something he'd forgotten forever, pure joy. All the pain and heartache he lived with from the loss of Little Rain fell away in an instant and was replaced with the happiness he once had. His whole life flashed before him and he returned to the place in time when it was just Little Rain and him paddling towards a new beginning, and this girl was theirs, the first of the many they would have in their new home. Peter felt a profound sense of contentment in the face of this young toddler.

"Peter?" Sam asked. "You, okay?"

Peter came out of his trance and shook his head, saying, "She's beautiful." He looked over at the girl's mother and smiled.

"She reminds me of . . . a girl . . . a woman, I once knew when I worked for the company."

"When was that?" Sam asked. Peter looked out over the water then gazed at Catherine.

"Oh, that was so many years ago I can't remember," he replied, bouncing the toddler on his knee. Just then Mr. John, barking happily, bounded into their circle, causing the little girl to squeal and try to wrench away. Peter grinned and gently handed her back to her mother.

For the next few hours they steamed clams over the fire and talked and laughed in the warm afternoon sun. Peter hadn't felt so good in years, he'd discovered again what life should be about. He felt happiness and inclusion, it felt like he was finally part of a family and he relished in the day.

After the main course of clams, corn, and sourdough bread, Teresa produced a linen packet from her basket and unwrapped it to reveal multiple pieces of sliced dark brown salmon. She handed everyone a long, thick piece. Peter gladly accepted the fish and, tasting it, was overwhelmed by its purity, its simplicity. It was

361

perfect. He licked his lips and grinned.

"That's the best dried salmon I've ever had! Thank you."

"It's smoked silver salmon, the boys and I made it," Teresa said with pride.

"Oh, smoked, is it? Far better than dried, moist and such a sweet crust. Is that sugar? Or molasses?" Peter asked. Teresa smiled a silly little grin.

"Oh, that's a secret!" she said, and everyone laughed. Peter looked over to her two sons.

"You boys helped your mother smoke that salmon?"

"We did," Luke answered, beaming proud, "all the time."

"Could I buy some?" Peter asked. The two boys looked to their parents. Sam nodded to them.

"Sure," they both replied, smiling wide.

"How's two dollars sound for, say, a few pounds worth?"

Luke and Nathan leapt to their feet and walked over to Peter, sticking out their hands.

"Shake on it," the older boy Luke said. Peter shook his and then Nathan's hand.

"And if you paddle it over to the island for me, I'll give you an extra dollar." Both boys looked at each other and then their dad, who nodded his head in approval.

362

"Deal," Luke said. "We'll bring you some when the next batch is ready."

"*Fantastique*!"

XXVII

Priest Point
čхаʔqs
November 15, 1875

At the mouth of the Snohomish River, Thomas McPherson leaned across the lip of the canoe to scan the foggy bay, squinting hard through the mist for Gedney Island. To the north, in a cleared off area on the slope of a hill on the mainland, a column of wood smoke was rising from a structure.

"Let's head over there," McPherson said, pointing with his paddle, "you see that?" Pierre turned and peered through the haze.

"I see it there," Pierre replied. "That's not an island."

"I know that! But where there's smoke there's fire, and where there's fire there's someone who can help us, willingly or not."

By the time they'd gotten close to the shore the sun had broken through the clouds, and by its light they could more clearly see what they were approaching. It was a small, windowless log cabin just above the beach, and an aging Indian woman wearing a long black dress with a white shawl around her shoulders was hanging laundry on a clothesline. The two of them stopped paddling and conferred.

"Go talk to her," Pierre quietly suggested.

"And say what?"

"And ask here where Gedney Island is."

"Too risky, too suspicious. Why would we let her know what we're looking for it?" McPherson asked.

"Well, if you're not going to talk to her then why'd we paddle over here?"

"I don't know, I guess I just had a feeling that we'd see something, or learn something."

"Learn something? How about this — this whole thing is stupid and I'm goin' home," Pierre complained. "I've learned all I'll ever learn from you. I'm not going to do this anymore."

"No . . . We already talked this out, we've agreed on the job. We found out where he is, right? That's good progress. Give me a few more days, we'll get it done."

"Then go and talk to her," Pierre said. "I'm tired of this." He sat silent in the canoe, staring at McPherson, and then at the log cabin, and then back to his cohort.

"Lemme think for a minute," McPherson said.

"We already came all the way over here. I'll give you that minute but not much more. But I ain't gonna go talk to that squaw! It's your thing, you do it."

"Alright, okay. I'll go see what I can find out," McPherson said, starting to paddle towards the shore.

After they hit the beach, McPherson climbed out of the stolen canoe while Pierre waited. McPherson walked up the bank and over to the woman.

"Hello!" he said. The woman turned around with a scowl on her face. She immediately eyed the stranger warily and put her hands on her hips.

"Ah, we've lost our way, *ne-si'-ka tso'-lo*," McPherson said, smiling and removing his hat. But the woman didn't answer, instead she pinned another white cotton shirt to the line then picked up her basket and started to walk towards the cabin.

"Ma'am?" McPherson asked, his hat in his hand. She started to climb the stairs when the door opened, a large middle-aged man wearing the same kind of white shirt stepped out on the porch.

"What do you want?" he asked, as the woman walked past him and inside.

"Oh good, you speak English . . . I 'um, we're looking for the, I'm a, we're off-course, and needing directions for . . . the closest outpost or general store."

"Just head south and follow the shoreline. You'll find it," the fellow replied. He turned, went back into the cabin and closed the door. McPherson could hear the latch lock.

He turned around, threw up his hands and looked to Pierre, squinting in the sunshine that was breaking through the fog.

Pierre shook his head and yelled, "What'd he say?"

367

McPherson shrugged and answered, "Nothing," then put his hat back on. He stood in front of the log house and gazed out over the Sound, searching his mind for what to do next when he saw it. A billowing tower of black smoke coming from the top of an island to the southwest. He grinned a devilish grin but kept silent. He walked slowly back down the bank to Pierre.

"I think I know where he is," McPherson said, pushing the canoe into the water and hopping in.

"How? I didn't hear them say anything."

"Not what they said, what I just saw."

"You saw? You saw what?"

"Turn this thing around and I'll show you." With a few paddle strokes, they were facing south and McPherson waited for Pierre to say something, but he didn't.

"There in the distance. You see that island? Can you see all that smoke?"

"Ah, *monami*," Pierre said with a sign of relief. "I see it. I see it."

"That's got to be him, I can feel it in my bones," McPherson remarked. "But we still need to come up with some kind of plan. What if there's other people living out there with him?"

"I do not care about others," Pierre quickly said.

"Well," McPherson said, contemplating, "if he has a woman out there or if others live on the island, then we need to hide somehow or sneak up on him some way, maybe at night."

"Paddle out there at night? No, too many things could go wrong. I don't like the darkness, hate it. Besides, you said we also needed an escape. I'm not going to escape into darkness. I need to see where I am going. We do not know these waters."

"Well, now that we think we've found him, let's go up this shoreline and find a place to camp for the night, talk things over and come up with a plan."

A lazy hour of paddling later they'd come upon a long sandy beach at the base of a cliff. "What's that?" Pierre asked.

"What's what?"

"There's a cross up on the hill with stuff hanging all over it."

McPherson stopped paddling and cast his eyes upward. It was Little Rain's monument. He turned his gaze back to the water and replied, "Looks like some kind of totem." He looked up at it again and said, "There must be a tribe in the area."

"But the craftsmanship. It doesn't look like any Indian totem I've ever seen."

"With that cross it looks like a Christian totem."

"Ah, it does. Maybe it was built by a white man who thinks he's an Indian."

"Maybe so."

They continued on and found themselves at the entrance to a bay. When they paddled into it, they found a small community. First, they spotted a two-story building with a waterwheel on the side of it where a man was loading lumber in the back of a horse drawn wagon. Then at the southern head of the bay a gentle slope of sparse trees and stumps ran up to what looked like a church and more buildings, some large and others small, most of them painted white with smoke drifting out of chimneys. As they made their way towards them, they could see people milling about and children playing.

"Those are all Indian kids . . . we're on a reservation," McPherson remarked.

"Yes," Pierre replied. "I believe you are right, but we cannot camp here tonight." Pierre turned around. McPherson was staring intently at some boys on the beach.

"Look at them," McPherson said. "They're all wearing the same thing. White shirts and black pants." Pierre looked at the kids.

"So?"

"So, that woman in the yard, she was hanging up those same kinds of clothes. If we go out there wearing white shirts like that, we could get closer to him, he'd think we're locals. It's the perfect disguise!"

"Ah, *monami*, that's brilliant!"

"We need to turn around and head back to that woman's laundry line and steal a couple of her shirts, then come back up this way and make camp."

XXVIII

A Skin for A Skin
Pro Pelle Cutem
November 16, 1875

Pierre Kannaquassé woke up quickly, groggy and sore after a fitful night's sleep in his filthy clothes on the beach. It was early morning, the gray light of dawn lay heavily, unhappily, on the clouded skies and the dark but calm waters of Possession Sound. He was greeted by the sight of his comrade cooking up bacon, biscuits, and coffee on a small driftwood fire. Pierre pushed himself up off the ground and stretched, then took his long knife and whetstone from his rucksack and started sharpening it.

"You won't be needing that today," McPherson remarked, turning a piece of bacon.

"Maybe Frenchy would like his leg sliced open, like happened to me thirty-years ago," Pierre remarked, not looking up. He stroked the blade across the flat stone then felt for the sharpness with his thumb.

"Today we are only thieves, and if you concern yourself with other matters then I will hold back your final pay. Savvy?"

Pierre held the blade of the knife straight up in front of his face and slowly turned it with a rapturous gaze. Once satisfied, he slid it back into its sheath. Not looking at McPherson he said, "After we're done here, I'm leaving and going back east. So when it's over, we split up the loot, you pay me what I'm owed and we won't see each other again."

McPherson glanced at Pierre and nodded, not saying anything, and returned to his bacon.

An hour later, after their meal, McPherson was busy in the bushes, taking his morning constitutional. Seeing his opportunity, Pierre dug through his rucksack, found the .22 Short rimfire pistol he'd kept concealed the whole time, and shoved it behind his belt under his coat, then started to break camp.

Before they pushed off, McPherson tossed one of the white shirts they'd stolen the day before at Pierre. "Here," he said, "before we land, you need to put that on."

"Ah, *bien!*" Pierre replied, grinning, catching the shirt. "We will fool the Frenchy today!" But as he climbed into the canoe his expression changed to an evil-minded look.

Halfway across to the island the sky turned dark and full of doubt, a slight breeze began to blow. Soon the flat water of the bay was rippled with wind chop.

In the distance, black woodsmoke could be seen coming from the top north end of the island. Once they were about a quarter mile off, McPherson took off his old military coat and put on the white shirt.

"Get that shirt on," McPherson said. Pierre stopped paddling and then very carefully took off his coat and put on the white shirt.

As they resumed paddling no one could be seen on the island but the same smoke they'd spotted earlier coming from the upper reaches, was even blacker now and growing thicker. They paddled farther west towards the smoke, hugging the shoreline.

"Since we're disguised as locals," McPherson said, "I'll use some jargon to call him out."

"Klahowya!" he yelled up towards the smoke, just above them. They waited for a reply but heard none. While they waited, they scanned the island for any sign of life.

"Look!" Pierre said, pointing. "Is that the roof of a cabin?"

"It is, I see it back over there," McPherson replied. "I'll try again."

"Klahowya Peter, *me-si'ka yuk'-wa?"* McPherson yelled once more.

"Luke? Nathan? Is that you?" a voice called back. "How come you're not speaking English?"

"Is that him?" Pierre asked quietly, but with an eager tone.

"Maybe," McPherson answered, "let's land the canoe but not get out. And let me do the talking."

Ten minutes later a tall and lanky man, bent with age, appeared at the top of the beach with a knit cap on his head and a dog following behind. The man was walking slowly and his dog even slower. As soon as McPherson could get a good read of him, he knew it was Goutre.

"I was pruning and burning up top in the orchard!" Peter hollered, walking around and stepping over all the logs at the high-water mark to be closer to them. "Got too much work to do. Did you boys bring me my smoked salmon?" He squinted at the dugout, it looked like the two figures weren't getting out. Mr. John wandered up to Peter's side and sniffed the air, he let loose a few hoarse old barks.

"That's okay, boy, it's only the Keokuk kids here to pay us a visit with some fish," Peter said to his dog. "Did you bring my salmon?" he yelled again. "Come on! Let's go in the cabin and get out of the weather, there's fresh thunderheads building!"

McPherson looked at his comrade, grinned, and then searched in the stolen canoe for the previous owner's gunny sack that was already in it. Holding it up above his head he pointed to it with his other hand. Pierre smiled back as he understood the deception.

"Good," Peter replied, rubbing his eyes, looking at the out of focus brothers. He couldn't put it in words, but he was feeling jubilant, part of a family — "Come on, boys!" he shouted again, motioning with his arm, "The sooner I'm eating that salmon of yours the better!"

Swooping down from the sky a raven flew close to Peter's head, cawing loudly. It darted back over to his cabin, landed on the roof and began walking back and forth while wildly flapping its wings. But Peter didn't notice, so it took flight once more. This time it circled around the beach then returned and landed on the sill outside of the window, it started pecking on the panes of glass, Peter still didn't notice. But the Changer, *Dukwibal*, was paying close attention.

McPherson and Pierre began to get out of the canoe and walk up the beach towards Peter, still standing in all the drift logs. As they did Pierre slipped behind McPherson just as the wind picked up, then it began to spit rain.

374

Peter turned and slowly began to walk around the logs towards his cabin. McPherson picked up a little speed and, snatching up a club-shaped piece of driftwood in his right hand, he jumped over and ran around the logs and closed on Peter. Then he threw the sack in front of him. Peter stopped to look at it. Unsure of why one of the Keokuk kids would throw his smoked salmon at his feet, he turned around and tried to focus his failing eyesight on the boy. Luke seemed taller than he remembered.

"You son of a bitch, you stole everything from us!" McPherson hollered, raising his club, threatening Peter with it. "And now we're here to collect our due."

"What? Wait!" Peter said into the wind and rain, staring at the two fuzzy looking forms. He glanced down at the gunny sack. "What are you talking about? I just want my salmon."

"Some things never change, even a thief like you!" McPherson snarled. "I said you stole our lives from us and now we want it all back! You ruined us, Goutre. You took everything you could and then burned the rest of it down at Stikine!"

"Stikine?! What are you talking —" Peter replied, then it hit him. *These aren't the Keokuk boys. It's somebody from Fort Stikine years ago — it's McPherson and Heroux!*

"Yeah, Stikine, you dumb old bastard!" McPherson spat.

Peter's mind reeled, he shouted, "What are you talking about? I don't have anything of yours!"

Sensing his master was in trouble Mr. John started to run towards the two intruders, firing a barking salvo of angry warning bursts. But McPherson was too fast, he hit John in the side of his head with the driftwood, knocking him down, unconscious between some beach logs. It started to rain harder.

"JOHN!" Peter shrieked, stepping towards his dog.

At the same time, Pierre pulled the .22 rimfire out from under his belt and stepped over a beach log towards Peter. He leveled it on him.

"NO!" McPherson screamed. "What're you doing? Where'd you get that?"

"Shut up, Thomas, I'm in charge now," Pierre uttered, smirking and pointing the gun at McPherson. "Drop it," he said, motioning with the gun at McPherson's club, he let it fall to the ground.

When Peter saw the pistol he stopped, then instantly reacted as if he was still a trader up north, he reached for the old flintlock he used to carry at his side; it wasn't there. He looked up and saw a pock-marked face, and depraved eyes showing the emotion of a madman, a grotesque bent on revenge. They were the same eyes he'd seen years ago at Fort Langley when —

Ka-POW! the sound of Pierre's rimfire filled the air. Goutre stumbled from the bullet and dropped to his knees grabbing his neck, he pulled his hand away, covered in blood, the bullet had ripped a deep wound in the side of his neck . . . Thunder instantly began to rumble in the sky! It rolled across the water from Skayu Point and resounded overhead.

"Damn you! I told you we are only —" McPherson sputtered, glancing at the club on the ground. Kannaquassé pointed the gun at him, saying, "Don't pick it up." McPherson took a step back. Pierre turned to Goutre.

"A skin, for a skin, Frenchy," Pierre seethed. "And now you shall receive the same pain you inflicted on me because death is all you have."

Peter realized it was Pierre **Kannaquassé**, not Urbain Heroux and fumed, "You dirty bastards, go after my dog will you," glaring at **Kannaquassé and then McPherson**, looking down at John, holding his bloody neck. "And what happened to Urbain?" he probed, raising his gaze. "He killed McLoughlin, didn't he."

"Urbain's dead and gone," Pierre replied, aiming his pistol back and forth at Peter and McPherson.

"Did Simpson send him to prison and have him shot?"

"Oh, Urbain went to prison alright," Kannaquassé said, looking nervous, "but because Stikine was on Russian soil Chief Manager Etholén didn't care about any of it, so he didn't prosecute him. He let him go and Heroux went back to Trois-Rivières where he died."

"So you sons a' bitches got away with it. You killed McLoughlin and walked away scot-free, didn't you?"

"No," Pierre countered, "nobody walked away scot-free. Antoine spilled the beans after **those God damned Kanakas from Fort Durham claimed they saw it and ratted Urbain out weeks after it happened**. But Simpson didn't go after us and blackballed us instead. We never got to be rich like you. You're the one who got away with everything."

"The Kanakas from Durham?"

"Mr. John brought back two canoes full of Kanakas workers and a couple of them claimed that they saw Urbain kill McLoughlin. And you got rich out of the deal."

"Rich?" Peter said, trying to laugh but it hurt too much. "What are you talking about? I'm not rich you ignorant bastard. I should have slit your throat when I had the chance."

Pierre limped towards Peter so McPherson took a step towards Pierre, Pierre wheeled on him and yelled, "I've waited long enough, it's time for him to pay! Don't deny me my right!"

"Your right? We didn't come here to kill him!"

But Pierre's eyes told a different story. With a searing look that burned into McPherson's soul, Pierre aimed square at his head. "Get back!" he screamed, cocking the pistol. This time McPherson stepped away farther with his hands raised. Pierre picked up the driftwood club and tossed it as far away as he could.

Then Pierre turned to Peter but he was back on his feet, stumbling over the shanks of driftwood that littered the upper shore, heading towards his cabin. He pulled a pocket knife from his trousers and opened the blade, thinking he might be able to hide it and then stab one if they got close enough.

Pierre limped as fast as he could and cut him off. "That's it!" he barked, aiming at Peter.

"But I have no money, everything I took from the cabin up at Bitter Water was stolen from us by Haida raiders. They took everything and took my wife . . . killed her," he moaned, then he glanced over at the emergency bonfire piles. "I worked years for this island, with my own two hands. Come a little closer so we can talk this —"

"Shut up!" Pierre hollered, spit flying from his mouth. "We know you've been living like a King and now we want to do the same."

"A King? I'm not a King by any means. Look around, does this look like someplace a King would live?"

"You're a liar, Goutre! We know your cabin is full of gold and all the jewels you stole!"

"No, it's not," Peter said faintly, his hand against his neck trying to stop the flow of blood but he couldn't. He began to feel dizzy and faint, he dropped down on his knees. It was then that his life flashed before him: there was Little Rain in his mind's eye, her smile and gentle way and the young toddler, Catherine Rose, she was bouncing on his knee. Then the wilderness he spent his life in and loved, rugged, and beautiful. The mill, Isaac Ebey, his island, and My Man John.

Pierre turned his head but kept the hand gun aimed at Peter and said to McPherson, "Go check his cabin."

"Check it yourself," McPherson grunted.

Pierre spun around and CRACK, he fired his pistol in the air. "DO IT NOW!"

McPherson scowled and then slowly walked around the last of the beach logs towards the cabin with a stiff gait. Once there, he saw an unlocked padlock on the hasp of the door but he kicked it open anyway. It instantly bounced back on him so he pushed it and held the door open against the wall with his arm, then glanced around. The floor of the small one room hovel was covered with sand and bits of seaweed, the wood stove still had a few embers from a steaming pot of cabbage soup. A messy bed that was half-covered by a filthy quilt rested in a corner. He went over and looked under it, saw nothing, only a sand and dog hair covered floor, so he stood up and scanned the room. There was a table with a kerosene lamp and a small plate with some bright pebbles on it, two bowls; one with biscuits and the other held some apples, two chairs were on either side. He saw a box of whiskey bottles then opened a few metal containers but there was only flour, sugar, salt and pemmican. Some clothes were hanging on a wall. McPherson found nothing of any value and went back outside.

"There's nothing here," he yelled from the cabin door.

"You see," Peter uttered, "I told you I don't have anything."

"What do you mean? There's nothing?"

"There's nothing, it's just a shack. He lives like a pauper."

"He's right. I have nothing . . . no money, no gold . . . you've came here for nothing, you dumb bastards," Peter stammered, bleeding and weak. He glanced up at Pierre and then over at McPherson. "The two of you are fools."

"Fools? That's it, I've had enough. You've got it buried, don't you? Tell us where's it's all at! All the emeralds and safire, the sterling and nuggets, the gold rings! Where is it?!"

"There's nothing buried here! When I beat the hell out of the two of you at Fort Langley was I with my wife? No, she wasn't there because like I just told you we were ambushed by Haidas on our way south. They took everything we had, including her." He glared at Pierre and seethed, "So get off my island you —"

Ka-POW! . . . Pierre shot him in the chest. Peter rocked backwards on his knees and dropped his pocketknife. But he pulled himself forward then clutched his chest, he looked up at Pierre and scowled at him as he gasped for air.

"You little coward," he coughed, trying to inhale, spitting up blood onto his beard. Peter turned his head upward to the darkening sky and rolled his eyes, then closed them and murmured a few soft words of prayer to Mother Mary and, as he did, he began to sway side-to-side. A moment later, the swaying changed and he started to revolve in a circular motion, slowly, his eyes still closed, pivoting on his knees and rotating ever so slightly. Pierre watched in disbelief, mesmerized, his mouth agape. Not only was he astounded by the sight of him still alive, but by his transfixing movement until Peter stopped rotating. With every ounce of strength left in him he opened his eyes and sputtered with bloody defiance, "Why are you . . . still here? I just told you to — get off my island."

"I'm not going anywhere, Frenchy, *enculer,* you *bâtard.* You're the one who's leaving," Pierre spat. He lowered his .22 Short, aimed at his head, squeezed the trigger and — CRACK! Peter jerked backwards, he awkwardly fell away from the gunman onto some driftwood between beach logs. In a flash of wickedness, French Peter's life, and his long journey, was over.

"Wait! Don't!" McPherson screamed, running towards him. "Are you mad?! Why'd you do that!"

Pierre wheeled on McPherson, aimed at him and yelled, "Stay back! I'll do it!" McPherson raised his hands and took a few steps backwards, shaking his head and muttering.

Pierre stood next to Peter's body, the tight smirk of heinous satisfaction on his face. Peter's marriage stick had slid up to his neck when he fell and was now exposed. Pierre reached down and ripped the sanctified artifact from his neck, breaking the unbreakable bond and sinew that had held it close against Peter's heart for over thirty-years and . . . BOOM! A clap of earth-shaking thunder reverberated from the sky above Little Rain's monument — she began to tremble, her draped artifacts swaying to and fro from the sudden rumbling. Chain-lightning flashed across the heavens, from Skayu Point to Peter's Island and back again like a ricochet, filling the sky with the wrath of fire and creation from The Changer *Dukwibal*.

The sky lifted up and fell back down, then *Dukwibal* sent a strong wind. It enveloped Little Rain's totem like a tornado, but the whirlwind stayed outside of her body. The starfish and clam shells at her base were swept up in its wake — spinning a tempest around her while the raven feathers on her headdress barely moved. They gently swayed about until Little Rain's obsidian eyes began to cry and melt as trails of black tears trickled down her face. At that moment The *Changer's* wrath became whole, it rose up above the sacred monument and soared across the Sound's darkening waters towards the island.

Jolted from the thunder and lightning, Pierre covered his head and inadvertently let go of the marriage stick, it dropped on the sand next to Peter's body. Seeing his opportunity, McPherson ran up behind him undetected and violently, quickly, ripped the pistol from his hand, then pointed it at him. Pierre raised his hands just as hail began to pour straight down on them in a blizzard.

"You idiot! This is what you wanted to do the whole time," McPherson cried, his voice thick with panic and confusion, the hail bouncing off the logs and sand, the wind swirling around them. He swallowed hard and tried to regain control, "Get back to the canoe! Now!"

"What are you doing? Don't shoot me, you wanted him dead too! I know it!" Pierre hollered into *Dukwibal's* storm, taking a step towards McPherson.

"STOP!" McPherson yelled, pulling back the hammer. "I'll kill you and leave you here to rot! Now get back to the canoe!"

"Ah, *monami*," Pierre said with a devilish smirk, "but I am —"

"Don't give me that *monami* crap! Move it! NOW!"

Pierre took his meaning and started to limp away from him. "Okay. I will go back to the boat to put on my coat and wait for you," Pierre replied over his shoulder with a sly grin.

McPherson watched and waited for Pierre to reach the canoe, then he went over to Peter's cabin again. He shoved the small revolver behind his belt and frantically looked around the cabin one more time, thinking he might find some clue as to where Peter kept his valuables. As he searched, he glanced out the lone window but didn't see Pierre.

Leaving the cabin he trotted towards the beach but the canoe was gone. Startled, McPherson scanned the bay. *Dukwibal* had whipped up the waves, they were building and a howling wind blew through the trees behind him, snapping limbs and sending debris flying through the air. The hail was replaced by pounding rain and, bobbing up and down in the waves fifty-yards offshore was Pierre, paddling furiously in *Dukwibal's* cold, driving storm.

"That wretched little —" McPherson muttered, he pulled the .22 Short up, aimed and . . . CRACK! Pierre ducked, but started paddling again.

McPherson scanned the beach, two canoes were tied up down the way. He ran, stumbling, as fast as he could through the beach logs then over the rocky, slippery shore. In a frenzy he untied the smaller canoe and set out on the bounding surf.

The Changer's whirlwind plummeted from the sky, then hovered over My Man John until it ever so slowly descended upon him. As it did, sand, shells, and bits of seaweed were lifted up and began to swirl in its spinning funnel. Once Mr. John was fully encased in the tornado vengeance of *Dukwibal*, the grey hair on his snout changed to black, and his weak old legs turned strong, then his body twinged and his eyes opened. Mr. John jumped up with a start, young and spry again. He bounded over to Peter's lifeless body and pushed his shoulder with his nose, but Peter didn't move, so he licked his face, Peter didn't wake up. Realizing he was dead, John growled and his eyes turned fiery. In anger he raised his head and let out a HOWL! of rolling thunder . . . then he sniffed the swirling wind.

Pierre turned south, but McPherson was the stronger of the two and had a lighter craft. Soon he was thirty-yards off Pierre's stern. He set down his paddle, got on his knees, aimed the gun at Pierre's back and fired.

But the waves slamming the canoe were rocking it too much, he missed. McPherson opened the pistol's drum, there was one unused bullet left. He started to paddle again, he needed to get much closer.

Just then McPherson heard loud barking. He turned his head and was shocked to see that it was Peter's dog! Back on his feet, young and strong, running along the shore, soaking wet and covered in sand. As John got closer, he started snapping his sharp white teeth and growling with the power of cannon fire, determined to sink his fangs into the men who were responsible for his master's death.

At the south point of the island, the waters opened up and the rage and fury of *Dukwibal* had reached a crescendo. Stinging stiletto rain slashed sideways and the churning white caps were now stacked up with nearly no space between them, turning Possession Sound into a roiling broth of Hell. They crashed over the bow of each canoe, both men breathing hard and drenched, the numbing cold making it hard to even hold on to their paddles.

Pierre glanced over his shoulder, McPherson was bearing down on him. He looked to the west and then the east, he saw nothing but dancing vertical waves, the wind was so fierce it ripped the white water off the tops of each one, it flew sideways through the air, the sky black with wickedness. Pierre instantly decided he'd never make it to the mainland, he started to turn around and go back to the island.

Just as he turned in a trough between waves, he glanced at McPherson when *Dukwibal's* funnel of wrath whipped the waves into a frenzy, lifting his canoe then dropping it, causing the dugout to capsize and sink. Pierre gasped for air and flailed at the icy cold water, but his heavy wool coat pulled him under, his lungs filled with water and he disappeared.

"You bastard!" McPherson screamed, just as the whirlwind bowled over him and scuttled the small canoe. He thrashed in the frigid surf and tried to swim to shore but soon, he too was in the downward pull of the current. It sent him into the depths of Whulge, where his evilness was consumed by The Changer *Dukwibal*.

Mr. John stood and watched each canoe get swallowed in the

Sound, the men sinking away. He waited, then barked one time into the wind and rain. Finally, he bounded back up the beach to Peter, where he found the marriage stick, picked it up in his teeth and dropped it on his chest. Instantly, John's snout turned back to grey, his body became old again, and the furor began to calm. He sat down and stayed by his master's side, insensible to the rain.

XXIX

After the Storm
Kim'-ta Snass
November 26, 1875

Brewery owner Joe Butterfield stood at the top of the beach in Mukilteo and looked out over the water towards Gedney Island, hoping to spot some sign of French Peter and his crop of apples. Seeing only the wide smooth Sound before him, he shook his head, turned and went back into the trading post.

"Still no sign of him," Joe reported, closing the door and walking over to the counter.

"That's odd," Morris replied, "he should've shown up by now. John Ross said the same thing and you know, nobody's seen a touch of smoke coming from over there either. His new eye glasses came in the other day and I'm sure he could use them. I think we need to send someone over there to check on him."

"I agree," Joe said, rubbing his chin, the look of concern on his face. "Those apples were due in days ago, and we all know that Peter would be late to judgement day if he knew someone on earth still had some money for him. I'll go see if Hank Vining will go over there."

Two of Joe's best customers, and friends, were having coffee at the front table. "If you can't break away then I'll go," Bob Niles said, pushing back his chair. He stood up and looked at his cohort.

"Come on, get up. What else you got to do today?" Jack Wiggins sighed and shrugged, then stood up.

"Alright, but the beer is on you, Butterfield!"

The three men left and walked over to the salmon-salting warehouse, where they found the proprietor maneuvering new empty barrels from the front of the building to the back.

"Afternoon Hank," Joe said, greeting Vining. "How soon before those are filled with fish?"

"Not soon enough, got another order to get ready for. What're you fellas doing? Here to help?"

"Oh," Joe said, "I'm, I mean, we're worried about French Peter. Nobody's seen him since the end of last month and he's supposed to be bringing over some bushels of apples for a batch of cider for me."

Hank stopped what he was doing and put his hands on his hips, "I do believe this has got to be the first time anyone's ever been worried about that old cuss."

"Hank, some tree could have landed on him over there, he could be crushed and dead under some uprooted hemlock for criminy sakes! That storm was one for the ages," Butterfield reiterated.

"So what're ya' sayin'?"

"He's sayin'," Bob said, breaking in, "that somebody needs to go and check on him."

"Somebody who?" Hank asked.

"I can't, I've got a-hundred bottles of beer to fill, cork and wire this afternoon, so I shouldn't even be here right now," Joe answered.

"But the point is Peter could be in big trouble over there and need help."

"Yep," Wiggins added, "It ain't like him to be not showin' up where he can make some money."

"Or save some money."

"Or come out better on some trades don't ya' know."

"Okay, your next batch of brew is of utmost importance, so how many need to go?" Hank asked, finally warming up to the idea.

"With three paddlers on the flood tide we could get over there in about two hours, I figure," Bob remarked.

"Okay, whose canoe?"

"Use mine," Joe suggested, looking at Jack Wiggins, "it's light and a whole lot faster than that tub of yours."

"What'd you mean?" Wiggins asked. "My Skagit is a damn fine vessel." The other three men chuckled.

"Why indeed Wigs, that boat of yours is a fine ship. Hell, I'd take that thing all the way to Olympia and not worry a lick! Might take me two months, but —"

After the laughter died down, Bob said, "Thanks for offering Joe, we'd be pleased to use it. But it's already 10:30 so we need to get going, it'll be dark in six more hours."

"And," Jack said, "the tides still coming in so we should go right now."

"Joe," Hank said, "can you tell Morris that we're headed over there? And that if we're not back by nightfall have him put a lantern in the window."

"Will do."

The three men headed straight for the beach and found Joe's canoe. Bob and Jack hopped in and Hank pushed them off.

"Any bets how long it takes to get over there?" Bob asked, picking up a paddle.

"Oh I'm thinkin' Joe was right, probably about two hours," Wiggins answered.

"Yeah, well," Hank said, "good thing we ain't in that old waterlogged floater of yours, Wigs."

"Ha! Real funny," Wiggins replied, "I'm thinkin' we'll get there sooner with less chatter and more paddling."

An hour and a half later they were approaching the northeast end of the island. As soon as the south side of French Peter's weather-beaten cabin came into view, uncrushed by a tree, they saw a raven skip-hop walking back and forth along a drift log flapping its wings. Then Peter's dog saw them and popped up from behind another log, he started viciously barking at them so the raven flew off.

"He doesn't sound too happy," Wiggins remarked.

"No kidding," Vining added, as they drifted closer.

"Look!" Hank exclaimed, "the front door is open."

"Damn, that's no good," Wiggins said, staring at Peter's abode.

"Hey Peter! Where are ya'?" Vining hollered.

They floated just off shore, near where Peter's big canoe was tied off, yelling for him for a few moments while Mr. John slowly worked his way along the beach and over to them, barking nonstop.

"Jeez, he's pretty mad," Bob said.

"And old too," Hank added, "that thing must be 15 or more."

"If Peter's got a broken leg up top at his orchard and can't walk then I bet his dog is probably starving, both of them for that matter," Bob said. "We should've brought something, a steak or some chicken. What's this dog's name?"

"Peter calls him John, or Mr. John, sometimes," Wiggins replied.

"It's alright, John, easy boy," Bob said. But Peter's dog wouldn't stop barking, and the closer they drifted to the shore the more John snapped at them.

"Well, we sure ain't turning around, and I ain't landin' with him goin' at us like that. We've got to get him to skedaddle so we can go ashore," Vining remarked.

"Just because he's a barker that doesn't mean he's a biter," Wiggins observed.

"Oh, yeah!" Hank laughed, "if he's anything like his master then I bet he'd sink his teeth into you in a heartbeat."

"That could be, but my knees are killin' me right now and I need to get out of this boat," Bob Niles said. "I'll get him to stop."

"How you gonna do that?" Wiggins asked.

"Let's get into some shallower water and I'll jump out and use my paddle to fend him off," Bob offered.

"Sounds fine by me," Niles said.

They paddled closer to the shore while Mr. John continued to object. Once they were in less than two feet of water Niles jumped into the surf with his paddle and started to advance on the dog, jabbing at him like he was in a fencing duel. But John sunk his teeth into the blade of Bob's oar, growling and shaking his head. Bob pushed against his paddle and the dog and forced him to back up a few yards. During the struggle, Hank and Wiggins jumped out of the canoe and started to pelt rocks at Mr. John, one hit him in his rear leg and finally with a yelp, he gave up and ran off back up the beach to where he was first sighted.

"Holy crap," Bob belched, "he's a real scrapper."

"No shit, he's a tough old guy," Wiggins said.

"Just like his old man," Bob added, looking around.

"We should do a search."

"Let's check the cabin first," Hank suggested, pointing at Peter's abode. They walked over to Peter's little hovel, there were baskets full of apples outside and Hank found the padlock from his front door lying on the ground. He picked it up.

"That's odd, why would his front door be wide open with the lock in the dirt?" he asked.

Inside, nothing had been disturbed and a large pot of vegetable soup was sitting on the top of a cold stove. His bed was unmade and his rifle and two shotguns were hidden, leaning against the wall behind the door, his two chairs were standing upright at the table where a small plate with some colorful pebbles and two bowls sat, one with a batch of biscuits, the other held some apples. Everything seemed to be in its place.

"Mr. John would like these," Hank remarked, picking up the bowl of biscuits.

"I bet he would," Wiggins agreed.

"I don't get it," Bob stated. "A tree didn't land on his cabin and he was cooking soup it looks like. This don't add up."

Bob and Wiggins walked out of the cabin and started to search around outside. Wiggins found the trail that led up to Peter's well and orchard. He took a few steps up it then turned around.

"I'm gonna hike up this way and see what I can find," he called out, pointing up the trail. "I think his orchard is up there."

"Okay, I believe it is," Bob replied. "We'll search the beach."

"I think I'll take those biscuits over to Mr. John, maybe try to make friends and then look that way," Hank said, going back in the cabin and getting them.

"That's a good idea," Bob remarked. "You do that and I'll head the other way down the beach."

Up at the orchard, Wiggins found what was left of a few burnt up bonfire piles and dozens of chickens scratching and scurrying about. A half dozen head of cattle were grazing close by and four hogs were rooting around in their paddock, their feeding trough stood empty just inside the fencing.

Down below, Vining walked the biscuits to Mr. John, he sat up when he saw Hank approach. John raised his nose and started sniffing the air.

"Come on, boy," Hank said, tossing one on the sand nearby. "Here ya' go."

Hank took a few steps back as John stood up. He walked in the opposite direction so the dog wandered over to the biscuit with his tail slightly wagging and inhaled it with one bite.

As soon as he did, Vining stepped up on a beach log and walked along it towards where Mr. John had been, then jumped over to another and continued until he saw French Peter's lifeless body, lying on its back across some driftwood with one leg pinned under him. Vining's heart skipped a beat then it jumped up into his throat, he dropped the bowl of biscuits inadvertently into the dirt, Mr. John immediately walked over and gobbled them up.

"Holy mother of God," he whispered to himself. Hank stood there stunned, unable to process the sight before him. There was a gunshot wound in his neck and chest, and the right side of his skull was shattered, his knit cap was akilter on his head. Stepping closer he could see there was a bullet hole in it.

On Peter's chest was his marriage stick, the braided sinew necklace broken and worn, a pocket knife was lying on the ground next to him. Hank got down on his haunches next to the body.

"Lord Almighty," Vining said quietly to himself. "Looks like French Peter's been murdered." He took his hat off and said a few words of prayer, then he stood up and looked down the beach.

He put his hands to the side of his mouth and yelled, "Hey Bob! Get over here! I found him!" He waved at him and yelled again.

Bob turned around right away and then raised his hand in the air in acknowledgement, he started walking in Vining's direction. Hank yelled up the hill to where he thought Wiggins was.

Soon, the three of them were standing over French Peter's body, it was a horrible sight to look upon.

"Criminy, this don't look good," Bob said.

"Looks like he was executed to me," Wiggins added.

"We shouldn't touch anything. A crime's been committed here,"

Hank remarked. While they talked Mr. John had wandered over to them so Hank started petting him.

"Sure looks that way," Wiggins said. "What should we do?"

"Head back and tell Morris," Bob replied.

"Yeah, we need to come back with a coffin and give him a good Christian burial," Hank said.

"A good Christian burial? Really? For French Peter?"

"He told me once that he was raised Catholic and that he learned his letters in church," Bob said.

"No kidding."

"Yep, he was pretty drunk at the time but I believed him," he added.

"French Peter could read?"

"Yep, that's what he said."

"No wonder he was always so sharp in trade."

"And what about Mr. John? We can't leave him here to starve," Hank said.

"Well, if we can get him in the boat then we should take him back," Wiggins offered.

"He might like that soup in Peter's cabin. Or, maybe we could find something else for him. If we do, we should be able to get him in the canoe with some more food," Bob suggested.

"What's that over there?" Wiggins asked, pointing at a lump of something lying near them by some logs. He walked over to it, picked it up and looked inside. "Looks like a bunch of dirty clothes," he said, holding up the gunny sack.

"What?" both men said at the same time.

"Why would a sack of dirty clothes be out here?"

"Maybe he was gonna do his laundry down here on the beach?" Wiggins asked, pulling a filthy white cotton shirt out, he held it up. It was small, much smaller than Peter.

"That looks kind-a little for a man as tall as old Pete."

"This is getting strange. I think we need to get the authorities over here right away."

"We do," Hank added.

"Okay, well let's see if we can find Mr. John something else to eat and try to get him in the canoe."

Wiggins dropped the gunny sack next to Peter and started walking towards the cabin while Mr. John followed at a distance. In Peter's cabin Wiggins found some pemican stored in a metal container.

"Good," Hank said, "that should work, let's give him a piece, see what he does."

Wiggins tossed Mr. John a piece of pemican and he promptly gobbled it up. He took a step closer and tossed him another. By the fourth piece Wiggins was standing right next to Mr. John, feeding and petting him.

Wiggins looked up and smiled, "I think he likes us now." Then he started walking towards the canoe while holding out a piece. At the shoreline he tossed it inside the dugout. Energized by the food and an extra lift of his hind quarters by Vining, Mr. John got on board and they headed back to Mukilteo.

Island Requiem
čəčəs ḱáyu
November 27, 1875

The next day Joe Butterfield and Jack Wiggins struggled with getting the long, odd-shaped coffin out of Morris' backroom. "How heavy is this thing?" Wiggins groaned, trying to maneuver the big wooden box around a corner and out the rear door.

"I'd say a good sixty 'er seventy-pounds," Joe answered.

"Yeah, well, I'd say more like a-hundred, and why can't these things have handles?"

Once outside they set it down on a small cordwood pile and caught their breath. "They should," Butterfield said, "but all we gotta do now is get the thing down to the beach and in the canoe."

"Easier said than done, my friend," Jack said, bending over and grabbing hold of one end.

Down at the dugouts, Sheriff Ben Stretch was already there and wasn't too pleased with having to paddle all the way out to the island, Bob Niles was waiting with him. When Wiggins and

399

Butterfield showed up with the heavy casket, breathing hard and stumbling on the rocks, the sheriff spit in the sand and bellowed, "Come on you two! Hurry it up! It's bad enough I had to come all the way out here but now I gotta wait on the both of you."

"Yeah, yeah," Wiggins sighed.

"That thing can't be as heavy as it looks!" Stretch remarked.

"Oh, it is, Sheriff," Joe answered, walking into the surf with Wiggins and setting the long box in his canoe. Then both of them bent over at the waist and put their hands on their knees, breathing deeply.

"I hear his dog gave you quite a time yesterday," Stretch said.

"He did at first. But once we got some food in him his orneriness went away," Wiggins replied.

As soon as they landed at Gedney, Butterfield and Wiggins carried the coffin up onto the beach and set it down across two drift logs, Niles carried the shovels and pre-made wooden cross. Then they led the sheriff over to the body.

"There's the poor son of a gun," Jack said, pointing at French Peter's body lying face up.

"Jesus," Stretch mumbled. He got down on his haunches and looked at the bullet wounds first, then flipped the marriage stick over and flicked it around on Peter's bloody chest with an index finger. The Sheriff looked at it closely, then picked up a pocket knife on the ground, saying, "And you fellas found him like this?"

"Yes, sir," Niles responded, leaning on the end of a shovel handle. Stretch reached into Peter's front trouser pocket and pulled out some keys and another pocket knife. He stood up, put them all in his trousers and then looked at the gunny sack. "What about that," he asked, motioning at it, "where was that found?"

"I found it yesterday over by those logs," Wiggins answered, pointing. The sheriff picked up the gunny sack and looked inside.

"Clothes? Strange way to do laundry. Maybe he had them bagged up for someone," he mused. He dropped the sack on the ground and then got down on his haunches again and took a closer look at Peter's head and chest wounds. He took a pencil out of his shirt pocket with a small leather-bound pad of paper and began to take some notes.

"So, ah, sheriff," Wiggins said, "I noticed yesterday that one of Peter's canoes ain't here. His big boat is right where he usually keeps both of 'em, but the smaller one's gone."

The sheriff stopped writing and looked up, "You sure he didn't trade it away? But then . . . I guess the storm could've broken it free."

"Yeah, I guess so, but I don't think he'd get rid of it," Wiggins replied. "You know, though, now that I think about it, in a storm like that one he would've done his best to pull both of 'em up on the shore."

The sheriff paused and looked out over the water, he said, "I could see a man doing that but, if he didn't trade it away, then maybe he was dead before the storm hit?"

The three men stood over the sheriff and all nodded their heads at the same time.

"How 'bout if you fellas find a good spot to bury him so's I can do my work?"

"You heard the man," Joe said, picking up his shovel and resting its handle on his shoulder, "let's go find a nice spot for French Peter."

The three grave diggers went a dozen paces to the west of the cabin and found a sandy bank against the hill. Wiggins pressed the tip of his shovel in the soft ground, pushed it into the soil and then levered the handle. He stopped, looked at his friends and, half laughing, asked, "Think we'll find any gold?"

Everyone started to chuckle and Wiggins tossed the dirt aside.

"Maybe!" Niles said, "They always said the Government paid him a big heap of money for his land at Tulalip, and Lord knows he never spent a cent he didn't have to. He musta' buried it away somewhere here. Then of course there is all that talk of gold."

"And what are we gonna do about it? Huh? Dig up the whole damn island looking for it?"

"Well no, but Wiggins is right! We know he had the gold and we know he was the flintiest son of a sailor in the territory, so it stands to reason that it must be here somewhere."

"Maybe he was murdered for it."

"What? You mean for the gold and the reservation money?"

"Sure! People have killed for less than old Pete probably had stashed over here, happens all the time."

"What'd ya' mean, all the time?"

"Okay, well, take for instance old man Seybert. He got murdered."

"Aw, that were different. That wasn't about money, his kid did him in because he was the worst all-out bastard this side of the Cascades! There was no gold involved, or even love for that matter."

"Then what about T.P Carter, he was murdered! Stabbed to death in his trading post for guns and ammo!"

"Oh, Jesus, Wigs, that was a long time ago. Stop it with the theories would ya'!"

"Yeah, well, anyway . . . we could still hit golden treasure with the next shovel full," Wiggins countered.

"If you could just listen to the two of you cackling hens," Bob said. "Why I never heard such a pitiful sound. All you two can do is go on about murder and money like you were a couple of little old ladies in a parlor room. Aren't you even the least bit concerned that there's still a killer or two on the loose? Or better yet, how 'bout if you both have a little respect for the dead."

Butterfield and Wiggins looked at each other and shrugged. Jack opened his mouth, and was about to say something but stopped, rolled his eyes, and then quietly said, "Guess I hadn't thought about someone still on the loose . . . Hell — Is it you?"

The three of them laughed heartily so Wiggins kept feeding them line after line of talk. "You know, I guess he was married once," he stated, stabbing the earth with his shovel and then jumping up and landing with both feet on it.

"Married? French Peter?" Joe asked. "Impossible."

"Yep, Brigham told me that years ago. Said he built a cabin door for him, brought it out one day like a surprise and hung it. They had a few drinks and Peter told him."

"Really? He said that French Peter was married?"

"Yep, to an Indian girl, Tlingit, from way up north when he was a trader for Hudson's Bay."

"No kidding."

"Unless Dennis was kidding me, but I'd never take him as a fabricator."

"And what happened? No one ever saw a wife around here."

"He told Dennis that she passed away, right after they were hitched."

"What? How?"

"Yep, that's what Dennis said, but Peter didn't say how."

"From like smallpox, maybe?"

"Didn't say, he apparently took it pretty hard though."

"I'll be damned, never saw him as a married man."

"Me neither, who did? We can ask Dennis about it the next time we see him."

Just then Sheriff Stretch walked up and looked in the hole. "That looks like easy diggin'."

"Easy for you to say," Wiggins quipped.

"I'm gonna head over to the cabin and see what I can find. You boys should be all done by the time I get back."

"So Sheriff," Jack said, "what'd ya' think about Peter?"

"About what?"

"Well," Wiggins continued, leaning against his shovel, "about who shot him, or why? Bob here said yesterday that it looked like he was murdered but I think he was executed."

The Sheriff stared at Wiggins for a moment, he took off his felt hat and rubbed the liner band with his free hand to wipe away the sweat then put it back on.

"So, ah, the bullet in his chest didn't kill him because the one in his head would have instantly, so the head shot was the last one. And the bullet hole in his hat couldn't have happened unless his killer was ten-feet tall . . . so he was probably on his knees, plus, I didn't see any sign of a struggle. Peter didn't look bruised or injured at all beyond the bullet wounds and there's no damage to anything else in the vicinity, so I'd say it looks like someone took him by surprise, shot him in cold blood. Probably somebody he knew; it all leads me to believe that someone could have executed him."

"You see!" Wiggins exclaimed, "I knew it. I thought it looked like he was."

"Oh jeez," Joe said, "this is gonna go straight to your head. I can hear you already back at Fowler's jackin' your jaws about this."

"That's a-right!" Wiggins replied. "Hell, you better watch out Sheriff, I might just have to launch my campaign to run against you next election. Seein's how I'm a crime-solver now."

Even the sheriff laughed as he walked away and over to the cabin. The three gravediggers continued their task and soon they had a deep and long enough hole for the coffin. Wiggins tossed up his shovel and the other two helped pull him out.

"Good thing I've got plenty of rope in the canoe," Joe stated as the three of them walked away towards the beach.

"Rope!" Jack exclaimed, "What 'er ya' so damned depressed about French Peter that you're gonna go and hang yourself now?"

"No, to lower the coffin in the grave, ya' dummy."

"Oh fer' cryin' in the night, Butterfield, I know that. I was just hackin' on ya' is all."

Jack and Bob lifted the coffin and started to carry it towards French Peter while Joe got the rope. Once they were at the body Wiggins and Niles set it down on two logs and both of them sat down next to it.

"I think it's gonna take all four of us to get him in it," Jack said.

"Each one lifts a limb, huh?" Niles suggested.

"And have the rope under the coffin so's we can all lift and then lower him down, I guess," Joe said, dropping the rope on the ground.

"Do we put him in the box here, or take it over to the hole and carry him over to it?" Wiggins asked, looking at Bob.

"Don't look at me! I ain't never done this before."

"Oh, Jesus, you two, this can't be that difficult to figure out and besides, it's gonna take all four of us so the Sheriff . . . why speak of the devil, here he comes right now," Butterfield said.

The other two turned to look and saw Sheriff Stretch walking towards them, but then he stopped and pulled out his writing pad and jotted something in it, stuck it in his back pocket, and then walked over to them.

"What'd ya' find? Any clues?" Wiggins asked.

"Not much really. All I can say for sure from the looks of his cabin is that French Peter wasn't much for housekeeping. But I did find a double-barrel pistol between his mattress and bedframe as well as a double-barrel shotgun, a rifle, and his old musket behind the door. This situation is asking me more questions than I can answer."

The Sheriff looked at the two large slash piles of wood over on level area south of the cabin, "I'm guessing that those two bonfire piles were for signal fires in case he ran into trouble, or got himself hurt but he never lit them . . . and his padlock was unlocked on the ground and the keys for the front door were in his pocket, plus his pocketknife was in the dirt."

Then he pointed over at Peter's chest and said, "That soapstone thing that I guess he wore around his neck's got a broken lanyard and I'm sure his dog didn't break it free . . . And that's in addition to the main thing of it, which is that his house wasn't ransacked! Like he walked outside, got shot, and then the murderers just left. If they came for money or gold, then why didn't they tear the cabin up looking for it?"

"So, what's all that mean, sheriff?" Bob Niles asked.

"Well, I believe it means that he knew his killer — and that he got caught off guard so he couldn't torch off those wood piles or get to the cabin for one of his guns."

"Sounds like a real mystery," Wiggins said.

"Aw, Wigs, right, there ya' go again," Butterfield replied.

"So! How we doing on the hole?" Stretch asked.

"We's ready," Wiggins answered, standing up.

"Okay, so! Take yer' rope over next to the grave site and loop it back and forth on the ground so we all have an end to lift with, then take the coffin and set it on the rope."

"You see, nothin' like having an experienced man to lead the way I always say," Wiggins remarked.

"Oh, the hell you do! I ain't never heard you say such a thing, ever," Joe noted.

"And after you do that," Stretch added, "we'll carry the victim over to the coffin and put him inside. Oh, any of you bring a hammer and nails?"

The three gravediggers glanced back and forth at each other with blank faces. "I bet Pete's got a hammer and nails around here somewhere," Wiggins offered.

"Okay, you boys get everything set up and I'll go find us something to use. We wouldn't want that coffin lid pried off by some varmint," the Sheriff commented, walking away.

By the time he got back from the cabin with a hammer in his hand and some eight-penny nails in his pocket the coffin was resting over in its rightful place on top of the rope and the three diggers were standing over French Peter's body.

"The coffin would be too heavy with him in it so each one of us is gonna grab a limb," the sheriff said, bending over and picking up a foot. "And then we'll carry him over and set him inside. Okay, everybody on three. One, two, three."

As soon as Peter's body was off the ground his head fell back, the knit hat fell off, and some of his brains fell out of his skull and onto the ground.

"Jesus, we didn't need to see that," Bob said, looking away while they all slowly walked over the beach logs towards the casket, groaning from the weight.

"This is good, set him down," Stretch said. "We need to have him in line with the coffin so we can be on either side of it, we'll walk him to it head first and then set him inside. Ready? One, two, three."

They lifted him again and walked him straight over the box and set him down inside with his marriage stick still on his chest. The Sheriff went back to get Peter's knit hat, came back, and put it on his head.

"That's better."

The four men stood over French Peter for a few moments, just looking at him, until Niles picked up the lid and slid it over the top and into place. The Sheriff started to nail it down while the three men sat on the closest beach log and took a break.

"Either one of you gonna have anything to say once we put him in the ground?" Bob Niles asked.

"Oh, I'm sure Wigs does," Joe answered, looking over at his friend. "I don't, not much for that kind of thing."

"I might be able to come up with a few fittin' words. After all my momma always thought I should-a been a preacher," Wiggins replied.

"It just never stops with you does it," Butterfield said. "Ever since I met you ya' been speechifyin' and preachifyin' every day, all day."

"It's just my nature is all, besides, I always liked French Peter. That's not sayin' I looked up to him or anything like that, I just always thought that he had himself one hell of a life, just livin' out here on his island would-a been more work and adventure than any normal person would put up with. And that's not to mention all the gold we've talked ourselves into believing that's buried out here. Someone's gonna find all his money, someday. Mark my words."

"Alright fellas, time to lay his body away," the sheriff said, standing up and tossing the hammer off to the side.

The three men got up and stepped over to the coffin just as the raven flew up and landed on a hemlock limb right above the grave. It bobbed its head a few times then watched the four of them bend over to pick up their end of rope. "Okay, here we go. One, two, three."

Once the casket was off the ground, they slowly walked it over the hole and began to lower it into the grave, when it was at the bottom, they tossed the rope in as well.

Bob nodded at Wiggins and said, "Okay preacher, time to say a few words." Jack took off his frumpy felt hat, held it in front of himself and started.

"Okay, so . . . we all knew him as French Peter, but Peter Goutre was a traveler, and now he's travelin' home to heaven," Wiggins began, looking up to the sky. "He didn't have many friends but I'd like to think that I was one."

He glanced around at the three men, they had their hats off and heads down. Jack continued, "Lots of folks round here thought of him as a hermit and a miser and, because he was so sour, I think people were afraid of him. He lived alone and I think maybe he liked that and because of that he didn't really have many friendships but I always liked him, he was the most interesting person I ever knew."

Then Wiggins opened his eyes and glanced around at the men again, they still had their heads down. He glanced up into the tree and the raven was still there overseeing the proceedings, he kept going.

411

"Peter looked at things and at life differently and chose to live like he did. But he was true to himself and true to how he lived out here with just his dog. I guess if French Peter had a philosophy, it was his fundamental love of nature and living in the wilderness. I think life had more meaning for him over here on —"

"Ahem," Sheriff Stretch coughed, clearing his throat. "Okay Wiggins, let's not take all day."

"Yeah, alright Sheriff. I'm just about done. Where was I? Oh, so let me finish like I began. French Peter was a traveler. When he was a young man, he traveled by foot and canoe on the York Express out here to the Pacific Northwest. He worked as a trader down at Fort Nisqually and up at Stikine, and if that's not enough he rode the high seas and was a sailor for many years. If you knew French Peter you just had to accept him for what he was, one of the originals of this area, a true pioneer, a hallmark to the past and the way things used to be. Peter loved the world he lived in, he loved Puget Sound and all the Natives. Hell, I think he was more at home with the Snohomish Indians than any of us white folk. He was a very real man and I don't think there'll ever be another one like him again."

"So, in closing, we don't know what happened here . . . if Peter was killed for greed, or for revenge, or some kinda' dumb little thing then I guess we'll never know about it. But no man deserves to end up on the wrong end of a gun, armed with just a pocketknife, so please Lord, take French Peter into your grace and let him rest in your arms in heaven . . . Amen."

"Rest in peace, Peter Goutre," Joe added.

The group was silent for a moment until Bob Niles spoke up, "Good job, Wigs." He put his hat back on and grabbed a shovel.

"Yep, your mama was right Wigs, you probably should've been a preacher," Ben Stretch offered, starting to walk away. "I've got the keys to his padlock so I'm gonna go and lock up the cabin. By the time I'm done you boys should be finished."

Bob and Joe started shoveling dirt into the hole while Wiggins used the back-side of his shovel to pound the cross into the ground.

When they were done and heading for the canoes the sun broke through the clouds, its living warmth shone down brightly on what would always be French Peter's Island.

Like the wind, the Raven took to flight and flew close to the men's heads, counting coup, cawing loudly — it winged up and away from the past and into an uncertain future. As it soared above the emerald waters of Whulge, the Raven felt troubled. It had tried its best to watch over Little Rain and Peter, to guide them in their travels and warn about danger, yet it had failed. But the Raven was sure of one thing, it knew the warm comforting solace that its spirit needed that day still stood high on the cliff overlooking the rippling waves of the great Salish Sea, knowing that its lofty perch in the welcoming arms of the Princess of Possession Sound would be there, until someday when it was gone. Because the Raven knew that the world was changing. Soon, it would no longer be wild, open, or free.

Acknowledgements

I would like to thank and credit Snohomish County Historian David Dilgard for encouraging me to write about Peter Goutre. Thank you, David, for handing me a copy of your publication Dark Deeds years ago, it provided the spark I needed to take on this subject. I couldn't have done it without your encouragement. I just wish you were here to see this project completed.

I'm eternally grateful for my creative team: Skyler Cuthill, Susan Harrell, Steve K. Bertrand, Gene R. Fosheim, Steve Breeden, Rebecca Dickinson and Susie Uhl. Thank you all for your help, guidance, support, and design and artistic talents in helping bring this project to life.

I wanted to thank Cassie Rittierodt of the Island County Historical Society and Lisa Labovitch of the Everett Public Library Northwest Room for all their help and assistance in my research for this publication. Thank you, Cassie and Lisa.

The speeches by Chief Seathl and Isaac Stevens on Jan. 22, 1855 were originally recorded with the U.S. Department of the Interior Bureau of Indian Affairs as notes of the proceedings of the Treaty of Point Elliott. For this publication they were pulled from: The Many Speeches of Chief Seathl by Eli Gifford (2015) and Isaac I. Stevens: Young Man in a Hurry by Kent Richards (1938).

Historical Notes

The following pages were provided courtesy of The Everett
Public Library Northwest Room and Lisa Labovitch. The first
two pages were written by Morris Frost, who was a justice of the
peace, they are a statement of fact finding in the days directly
after Mr. Goutre's death and written by Frost on November 28th
1875. Next is an accounting of Peter Goutre's Estate and a
probate court newspaper notice followed by a short poem that
was published shortly after French Peter's demise.

Muskillie
Nov 28th 1875

Dr Sir

On friday last about 10 A.M
I was informed by John Kely and his friend
that something was wrong at Peter Goutrie
on hat Island as the house was broken open and
no one to be found—we immediately dispached
a boat and the men—viz—Robt Niles H C
Vining and Robt Wiggins—on landing at the
house they found it open but nothing appeared
to be disturbed—the remains of Mr Goutrie was
soon discovered by Mester Vining lying amst two
pieces of drift were about six rods west of his
house guarded by his faithful dog. he called
to Niles and Wiggins, and puting the dog. got
to the bodsly—a horible sight to look upon—
a heavy charg of buck-shot had penetrated his
neck and brest and the right side of his face
and head was entirely bown away—so that
most of his branes had fallen out, his hat
was on his head and one or two shots has

418

...the men proceeded to the remains in the
most decent manner, the circumstances would
permit having taken a box or coffin with
us — we found a dry sandy bank about ten rods
west of the house — a very suitable place and not
likely to be disturbed, the remains were some
what decomposed —

It is necessary that some suitable person
persons should be appointed to take charge of
and remove some of the property to a place of safety

Circumstances show that he or was gathering his
apples, and was called from the orchard to the scene
of his death for the purpose of killing him — we put
up the fence to secure the remainder of the apples from
the cattle — I will send two men tomorrow to
take care of the remainder of the apples and other
exposed property —

Respectfully yours
H. H. Frost

419

Schedule of All the Property Personal
and real found by me composing the Estate of
the late Peter Gourie of Snohomish County Wash Try

7 Cows	9 dry hides
5 yearlings	2 Barrels
2 two year old steer	1 Stone jug
2 two yearolds — wild	6 old axes
1 Calf —	1 dog —
4 hogs —	3 augers
125 bushels of apples—supposed	1 Brush hook
1 Grindstone,	2 Cow bells
2 Double Barrel Shot guns	2 Bowls and other dishes
1 Single Barrel	Trumpery not worth enumerating
1 Musket	1 Trunk and contents
1 Cross Cut Saw	1 Pair of Skates
1 two Barrel pistol	Farm 153 50 acres
1 Broad ax	U S Patent homestead
1 Jack Plane	there is a quantity of fern and
1 hammer —	Stuff intended for hay — not
1 Hand Saw	worth appraising which I
1 Square	deemed best to feed to the
3 half windows	Cattle, which is being done —
8 yards Sheeting	there has no papers of
10 pounds nails	any value come to my
1 feather bead & 5 sacks feathers	possession and I think there
1 canoe	are none — as Peter done
3½ M Shingles	no credit business. All the
19 Fowles or chickins	papers I have found are tax
1 Scow boat & chane	receipts and bills of goods bought
	M H Frost

420

Estate of Peter Goetry
To Finest & Fowler &c

1874				
Dec 4	1	Bot Whiskey	1 00	
1875 Jany 4	1	lb Tobacco	1 00	
Mar 10	1	Scythe	1 50	
	6	lbs Sugar	1 00	
	3	" Coffee	1 00	
	20	" Bacon	3 20	
	1	Bot Oil	25	
		Meals	1 50	
	1	lb Tobacco	1 00	
	1	Bbl Salmon	5 00	
		Bar bill	2 00	
	1	File	25	
		His man Johns bill	2 00	
April 7	1	Bot Strychine	1 00	
May 1	18	lbs Bacon	2 88	
	1	Bot Whiskey	1 00	
		Bar bill	25	
		Yeast Powders	25	
June 1	6	lbs Sugar 1 20 3 lb Coffee 1 00	2 00	
1876	1	" Tobacco 1 00 18 lb Flour 2 00	3 00	
Jan		Lumber for Coffin	1 00	
	1	Bushel Wheat 3 . Chickens	1 25	
			$33.33	
1875 June 14		By Cash	20 00	
		To bal.	$13.33	
		" use of Boat 2 Days Carre $3 00		

I M W Fro' being duly sworn say that the above
account is just and true and that no part thereof
has been paid and that there are no opsets against
...

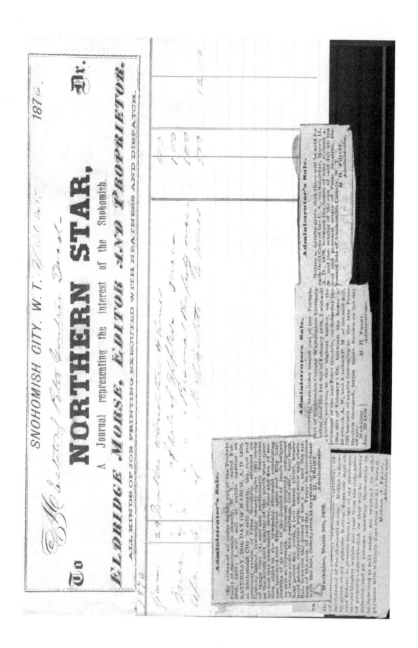

SNOHOMISH CITY. W. T. _____ 187 6.

To _____ Dr.

NORTHERN STAR.

A Journal representing the interest of the Snohomish.

ELDRIDGE MORSE, EDITOR AND PROPRIETOR.

ALL KINDS OF JOB PRINTING EXECUTED WITH NEATNESS AND DISPATCH.

There was an old man called French Peter
Who was shot gunned from less than a meter
While few were offended
That his life had been ended
Some were vexed that it wasn't done neater

— Seattle Evening Dispatch, Nov. 30th, 1875

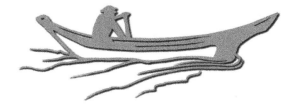

About the Author

Hibulb Cultural Center
Tulalip, Washington
Point Elliot Treaty Exhibit

Malstrom Award winning author JD Howard was born in West Seattle and raised in Everett, Washington. He currently lives in the foothills of Snohomish County. Other works include: Both Sides of The Wish (2013) Sawdust Empire (2016) The Pride of Monte Cristo (2019) and Paper Highway (2020).

Made in the USA
Monee, IL
28 October 2021

80461130R00246